CALIGULA

A born and bred Yorkshireman with a love of country, history and architecture, Simon spends most of his rare free time travelling around ancient sites, writing, researching the ancient world and reading voraciously.

Following an arcane and eclectic career path that wound through everything from sheep to Microsoft networks and from paint to car sales, Simon wrote the Marius' Mules series. Now, with in excess of twenty novels under his belt, Simon writes full time. He lives with his wife and children and a menagerie of animals in rural North Yorkshire.

SIMON TURNEY

First published in Great Britain in 2018 by Orion Books,
an imprint of The Orion Publishing Group Ltd
Carmelite House, 50 Victoria Embankment
London EC4Y 0DZ

An Hachette UK company

1 3 5 7 9 10 8 6 4 2

A CIP catalogue record for this book
is available from the British Library.

ISBN (Hardback) 978 1 4091 7516 2
ISBN (Export Trade Paperback) 978 1 4091 7517 9
ISBN (Ebook) 978 1 4091 7519 3

Typeset by Input Data Services Ltd, Somerset

Printed and bound in Great Britain by Clays Ltd, St Ives plc

www.orionbooks.co.uk

For Tracey, who keeps me right,
and for Marcus and Callie, who keep me left

DAMNATIO MEMORIAE

Upon the death of an emperor, it became practice for the senate to confer apotheosis upon his name, granting him divine status and a cult of his own. If the emperor had been despised, however, the senate could choose the precise opposite and vilify rather than deify him – damnatio memoriae *(a modern term) would occur. Without hesitation or ceremony, the emperor's name was erased from all public inscriptions (a process known as* abolitio nominis*), his image would be scratched from frescoes, his statues smashed. Sometimes even coins bearing his image would be defaced. The damned emperor was not only denied an ascent to heaven, but wiped from history. Such was the fate of the wicked, the unpopular or the unfortunate.*

A sestertius from the reign of Caligula, showing his sisters on the reverse: Agrippina on the left, Drusilla in the middle, and Livilla on the right.

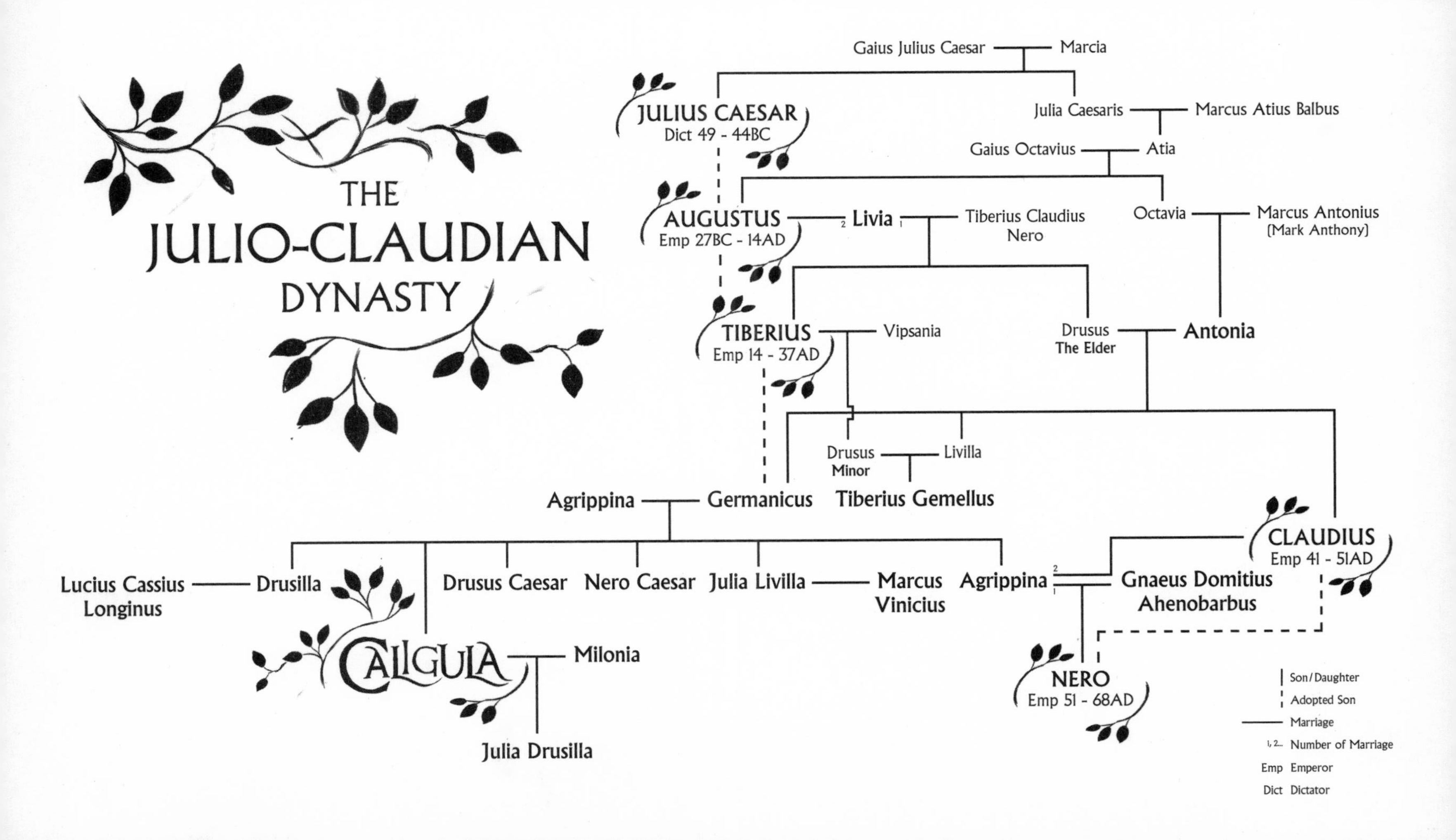
THE JULIO-CLAUDIAN DYNASTY
Gaius Julius Caesar
Marcia
JULIUS CAESAR
Dict 49 - 44BC
Julia Caesaris
Marcus Atius Balbus
Gaius Octavius
Atia
AUGUSTUS
Emp 27BC - 14AD
2 Livia 1
Tiberius Claudius Nero
Octavia
Marcus Antonius
[Mark Anthony]
TIBERIUS
Emp 14 - 37AD
Vipsania
Drusus The Elder
Antonia
Drusus Minor
Livilla
Agrippina
Germanicus
Tiberius Gemellus
CLAUDIUS
Emp 41 - 51AD
Lucius Cassius Longinus
Drusilla
Drusus Caesar
Nero Caesar
Julia Livilla
Marcus Vinicius
Agrippina
Gnaeus Domitius Ahenobarbus
CALIGULA
Milonia
Julia Drusilla
NERO
Emp 51 - 68AD
Son/Daughter
Adopted Son
Marriage
1, 2... Number of Marriage
Emp Emperor
Dict Dictator

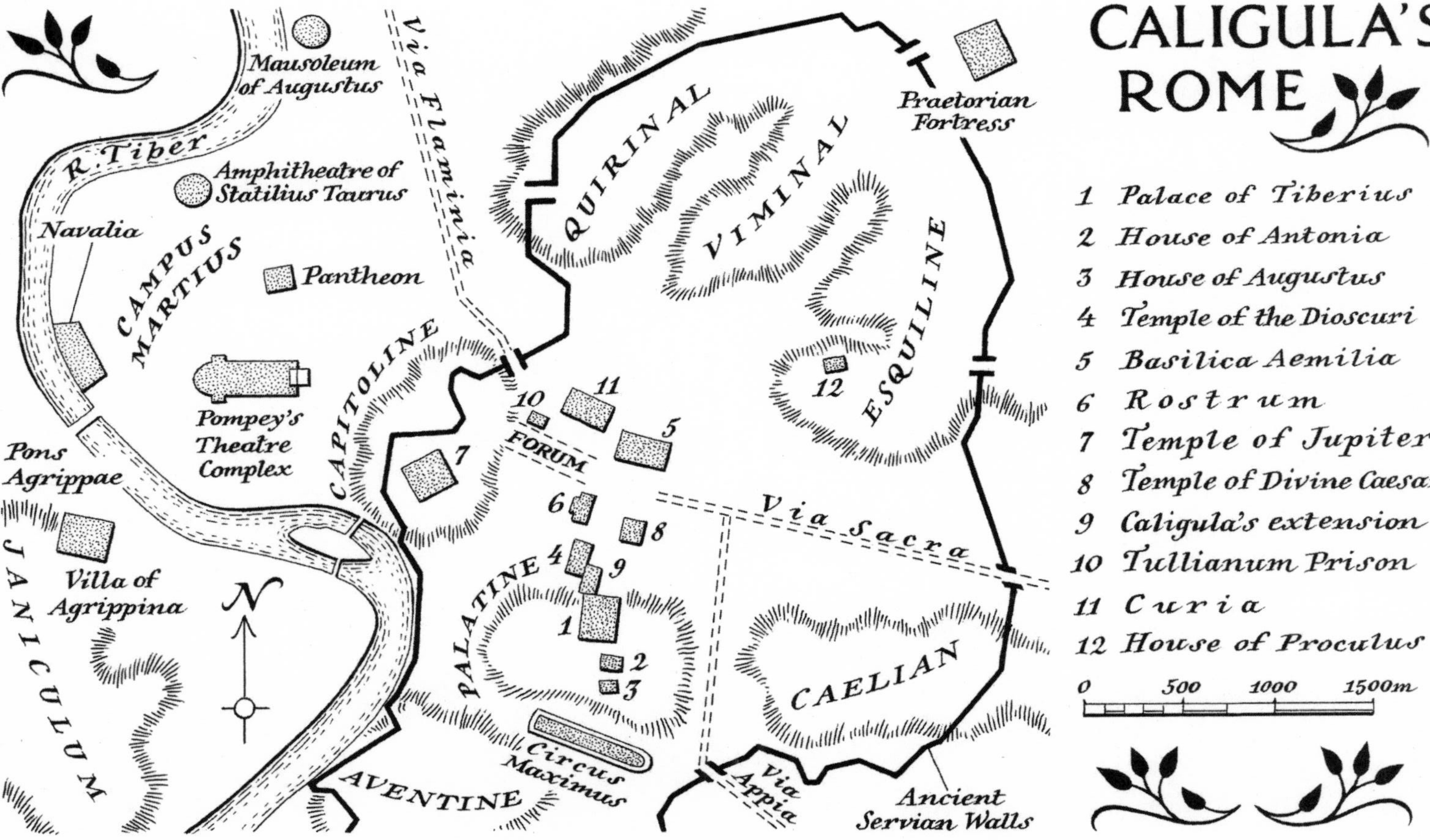
CALIGULA'S ROME
1 Palace of Tiberius
2 House of Antonia
3 House of Augustus
4 Temple of the Dioscuri
5 Basilica Aemilia
6 Rostrum
7 Temple of Jupiter
8 Temple of Divine Caesar
9 Caligula's extension
10 Tullianum Prison
11 Curia
12 House of Proculus
0 500 1000 1500m
Mausoleum of Augustus
Via Flaminia
R. Tiber
Amphitheatre of Statilius Taurus
Navalia
CAMPUS MARTIUS
Pantheon
Pompey's Theatre Complex
Pons Agrippae
Villa of Agrippina
JANICULUM
N
CAPITOLINE
QUIRINAL
VIMINAL
ESQUILINE
Praetorian Fortress
FORUM
Via Sacra
PALATINE
Circus Maximus
AVENTINE
CAELIAN
Via Appia
Ancient Servian Walls

It starts with flashes.

Blinding, eye-searing flashes of red and white, which gradually resolve into a canopy of crimson with the brilliant sunlight of a Roman summer slashing through like a blade. The world below that shelter is a dreadful scarlet, battered and stabbed by those sharp beams of light.

The roar of a crowd is still audible as a din in the background.

I am moving, walking casually, calmly.

I am filled with a strange ennui, though that itself is just a boat of emotion bobbing upon a sea of despair that has always been there, dark and immense, threatening to engulf me. But now that is changing. The untroubled nature of my mind is cut through with new emotions . . . stark, terrifying ones.

The unexpected. A shock. Horror, even. How can this be?

My hand goes out to ward off the unseen threat. No! I am surrounded only by the trusted. This cannot happen. Such threat is the province of enemies, not friends.

Gleaming metal – blue Noric steel shining with that sickly all-pervading red glow – lances towards me. I lurch away and the blade that seeks my heart instead cuts through flesh and grinds against bone.

Agony. Flashes of agony and panic. Disbelief and terror.

There is blood. My hand comes up and is oddly black within the red of my enclosed world. So much blood. I try to react, but I am prevented. I am stopped.

I am helpless, and it is trusted ones that seek my end. Why? What have I done to deserve this?

I shout, but that shout goes nowhere, gathered up by the limp crimson canopy and hurled back at me. The myriad voices far away cheer still, unaware that I am imperilled.

Panic is all, now. There is nothing I can do.

That blade, given an extra scarlet tint by my life's blood, is pulling back, the face behind it feral, the teeth bared like a wolf defending a half-eaten kill from its pack mates.

I am still trying to react, to fight, but I am failing, restrained. The wound that daubed the blade before me is a searing conflagration in my flesh, sending tendrils of pain throughout my body. To see my own life coating a sword . . . I catch my face briefly reflected in the oily red sheen. I do not look panicked or agonised. Just sad.

But it is not that *blade I should fear.*

The blade that robs me of my world is the unseen one. It scythes through flesh and I can feel it cutting the threads within that bind life to this earthly shell. My heart stops – a steel point transfixing it.

My eyes are wide. The feral face comes closer. I am already dead, but still standing – I can still feel as that animal drives in his blade once more. Another comes from behind. And another from the side. Each blow is an insult now, nothing more, for death has been dealt. Each new blow is a statement from those I had loved and trusted.

Thirty blows in all. Thirty wounds that go deeper than mere flesh, that carve my very soul.

I am falling now, the scarlet canopy receding, the flashes of dagger-like sunlight unable to warm me. Nothing will ever warm me again.

I can see the most familiar of faces . . .

*

I wake sharply, my pallet drenched with the sweat of terror. Was it just a dream again? Or was it something more? I remember now. I remember who I am. And I remember how it began.

PART ONE

THE CHILDREN OF GERMANICUS

'He who was born in the camp and reared 'mid the arms of his country, gave at the outset a sign that he was fated to rule'

– Pliny, quoted in Suetonius: Life of Caligula

I

ASHES AND A HOLLOW HEART

My name is Julia Livilla, daughter of Germanicus and sister of the emperor Gaius, who they called Caligula. And if I am to start this story anywhere sensible then it must begin with my first memory of him.

My father, the great conquering general beloved of Rome – if not of his emperor – had spent a year in Syria as its governor before passing rather suddenly from the world through illness. Or by the emperor's poison as some, such as my mother, would have you believe. I have no memory of that dusty land, of course. I was a mewling baby when my father died and my mother gathered her children and returned to Rome with her husband's ashes and a hollow heart.

So I came to Rome with the others, nestled in the arms of my mother in the year of the consuls Silanus and Balbus – an entourage of death returning from distant lands to a mourning city with a wicked emperor. We landed at Ostia and transferred to Rome, where we moved through the city at a stately pace, a sombre family amid the wailing crowds that had turned out to see the beloved Germanicus come home for the last time. We were stony silent and dour, Drusilla and Agrippina, Gaius and myself, Mother and the numerous slaves and attendants. I was still a babe of course, yet to form true memories, and one image is all I can claim from that day: my brother gathering our weary sister Drusilla into his arms to save her tired young feet, and carrying her across the forum beneath a glorious rainbow that arced incongruously through a deep blue sky.

A single snatch of early life: a rainbow, noisy crowds, a burial and my brother at his glorious best.

Four years passed then, with us living in Rome as a large, peaceful – if not always harmonious – family. In addition to the wealthy town house we had on the Palatine where my father had grown up, my mother also kept a well-appointed villa with extensive gardens on the far side of the Tiber, within view of the great curve of the theatre of Pompey, and it was this semi-rural location that my mother favoured. I liked to think – probably in the naïve, childish way of a five year old – that this was because she wished to live out the rest of her life in a place that harboured only joyous memories of her husband. Agrippina and Caligula, both of whom were ever more subtle and intuitive than I, maintained that the real reason was that she persisted in the conviction that Tiberius had ordered the death of her husband, and would never countenance even the idea of living on the Palatine alongside him.

At five, I was just grateful for the extensive gardens and the relatively clear air on that side of the river, away from the summer stink of Rome's huddled streets. As I had grown into a happy girl, playing with the family's pet hounds that roamed the grounds, absorbed in an endless series of games that resulted in torn and muddied clothes, so too had my brothers and sisters grown. Nero and Drusus had both taken the *toga virilis* while we were in Rome, becoming men in the eyes of the city, and each roamed the villa's corridors pensively, impatiently awaiting a posting to the legions as a tribune. Agrippina, now eight, was already exhibiting all the signs of a competitor in the game of power. She played off one slave or servant or former client of our father's against another constantly, for her own amusement and always for an advantage. Drusilla, a year younger, was just happy to play with a small circle of friends, holding her own court as though she were an empress. The former consul's son, Marcus Aemilius Lepidus, who was often at the villa, had begun to moon around Drusilla as though the very ground upon which she walked might sprout roses. Even at such a tender age, I remember the first flowerings of jealousy over my placid sister. She had to do nothing to attract the attention of everyone, whereas I was often overlooked. Would that I had been closer to Drusilla then, and far more wary of Agrippina.

There was a tense time for a while when Caligula, now a rangy boy of eleven, began to prowl around Lepidus, contending with the handsome visitor for the attention of our sister. Agrippina and I held our breath at every visit, waiting for our youngest brother to launch an assault upon Lepidus in defence of his relationship with Drusilla. Caligula was ever quick-tempered, you see, though that was just part of his nature. He was as avid and forthright with every emotion: quick to anger but expansively loving, exuding sympathy yet tightly, even acerbically humorous. In the end our worries proved unfounded. One morning, as Lepidus entered the house, he brought Caligula a gift – a jewelled knife. It was a small thing, expensive and decorative, intended for use as a handy work blade for all its silvered hilt, but it was given as a gift of friendship and it sealed such with our brother, who was rarely without the blade thereafter. From that day on he shared Drusilla with our friend, and the matter was settled, even if it did little to diminish my occasional pangs of jealousy over the attention my pretty, delicate sister constantly received.

They were happy days, but things began to change in the year of the consuls Pollius and Vetus. While the older boys and our mother kept themselves occupied in the villa, the younger children and some of our friends were busy playing in the Courtyard of the Fountains when the heavy bronze knocker at the gate rapped loudly twice, sharply, announcing visitors. The bow-legged doorkeeper shambled out of his hut, the fingers of his left hand drumming on the stout ash-wood club at his waist, and crossed to the gate, opening it a crack. Moments later, and after a very short, terse exchange, he swung back the gate to admit the soldiers.

It was the first time I had encountered men of the Praetorian Guard – since I'd been old enough to understand, anyway. And they were so *clearly* soldiers, despite their civil garb. Each man wore his toga like armour, impenetrable and marble-white, his hand hovering near the tell-tale lump that betrayed a sword hilt. Each one had the grim face and square jaw of a hard man, and their feet crunched on the gravel with the sound of hobnailed soldier's *caligae* boots. I knew that sound well. Soldiers did not visit a villa without cause, and soldiers of the Praetorian Guard, no less?

I felt panic thrill through me at the sight. Everything Mother had said about our father's death suddenly seemed more plausible with the emperor's own troops in our garden. Perhaps I shrieked, for Caligula reached out and grabbed me, pulling me close and holding me tight in a protective embrace, murmuring calming words with no substance beyond the sounds of his voice. He always had a slightly hypnotic tone – unless he was angry.

We watched, our games forgotten, as the soldiers entered the house, their rough boots clacking across the marble. They were in there for moments only. Mere heartbeats. The message they delivered must have been as forthright and brief as their manner, and no sooner had they exited the grounds to wait impatiently outside, than Mother hurried from the door with our major-domo at her heel, a gaggle of slaves following on. At the rear came Nero and Drusus, both in togas and wearing swords beneath them in a disturbing echo of the Praetorians.

'Lepidus, Callavia and Tullius, I am afraid you will have to leave. Hipsicles here will see you back to your families.' Mother turned to us, and her expression was steely. 'Children, go into the house and change into your best clothes as fast as you can. We are summoned to the emperor.' Her eyes played across us and settled on me, narrowing. 'Livilla, how is it possible to acquire such filth in such a short time. Wash your face and comb your hair. And be quick about it, all of you. Emperors do not expect to be kept waiting.'

As we rushed past her into the house to make ourselves presentable as fast as possible, and Hipsicles, our major-domo, gathered up the friends to return to their own houses, Mother seemed to notice our oldest brothers for the first time.

'What in the name of sacred Venus are you two doing?'

Their blank looks betrayed their puzzlement.

'The swords?'

Nero frowned. 'But the Praetorians are wearing swords.'

'*No citizen*,' Mother explained in a strained hiss, 'bears a weapon of war in the city. It is ancient, inviolable law. The Praetorians are exempt by imperial order, for they must bear a blade to carry out their very duties, but you are just private citizens. Now take those swords off before you get yourselves arrested.'

As our older brothers struggled out of their togas, removed their blades and then rehung the draped garments with the help of the slaves, we hurried to prepare ourselves for the emperor. With surprising alacrity, we assembled out front once more, dressed finely, clean and tidy. Mother marched up and down in front of us like a general inspecting her troops. Was this what my father had been like, I wondered. Her eyebrow rose at the sight of that silvered knife sheathed at Caligula's belt, but she let it pass without comment – it was not a weapon of war, after all.

We were escorted to the large carriage that had hastily been made ready and moments later we were bouncing off through the gate at a steady pace, escorted by the emperor's Praetorians, into the city. As we moved onto the Pons Agrippae, the soldiers were obliged either to march ahead or drop behind by the press of the traffic, and the moment they were out of earshot Mother was jabbering at us in hushed tones.

'Beware *everything* at the palace, children. The emperor is a dangerous old man and with the passing of his son last month, he is worse than ever. His court is a pit of vipers, each as bad as the next, presided over as much by the dangerous Praetorian officers as by the emperor himself. Say nothing unless you are addressed directly, and then be circumspect with your replies. Be polite but not fawning. Be truthful, but economical with it. Above all, be careful. Remember that this is the man who had your father poisoned.'

She clearly had more to say, but we had crossed the bridge and the soldiers were closing in, so she fell silent and locked her eyes on the distant rise of the Palatine. We travelled in strained silence and by the time the carriage pulled up outside Tiberius' great palace we were all quite tense. The grand façade, with its false columns and marbled architraves, was interrupted at the centre by a high portico with a grand pediment that showed the emperor himself as a young general butchering Germans.

I have to admit to shaking with nerves as we passed up the steps and into the shade of that portico. The presence of armed and armoured soldiers who could have killed me before I managed a scream unnerved me as a five-year-old girl.

Caligula was there next to me, a soothing hand on my shoulder, trying to take away my fear. It worked, too. I began to calm down and, once the trembling subsided, he moved on and took Drusilla's hand. I felt a thrill of jealousy again. The closeness the pair shared went beyond what we had, and I envied my sister that, for he was truly the golden boy of our household.

We entered a courtyard where white travertine paths cut across beds of chippings of golden African marble, carefully tended poplars at both ends in neat, orderly rows. Then we were across and inside, letting our eyes adjust to the dim interior. The main building of the extended palace complex, a rectangular *domus* at its heart, was exquisitely designed, lofty and spacious, sumptuous without descending to the gaudiness of eastern princelings. It was grander than anything I had ever seen and my eyes roved as though they had a life independent of mine.

At some point, unnoticed by me, we passed from the control of the Praetorians to the emperor's German bodyguard. Though we still had an escort of four Praetorians, their comrades were no longer in evidence around the building. Instead, bristly northerners with red-blond hair and suspicious eyes occupied the various niches and doorways, watching us as though *we* were the foreigners, and not them. It struck me as darkly humorous that these barbarians guarded the very man who was shown on the building's pediment cutting their fellow tribesmen to pieces. Caligula's eyes narrowed as we passed so many armed men and his expression suggested we were walking willingly into the festering maw of a beast.

I was still contemplating the reason for a guard of such brutish barbarians, while our own elite Roman unit were so readily available, when we were ushered into a great room hung with banners of purple, white and gold. Braziers burned in the corners, giving the place a cosy atmosphere, if a little smoky towards the ceiling. At the centre of the room a fountain in the form of a statue of three unrealistically endowed Greek females – the Furies, possibly – poured wine into a catchment area below, whence slaves would periodically scoop a rich cup for the emperor or one of his guests, cutting it with water before handing it over. The extravagance was astounding, though the sheer wastefulness of it was beyond my tender years.

It took me a moment to locate the emperor. I did not know any of the people who were there with him, though I presume they were highly placed, given how freely he spoke in front of them.

Tiberius looked to me like a cadaver. If he had rotted and crumbled away before my eyes it would not have surprised me. And it was not simply his age, though he was far past youth, now – I have known men who were older than he was then. It was a combination of his age, his bitterness, his acidic temper and, I think, a number of chronic ailments that had begun to plague him by that time. He was drawn and grey, with that thin leathery look to his skin that I have always found distasteful. But for all the corpse-like nature of his body, when I caught his eyes, there was a fierce intelligence in them, and a sharp cruelty, too. Again, I began to tremble, and made sure to lose myself behind my taller brothers.

'The lady Agrippina,' the emperor said in flat tones, meaning my mother, and not my sister who shared her name.

'Majesty,' Mother acknowledged with a rigid politeness that was just a hair's breadth from being brusque and a bow of the head that stopped short of respect by a fraction. The emperor saw it, and I noted his eyes harden.

'You are late.'

'Forgive me, Majesty. Your guards failed to mention a deadline. We came as fast as we could.'

That was the first time I really noticed Sejanus. The emperor, beaten in this verbal contest, flashed an irritated glance at the Praetorian prefect, who stood, armoured, close by, lurking in a shadow. I trembled at the sight of that man in the gloom.

'You are forgiven,' the emperor said with a magnanimous swoop of a hand and a smile that barely touched his mouth, let alone any other part of his face. 'Have your brood relax. There are couches and cushions aplenty. And you, dear Agrippina, please do sit.'

Dear Agrippina? My eyes for some reason slid to my brother Caligula, and I noticed that his fingers were toying with the chape of his knife's scabbard on his belt. I prayed that none of the German Guard noticed, for it would be very easy to see it as a threat.

We were seated, my sister 'Pina to my left, Caligula to my right, Drusilla beyond, all on one couch. Mother sat stiffly on another, not reclining as expected, and my two eldest brothers sat beside her.

'You were not at my ceremony of mourning?' the emperor threw out in an offhand manner, though the bile behind the words was unmistakable. Caligula's eyes, I noticed, were darting around the room, taking in each expression. While our older brothers sat, respectfully riveted to the emperor's presence, Caligula was more interested in the reactions of those around him, using them, I know now, to judge the emperor's own true moods and motivations, without having to peel away the mask the bitter old man wore by nature.

'Again, my apologies, Majesty,' Mother said. 'I was unwell and unfit to travel.'

'Travel? To the forum? Just how unwell *were* you, dear lady?'

There was an awkward silence. Mother was not going to collapse under the pressure of the old man's words. It was plain to all present why she had not been there, but no one dared say anything about it. The emperor sighed.

'I mourn the loss of my son, Agrippina. I mourn darkly and I mourn hard. I do not sleep. I cry often.'

It was such a sudden change that it took us all by surprise, even my mother, whose shell of silence cracked.

'No parent should have to bury a son, Majesty.'

There was another silence, a pause filled only by the gurgling of the wine fountain.

'Agreed,' he said finally. 'Unfortunately, I am not to be given the luxury of grief. Rome demands. She *always* demands. She is ever hungry and I can never give her the peace that I would have from her. My advisors and those in the senate with the more insistent voices remind me constantly of the succession. I believe they fear that I am on the point of death, simply because I am no longer a young man. We have had half a century of internal peace in the empire since my illustrious forebear wrestled control of the empire from that dog Marcus Antonius and founded a dynasty.'

I caught the hardening of my brother's jaw as his fingers rested on the hilt of his knife. Caesar's great friend Antonius was, after all, another of our great-grandfathers, and the comment was almost an open insult.

'And my dynastic progression died with my son,' the emperor said in a cold, flat voice. 'So the succession hangs in the balance and the blabbering old senators fear a new civil war if it cannot be put right.'

'The senators are astute, Majesty,' Mother said quietly. 'The succession is of prime importance.'

'I am *not* on the verge of death!' snapped Tiberius with anger that seemed to turn into smoke and drift about the room. He sighed again and slumped. 'I have made my decision, Agrippina. Despite the differences between you and I, your husband was my nephew and I loved my brother – his father – above all men. And since Germanicus' tragic end I would not see your line fade. You are of the house of the divine Caesar, after all. I have already logged my intentions with the senate. Your eldest boys – Nero and Drusus – will be appointed as my heirs in my son's place, and before you ask why, I will explain something to you, Agrippina. I *know* that you do not like me and do not trust me. And I mirror your dislike to some lesser extent. But you have ever made your views known to me, and despite our enmity you still treat me as your emperor and a distant family member. In four years in the city you have never plotted against me or involved yourself with my enemies, and neither have your children. I have those in my court –' his sweeping arm took in the nameless lackeys in the room '– who profess to be my closest friends and greatest supporters and who have made moves against me that they do not think I am aware of.'

I was startled by a sudden gurgling noise and my gaze – along with that of all others – snapped in the direction of the sound. A young man in a rich toga was suddenly jerking and spasming as crimson began to soak the white folds of his attire. Above him, Sejanus, the Praetorian commander, withdrew his blade from the man's neck, wiped it carefully on a rag and sheathed it as the body of the unfortunate courtier collapsed, slicking blood, to the floor.

I felt nauseated with the shock of it. The tang of the blood filled the air with its cloying scent even amid the stink of his voided bowel. But it was neither the smell nor the sight that sickened me as much as the realisation that a life had been snuffed out before my very eyes. Ended viciously and coldly. I think I threw up a little.

It was the first time I had ever seen someone die. It was to be far from the last.

Beside me, Caligula's attention was, oddly, not on the blood-soaked body, but on the dark killer behind him. I felt certain my brother had committed to memory every tiny facet of the prefect's being.

Then the emperor was talking again as though nothing had happened, and my mother instantly returned her attention to Tiberius.

'So you see,' the emperor said diffidently, 'I would rather place my trust in a reliable enemy than an unreliable friend. Nero will be my heir apparent, with Drusus as his second.'

'In case one dies,' my mother said in a flat tone. Heirs died for many reasons, and I think Mother did not relish the idea of the increased danger in which such an appointment put her boys.

'I have been caught unprepared once, Agrippina. Do not contest me over this. Think only of the honour I do your children. The deed is done, anyway. I am seeking neither your permission nor your approval. I am informing you of what has been decided.'

Nero and Drusus were staring wide-eyed at the emperor. Can you imagine what it must be like to be told that you have been plucked from among so many with equal or better claim and made heir to the whole world? All I could think, though, was how my youngest brother must feel.

As the emperor continued his conversation with Mother, I turned to Caligula, catching with distaste the sight of Sejanus clicking his fingers and slaves dragging away the body, leaving a gleaming trail of blood across the marble.

'Why them and not you?' I whispered.

My brother, his fingers no longer on his knife, turned a quizzical look on me. 'Sorry?'

'Why Nero and Drusus and not you? If it is safer for the emperor to have two heirs than one, would it not be even safer with three?'

Caligula frowned for a moment, and then fixed me with an easy smile. 'Drusus and Nero are men, Livilla. Sixteen and seventeen years old. They are about to be made tribunes in the army. They are ready-made successors. I am but eleven, remember, and not yet a man in the eyes of state.'

I couldn't see how he was so calmly accepting of it, though, and I drove on. 'Doesn't it annoy you?'

'Far from it, little sister,' he replied, lowering his tone to a barely audible level as we pulled away from any unwanted ear. 'Do not fret, for I envy neither Nero or Drusus their unsought windfall. In fact, I would quite hate to be in their position. The court is a dangerous place, as you must by now have noticed. Nero and Drusus will have to be vigilant. Their every word and gesture will be the subject of scrutiny and they will have to navigate the tides and currents of the emperor's court with great care.'

My eyes drifted first to Nero and Drusus who had hungrily involved themselves in conversation with the emperor – were they capable of the caution Caligula was advocating? – and then to the bloody streak across the floor, which was all that remained of a Roman nobleman. In the deep shadow beyond, the prefect Sejanus stood with his arms folded, surveying the room.

'And watch *that one*,' Caligula whispered at my side. 'He will not stop advancing until he outranks Jove himself.' I watched Sejanus for a moment longer, then flicked a quick glance at my brother, but he was already deep in conversation with Drusilla. I turned instead to 'Pina at my other side, but she was busy listening in to the conversation of state as though it might provide as useful information as her intelligence-gathering at the villa. I was effectively alone, and all I could do was look at the emperor, the ageing ruler who had just named my brothers as his heirs, and at Sejanus, who seemed so comfortable in the gloom that he might have been made of shadow.

And I started to shiver all over again.

The following seasons passed surprisingly swiftly, despite the ever-present, lurking fear of interference from the emperor or the Praetorian prefect. Once the old emperor had named my brothers as his heirs, Mother called in favours to secure Nero and Drusus their tribunates as quickly as possible. It would have been obvious even to those unversed in our family's ways that she was attempting to keep her sons as far from the perils of court as possible. It had not escaped my notice, though, that if our father *had* been poisoned on the orders of the emperor, he had been serving in Syria at the time, and so clearly distance was no real protection. Tiberius had been distinctly unimpressed that, within a month of his announcement, his two new heirs had left the city for military posts, but he could hardly complain about a young Roman following the traditional steps on the *cursus honorum*.

And so Nero had taken up his posting as a tribune with the Third Augusta at Theveste, his brother Drusus accepting a place with the Third Cyrenaica in Aegyptus. The whole of Africa was in turmoil at the time with the rebellion of the barbarous King Tacfarinas, and Nero at least would become involved in the war, if not Drusus as well, yet Mother was not as worried as I expected. Not only were tribunes hardly expected to fight in battle, but also, in her opinion, a desert full of Berber tribesmen posed less of a threat to the family than one Praetorian with a knife.

I had watched my brothers pass through several stages of reaction to the emperor's pronouncement. Disbelief merged quickly into a certain smug satisfaction, unintentionally aimed often at Caligula and Lepidus. Then, as the shine wore off and the reality of what the succession truly meant, and the dangers it would bring, sank in, they moved to a nervous, jumpy acceptance. By the time their tribunates were secured and they left Rome, I think both were pleased to go. Drusilla and I watched them leave with sadness, Caligula with a calculated understanding, and Agrippina with disappointment. I think she had been expecting that their rise in status would positively affect her somehow. It had not, and with their departure it seemed likely nothing would come of it at all.

Despite four of us remaining at the villa with Mother, the absence of our two older brothers left a sizeable hole in our lives, and things seemed unnaturally quiet. We went on as always, if with less enthusiasm, playing with friends and learning what would be required of us when we were older.

I suspect that Mother despaired of me in that regard. Agrippina was a good student, absorbing everything she could, storing it away to retrieve when she needed it, calculating girl that she was. We all knew that she would excel at marriage in the way she excelled at anything, because she was so single-minded and manipulative. To some extent I pitied her future husband, since I could hardly see her settling meekly into the background in any marriage. The man who took Agrippina to wife would certainly have his hands full. Drusilla, conversely, would make the perfect Roman wife, damn her. She learned every bit as well as our oldest sister, but she was learning in order to be good at the role, rather than to see how the role could be made to serve her, as Agrippina so clearly did.

Me? I wasn't sure I would ever marry. I had managed to convince myself that Mother would be sick of the whole process by the time she had arranged everything for Agrippina and Drusilla and got around to me. I was headstrong and liked my freedom. I would be a less-than-perfect wife, and I knew it. My family was more important, and it always would be. I listened half-heartedly as I was told what would be required of me and was taught how to do the myriad things a wife needed to do to keep her husband's house in order. Frankly, I was more interested in the things Caligula was learning: oratory, history, mathematics, even a little practice with a sword when Mother was feeling generous.

To lighten the mood after our daily studies, our friends would visit. The games were different these days, of course. Caligula was thirteen now, and expecting to take on the man's toga soon. We girls ranged between ten and seven, with myself always struggling along as the youngest. Our games became more elaborate and less childish. Our friends Callavia and Tullius were starting to lose interest in the things that entertained me, one with an eye for boys and the other with a desire only to pick up a practice sword and test his strength, and Lepidus seemed to have no time for anything but standing and staring moon-eyed at Drusilla. For her part, she did nothing to discourage him, and I think that even then the attention she paid to her lessons was simply in preparation for netting our handsome young companion. Lepidus and Caligula remained firm friends, often taking afternoons out riding or at the races with some of the more trustworthy staff from the villa.

Two years of this, from that day we had left the emperor's room in astonishment with brothers in the imperial succession. It was not a bad time, but it lacked some of the youthful exuberance of the previous years, and the absence of our brothers affected us in subtle ways.

The world changed slowly as I drifted along in my family life, largely unaware of the vast implications of what was happening beyond our walls. The winter of that year rolled on into the spring of the next, and after a long hot summer of no news from our brothers in the south, finally the war in Africa ended. Mother almost collapsed in relief at the knowledge that her sons would no longer be racing across Mauretania chasing down rebels, but then spent months waiting impatiently each day for the riders of the *cursus publicus* who might bear news that one son or the other had fallen in the last days of the war. Again, when letters arrived in consecutive weeks from both Nero and Drusus, Mother sagged with relief.

Closer to home, the snake Sejanus began to move more into the light. The prefect had long been involved in an affair with the emperor's niece, Claudia Livia Julia, though I had paid scant attention to such talk at the time as unimportant. Now, with a respectable period of a year having passed since the death of her husband, Sejanus petitioned the emperor to marry her. The importance of this move still passed me by until I found Mother and Caligula both fretting over it and asked my brother why it should matter to us. Caligula told me in the most grave tone: such a marriage would make Sejanus a member of the House of the Julii and place him in the line of succession, probably above my brothers. Personally I saw that as a good thing, since it might make them less of a target, but it seemed I was wrong. Sejanus would then, my brother confided, attempt to remove all other claimants until he was the only heir.

The panic came to naught in the end as the emperor denied

Sejanus his marriage. I can only imagine how the prefect had taken the news. Quietly respectful, I imagine, bowing to the emperor and making obeisance until he returned to his own house, where I can picture him tearing down the drapes and smashing the furniture in his rage at being denied a place in the succession.

Now aware of the importance of the prefect's attempted matrimony, I paid more attention over the following seasons, and began to understand a little of how my brother saw the world. Every tiny piece of news fitted into a web, and when you understood the positions in that web held by you and your enemies, you could begin to prepare against eventualities. Over the following winter we watched the prefect slowly but surely undermining the emperor's authority, securing allies in useful stations, increasing his list of clients and appointing his lackeys to positions of power. At the same time he began to pour honeyed words into the ear of Tiberius, feeding the old man's mourning misery and his increasing mania, persuading him ever more to step back from the direct running of the empire.

Every month saw more power in the hands of Sejanus and Tiberius a little more removed from his empire. I was horrified. Though I had no love for the old emperor, the thought of Sejanus on the throne was shudder-inducing; more than once I asked Caligula why no one did anything.

'What can anyone do?' he replied bleakly one time. 'Anyone who speaks out against the prefect disappears or is arrested on fabricated charges. And the emperor still trusts Sejanus, enough to more or less let the man run the empire for him. The best anyone can do is to hope and pray.'

So I hoped. And I prayed. And all I received was silence.

II

JUST SCRATCHES

The summer that followed – the year of the consuls Lentulus and Agrippa – saw the most social occasion we had experienced for some time, as well as one of the most eye-opening and prophetic. Our brothers came home, and for a month that summer the house exploded with life and light. Nero and Drusus seemed to have grown immeasurably, truly becoming men during their sojourn in the south.

Nero had seen action with his legion more or less continuously since his arrival. The Third Augusta had ranged across Africa from Theveste in an attempt to put an end to the Berber king, Tacfarinas, and then spent a month rounding up pockets of resistance and putting out the fires following the rebel's defeat. He was full of tales and exciting anecdotes, and bore two small scars to prove that he had done more than run errands for the legion's commander as Mother had expected. His skin had become burnished bronze in the glare of the African sun and his hair had been bleached almost blond. He also bore more than one decoration for military achievement. Mother exuded an interesting mix of pride and horror as she beheld her son the war hero, glorious but scarred.

Drusus, conversely, was unmarked, though his colouring had changed similarly. His posting at Nicopolis on the coast of Aegyptus had been peaceful. He had been involved in a few tiny clashes with the ever-troublesome groups of Alexandria

– Jews, Berbers, Phoenicians and the like – and had run occasional missions upriver into the heart of that strange land, but had escaped battle entirely, and with it any hint of danger or hope of glory. He never begrudged Nero his success, of course, but his quiet disappointment was palpable.

Their stories were exotic and vivid to me, with no memories of the world before we arrived in Rome.

'The old legate, Blaesus, was called back to Rome without having finished the job,' Nero said between mouthfuls of cumin-spiced Parthian chicken. 'Even with reinforcements from the Ninth Hispania. But the new proconsul when he arrived was a different proposition entirely. Dolabella is a hard man. Within months of taking up his post, we had Tacfarinas fighting for his life. The rebel had taken Thubursicum and overrun the garrison, and the proconsul was quick to respond. We were a hundred miles to the south-west, but parts of the Ninth that had been sent to bolster our numbers were close, only thirty miles away from the city. The Ninth engaged the enemy at Thubursicum and held them until we arrived. It was glorious, Drusus.'

I caught Drusus' look of envy before he plastered a supportive smile across his face.

'Anyway, I got this scar above my eye at Thubursicum. The Numidian cavalry broke them, but there was still heavy fighting for the infantry, forcing them from their positions. We retook the garrison easily enough, but driving them out of the streets of the town on the hillside was wicked work. I remember running alongside a centurion – an old fellow with a missing ear called Pansa – up a steep street, chasing a bunch of native spearmen, with the best part of a century of men at our back. Then, completely without warning, a second group burst out of a side alley and tried to cut us off from our men. We nearly lost then, when the ones we'd been chasing turned and came back for us, but the men of the Third are tough and quick. I put down two rebels myself, one in the throat and one in the armpit, before I was suddenly surrounded by my men again. I was covered with blood and I had to check quite carefully to make sure it was all theirs, not mine. But the scar on my forehead was from one of their spears in that fight.'

We children were rapt, listening. All but Caligula, I think, who fiddled absently with his silver knife and drummed little tattoos on his knees. He, of course, had travelled with Father on his campaigns in Germania, wearing his 'little boots', and had seen war, albeit from a distance. I don't think he ever really liked soldiering. Mother was aghast.

'Precious Juno, my son, but do you have to put yourself at risk so? Tribunes are not expected to fight. *Centurions* lead from the front, but they are career soldiers. I did not send you so far from court only for you to place yourself in even greater peril. You are destined for great things, Nero!'

My eldest brother just smiled at her. 'And a man who seeks to rule the world should sweat and bleed for his nation, Mother. Do not forget that Caesar himself fought alongside his men against the Belgae. And Augustus was on a ship at Actium. And even old Tiberius campaigned successfully and gloriously in Germania as a young general. All our illustrious predecessors have won glory in the field before sitting upon a throne. You cannot expect me to do less.'

'Be very careful, young Nero.'

We all turned in surprise at the voice, its parchment crackle telling us who the speaker was before we saw her. Our great-grandmother, Livia, Rome's first empress and wife of the great Augustus, was standing in the doorway. Livia was one of the greatest women in Rome's long history, and a woman on whom I have to some extent modelled myself, or at least tried to. She was over eighty years old at the time of that visit, and yet when a slave rushed over to help her into the room, she snapped something about not being useless at him and pushed him away with her stick, ambling into the chamber and taking a seat with a groan and a creaking of joints.

'Grandmother,' smiled Nero, 'they are just scratches. Nothing to worry about.'

'Not careful of *swords*, boy!' snorted Rome's great dame. 'Careful of *success*!'

Mother was nodding her agreement, but Nero just sniffed. 'I cannot be one of those men who stands on a hill while the fighting happens, fetching footstools and drinks for my superiors. There's too much of Father's blood in me. You know that, Grandmother.'

Livia coughed for a moment, dabbed her lips dry, and turned a shrewd frown on our oldest brother. 'I am not telling you not to fight, boy. It's in your blood. Your family were always fighters. Just do it quietly. Try not to win awards and praise. Stick your sword in the Berber gut if you must, but do not stand on their parapet and wave your flag. Attention is your enemy. Success can be dangerous in sufficient quantities, and Tiberius is an ungrateful snake at the best of times—'

Mother cut the old woman off sharply.

'You cannot *say* things like that, Livia.'

The old woman snorted again. 'At my age I can say anything I damn well please. And Tiberius is my son. If anyone has the right to label him a venomous reptile, it is me.'

Mother was still horrified, her eyes raking the room as though imperial agents were hiding behind the curtains listening out for signs of dissent. Perhaps she was shrewder than I often give her credit for, in retrospect. But that day at least we were unobserved, and Livia was unabashed.

'Tiberius is a dangerous animal, children. Never think of him as a frail old man. Even frail, he could have you peeled and thrown in the Tiber, nor is he above such things. Your mother remains convinced of his complicity in the death of your father, and she may not be mistaken. I remember watching Tiberius slide into jealous hatred of your father's success, and even now he displays those same signs again. The senate sings the praises of the sons of Germanicus, and every cheer the senators give pushes Tiberius a little further into the darkness. Every salute is another log on the pyre he builds for our family. Your mother is not being over-protective . . . she is being uncharacteristically wise.'

Mother shot a sour glance at the old woman, but said nothing. Over the decades she had become familiar with Livia's rather acerbic and very forthright manner, something that Caligula inherited down the line – just as I inherited Mother's eye-rolling – for all that he hid it well for some time.

'You are jumping at shadows, Grandmother.' Nero smiled indulgently, and then shrank back as Livia's stick neatly rapped him on the forehead.

'Don't be a fool, boy. The emperor is already starting to see you not as an heir but as a threat. And the bigger the name you make for yourself, the worse things will get. Take to the background. Let others win glory. You are his heir now, but there are others with a claim, and if you appear to be too much of a threat to my son, you may yet find yourself supplanted. Your own eyes should be set not on the journey but on the destination: succession. Do not let pride get in the way. That was the undoing of Caesar, after all, and I have no wish to see another member of my family lying on the steps of the senate house, riddled with stab wounds.'

Nero was about to reply, but Drusus cut in this time. 'There will be precious little glory to win anyway, Grandmother. The African war is over and Nero will be settling into garrison life just like me. We will be quiet and unassuming, not by choice, but by accident.'

'See that you do. I have no desire to witness my great-grandchildren slain by my son. We are not some Hellenistic tragedy – we are the Julian family, and it is our place to rule the world.'

As they petered off into more petty conversation I caught Agrippina frowning as though working through a problem. At the time I was blind to the nature of her inner discourse, though it seems clear she was calculating how to become another Livia in her turn – a masterless matron, feared and adored by an empire. Secure a husband with noble lineage, sire a child, remove any competitor with a stronger claim to the throne. Better to control a living emperor than have to survive one, after all. As my eyes slipped past smiling, taciturn Drusilla, a thought occurred to me and I turned to Caligula, who sat still, drumming his fingers on his knees as though in deep contemplation.

'Will you be a tribune?' I asked quietly. My brother turned a frown on me, and I shrugged. 'I mean, you're thirteen, so you'll be taking the toga virilis soon, surely? And then will you seek out a post with the legions like Nero and Drusus?'

Caligula pursed his lips and the fingers came to a stop. 'Listen to what our great-grandmother says. She is a clever one, Livilla. She knows how to survive. I will do what is required of me and no more. Let Nero and Drusus have their glory. If I must take the toga, then I shall, and if I must accept a posting, then I shall, but I shall be chary in everything I do and shall provoke no one. And if the toga virilis evades me a while yet then I am content not to hunt it down. My legal status as a child is my greatest protection from intrigues right now, and I value it.'

As I absorbed his words and his fingers went back to their rhythmic drumming, I turned to the gathering and looked from one brother to the other. I knew them both well enough to see how they might doom themselves. Nero could no more stay out of the public eye than a fish could decide to fly. And Drusus, for all his staid career so far, was twitching to step up beside his elder brother. Was Great-Grandmother right? Would the boys' success carry them into danger? Caligula seemed to think so.

Mother retired early that evening with a headache, which she blamed on Livia's unusually strong proportions of wine to water, and her children gathered in the garden. We had been accorded a most unusual freedom with Mother's early bed, since Livia had also dozed off in the *triclinium*, and we had taken what opportunity we could to talk without the matrons of the house overpowering us. Drusilla and I were still too young to be given such liberty, in truth, but our older brothers were adults now and as such were free to do as they pleased, within reason.

'You have grown, Gaius, in just two years,' Drusus said with a smile, taking a pull on well-watered wine. 'And not just in stature. You seem very sure of yourself, almost to the point of arrogance? Remember what the Greeks taught us about hubris.' It sounded harsh, but there was a slight smile on his face that told of a gentle ribbing. Over the years, Drusus and Caligula had developed something of a habit of good-natured argument, though from time to time it would escalate and end in a row, either Drusus asserting his seniority and stalking off or Caligula losing his temper and snapping in a tart manner. Not tonight, though. Tonight they were both smiling.

Agrippina reached for the jug, and Nero used an ankle to slide it away from her. 'Ah, ah, ah. If Mother wakes to find her girls drunk it will be Drusus and I who are for the back of her hand.'

Agrippina snorted derisively. 'If you believe for a moment that I would drink enough not to be able to control myself, then you are fools, the pair of you.'

Nero and Drusus looked at one another and chuckled. I did not. I believed her. They had been gone for two years and had not seen our oldest sister already playing the villa's staff against one another. Agrippina, I felt, would never let her guard slip. She was too clever for that by far.

'I have grown . . . careful,' said Caligula with an odd smile in reply to his brother's comment. 'You may have faced death in the form of screaming nomads out in Africa, but the danger in Rome is no less real, and innocence is no defence against it.

Were I to don the toga virilis tomorrow I would be watching every set of eyes I passed, waiting for a knife in the dark. Probably a knife with a scorpion on it.'

I flashed him a look. Perhaps he had not grown quite as careful as he believed, to say such things in the open air. The scorpion was the symbol of the Praetorians, and it was unwise to speak openly against them in these days of Sejanus' power, as we had seen first-hand in the emperor's court. He immediately realised what he had said, his eyes darting around the garden, seeking stray ears listening in. Nothing moved but a few leaves in the gentle breeze and after a moment we all relaxed.

Nero and Drusus shared their look again. 'We go abroad for two years and our family turn into politicians and plotters in our absence,' Nero chuckled. 'Next Drusilla will tell us she is training to be a gladiatrix!'

As Drusus laughed and choked on his wine, a voice from the doorway said, 'Drusilla is training to be the most radiant flower in Rome's garden.'

We turned to see Lepidus standing there in a grey tunic and woollen cloak against the night breeze, with the doorman behind him, looking somewhat disgruntled.

'Aren't you out a little late?' Caligula murmured in a friendly, teasing tone.

'I'm older than you, Gaius *Little Boots*,' laughed Lepidus as he waved away the doorman, who stumped irritably back inside.

'Lepidus?' said Nero in surprise, gesturing at our friend. 'I'm surprised to see you. Thought you'd be off filling a tribunate somewhere by now?'

Lepidus glanced down to where Nero pointed and grinned. He no longer wore the *bulla* of childhood, something that I think bothered Caligula, though he'd never let it show. 'I am!' Lepidus laughed. 'Don't you know how important my father is? I'm on the rolls as a tribune of the urban cohorts.'

'Cushy,' snorted Drusus, now he had recovered from breathing in his wine. We all smiled. 'On the rolls' was the perfect description. Lepidus had been a tribune of that force which policed the city of Rome for two years now, but we had not once seen him don a uniform or visit their barracks. In fact, he lived what appeared to be a life of simple ease with a martial title that involved some kind of illusive and seemingly fictional effort.

'Well now, this is nice, having everyone together. It's like the old days,' smiled Nero as Lepidus strolled over and took a seat on the far side of Drusilla to his best friend. My quiet sister flashed a smile at Caligula and then turned her doe eyes on him. He was lost to conversation for some time, until she saw fit to release him.

I caught a flash of something I couldn't name in Agrippina's eyes as she looked at the pair of them. Bitterness? Envy? Nothing that might reveal her true feelings ever stayed on her face long enough to pin down.

'Make the most of it,' Caligula said in an odd tone.

'What do you mean?' Drusus asked, taking another sip of wine.

'By the kalends you'll be on your way back to Africa. The next time you both get furlough at the same time I shall likely have been sent somewhere with a command of my own, Agrippina will probably be married, and the other girls will be preparing for the same. And Lepidus? Well in fairness, he'll probably still be lounging around, shirking duty and pretending to be a tribune of the cohorts.'

Lepidus tried to put on a hurt expression, spoiled only by his grin. I flashed a look at Agrippina. Yes, she was almost of an age for marriage now. Soon Mother would be receiving offers. Or would it be the emperor who arranged matters, as the nearest thing we had to a *pater familias*?

'There will always be occasions for the family of Germanicus to gather,' Nero said confidently, drawing nods from Drusus.

Gooseflesh prickled my skin, though I blamed the breeze and not my increasing feeling that the gods were watching us intently.

But such an occasion seemed increasingly unlikely in the months that followed. Our two oldest brothers went back to pursuing fame and glory on the dusty plains of Africa, Lepidus continued on his leisurely course for a further half year, but was then drawn into real service in the cohorts when one of the existing tribunes departed for public office. A new youth had been granted a commission and suddenly Lepidus was no longer the junior and least important. Of course, our friend was both likeable and clever, so it did not take long before he worked out how to carry out his duties and yet maintain a healthy quantity of leisure time. But he was not at the villa as often as he had been, and we could see the change in Drusilla as she took to moping in his absence, even when Caligula was with her.

Our golden brother continued to grow wily, learning from Livia whenever she would give him time. He started to exhibit something of her dry wit, and I was not sure how much I liked that in him. When she was acerbic it came over as clever and ingenious. Combined with his quick temper, when Caligula followed suit it more often manifested as acidic and harsh. Still, he was learning.

I learned little other than the drab day-to-day matters of how to run a household and manage the affairs of a husband from equally drab tutors. I took to sitting in front of the *tablinum*'s east-facing window for my morning instruction. The glare was horrible and off-putting, but at least there Agrippina could not copy my work – a habit at which she was adroit and ingenious. For some time she took to waiting until I had gone, then scratching out the name on my work and replacing it with her own. Our handwriting was remarkably similar, and she managed to get away with it for a while. I was curious as to why she did such things, since she was easily cleverer than I, but it became clear that she was simply saving time so that she had more opportunity to build and maintain her webs of control among the staff and our less witty friends.

I think even I, who had always been more aware of Agrippina's calculating mind than most, was surprised when one of her schemes at the villa came to a head. One of the slaves – a Bithynian girl, the daughter of our head gardener – possessed a brush that 'Pina coveted. Yes, the property of a slave is the property of their owner, but of course Mother was the girl's owner, not my sister. When 'Pina haughtily took the brush from the girl one afternoon, Mother gave her a clip round the ear and returned the slave's only possession, reminding our sister that she had dozens of brushes of her own. Sometimes, Mother said, it is best to let the slaves have their small things, for it makes them grateful and hard-working, rather than sullen and troublesome.

Agrippina had seethed for a while and then apparently forgot all about it. Over time, though, I uncovered how my sister had proceeded and I was impressed, though in a rather worried manner. She had monitored her network of slaves in the house until she discovered that two were regularly having congress in the wine store. Promptly, she blackmailed them into stealing one of Mother's necklaces when they were about their business.

Lo and behold, that necklace turned up in the Bithynian girl's bed. She was beaten while her father was restrained, wailing, and was then taken to the market and sold at a reduced price for farm labour. Two days later the girl's brush appeared on Agrippina's table. Only I noticed. It had been half a year and everyone else had forgotten that small incident. My sister had essentially condemned a slave girl to be worked to death and torn from the company of her father, and for what? For a brush, which I doubt she ever used once she had achieved possession of it.

I think the whole household breathed a sigh of relief when, at Saturnalia, Mother announced that she was seeking suitors for Agrippina. Even I felt less tense, which is a wicked thing to say about your own sister.

As the months wound on, the world changed in ways that were, while seemingly imperceptible in our enclosed domain, vast and far-reaching for the empire. Tiberius, the old monster, had grown ever more reclusive with the constant nudging and wheedling of Sejanus, and had stopped appearing in public entirely. Then, in a move that shocked the people of the city, he quit Rome altogether. Taking to a galley with his court and his guards, he sailed away down the Tiber and the coast to the isle of Capri, one of his favourite summer retreats, where he had many villas.

'Is Rome free now? Safe?' I had asked Caligula in the privacy of our villa upon hearing of the old man's departure. How naïve I was.

'Hardly,' sighed my brother. 'Thus far the Praetorians have been bound by their duty to the emperor. Now, with him gone, their command becomes the responsibility solely of Sejanus. He will be unrestrained, I think. More dangerous than ever. I already hear that noblemen and senators are retiring to their country estates, fearing what is to come.'

'Surely the emperor will still control them, even from his island?' I prompted. 'Sejanus will still answer to him.'

Agrippina, busily scribbling something in the corner, looked up sharply. 'What makes you think the emperor *ever* controlled Sejanus, even when he was here?'

I frowned, but my brother was nodding. 'Mark my words, Livilla: Sejanus has just become the most powerful and dangerous man in the empire and, until Tiberius chooses to return, he will likely stay that way. And having been denied a place in the succession, watch as he manoeuvres himself into it another way. I fear for Nero and Drusus now more than ever.'

My thoughts sank into a mire of tense unhappiness. The news of the emperor's leaving Rome had seemed to me a boon. We would no longer be under his direct scrutiny, Nero and Drusus would be safe, and Rome would flourish. If my brother was right, though, Rome was heading instead into dark storm clouds and our family stood in the prefect's way.

Things became tense for some time and the mood only lightened a little in spring, when word reached us that our brothers were coming home once more.

III

TROUBLE

The *navalia* was extraordinarily busy the morning we went to welcome back our brothers. Of course, as the military shipyard and main docks of the city, it seethed with life at all times, but that particular day was unusual; carts and wagons of supplies backed up into the streets beyond and soldiers scurried around trying to hold everything together. I remember asking Mother why there was so much activity.

'Fidenae,' she replied in an offhand manner, as if that explained everything. Her attention was centred on other things, such as herding the four of us through the crowded space, with the aid of six heavyset attendants and four slaves.

I pressed for more, my curiosity overcoming my common sense. 'What about Fidenae?' I knew it was a town a little upriver from Rome, but little more than that.

Mother turned an exasperated face on me as she grabbed Drusilla to stop her wandering off.

'The amphitheatre at Fidenae has collapsed,' she announced blandly.

It seemed that was all I was likely to get as she turned once more to call Agrippina closer. As she steered us on, Caligula moved near. 'I hear it was a true disaster. Thousands dead. The whole structure in ruins. They say the military has been mobilised to sail upriver and help in any way they can.'

The thought of so much death and ruination was sickening.

But, as I say, we were there for other reasons – to welcome back our brothers from their completed terms of service in the legions. The trireme from Syracusae that had brought in the men from Africa had already docked, and the ramp had been run out. Soldiers returning to the city either on leave or at the end of their term waited patiently on the ship, their kitbags slung over their shoulders. And at the forefront, close to the ramp, stood Nero and Drusus, bronzed and with sun-bleached hair, looking more like Berbers than Romans, in full uniform and thoroughly impressive. Their personal slaves stood close by carrying their armour and gear. The rest of their bounteous possessions would be following on by pack animal in due course. The majority of the soldiers on board kept back a respectful distance from the two tribunes, but one man who carried a helmet with a centurion's crest atop it stood with them, chatting as though every bit their equal. I saw Nero chuckle at some comment and the centurion grinned rather lewdly.

Beside me, Agrippina clucked her disapproval, which made me roll my eyes. 'Pina was now preparing for life as a Roman matron, and she seemed to be taking that role a little too seriously for my liking. She had been promised, as soon as she turned thirteen, to Domitius Ahenobarbus, a distant cousin almost twenty years her senior and with a dreadful reputation in almost every respect. Despite this, Agrippina was determined to make the best of the situation, planning to use her new husband to climb the social ladder and position herself well. I had little doubt that she would, and that she would learn to handle the dissolute and despicable Domitius with ease.

Drusilla was grinning from ear to ear, watching our brothers as they laughed with the centurion and waited for the all-clear to descend to the dock. Caligula's attention was elsewhere.

As I looked at our youngest brother, standing slightly back from the rest of us, I felt a tingle of anticipation run up my spine, for he wore a frown that I knew to mean trouble. His eyes were not on the ship or his older brothers, but were scanning the crowd around us, pausing here and there. A series of calls and whistles on the trireme seemed to indicate that it was now permissible to disembark, and the activity began. Drusilla was almost vibrating with excitement.

'I do hope that grizzled old man is not coming with them,' Agrippina muttered, eyeing the veteran centurion as he prepared to come ashore in the wake of the two senior officers. Mother replied with something, but I wasn't really listening by that time. I was looking at my other brother, wondering what was causing him such disquiet. As the family moved forward to greet the returning heroes, the hired men and slaves spread out, forming a cordon to protect our family from the huge crowds of the port. Caligula still hung back, squinting into the periphery of the complex.

'What is it?' I whispered nervously.

'Trouble.'

I waited for further elucidation, but it seemed not to be forthcoming, so I tried to follow his gaze. For a moment the crowd parted, and I caught a glimpse of half a dozen men standing on the steps of a large porticoed building. We were outside the *pomerium* here – that invisible boundary that marked the sacred limits of Rome – and so the restriction on weapons was not in effect. The six men were clad in plated armour, with white tunics and shields of blue, bearing the stars and the scorpion of the Praetorian Guard. One of them, a man with a tall white crest of feathers atop his helmet, was gesturing through the crowd. Caligula's eyes were on the move again and I followed them once more. Praetorians were in evidence in small groups of twos and threes, mainly around the edge of the navalia's open square. What were they looking for?

'Is it the Praetorians?' I asked quietly. I knew it was, of course, but I saw nothing perturbing about the presence of the emperor's guard, especially with Tiberius himself currently residing in his sumptuous villa on Capri, far to the south, so I wanted to prompt Caligula to explain.

'Of *course* it's the Praetorians,' he replied in a whisper.

'What about them?'

He turned to me then and I was startled to recognise actual fear in his eyes. 'Livilla, why do you think they are here?'

I shrugged, frowning myself now. The Guard were a chillingly common sight in Rome, though usually on the Palatine, or in the forum, or up at their own fortress, that great, brick block of brooding power that had been the contrivance of Sejanus and the emperor. The Praetorians were rarely present in force elsewhere without Tiberius being there in person.

'Is the emperor here?'

'No. You think he'll leave his island now?'

'They must be preparing to go and help with the disaster at Fidenae, then?'

'Think again, sister. The emperor and his prefect do not dispatch the elite Guard to help clear up rubble and burn bodies. That's a job for ordinary soldiers, marines and labourers.'

'What then?' His nervousness was beginning to affect me now. The crowd parted again momentarily. The six Praetorians had become nine.

'I cannot say, but I find it difficult to believe their presence at the return of Nero and Drusus a coincidence. Brace yourself for trouble, Livilla.'

I went to reply but our conversation was drowned out by our older brothers as they rejoined the family, embracing us all. Agrippina pulled a sour face as Nero enfolded her in his arms, huffing and pinching her nose.

'Did you sleep in a basket of dead fish, brother?'

Our oldest sibling chuckled. 'My, but how you've grown again, 'Pina. It is the scent of the sea upon me you smell. What did you expect? I have been on two ships almost constantly since I left Carthage, all the way from Africa to Rome.'

Drusus was there then, hugging me tight.

'I've missed you, little sister. You're so grown-up, now. How old are you?'

'Almost ten,' I replied.

'Jove, you're almost a woman. I had no idea we'd been in Africa so long.'

'I have your rooms ready and fresh clothing laid out for you,' Mother told her sons. 'Sallustia has been at work since before dawn with her cohorts to put together a homecoming meal fit for the pair of you, but the first thing of import is to get you to the baths. You cannot sit in our triclinium stinking of the docks.'

'The first thing,' Nero said with a smile, 'will be to present ourselves to the emperor. We carry dispatches from the proconsul at Ammaedara that it is our duty to deliver before attending to any personal concerns. Only then are we free of our posts and once more private citizens.'

I nodded with an easy smile. It would be nice to have the pair of them home once more. They would no doubt angle for another posting as soon as possible, but we could enjoy their presence and their stories for a while at least.

'Your duty will have to be carried out by another,' Mother said, and when Nero and Drusus frowned, she sighed. 'The emperor has retired to his villa on Capri in some sort of self-imposed exile. You had not heard?'

'Word reaches the desert outposts of Africa slowly, Mother. Has he gone mad?' Drusus asked in surprise.

'Shut up, boy. There are ears everywhere. *Never* speak ill of Tiberius. Never! He simply lives on Capri now. But . . .' Her voice dropped to a barely audible whisper as she drew both the older boys to her. 'Sejanus runs Rome now. The Praetorians control the streets and their prefect's word is law. He doesn't even bother ratifying his decisions with the emperor any longer.'

And suddenly I felt the cold stone of fear settle in my belly. Caligula was right. The Praetorians being here as Nero and Drusus returned could be no coincidence.

'Mother,' Caligula said, interrupting her.

'Gaius, you mustn't—' But as she turned to deliver a lesson in manners to her youngest son, she took in the look on his face and her eyes passed over him, widening at what they saw. I followed her glance and felt panic grip me.

More than a dozen soldiers in white bearing the scorpion insignia on their shields were marching across the square directly towards us. The man with the crest was some sort of officer and as they approached, the crowd melting out of their way like snow before a conflagration, he bellowed to our slaves and hired guards to stand down. I was impressed that they did not immediately do so, and the Praetorians had to stop for a moment, but within a heartbeat Mother was ordering our people to step aside. The slaves complied immediately, of course, but two of the hired men – both veterans of the legions – remained steadfast, drawing the clubs from their belts.

'Stand down!' snapped Mother, but she was too late to save them. The guardsmen already had their weapons drawn and two of them stepped forward, catching the rough club swings on their shields and deftly driving their gleaming blades into our people. The two men fell to the ground, blood pumping from neck and armpit as they died in gasps and gurgles, a river of crimson filling the gaps between the cobbles, racing away from the bodies as though through a labyrinth.

I stared in horror. My gorge rose at the ferrous smell of blood and I tried not to look at the convulsing men. I had seen a man die, once, years back in the emperor's court at the hand of the shadowy Sejanus, but that had been at the request of Tiberius himself and, at least to some extent, a state execution. Never had I seen such open, wanton bloodshed as this. The private staff of a noble Roman family cut down in the street. I was cold as ice.

Mother pushed us behind her as she approached the scene, treading carefully to avoid the slick of red. As the officer stepped forward and his men lowered their blood-coated blades to move aside, Mother pulled herself up to her full height, matching the officer and meeting him eye to eye, her gaze full of steel.

'What is the meaning of this?'

There was a momentary pause and I realised then that the whole navalia was silent. The crowd had stopped everything en masse and was watching the scene unfold. The Praetorian officer cleared his throat.

'On the orders of Lucius Aelius Sejanus, Prefect of the Guard, right hand of the emperor, I bear a warrant for the arrest of the lady Vipsania Agrippina and of her son, the tribune Nero Julius Caesar Germanicus.'

I felt my panic ascend to new heights. This had to be a mistake.

'Nonsense,' snapped Mother. 'I am the daughter-in-law of the emperor, officer. I recognise no authority above his, and most certainly not that of Sejanus. Return to your master and tell him that I will submit to your warrant when it bears the seal of Tiberius.'

Caligula was suddenly next to me and my sisters, his arms out as if to protect the three of us from this man. I truly believe that he would have taken a Praetorian sword that day to defend us if he had to. But it was not us the officer wanted.

'Sejanus bears the emperor's authority in all things, Domina,' the Praetorian said in leaden tones. 'You will submit to the warrant and come with us peacefully, along with your son, Nero, or we will be required to take you by force. That would be unseemly and very unpleasant for all of us, and I urge you to submit.'

Again, Mother opened her mouth to deny him, her face full of imperial hauteur, but Nero pushed past us all to stand beside her.

'Peace, Mother.' He turned to the officer. 'What are the charges?'

'You are both charged with numerous offences of treason under the *lex maiestatis*.'

'Pah!' Nero snorted. 'This is ridiculous. I have spent the past four years on the border of the empire, fighting the emperor's enemies. I have had no *time* to commit treason, let alone desire. And my mother has done naught but raise a family in these difficult days. Our advocate will wipe the basilica floor with these charges.'

The Praetorian's eyes narrowed slightly. 'There will be no advocacy. You are both to be escorted to your family holding on the Palatine, where you will remain under arrest until such time as the prefect decides your penalties.'

Again, Mother began to speak, but Nero was there once more, attempting to calm the situation. 'Be patient, Mother. If we must remain at the Palatine house then we can do that. It will give us time to prepare a case and send off an appeal to the emperor.' He turned back to the officer. 'Put away your blades. We will come peacefully.'

The rest of us just watched, dumbstruck, as our mother and oldest brother were marched off towards the city's heart. The officer remained for a moment, his suspicious gaze sliding across the five of us: three girls, Caligula and Drusus.

Of all the ruinations my heart has experienced, that moment was one of the very worst: watching my mother walking away, a haughty nobility to her step even at this dreadful juncture. The back of her head with her naturally wavy hair pulled into tighter ripples and pinned at the nape of her neck. Her simple white tunic and her rich yellow *stola*, made all the more delicate by the indigo *palla* wrapped around her.

Effortlessly elegant. My eyes filled with tears, my vision blurred.

'What are we supposed to do now?' Drusus asked the Praetorian archly.

'It is the prefect's command that you be separated from your mater. You may not visit the Palatine property, and the villa beyond the Tiber is hereby impounded until such time as its future is decided. You shall take your siblings and lodge with the lady Livia at her villa.'

Drusus nodded slowly. His face clearly informed us that he wanted nothing more than to argue with the officer, but that he was also under no illusions as to where that would lead. The Praetorian turned and strolled off through the wide avenue left in the crowd by the retreating guardsmen.

'We shall send to Tiberius,' Drusus said firmly, 'and enlist the help of every great advocate we can find.'

'It will be of no use,' Caligula replied in a flat voice. He pointed, and we all followed his gesture.

I felt sick.

As he crossed the square, the Praetorian officer met up with the very centurion that had stood beside my brothers on the ship. No money exchanged hands, only words, but the situation was clear. The veteran centurion could only be a respected citizen by his very position, and his word would be admissible evidence. All he need do was condemn my brother and every word from his lips would be a nail in the cross upon which Nero would be hung.

'The devious bastard,' Drusus spat. 'Rabirius has been with Nero for two years now.'

'And how long do you think he has been reporting to Sejanus?' muttered Caligula. 'Nero was cautioned by Mother and by our great-grandmother, but it seems he has not been careful enough. Pray to Minerva that you have been tighter-lipped, Drusus.' Our middle brother stared at Caligula, his eyes betraying his nerves as he attempted to think back over two years and more at Nicopolis to what he might have said, and to whom.

'And Mother?' Agrippina whispered. 'Why her?'

Caligula shrugged. 'It would not be difficult to provide evidence from among our staff at the villa. A slave's word may count for nothing, but there are plenty of freedmen and citizens that attended Mother daily. I say again, all of you, take note of this example. Be more than careful what you say and before whom you say it. You, Drusus, are now the prime candidate for the succession, after all.'

And he said no more, keeping to his own advice. We all knew what he meant, and why it couldn't be spoken aloud, for hadn't he said as much when the emperor had departed last year? Sejanus now saw himself as the emperor's successor, and while Tiberius languished on Capri, Sejanus ruled in Rome. Nero had been an obstacle in the succession. And so was Drusus.

'At least we should be safe to speak openly at Great-Grandmother's villa,' Drusus muttered. 'There we can plan. She lives six miles from the city and if her staff were unreliable, with *her* tongue she'd have been arrested years ago.'

'Do not be so sure about that, Drusus,' our younger brother said quietly. 'Though the act is Sejanus', the emperor still trusts his prefect implicitly. No appeal to Capri is going to change Nero's fate, nor Mother's, now, and you know how much Livia and the emperor dislike each other. I have the feeling that somehow either Sejanus or the emperor are putting all the eggs they fear to be bad into one basket.'

'There must be something we can do?' Drusus said desperately.

'No,' snapped his younger brother forcefully, the suddenness and heat of his anger startling us all, so rarely did his calm mask slip. But as soon as the ire had appeared, it was gone again. 'No, Drusus,' he repeated, this time calmer. 'Moving on this would just further endanger us.'

All I knew was that Mother and Nero were gone. I didn't know whether we'd ever see them again and, though cold fear still gripped me, I felt certain that the gods who so loved my father could not let wicked men do away with my innocent family.

Gods are capricious, though.

IV

THE OLD ROME PASSES

We did as we were bidden, moving to the estate of our great-grandmother. We lived in a strange state of tension in that grand villa north of Rome, in the green valley of the Tiber and away from the stink and the machinations of the wicked. Livia, even at her advanced age, was a woman always given to fascination and new things, and her house was correspondingly busy and interesting with a steady stream of famous and important visitors over the months. Despite her fearsome reputation – some said, albeit under their breath, that Livia had been far more than an emperor's wife and had killed more people than the bloody flux – she was a generous and kind hostess to the four of us.

Of we girls, Drusilla and I remained at her house, and Agrippina, who married Domitius Ahenobarbus only a month after mother's arrest, went to live in his household. It was an interesting wedding, to say the least. It had been Tiberius who had selected the groom, of course, as our nominal pater familias, and consequently the ceremony took place in his household on the Palatine, though the wedding of someone so distantly connected had not even drawn well wishes from Capri, let alone the emperor himself.

Consequently, Sejanus was the master of the household, which sent shivers through us all. He stood like the figure of Hades at the periphery of it all most of the time, his eyes permanently roving across those present while those observed threw him nervous, ingratiating smiles.

I was dressed in a dark blue stola that made my skin look like sickly alabaster, with a pale blue palla over the top. My hair had been attacked time and again by the slaves in an attempt to make me look like anything but Medusa, though they had largely failed. Coils of it kept falling across my forehead and I constantly had to brush them behind my ears.

As the ceremony itself was concluded – the ten witnesses rather tellingly drawn from the ranks of the Praetorian officers – the feast was made ready and I found myself at a loose end. Agrippina was taking charge of things, directing the slaves hither and thither, Caligula was nowhere to be seen, Lepidus and Drusilla were together – I was alone in a sea of people, most of whom I did not know. As I looked around, wondering what to do and avoiding eye contact with the Praetorian prefect, Caligula appeared in a doorway and gestured to me.

'Can you find the groom? There is a senator here who wishes to speak to him.'

I frowned. My brother had obviously been trapped in a conversation, but I was unoccupied. Perhaps it was unseemly to ask a Roman lady to run errands at a feast, but I had ever been practical and I was the bride's sister, after all. I hurried over to Agrippina, who had just slapped a young slave for having spilled wine on the cloth and was now glowering at the timid girl.

'One of the senators is looking for your husband. Do you know where he is?'

'He went to change his tunic,' said 'Pina absently, waving at a door.

I nodded and crossed the room, knocking at the door in case I entered and found my new brother-in-law half-naked within. Ahenobarbus' gruff voice called for me to enter, and I did so.

'My brother is with one of the senators. He . . .'

My voice tailed off. Ahenobarbus was dressed again as two half-naked slave girls helped settle his toga into a more proper position. But my eyes were not on him. They were on the slaves. The two who were adjusting his dress had been beaten, one with a bloody lip and the other with an already blossoming black eye. Both exhibited bruises old and new across their flesh, which were easy to spot given their state of half-undress. A third girl lay on the floor weeping quietly, her hair matted with blood.

What monster had the emperor betrothed my sister to?

'Well?' snapped the man, brushing off the slaves and finishing the job himself, heedless of the violated girls around him, as though they were nothing of interest.

'I . . . Gaius. He is with a senator. Uh . . . he wanted me to find you,' I stuttered. 'They are in the circular tablinum.' I felt shocked to the core.

The man simply nodded and walked past me, opening the door and returning to the guests with a horrible leer plastered across his face. I stared agog for a moment at the three poor girls, and then scurried out. By the time I caught up, Ahenobarbus was in the room with the senator and Caligula was strolling back out, looking relieved to be freed from the conversational trap.

'I am aghast,' I hissed at my brother, taking him by the arm and steering him to the quieter end of the room.

'What is it?'

'That man. He has forced himself upon three slave girls while his guests waited for him. And he beat them all too. Agrippina should know about this.'

I was surprised at the look on his face. He seemed unsure, as though weighing up possibilities.

'Gaius?'

'It's not our place, Livilla. The match was made by the emperor. You and I are not even adults yet, let alone with adequate authority to interfere. And Sejanus is monitoring all the proceedings. See how his eyes follow every movement. Do not cause waves.'

'She has to know,' I snapped peevishly and stalked over to our sister, who was adjusting a garland at the table and waving away a slave who had apparently not done the job to her satisfaction. I tried not to be irritated that my brother followed me.

''Pina,' I said in an urgent hiss.

'What?'

'Your husband. I just found him . . . He was with the slave girls. He despoiled them and beat them!'

I was dumbfounded when our sister shrugged carelessly. 'They are slaves.'

'Well, yes,' I replied. He was well within his rights, after all, and I was no radical lover of slave freedoms myself, but that was hardly the point. 'But if he is that sort of man . . .'

'My husband's reputation precedes him, Livilla. We all knew what he was going to be like. I consider what you found a boon. If he is attacking the slaves, then he is not hurting me. I will throw slave girls at him if need be.'

I blinked. Gods, but that was a cold way to think, and yet it was a practical solution, I had to admit. Caligula held her eyes for a long moment.

'You are strong-willed and clever, and I trust you to keep yourself safe, 'Pina, but know that if he truly hurts you, I will visit the same pain upon him.' And with that, he strolled off. I stood, turning to find the prefect, Sejanus, watching me with his icy eyes.

I did not enjoy the wedding feast at all.

We saw her intermittently for family visits after that, and every time she had acquired a new bruise for which she haughtily threw out some implausible explanation. When Drusilla and I suggested that perhaps there was a way she could seek to have the marriage annulled, she told us to mind our own business. Of course, it is the right of a husband to beat his wife if he wishes, but I am sure that Livia could have done something had Agrippina but asked. Still, she had her own plan in place – her own ladder to climb – and she did not wish us to interfere with it.

Caligula remained with us, and remained nominally a child, free of his toga and the dangerous responsibilities it brought. Despite his pragmatic attitude at the wedding, he had almost needed to be restrained during one of her visits with her new husband, when she sported not only bruises but a neatly stitched gash in her neck. She explained it away as an accident with a fruit knife. She fooled no one, and Ahenobarbus did not even bother to hide his expression of satisfaction. Caligula had excused himself from the gathering, but not before spitting a barbed insult at the man under his breath.

Drusus stayed at Livia's villa with us too, though with permission from the emperor he had married Aemilia Lepida, sister of that handsome young man who still came to visit us and hang around Drusilla like a puppy with his tongue lolling out. And with his new bride and a façade of loyal imperial subject to maintain, Drusus was hardly about to attack the unpleasant Ahenobarbus on behalf of our sister whenever she visited with a new injury.

Our sojourn with the grand dame of Rome might have been joyous, but life was tainted for us by the overhanging shadow of Mother and Nero. Both had remained in her Palatine house, removed from us and awaiting some arbitrary judgement from the Praetorian prefect, until early that year when, as the snows began to melt, the emperor confirmed the decision of Sejanus.

'Exile?' I said in disbelieving tones.

Caligula nodded, reading the missive from the palace with an inscrutable expression on his face. 'Separate islands. Pandataria and Pontia.' He erupted in a sudden bestial snarl, and cast the letter to the table. I picked it up warily, watching my brother for another outburst, and re-read the words.

'At least it is exile,' I said in a small voice, clinging to whatever small hope I could find. 'Plenty of great men and women have returned from exile over the centuries. Cicero, for example. Or Marius.'

'These are not the days of Cicero and Marius, sister,' Caligula replied in a dark voice. His eyes strayed around the small winter triclinium, though we were alone and relatively safe in the house. 'The senate are not going to lift the exile like they did for Cicero. And Nero is not going to march on Rome like Marius. They are alone and vulnerable and, with the emperor *in absentia*, it is Sejanus who dances the puppets in Rome. Exile is not the punishment he imposes. It is just the subtle first stage of a slow and quiet death sentence.'

I felt cold disbelief settle upon me.

'But I have seen Sejanus – the Praetorians of his – kill people. They do so surprisingly often. If he were going to kill them, surely . . .'

'If he were to kill the wife and the son of Germanicus, the emperor's heir, there would be a public outcry. Sejanus is powerful – the most powerful man in Rome – but even he cannot afford the scandal that would cause. No, he will shuffle his enemies somewhere far away where they will soon be forgotten by the populace and can die quietly without an outcry.'

He rose and left the room, and I suddenly realised what the isolation of an enforced exile might be like.

I wept often after that.

With her usual sharp mind, until the spring of this last year of our time in the villa, my great-grandmother Livia attempted to lift my spirits whenever things got to me by parading a line of suitors before me, asking whether any of them took my fancy.

Mother would not have asked such a thing, and Agrippina had not been consulted over her marriage. Needless to say, I had no interest in any of them, no matter how pleasant they seemed. Though Livia had weeded out the grasping, the vapid, the cruel and the immoral, even the best of Roman youth that remained interested me little. How could I consider giving up my family and joining another when my own was diminishing and teetering on the brink of extinction?

With the change in season came a withering of our great-grandmother. Her body seemed over a period of months to relinquish the will to go on, though her mind and her sharp tongue and acerbic wit never faltered. Indeed, if anything, she became ever more forthright and shocking in that time, leading to a thinning of the ranks of important visitors. I wonder sometimes whether, had we not spent that time in her house, Caligula's later life might have worked out much differently, for he acquired every bit of her wit and sharpness over our time there, and that acid wit was very much part of his trouble.

A series of Rome's very best physicians came to see Livia. She decried the opinions of the Judaic ones as worthless since they were impious and wouldn't recognise the true gods of Rome, the Greek ones she considered dissolute, and the Aegyptian ones she said reeked of 'Marcus Antonius and his ilk'. That left only the Roman-born physicians, and everyone knows how inferior they are to Greeks, Jews and Aegyptians in the healing arts. Thus Great-Grandmother declined slowly.

By the time the summer truly hit, bringing with it that cloying, hot dusty stink that pervades the city, Livia was too ill to retreat to the coastal villa as had long been her habit, and as we watched the leaves in the garden begin to turn and the world to pass from green to golden, she finally became unable to leave her suite, then her room, and finally her bed.

We were brought into her presence then. I think it was two days after the Ides of September. The trees at the edge of the villa estate were burnished copper and blended almost seamlessly with the golden sunset of that evening. Livia had not left her bed throughout the day and for the first time the slaves were worried for her, as all her food and drink had been removed untouched. Livia called for her family, which is always the worst sign. Agrippina had been summoned from the house of Ahenobarbus, and the five remaining members of the family of Germanicus who were not languishing in an island prison stood in Livia's chamber, alone with our great-grandmother in glowing lamplight.

'Livilla,' she said, and I remember being startled. As the youngest I was used to being addressed last in any group, and certainly not first. 'Livilla,' she said, 'I know that you still weep for your mother and your brother, and that despite everything you know and have been told, you continue to harbour the hope that they will be returned to you. I shall tell you here and now: that will not happen. Their time is done and you must harden your heart to that fact. *All* of you must. If Nero and your mother still live, then they are now counting out the days until they cross the final river. It is laudable to respect your family and wonderful to wish them well, but turn from them now. Forget them. You must now look to your own safety.'

At this she leaned back slightly, addressing all of us.

'I am dying and I shall not see another Saturnalia. When the snows come I shall be cosy in a jar somewhere in that great drum of a mausoleum. I have lived a long and very interesting life and I am comfortable with my ending, so fear not for me. I shall join your great-grandfather, who has probably already managed to find a way to rule in Elysium. But when I am gone, you will no longer enjoy my protection. I know you have felt safe here, but a great deal of that is due to my ongoing efforts and the shelter my very name gives you from snakes like Sejanus and Tiberius. You will be at risk from both of them. If you wish to avoid sharing your mother's fate, be wary in all you do.'

'Surely the emperor will not let Sejanus remove *both* his heirs?' Drusus frowned.

'If Sejanus does not, then it is very possible that my son *will*. You are his heir only because there has thus far been no better candidate. Do not trust Tiberius. Simply being part of his family will not save you. I have informed him several times of my impending demise and he has declined even to visit me. He will not hold a funeral for me and give appropriate orations, such is his hatred. I, the greatest woman in the history of our great empire, am to pass unsung.'

I remember catching the look in Caligula's eye then and swallowing nervously as he walked slowly towards her bed.

'*I* will hold your funeral,' he said loudly, with unexpected fervour.

'No you will not,' she replied calmly.

'I *shall*,' he insisted, and I could see the defiance set in his eyes. The simple fact was that though such a decision was incredibly dangerous and could quite easily cost him his life, my brother had grown and changed under Livia's keen wit, and he felt he owed her this. Throughout his life, Caligula always paid his debts, whether for good or for ill.

'And I shall orate at the funeral if the emperor is too weak and bitter to attend,' he added. 'Rome shall mourn and marvel at the grandeur of your passing.'

Livia narrowed her eyes. 'It is unheard of for a boy to hold funeral rites. It is not your place to do so and, if you do, then you will incur the wrath of Tiberius. You could bring upon yourself the very peril against which I am trying to warn you. You must not do such a thing, young Gaius. There are distant cousins who will do the job quietly and shuffle me off into an urn in a way that will not cause ripples in Rome.'

Livia then fell into a wracking coughing fit that drained her, and we were summarily dismissed. We left quiet and sullen, Caligula fuming impotently. For days afterwards we were repeatedly brought into the old lady's bedchamber and lectured on the best ways to keep ourselves safe when she was gone, who could be trusted – virtually no one – and who could not – every citizen of Rome and his dog. We were prepared in the only way Great-Grandmother could do so.

And then one day in September, while we were sitting sharing a small meal in the triclinium with the ever-present Lepidus, Caligula alone was summoned to our great-grandmother's bedside. We shared curious, nervous looks at this unexpected development, and my quiet, mouse-like sister frowned deeply as the door closed behind him.

'Gaius loves our great-grandmother,' she murmured – an odd statement, driven I think by the acknowledgement that his attention was for once on Livia and not on her. And while Caligula was ever protective of his little sister, seeing that 'Pina and myself were made of stronger stuff, he *did* love Livia too.

Our brother was gone for over an hour as his food became cold and our sense of dread intensified. Then, finally, he returned, his face drawn and pale.

'Livia has joined the gods,' he announced simply, five words that carried the weight of an empire, enough to crush even the strongest man. We sat in silence, not surprised, for we had all seen it coming over the days, but somehow unbelieving that the unstoppable power that was our great-grandmother had succumbed. And where it had been Drusus' place to perform the *conclamatio* and speak the lady's name back to her as the oldest child – Tiberius' place in truth, though that was hardly going to happen – the task seemed to have been given by her to the *youngest* male in the family. I think that even then, our great-grandmother saw something in him.

'Livia has passed,' Caligula said again, 'and the old Rome passes with her. The Rome we all know. The Rome of worthy men. The Rome of values and trust and morals. And whether you are with me or not, I will mourn both Livia and Rome, in public and in a manner befitting them: a funeral in the forum, public and grand, with appropriate spectacle and clamour. And Mars will have to brace his shield to save Sejanus or Tiberius should they try and stop me.'

I remember feeling a chill at the power in his words. A challenge to the emperor, no less. Drusus finally spoke quietly.

'You will bring doom down upon yourself, on *all of us*, if you defy Tiberius and laud his mother. Are you mad?'

'Hardly,' snapped Caligula. 'But the passing of the greatest blood in Rome cannot go quietly just because the whole of the empire quakes in fear of a tyrant. If it means my neck under a Praetorian blade, then so be it. I have been circumspect and held my own council all this time, and I would not risk my life for gossip, but some things are too important to ignore. Sometimes a line has to be drawn and toed. I shall not be turned aside from this.'

I shook my head at the insanity of it. Such foolishness. Simple closeness with our great-grandmother was surely not enough to drive such crazed notions?

Lepidus, remarkably, stepped up next to my brother. 'I will help. I will support you, Gaius. She deserves no less.'

And Drusilla went to him, for how could she hope to deny Caligula and Lepidus, the twin pillars that held up her heavens? And I, in the end, joined him. I quivered with fear at the very thought of what we proposed to do, but I stood firm by my family, and by my brother, for in that moment, defiant and honourable, Caligula was magnificent – the very embodiment of *romanitas*.

Drusus snarled his unwillingness to put his new wife's family through all of this and remained apart, and Agrippina pointed out that it would be Ahenobarbus' decision and not hers whether they attend. Caligula was so taut and angry and strong at that moment that he didn't even challenge our oldest sister over her willingness to adhere so to a man who beat her.

We all knew that Agrippina and Drusus would be there in the end, even if they said they could not, for Livia had been a great woman and a safe haven for us in a most terrible time.

The next ten days passed with increasing tension for those remaining in the villa. Our youngest brother took on the role of the family's pater familias, at least in terms of Livia's death and funeral arrangements, much to the shock of the servants and slaves, for he was still a boy – albeit a boy of seventeen, long past the age any son of Rome should have taken a man's toga.

Caligula spent those ten days pacing the house, firing out commands like a general on a battlefield, making difficult decisions and spending the money of Livia's estate as though it were his own, putting everything together for a grand funeral. Everything, that is, but a date.

Finally, one morning, Drusus found his brother in the garden where Drusilla and I were discussing the thorny subject of marriage and suitors. I remember the boys' exchange not for what it contained, though that alone should make it stand out, but for the clear change in the relationship between my brothers.

'Why do you delay?' Drusus said in an irritated tone.

'What?'

'Our great-grandmother lies in state in the atrium, unmourned, making entrance to the house troublesome and, frankly, beginning to smell a little. The autumn weather is still too warm to keep a dead body around for days. It is not healthy. Why have you everything arranged, yet nothing is happening?'

Caligula fixed his older brother then with a gaze full of Noric steel, unyielding and unbreakable. 'Because I am giving the emperor one last chance to be a Roman, a son and a human being. He will come. He must, for if he doesn't, all Rome will know him for a spiteful, ignoble coward.'

Drusus flashed a nervous glance around the garden, as though every shrub and flower were reporting our words to Sejanus. 'Do not say such things. Words like that kill whole families.'

Caligula's gaze lost none of its strength as he snorted. 'Worry not, Drusus. Your precious reputation will be untarnished, your new family safe. If Tiberius' or Sejanus' ire should fall upon me, I shall make sure to stop it spreading to you or your lovely wife.'

'He will not come,' Drusus muttered, abashed at his manliness being challenged so by his brother's manner.

'If he is not here before the ides of the month, then I shall make an extra niche in the mausoleum, for I shall be burying Livia, Rome, *and* the emperor's tattered reputation.'

Drusus stepped forward and grabbed Caligula by the shoulders. 'Brother, he *will not come.* A man who hides from the world on an island in his own exile and leaves Rome to sweat under the bloody blade of his Praetorian prefect cares nothing for his reputation. If we must defy convention and bury Livia ourselves, then let us do so now.'

There was a long, cold pause and Caligula shook his head slowly. 'I have to give him the chance, Drusus. I have to believe that there's enough spirit left in him to come, else the emperor is nothing and we are ruled by Sejanus. Don't you understand?'

'He is not coming, and Livia deserves better than to lie mouldering.'

Again, there was a pause. Drusus had hit the mark, finally, and Caligula nodded. 'One more day. I give him one more day, and then we hold her funeral.'

It was a defining moment for Caligula. I think that Livia's death and his subsequent decision to do the right thing despite the very real danger of utter destruction it carried with it was the first moment our youngest brother displayed both the will and the ability to command. I often wonder what he would have been like had he been a tribune in Africa like his brothers. He would, I suspect, have shined bright there.

*

In the event, Drusus was proved right. Not only did the emperor remain on Capri, but he declined even to send a representative or a message of condolence to any of us. It seems to me that he considered the passing of his mother a freeing from maternal shackles that had been plaguing him for years.

While the morning sun still climbed the vault of blue, the sons and daughters of Germanicus moved out of Livia's villa in a procession of comfortable carriages, the central one bearing the body, wrapped tight in perfumed linens inside her rich clothing, for her odour was becoming hard to conceal.

When we reached the city, we descended from our carriages at the Campus Martius where everything awaited us. Her body was borne from the carriage onto a litter, which was lifted by eight Numidian slaves taken in battle during that same campaign in which Nero had fought across Africa. Each slave was dressed in leopard skins and bronze accoutrements, and the litter was festooned with flowers designed to look wonderful but also to help drown out the smell of decay within. The display was impressive.

At the head of the long square that flanked the Pantheon and Agrippa's baths, the musicians waited patiently, twenty of them, each with their instruments ready. Behind them came a chorus of eight singers, hired at ridiculous expense from the most renowned theatre troupe in Rome, each armed with an hour-long song of remembrance of the deeds and qualities of the great empress we bore. Caligula had decided to forego the traditional jesters or comic players, feeling that Rome needed to consider the occasion a sombre one.

Then came two dozen actors from that same troupe dressed as the notables of our family for the past century, each wearing one of the death masks of Livia's – or her husband's – ancestors, such that her father, one of the *optimates* who had fought to maintain the Republic at all costs, walked alongside the same Caesar who had sought to end it in autocracy.

Behind the procession of musicians, singers and ancestors came the lady herself, and behind that came the family. There was some consideration as to the order of march. Normally the undertaker would settle any confusion but with there being no close or direct family here, Livia's great-grandchildren were all the family to be found. Neither Drusus' wife, nor Agrippina's husband came with us, though whether through fear or command, I cannot say. It was Drusus' rightful position to lead the column, yet with Caligula having organised everything, it was he who took the front place. In fact, through some unspoken desire to remain as inconspicuous as possible, Drusus brought up the rear, just before all the freedmen and slaves of her household. Torches were lit and passed to the bearers who flanked the procession all along the line and once my brother was satisfied that all was correct, he gave the order and we began our slow, stately procession through the city.

The crowds had gathered, for news of the coming funeral had spread throughout Rome a number of days earlier, and the previous morning's confirmation of the intended date and time had sent a thrill of anticipation through the populace. Almost certainly many of those attending were doing so in the mistaken belief that the emperor himself would be there, though no one seemed disinclined to take part in the wailing or the moaning as we passed through the region. The Campus Martius had, less than a century earlier, been mostly open grassland before this deceased traveller's own husband had filled that green swathe with grand monuments and buildings. We were, to some extent, passing through the legacy of our great-grandmother and her husband on the way to her funeral. And as we passed the *arx* and the Capitoline temples into the forum, the reminders of her great husband's works continued to present themselves. We passed the curia where the senate met and the monuments of the western end of the forum and arrived at the open square where the crowd was held back by hired guards. And there the funeral took place. There, with the Temple of the Divine Caesar behind us, the arch of Actium – Augustus' greatest military victory – to the side and, before us, the great rostrum constructed by Livia's husband and from which he had made so many speeches in his time. It was on this grand platform that she was placed, to the groaning and moaning of the crowd.

It did not escape my attention – in fact, it sent a jolt of panic through me – that members of the Praetorian Guard were in evidence at all junctions, high places and doorways, as though they sealed us all in. I couldn't see him at the time, but I think we all knew that Sejanus was there. And above us, atop the Palatine, the towering palace of Tiberius loomed, as though ready to fall on us for our insolence and impropriety.

The funerary song finally ended with perfect timing as the masked ancestors took their places around the rostrum and, with the end of the song and the music, the crowd fell into a hush. There was a long silence, and then Caligula began to speak.

'If the great and the mighty cannot lay their own to rest, then the pious and the true must take up the burden.'

There was a horrible silence. I stared at my brother but, for all the shock value of his opening remark, I understood and I could not argue. In merely arranging the funeral and agreeing to give the oration, Caligula had challenged the emperor already, and so there was little point in denying it. If he was going to put his life on the line for family honour, he might as well make it a grand gesture.

And the people of Rome received it in style. They stood in respectful silence as the young orator who now took centre stage in the forum began to list our great-grandmother's lifetime events and achievements. He began slow and quiet, such that the periphery of the crowd strained to hear, and yet he gave every line of his speech the power and presence of a significant moment of history.

I found myself standing in rapt silence along with everyone else. I had known Livia was a great woman, but I had not quite realised how many aspects of life in the empire and its leading families she had touched in some way. I understood then that when Caligula had been called into Livia's chamber on the day of her death, it had not been the first time he had attended her alone. Over the preceding months, the pair of them must have had many such meetings as my brother learned the history of our family from the beginning, which he now related.

It was simply stunning. And the crowd drank it in.

It took him an hour just to reach the death of Augustus, and for half an hour beyond that he told of how even as a widow with no direct power, still Livia had helped shape the Rome that now stood around us. And as he moved forward inexorably through time, so his voice gradually rose in strength and volume, such that he began to boom around the forum, his tone echoing from every wall and column. And as I listened to the deeds of this greatest of women, so I realised that he had been correct: the old Rome had died with her.

'These are the achievements,' he concluded, his voice reverberating around the façades and colonnades of the forum, 'of Livia, who is called Julia Augusta, empress, *mater patriae*, great dame of Rome. Four generations have flourished under her watchful eye and though the ship of state has navigated muddied waters and circled the maelstrom, with her hands on the steering oars she has weathered every storm.'

Such repeated digs at the emperor was a horrifyingly perilous course. Mater patriae – Mother of Rome – was a title that had been voted upon Livia, but which Tiberius had vetoed. Its use alone was a challenge to the emperor. And to all but accuse him of steering the empire into disaster?

The crowd remained intent and respectfully silent for almost two hours that day – even for the last quarter of an hour, as Caligula skirted treason in his denunciations of those who would not honour their ancestors, as he called Tiberius a coward, a poor son, a tyrant and a monster, albeit couched in nebulous terms such that a good advocate could argue his innocence. No one present, though, laboured under a misapprehension as to his meaning. My heart began to beat faster and the nervous tension crackled through my body as I listened to treason. My eyes jumped from one disapproving Praetorian face in the crowd to another. Something would happen soon, I felt horribly certain, and yet still no guardsman moved.

Then we gathered up the body once more and returned to the processional order as the musicians began again and we moved out of the forum and back to the Campus Martius, towards that same great drum of a mausoleum that had now held my father for a decade. Less than an hour later, those Numidian slaves bore their sad load onto the pyre that had been constructed beside the mausoleum, and those with standing in the city who were willing to risk defying the emperor came by in an orderly queue, carefully controlled by the hired hands and the slaves, to place gifts and spices and perfumes and all manner of valuables within the pyre.

There were fewer than might have been expected in better times, but more than I thought there would be that day, considering the overriding threat of the emperor's wrath, and the corresponding menace posed by those same Praetorians who had followed the procession to the mausoleum and now stood around the periphery here too. The threat we had felt in the forum had not dissipated, merely following us to this new location. Caligula lit the pyre. By this point, no one would have argued his right to do it. We watched as the great wood stack burned, fiercer and faster than I had anticipated – remember that this was my first funeral. Once all that remained was a pit of glowing orange embers atop a mound of ash, with a few grisly lumps of bone here and there, the wine and the water were applied, creating a column of smoke that must have risen a hundred feet into the air, marring the blue of that clear autumn sky. The crowd hailed Livia one last time and departed.

A group of slaves gathered up the ashes into a cloth, dried them as best they could, and carefully tipped them into the delicate and glorious urn that stood waiting. The ceremonial bone was buried by a priest with my brother's aid, and a pig was sacrificed to consecrate the ground. The villa staff broke out the funeral feast, and we sat on chairs prepared for the occasion and ate in silence as the undertaker and his staff tidied up and put things right around us.

Finally, as I finished, I looked around and my heart lurched. The crowd had gone. The Praetorians had not.

Indeed, the shadowy, wraithlike figure of Sejanus stood in the lee of the mausoleum and, as the food was tidied away, he stepped forward. Caligula rose and made to step towards him, but Drusus was suddenly in front of him, perhaps driven to take his appropriate place as pater familias despite his previous minor role in proceedings. Perhaps it was to protect Caligula. He met Sejanus face to face and I was immensely glad it was he doing it and not me, for I quailed even at the sight of the prefect, and could never have met his gaze even had I been tall enough.

'Your presence is in poor taste, commander,' Drusus said quietly. Sejanus' brow rose quizzically.

'And *your* presence is in contravention of the traditional code of conduct for such events, as well as a direct affront to the emperor.'

'This is a family occasion, Sejanus, and the funeral is now over, or will be once we return to the villa and make our offering to the *lares*.'

'That will not be possible,' replied the Praetorian prefect with a smile that put me in mind of a torturer weighing up his victim. I shuddered.

'Explain,' Drusus said in dangerous tones.

'You will not be returning to the lady Livia's villa. With her death, her property passes to the possession of her son, and the emperor wishes the house to be cleared of occupants.'

Caligula's eyes narrowed angrily and he stepped next to Drusus. 'If we cannot return and purify the house, then the funeral is incomplete. This is reprehensible behaviour, Prefect.'

Sejanus was smiling now. 'Be that as it may, the emperor's decision is made. That estate is no longer your home. Your uncle Tiberius wishes you to be moved to the household of your grandmother, Antonia. All of you.'

Drusus opened his mouth, bile-filled and angry, but now Caligula stepped in front of him, cutting him off. 'Very well, Prefect,' the younger brother said. 'I presume you will arrange for our possessions to be moved accordingly?'

'Any possessions not deemed property of the villa and therefore of the emperor, yes.'

Drusus was on the verge of exploding, and I noted with surprise Caligula press down forcefully onto his brother's foot, silencing him.

Sejanus laughed and motioned for his men to move out. We watched the Praetorians file off down the street back towards the heart of the city in silence and, once we were alone with the slaves and freedmen, Drusus rounded on Caligula.

'Why did you do that?'

'Because if I had not, you would now be dead. I could see it in his eyes. He was just waiting for an excuse and I was determined not to give him one.'

'Did Tiberius really throw us out of the villa?' I asked quietly.

Caligula shrugged. 'It was probably the order of Sejanus on his behalf, but the result is the same so the source matters not. Note how we are not even allowed to collect our possessions. The funeral has been marred because we could not finish it with our libations at the villa, and he will not grant us any opportunity to do so. That was a deliberate move by Sejanus, else he would have let us return. He ruins the funeral in the hope of riling us to the point where we push him into something precipitous. Do not let him get to you.'

'Who is Antonia?' I asked in that same small voice. There were many Antonias in our family, right back to the days of the high Republic.

Caligula turned with a sad smile. 'Our grandmother. Daughter of Marcus Antonius and niece of Augustus. She may be two decades younger than Livia, but if there is a woman in Rome with the power and personality to match her, it is Antonia. Great-Grandmother seemed to regard her highly, though in a somewhat opposed manner.'

'And will we be safe with her as we were with Livia?'

Caligula's half-smile slipped away. 'Now, Livilla, there is *nowhere* safe for us. Nowhere. Ever. Antonia lives on the Palatine, less than a *pilum*'s throw from the imperial palace where Sejanus now lives like a prince. We will be under the scrutiny of the Praetorians and the court at all times. Something dreadful is building in Rome, and to survive it we must be as shrewd and bold as Livia ever was. Be prepared. We are about to be thrown to the wolves.'

V

ANTONIA'S HOUSE

Antonia's house was utterly different to that of Livia. While the latter had entertained a regular succession of important folk but kept herself generally aloof and apart in the manner of a dowager empress, Antonia's house was lively – loud and exciting and full of characters. Having been born in Athens and with properties both there and in Aegyptus as well as in Rome, she was familiar with all things eastern, and she had no fear of the reputation a widow might be expected to acquire when her house was often full of male guests. Oddly, she never did achieve such a reputation, and I cannot truly understand why. Perhaps she was just too much of a force of nature to be tamed by Roman civility.

We were never alone there. We were not the only guests, and some stayed with her for months or even years. The expense she incurred must have been staggering, but then she had the funds to buy an empire had she wished, such was her pedigree.

Among those who were regularly part of her household we children of Germanicus made a number of friends who would stay with us for a lifetime – ours or theirs, at least. Perhaps most important of all was the handsome Julius Agrippa, grandson of King Herod of Judea, who had been fostered upon Antonia by that eastern monarch and who seemed thoroughly strange and otherworldly, yet good-humoured and exceedingly interesting. In addition to Julius, there was the young prince Antiochus of

Commagene, whose strangely angular face and olive skin made him look older than he was, and there was Ptolemy of Mauretania, that same king who had supported Rome in the war against Tacfarinas in Africa, where our brother Nero had acquired his scars.

These new companions were welcome. We had all felt the tension gradually mounting from the moment of Livia's death through to her funeral and beyond. We had begun to look in every corner before we spoke, half expecting to find Sejanus standing there. For none of us was it so bad, though, as it was for Caligula. While he still bore the bulla of childhood, even at eighteen years, and Drusus and Nero remained higher on the steps of power than he, what he had done at the funeral, defying the emperor and thumbing his nose at Sejanus, had made him the most endangered of us all. And therefore the most careful. But while most people saw only the Gaius Caligula he wished them to see, I saw him pacing at night when the panic set in and sleep fled from him like bats in sudden light. Now, gradually, with the influence of Antonia and the colourful foreigners she harboured, the world began to change.

There was a steady stream of visitors from Alexandria and the more peculiar Aegyptian regions up the River Nile. They were fascinating, though not over-friendly, and difficult at times to understand in their speech and their custom. Not for the lady Antonia, of course, who slipped effortlessly into their idiom when conversing with them.

And there were Romans. Not all her friends were strange easterners. Many of the higher-ranking Romans would call in or even stay for days or weeks. Not, I might add, the powerful or the rich in particular, but clearly the *interesting*. Antonia cared little for influence or wealth in her friends but she did insist on being entertained.

It should have been a happy time, and there were high points despite the death of Livia and the ongoing absence of the rest of our family. But Caligula remained tense for an entire year after that incomplete funeral, convinced that Sejanus was keeping the family under close scrutiny and that we could trust no one in Antonia's house, barring our grandmother herself. It was a strain living all those months in the presence of such a careful and tightly wound brother, and I can only imagine what it was like *being* Caligula at that time. As it happened, not only was he right, but that year of tension prepared him well for what was to come. Yet for me, used to him being careful but easy, watching this different Caligula was stressful. Even with his new friends, the eastern and African monarchs, my brother was guarded, never giving anything away and never speaking his mind over anything more important than the sourness of olives.

I could see the strain beginning to show from time to time. He would spend the day with his friends, his tongue carefully contained behind the barrier of his teeth, uttering only pleasantries and meaningless, friendly banter. Then, of an evening, when he was alone in the baths, he would almost silently, beneath his breath, tell the empty air all those things he could not say in public, his dangerous thoughts whispering away into the steam of the *laconium* and disappearing safely into oblivion. He was so guarded that even to release these tensions alone, he would make sure the baths played host to no other living soul – not even the slaves who tended the furnace. And how did he know he was safe? And how did I know that this was his habit? Because I was the one he employed – the *only* one – to keep watch while he bathed and unburdened himself to the silence.

It was an odd habit, but, strangely, it worked. Not once in all the time we were there did I hear him slip. Slowly, however, he began to open up to Julius Agrippa, never to the point of saying anything dangerous, but the burgeoning friendship between the two was obvious. Only one figure retained my brother's total confidence – other than Drusilla and I, of course – and that was Lepidus, who continued to visit and be a strong part of our lives, and persistently pursued Drusilla.

Despite the gulf in age between them, Caligula, Julius, Antiochus and Ptolemy gradually became ever firmer friends and during their long stays, they could often be found playing games of strategy in otherwise deserted rooms. To the pride of the family of Germanicus, Caligula won more often than not. Pride can be any family's undoing, though.

It was a strange thing watching my brother's progression in that house. In one way nothing about him changed. He remained guarded and careful, convinced that one slip would bring Sejanus down upon us. But at the same time, I watched him as he spent more and more time with the easterners. In their company he became less tense. Though his words were still careful, his manner became easier. He began to sleep through the night once more.

'In a way,' he told me on one occasion, 'their very foreignness is the thing that makes them most secure. They are royalty in their own lands, unchallenged by their lessers and at risk from no powerful magnate in their realms. And because of that, they owe no fealty to Sejanus and have no fear of him. Their status as foreign emissaries protects them, unless the emperor takes a hand.'

But while things seemed to be improving for us at last, the Fates were watching us carefully, and Morta was ever ready with her shears.

I remember the day things changed once again, and again for the worse. It was high summer, a time when by tradition all Romans of means fled the dusty, cloying, stinking streets of the city for villas by the sea or in the countryside. Yet Antonia continued to reside on the Palatine, reasoning that the hill full of wealthy housing was the coolest and least unpleasant of all Rome's regions and that nowhere in the countryside or by the sea had all the facilities to hand that Rome had to offer. The population of the house was at low ebb, with many guests away for the summer, but the arrival of some notable from Caesarea had prompted a spontaneous gathering and party.

I was busy with Drusilla, discussing in an almost philosophical manner the nature of love.

'Love is an all-consuming bloom that quickens the pulse and warms the heart, that fogs the mind and glazes the eyes,' Drusilla said, a dreamlike expression on her face even as her eyes automatically drifted towards Lepidus. 'Love is the driving force and the end goal. Love is everything that matters.'

I snorted. 'Love is an impediment. A means to an end. Sometimes it is the chains that bind us. Love is mutable and unpredictable, and it makes fools of us and drives us to idiocy. As Ovid says, "love is a thing full of anxious fear".'

My dark, opposite stance I know was in some small part driven by that ever-present jealousy I had for the charming Drusilla. But my words also held the core of my belief. Love for our family was the only love that drove me, and even then I knew into what terrible dangers it would draw me. Love was nothing but trouble, but I do to this day regret having so often attempted to one-up Drusilla and to tear apart her pleasant illusions. She did not deserve it.

Other conversations around the room were less philosophical. Paconianus, who seemed ever present at any social occasion where wine was freely given and nothing asked in return, was deep in a heated argument with Julius Agrippa about the validity of the Judean monarchy. I have no idea why I remember that so clearly.

I remember that Paconianus had gone so far as to prod the easterner in the chest while making a point – something that enraged Julius – just as the knocker clattered at the house's main door. For some reason it sounded like the knell of a great gong rather than a mere knocker, and it blessedly caused Paconianus to lose his train of thought and stutter to a halt. Antonia paused in the middle of some anecdote about an Aegyptian king from long ago and, as she stopped talking, the whole room fell silent. It felt as though she knew something was coming, though I suspect it was simply the fact that she was expecting no other guests and was intrigued at the arrival of visitors.

Then boots sounded in the atrium. Not just the soft leather boots of the doorman, but the clacking nails of military boots, and a chill flooded through me. I saw Caligula and Drusus over by one of the tables straighten and share a look. Drusilla and Lepidus and I turned to see.

It was a black and dreadful sight as the nine Praetorians filed into the large room, the doorman behind them looking shaky and panicked. The officer leading the group stepped forward and issued a curt bow to the lady of the house – a bow from the neck only. Then, producing two scroll cases from a large pouch at his belt, he removed his helmet, placing it under his arm, and approached Antonia. Something in her gaze stopped him several paces from her chair, and he straightened.

'Domina.'

'Commander.'

The silence could have snapped, it was so brittle. Finally, with a swallow so loud it almost echoed around the room, the Praetorian held out one of the scrolls, keeping the other with some difficulty in the same hand as his helmet. Again, the silence instilled itself and the officer frowned, clearly expecting the old lady who had sired an imperial line to clamber out of her chair and come to him. Antonia sighed and gestured at a man with a big nose in a fine toga.

'Vitellius, would you be a dear?'

The man, who was plainly of the finest Roman stock, nodded as though he were an eager lackey and retrieved the object from the soldier, carrying it across to the lady. Antonia peered at the scroll case and threw a questioning look at the officer, who remained immobile and silent. Frowning, she cracked the seal and withdrew the fine, expensive parchment.

'It is from the emperor himself. How rare and exquisite. I had assumed he had forgotten how to write.' Despite the danger in such words, she chuckled at the look on the Praetorian's face, and then fell serious once more, running her eyes down the lines of writing. Finally, with nothing to give away her emotions, she furled the scroll once more and slipped it into the case.

'Drusus? Gaius? You should have this.'

As my brothers strode across to retrieve it, Antonia drew a deep breath.

'The emperor informs me in a very matter-of-fact and emotionless missive that my grandson Nero has expired.'

I felt the call of fiery Tartarus as the floor ripped apart beneath me. I caught snatches of what followed, but not all of it, for my hearing was rather impaired by the blood thundering through my ears. I fell, my legs giving way in a faint, receiving a rather heavy crack to the back of the head from a wall decoration. As Lepidus and Julius Agrippa hurried to help me up, Drusus was reading from the scroll. Nero had died on the island of Tyrrhenia, where he had spent the last year. According to the blunt and unpleasant note, the jailor of our brother had stopped bothering to feed his ward, and Nero had starved to death in his room. There was some rubbish about the man responsible being punished, though that was clearly for show. No one in that room harboured any doubt whatsoever that Nero had been deliberately starved on the orders of either Sejanus or the emperor. My eyes strayed in my blurred panic to the huge tables groaning under the weight of the food for the soirée. I felt sick at the knowledge that we had glutted as Nero starved.

It took a long moment for the next thought to strike.

'What of our mother?' I asked rather weakly.

'There's no mention of Mother,' Caligula murmured as he scanned down the scroll.

'Very well,' Antonia announced. 'You have unburdened yourself, officer. Perhaps you would now remove yourself and your men from my house?'

'I am afraid, Domina, that I have further business.' He reached for the other scroll and held it out. This time Vitellius did not have to be asked. He scurried across and retrieved it, passing it to the lady. Antonia cracked the seal once more and slid out a second parchment. This was clearly longer, and yet her read was briefer. When she had finished, she straightened in her seat.

'The seal on this second scroll is that of your prefect. Has this come from Sejanus then, and not the emperor?'

'It has, Domina.'

'And you realise that I do not recognise your prefect's authority in matters such as these. This scroll should come from the emperor himself, not a vicious little lackey like Sejanus.'

To his credit, the Praetorian remained calm and collected. 'Be aware, Lady Antonia, that it is neither my business nor my concern whose authority *you* recognise, since the senate and the court recognise my prefect as speaking for the emperor in the city. This warrant holds and will not be contested. I am aware that your household includes almost a dozen hired guards – all ex-soldiers or former gladiators. They will avail you naught if you resist my authority, for I have a second unit like this one outside your door and if there is any resistance to the carrying out of my duty, two *contubernia* of Praetorians will do whatever they must to complete our task. It would be a shame if the rest of your family were to be arrested in order to save just one.'

And that chasm opened up fresh beneath me. Another of us? My heart pounded once more, and the chill was back. Lepidus and Agrippa held me tight, lest I faint again. It came as no surprise when Antonia turned to the boys and formed that first name with a dry voice.

'Drusus? This is a warrant for your arrest from the Praetorian prefect on spurious charges under the lex maiestatis. You are to go with these men.'

Drusus was shaking his head, angry and disbelieving.

'I can stop them taking you, Drusus,' our grandmother said loudly enough to make sure that the gathered soldiers heard, 'for they somewhat underestimate my staff. But the officer is right in one thing: if we stop them taking you, Sejanus will send a whole cohort and there will be half a dozen warrants then. If you wish to save Gaius and the girls, Drusus, you must go. I shall inform your wife and father-in-law of what has happened.'

Drusus was now staring helplessly from me to Drusilla, to Caligula, to our grandmother and back again, but his shoulders slumped in defeat, for he could see the truth in her words. He started to walk towards them, and I glanced from sibling to sibling in confused, desperate panic. Caligula was standing still as a statue, his face could have been carved from marble. But beneath his chin, muscles twitched. I could see his white knuckles where his fists were balled. I had seen that look before, but rarely. Fury. And not just anger, but that focused fury that was born of helpless desperation and grief. A brother dead and a brother taken in a dozen heartbeats. It was requiring every modicum of strength he had to contain it all and not either break down or explode.

I did not have that control. Something just snapped in me. I cannot say from where the strength came, for I was still woozy from the head wound and the fainting spell, but I managed to wrench myself free of the boys and was running across the floor towards the Praetorian officer, snatching a silver eating knife from the sickening banquet table as I passed. The officer drew his sword – a grave deed in such a situation.

I was saved from a gruesome death by my brother.

Caligula hit me mid-run, knocking me from my course and then grappling and restraining me, squeezing my wrist until I gasped and dropped the knife. I noticed with startled horror that his palms were bloody where his nails had bitten deep into them in containing his rage. The Praetorian sneered at me as he sheathed his weapon once more and Drusus walked towards him, shaking his head at me. I didn't care. I couldn't lose another brother, and I was determined to carve out the officer's black heart, with my fingernails if necessary.

Caligula held me tight. I had seen him training with a sword and exercising with Lepidus and Julius, and I knew that he was tall, but he always looked so thin that it baffled me how strong he turned out to be. He held me with ease as I struggled and scratched and bit into his arm trying to get him to let go. He did not.

'Livilla,' he whispered into my ear as I helplessly watched Drusus being taken by the Praetorians. 'Livilla, there is nothing anyone can do. What Livia once said holds true now more than ever: we must look to our own safety. If you oppose them, they will take you too.'

I stopped fighting for a moment, heaving in breaths and sobs in equal measure, and then I managed somehow to turn myself within his grip so that I was facing him.

'And you, dear brother?' I hissed beneath my breath. 'When they callously starve Drusus, you will be the only remaining male heir of Germanicus. You will become the last obstacle for Sejanus. How long then before the Praetorians come for *you*?'

He simply held me for a time, whispering to me, telling me that Drusus, although we would all change things if we could, had brought this upon himself, because no matter how often Caligula warned his brother to be careful, Drusus would insist on speaking his mind. And the house was never safe, for Sejanus had ears at every door. Only our caution would save us, and he was certain his own caution would save him.

I found it hard to believe that he could be so matter-of-fact over the loss of another brother, but in the years since, I have come to understand that he was right. He was almost always right, in fact. He held me for an hour, while I sobbed and collapsed.

The family of Germanicus had now lost one mother and two sons, and I finally accepted with the deepening of that hole in my heart that I would never see any of the three of them again. And that knowledge drew me ever closer to my remaining brother.

I hated the days that followed. Not for our living arrangements, which were every bit as exotic and fascinating as the previous year, filled with the eastern habits of the lady Antonia and the plethora of mesmerising visitors that endlessly filled her house. And, despite everything, not for the loss of our family, although the death of Nero, the exile of Mother, and the arrest of Drusus weighed heavily on our minds.

The *real* reason I hated that time was for the change in the atmosphere of the city of Rome.

I was now twelve years old and almost a woman in many respects. In another year, had I still a full and normal family, a match would be made and I would be married off. If we'd still had a mother and father, Drusilla would already be gone. But we were in a strange half-world with no direct pater familias, and as a guardian a woman who steadfastly refused to conform to the expectations of a Roman dame.

Caligula was eighteen now, and yet still a boy under Roman law, awaiting the toga of manhood. I had begun to understand what he had meant by the protection his status granted him. Nero and Drusus had gone, and with them the line of imperial succession, opening the way for the Praetorian prefect, Sejanus. The moment Caligula took the toga virilis, he would be in danger of a similar fate, for even without Tiberius naming him to the succession, he would remain the strongest candidate. The emperor's grandson was the most direct of the line, of course, but the eleven-year-old Gemellus was said to repel his grandfather, and had spent most of the six years since his father's death living in relative obscurity in Praeneste. He was hardly seen as a figure to rival Caligula.

My brother was untouchable. True to his word over the years, he never once let his guard drop, remaining loyal and above suspicion in every way. He was officially a child, protected by the authority of our grandmother. He was not a direct heir to Tiberius. He was popular and unblemished by suspicion.

And so began the campaign to ruin him.

Rumour began to circulate and, though we could not identify a source even with Antonia's power, there was never any doubt that the first words of twisted scandal came from the Praetorian fortress. The mood in Rome towards the children of Germanicus wavered. We had always been seen as a virtuous family, progeny of a great general and treated harshly by those who should know better. But now, with slander concerning our surviving brother spreading through the streets, those senatorial families who had supported us through hard times were starting to falter.

Not the *common* people, I hasten to add. The common people still saw us as paragons of virtue. But then, the common people do not have any power. And those who were in a position to affect us, for good or for ill, were beginning to turn their backs on us.

If one listened to rumour in Rome that year and accepted it all, then one would realise just how self-contradictory it all was. Caligula apparently shunned Roman womenfolk, for he was a lover of little boys, stealing them from their families to lie with and then sending them back ruined. But across the street, someone would tell you that he was such a savage lover of women that he forcibly took senators' wives and impregnated them while their husbands were away. Others still, and this really caught in the back of my throat, said that he had eyes only for his sisters and that we were his willing concubines, as though we were some Aegyptian dynasty. Some said that he was a thief, stealing from the Roman treasury – how they thought he managed such a feat I have no idea. Others said that he was a dissolute hedonist, spending the family fortunes on unseemly lavishness. It was all so utterly ridiculous.

At twelve, I was given plenty of space to myself and had taken to trips out to the forum and to social events at theatres, sometimes with only staff from Antonia's house, and other times with my sisters, my brother, or even friends such as Lepidus and Julius Agrippa. Travelling the streets was starting to become a sour and unpleasant experience. It was hard to equate the distrustful, superior looks of the toga-clad higher classes with those same people who had stood so sombre and supportive when we buried our father or the lady Livia.

Rome had become acrid.

It was sometime in late spring when trouble finally knocked on our door in person. The surly doorman had hefted his club but grudgingly admitted Paconianus. The man might not be welcomed by us, but he had been a guest in the lady's house many times – though on this occasion he came not to consume Antonia's wine, but to see my brother.

I was with Caligula in the peristyle garden when he entered. Drusilla was there, too, and Lepidus, never far from her side. We had been poring through a copy of Paterculus' new historical work and wondering whether the praise it lavished upon Sejanus was genuine admiration or acclaim brought about through fear, or possibly just simple, old-fashioned sycophancy. Oddly, it was the first time I really had cause to notice the name of Marcus Vinicius, one of the consuls that year and to whom the book was dedicated. It was far from the last.

The four of us were seated on curved marble benches that faced each other across a low table, and the manuscript was unfurled on the surface between us. I will swear to this day that I felt the temperature drop as Paconianus entered the garden.

He wore a look of concerned friendship and a simple toga, and yet I found him utterly repellent the moment I laid eyes upon him. Caligula stood as the man approached, and Lepidus followed suit a moment later. Drusilla and I remained seated.

'Gaius,' the man said, with no preamble whatsoever, as though we were kin or the closest of friends. I saw my brother's eyes harden at the familiarity, but he remained silent. 'I come bearing distressing news.' It is perhaps a mark of how bleak our lives had become that mention of such things no longer set us on edge. *All* news seemed to be distressing news for our family.

Lepidus made to step forward, but Caligula put a hand on his shoulder, motioning him to remain in place and be seated once more. I would learn games like this much later as I grew and became stronger and more wilful, and it surprises me that Caligula knew them even then, but he also sat once more so that the children of Germanicus and their friend were comfortable while Paconianus hovered on his feet like a plaintiff. It is a subtle way to shift the focus of power in a room, and the sort of thing at which Caligula soon became adept.

'Go on,' he said.

Paconianus' eyes darted around the colonnade at the garden's edge. 'Do you think we are being observed?'

Caligula's brow rose to an arch. 'I suspect the Praetorians have ears on us at all times, though I am happy to acknowledge that the number of such has just risen to the tune of two.'

It was a subtle dig, and one that seemed to completely pass the man by as he simply shook his head in bafflement and then forged on. 'Have you seen the letters?'

'Letters?'

Paconianus cast two vellum sheets to the table, each covered with text and marked with the signs of professional copyists.

'Save me the effort,' Caligula said with a sigh. 'Tell me.'

'Do you know the senator Sextus Vistilius?'

Caligula shrugged. 'I think so. Old fellow with one stray eye. Hair like a dandelion gone to seed, yes?'

Paconianus frowned at this humorous appraisal of an important and elderly nobleman, but in the end pursed his lips and shrugged. 'That does sound like Vistilius.'

'What of him?'

'He accuses you of misconduct. Publicly, in these letters which have been copied and made available across the city.'

'Pamphlets of idiocy and falsehood. What sort of misconduct am I supposed to have perpetrated? Did I sell him a lame horse, or did I make off with his wife? Such are the rumours of my life, or so I am led to believe.'

The man had the grace to look a little uncomfortable. 'No . . . Gaius, the senator accuses you of forcing him into sexual relations!'

There was a moment's silence in which my brother's face raced through a dozen different conflicting expressions, and finally he burst out into a peal of laughter, leaning back against the marble seat. 'Sexual relations? With *him*?'

'It is a *serious* accusation, Gaius.'

'It is a *ridiculous* accusation, Paconianus. I have heard more than once the rumour that I favour only the intimate company of men and, while in truth I have no inclination that way, I have known good men that do. But rest assured that were I a man to chase men, the very last specimen in the world I would hunt for gratification would be that daft old man with the lazy eye and the fluffy hair.' He chuckled again. 'Pah! Only a fool would give credence to such a tale, don't you think, Paconianus?'

The tall, willowy man standing before us fixed Caligula with a serious gaze. 'Do not discard such tales so lightly, Gaius. They could be your undoing.'

Caligula chuckled anew. 'What business is it of yours, anyway?' he asked, settling back and stretching.

'As a friend of the family –' the man paused, completely

failing to register the disdain that my brother projected at the very idea that Paconianus might be a friend '– I felt it my duty to warn you. And to offer my services.'

'Your services?'

'I remember the exact gathering – at this very house – at which Vistilius alleges your assault. And I know that on that particular occasion you were not present. The day after the Matronalia festivities, when the lady Antonia held a gathering to welcome some Aegyptian noble called "whoreboy" or some such.'

'Horbaef,' Caligula corrected him patiently. 'And you are correct. I was absent that day with a friend, for that friend and Horbaef share a mutual loathing, and it seemed prudent to keep them separate.'

'I am willing, Gaius, to stand at a hearing and proclaim your innocence, being a witness to the gathering, as I was.'

Slowly, nodding, my brother stood. He stepped forward until he was only a pace from Paconianus and reached out, putting both his hands on the man's shoulders in a friendly, supportive manner. Then, conspiratorially, he leaned in and spoke quietly, so that I had to strain to hear.

'I would sooner stand with only my own word in support than rely on evidence supplied by you, Paconianus. Why my grandmother ever let you cross the threshold of this house is beyond me, but let me tell you now that this is the last time you will do so. You are not welcome in this house or in my presence. Take your offer of aid and your unctuous, false smile back to Sejanus, and tell him that you have failed. I am sure he will be perfectly pleasant and forgiving. He has that reputation.'

Paconianus' face shifted from disbelief to anger.

'How dare you—'

He got no further, for my brother, his hands still on the man's shoulders, brought up his knee hard into Paconianus' crotch. So hard, in fact, that I heard a crunch. I hadn't known men's genitals could crunch, but that slimy weasel's did. He folded up, whimpering.

'Get out,' Caligula said loudly. 'My grandmother has a hired man who trained as a *secutor* in the arena and claims he can cut a man in half quicker than she can blink. If you are still here when I have counted a hundred heartbeats, I will put him to the test.'

The injured man, clutching his ruined testicles, staggered and almost fell, tears streaming down his face, but he managed with great difficulty and an obscene amount of pain to lurch back across the garden and into the atrium. Every step elicited a squeak as he went.

We sat in stunned silence as the limping, staggering figure disappeared, and our brother sat once more, rubbing his hands together.

'Can you do without his testimony?' Lepidus said quietly.

'As I said,' Caligula murmured, 'I would be better with *no* testimony than with his. Paconianus has been present at every important gathering in this house, with three notable exceptions. He was conspicuously absent for a while after Drusus was taken. I suspect he absented himself in order to avoid suspicion falling upon him. He has been the eyes and ears of Sejanus in our household for some time. He may not be the only agent of the Praetorians we have hosted, but he was most certainly *one* of them. I did a little digging into his background, and until three years ago, Paconianus had served as a Praetorian tribune.'

'So why would he offer to help you?' Drusilla asked, her brow creased.

'Dear, trusting, innocent sister.' My brother smiled, giving voice to my own thoughts even as I worked through the issue and unwrapped the truth. 'Paconianus had absolutely no intention of speaking for me. He was attempting to lure me into the court unprepared. I would trust to his evidence and prepare no case, and when presented with the accusation, he would then side with the old man and I would be hung out like a wet rag. No, Paconianus was trying to entrap me. But I have no intention of falling foul of such idiotic accusations. No one would believe them, and I have plenty of trustworthy witnesses. Why, you three were all at the gathering for Horbaef's arrival. You can all confirm that I was not there, and if that is not enough, Julius Agrippa will stand for me as witness, since it was he who was riding with me that day. And the emperor holds Julius in high esteem, so his testimony would be unchallenged, even by Sejanus. I am safe from any trouble in this matter.'

I felt chilled and frightened, though, by this turn of events. 'You are the oldest of us now, Gaius. You are the next in line. And the bulla of childhood no longer protects you. Sejanus is moving in for the kill. Gaius, I cannot lose you too.' I think I was crying then. The very thought that our last brother might be taken away like the others was horrifying.

'Sejanus is dangerous,' Caligula replied, 'but even he will not step beyond the bounds of his direct power, for the emperor still has an interest in our family. Sejanus is having to be circumspect since, while Nero and Drusus were easy targets as both were political animals, men of the court, and could be accused of intrigue, *I* am still a child, untouched by politics and with no direct link to Tiberius. If he simply arrested me, it would become obvious even to the blind that Sejanus was securing his succession. And so he must try and trick me into incriminating myself.'

He smiled and reached out, cupping my hands in his. They were as cold as the marble on which we sat.

'But I am brighter than Sejanus and more cunning than our brothers. I will ride out this storm as I have ridden out all the others.'

I was unconvinced, but I allowed myself to feel a little safer. Caligula always knew how to do that.

The enthusiasm of our gathering was gone, and none of us

seemed to have anything to say, so we split up and went about our business, the doorman still jabbering away at his mistress over our summary dismissal of an important visitor.

The next twelve days passed in a flurry of activity as the case against my brother was brought, shattered, and resoundingly defeated. Our reputation enjoyed once more a small triumph of righteousness in the public eye, and Paconianus and the daft old Sextus Vistilius were all but ruined in the process. Paconianus, for the record, lived the rest of his short, brutal and very miserable life as a eunuch, courtesy of my brother's knee. And as for the troublesome Praetorian prefect? We could almost hear Sejanus pacing in his fortress, furious at having been thwarted so easily.

We knew he would try again.

And that is why, when the news came twelve days later, I thought we had been saved, for Caligula and his remaining family had been summoned to the emperor's side.

PART TWO

THE EYRIE OF TIBERIUS

'Presently [Tiberius] broke out into every form of cruelty, for which he never lacked occasion'

– *Suetonius:* Life of Tiberius

VI

SCORPION

Capri is shaped like a giant saddle, rising out of the sea with horns jutting up at the near and far ends. We had set sail from Surrentum in good weather, though a gloomy black and orange sky out to the west and the wind battering our faces spoke grim predictions of a brutal storm on its way. It is but a few short miles from that charming coastal town to the island of the emperor, but every pace of that distance felt more and more tense.

Caligula had talked me through much of the history of the villas of Tiberius as we bounced and bobbed through the water towards the island. Where he himself had acquired such information, I could not fathom, but it was my brother's habit to be surprisingly well informed at all times.

'Agrippina used to say the emperor favoured a villa somewhere on the Latin coast,' I said, wondering at the old man's desire for such seclusion as Capri offered.

'Sperlonga,' he replied. 'Tiberius had a great villa at Sperlonga, but the cave ceiling collapsed while he was dining there.'

'Cave?' I prompted in confusion.

'The villa was an extension from a natural grotto and he had the cave turned into a giant dining room. He was eating his evening meal there a few years ago and the ceiling fell in.'

'He was lucky to survive.'

'Lucky? Pah!' Caligula waved his hand dismissively with a

quick look around the deck to make sure we were still unobserved and out of earshot of dangerous ears. 'Sejanus was there – one of the civilian guests. He pushed the emperor out of the way and saved his life. It was what earned him his promotion to the Praetorian prefecture.'

'I wonder if he regrets it now?' I mused, earning a hard, warning look from my brother.

'Guard that tongue, sister.'

Chastened, I leaned back silently.

'Sperlonga apparently soured for the emperor after that, but his family had land and residences here. Augustus had built five villas some years back for his summer retreats. Tiberius constructed more, until there were twelve villas, each as grand and sprawling as any imperial palace, and each named for one of the twelve Olympian gods.'

'Such extravagance,' I murmured. I had seen opulence, of course, and we ourselves were far from free of it, being one of Rome's most distinguished lines, but to own an island and fill it with palaces just for a place to retreat from the stink of Rome seemed excessive even for an emperor.

'Some see it as a facet of the old man's decline,' Caligula replied, dropping his voice to a whisper and peering around once more to make sure we were still unobserved, 'though they would never say as much in the open. Some even say that Tiberius dresses as whichever god he resides with that week, though I know this to be an untruth. I also understand that he only ever lives in three of them, preferring to give the others over to guests or important visitors.'

'How do you learn these things?' I asked, intrigued.

'I seal my lips and open my ears.'

I fell silent, taking his words as a hint and, sure enough, mere moments later, two Praetorians came over and stood close by.

The high end of the saddle that faced the mainland held the great Villa Jovis, perched like an eagle's eyrie high above the water on the brink of a thousand-foot drop. The very sight sent cold fingers up my spine as the ship slid beneath it, oars rising and dipping in time to the flautist's tune. Around the great white crags beneath that palace we sailed, skirting the island, in a race to beat that dark yellow-black storm to the harbour.

There is simply nowhere at the eastern end of the island to dock, for the cliffs rise almost vertically from the water and are utterly unforgiving. And so we moved into the harbour at the small settlement on the north coast, little more really than an overgrown fishing village, and yet equipped with the very highest quality piers and jetties, ready to welcome the most important figures in the empire to the home of Tiberius. I was never very good at sea travel. It does not turn me grey and make me vomit as it does my sister Agrippina, but I was never comfortable on boats. They make me nervous. And so I was immensely relieved as the oars were shipped and the helmsman used only the steering oars and our forward momentum to guide us in alongside the jetty, where we connected with the land with a stomach-jerking bump. Ropes were slung out and tied and the ramp run across. We were helped, teetering, onto the wooden jetty and then escorted to the stone dock. I stood on the edge and waited for the watering of my mouth to fade, and the urge to disgorge my stomach contents with it.

There we waited, while the crew unloaded the huge quantity of luggage we had brought. Carriages, wagons, pack animals and a veritable ocean of slaves awaited beyond the dock to convey both us and our belongings to the emperor's villa. We had brought everything we considered important and left nothing at our grandmother's that could not easily be discarded, for we were now used to being moved from one semi-permanent home to another, and it seemed more than likely that we would now be lodged in one of the empty villas on the island for a year or more.

Caligula was peering up at the high end of the island with a sense of nervous tension, while Drusilla and I stood looking around us in wonder at the natural beauty of Capri. They said the emperor had been driven to the island through the madness of grief, but I could not believe, as I beheld the place, that any kind of madness would be required to live here. It was beautiful. And I was almost beginning to relax.

Then I caught sight once more of the Praetorians who had escorted us from Rome and across the water to the island, and the tension returned. The island was made beautiful by the gods, but made corrupt and dark by men.

I had learned, oddly, to live without Mother, Nero and Drusus, despite the hole they left in my heart, but the ongoing absence of Agrippina cut me more keenly than I expected. Even once she had married, she had been with us as often as possible, even if only for respite from the chastising hand of her husband. However, with her now being part of the household of Domitius Ahenobarbus, the summons from the emperor had not included her. The family that had entered Syria twenty-one years ago as a household of eight was now arriving on Capri as a mere three.

'Our new home is apparently a secure one,' Caligula said, nodding at a two-storey structure of heavy stone that loomed nearby, white-clad figures moving about it. 'A barracks for the Praetorians to watch over the comings and goings at the harbour.'

I frowned. 'But surely these Praetorians are under the direct control of the emperor? They are far from Sejanus and on Tiberius' own island. The emperor has delivered us from Sejanus, so I cannot believe he would allow the man's influence to override his own *here*.'

My brother turned an odd, sad smile on me.

'*Delivered* us from Sejanus? Dear Livilla, do not think of it as deliverance. Be very, very watchful now, more than ever. Sejanus is a rat, sniffing around and causing trouble. But if Sejanus is a rat, then Tiberius is a scorpion, sharp and fast, and with a deadly sting.'

I looked around in panic at such outspoken words, but we were oddly alone in the noisy port, the officials and soldiers all engaged in the business of our arrival. I could think of nothing to say in reply to my brother's gloomy appraisal, but I found it hard to believe that life close to the emperor could be any worse than a life in Rome where Sejanus felt he could gradually thin the ranks of our family at will. I was, of course, as naïve as my brother thought.

Perhaps a quarter of an hour later all was made ready and we were helped into the carriages. A Praetorian officer gave a command and the long procession began to make its way from the port up to the great imperial villa on the crest of the eastern cliffs. It was a long and troublesome journey. Several times I asked to leave the carriage and walk, for the road that wound back and forth up the hill like a fallen strip of ribbon was pitted and rutted and, with the incline, much of the gravel surface had skittered off to clump in places by the roadside leaving bone-jarring cobbles that caused the carriages to lurch and bounce horribly. I had asked why the emperor allowed the road to be kept in such a state, and a soldier walking alongside the carriage explained that Tiberius moved around the island, when he did, by horse, but he liked to cause discomfort to the fat and indolent senators who visited him. I do not think the soldier meant the comment as an insult, but Drusilla – who was out of sorts with missing Lepidus – took offence anyway and yanked the curtain closed in a huff, obscuring my view of the orchards and vineyards that climbed the slope and leaving me with only the lurching and my fears.

It took over an hour to climb the great slope to the emperor's villa and, as we closed on the building, I had my first true view of the home of Tiberius. The palace, for it was far more than a villa, was a great square structure, built around a courtyard which, I would later learn, was constructed upon huge cisterns. Due to the undulating terrain, some parts of the palace – those towards the cliffs to the east – were two-storeys high, rising above the courtyard. Others, down the slope to the west, were as many as five storeys. And then, of course, there were various ancillary structures and external complexes. Somewhere behind, as we closed on our destination, there came a crack of thunder and I turned to see that that great black-orange cloud was already enveloping the far end of the island. We would just make it inside in time.

The road followed a ridge, climbing around the edge of the island until it reached the high point, where an elegant bridge carried it across a channel and to a wide doorway. I was so busy marvelling over this immense – and yet so delicate – building perched on the roof of the world that I had to be nudged by Drusilla when everyone else had already disembarked and begun to cross the bridge on foot, for there was no room for the vehicles, which would be taken around the lower regions of the grounds to the carriage house. I would learn the layout of those areas soon enough.

We entered and passed through vestibules, around the great courtyard, to a large exedra that arced out from the building, bulging worryingly towards the thousand-foot drop to the water. I was still marvelling over the stunning grandeur of the place as we were shown into a great semicircular hall with high, impressive shuttered glass windows – a rarity even in such great houses – and brilliant light yellow walls. Even with the sinking western sun hidden behind that roiling back storm cloud, the remaining light shone through those immense windows, setting the yellow walls ablaze and making the place bright and warm, despite the grumble of thunder.

It was so beautiful that it took me a moment to notice we had stopped, and I felt the flush rise in my cheeks as I realised we were in the imperial presence and I had just walked into my brother's back.

There were perhaps two dozen people in the room, though most of them were slaves. The emperor himself, looking more cadaverous than ever, reclined on a long couch of gold and purple, nibbling on some titbit from a plate on a low table. Behind him loomed a bulky figure in a grey tunic, with muscles that looked like whole sides of beef. His face was a network of scars and had probably never approached handsome even before the scars had come. At his waist was an expensive sword with an ivory hilt fashioned into the semblance of an eagle.

'Helicon,' Caligula whispered over his shoulder, 'the emperor's personal bodyguard.'

It says much about a man, to my mind, when his imperial guard – the Praetorians – were not trustworthy enough, and he had to surround himself with an extra Germanic guard, and even then must have a single personal sentinel within that circle.

That seemed to be the way of things on Capri. The Praetorians guarded the island. The Germans guarded the villa. Helicon guarded Tiberius. I looked around the room, discounting the Praetorians who had come with us, the four members of the German bodyguard at the chamber's edges, the slaves fawning and serving . . .

Apart from Tiberius and Helicon, only two figures of note remained. A tall man in a fine toga sat upright on his couch, his large ears folded back amid thin, iron-grey hair, narrow, cruel lips pressed tight beneath a sharp nose, dark creases under pale grey eyes. The very sight of the man made me shudder, for the air around him seemed to shimmer with wickedness and I could imagine no good thing ever coming from him.

On the far side of the emperor, on a rich couch and reclining with easy, flaccid languor, was a boy of perhaps my age wearing a tunic of purple edged with gold, a silver coronet amid his unruly hair. His face had seemed to me to be sneering as we entered, but then I realised that was just his natural look, as he *truly* began to sneer.

'Is this him?' snorted the boy, taking a swig of wine.

Tiberius turned a disapproving face on the boy, one eyebrow raised in a way that I would have considered a warning. The boy apparently didn't.

'He's dressed like a peasant!'

'Gemellus,' the emperor said in a quiet hiss that sent a fresh shiver through me, 'this is your cousin Gaius and his sisters. Remember who you are supposed to be, and act accordingly. If you insist on assuming the demeanour of a barbarian, then I shall send you to join them.'

Gemellus.

The emperor's grandson, who he supposedly despised, and yet who now sat at his right hand. Caligula, I noted, had straightened and suddenly seemed older, taller and far more impressive than I was used to. Of course, by comparison, my eighteen-year-old brother would always look more mature than this twelve year old.

'But, Grandfather, I cannot share the succession with an animal like this?'

I immediately understood, then, why the young Gemellus was so loathed by his own grandfather, for it had taken only one look and twenty words for me to revile him. But then, I had no great love for the emperor, either.

However, all my thoughts about the two of them and their value as human beings flitted from my mind at the sudden realisation of what had just been said. *Share the succession?*

Caligula and Gemellus? One too young for the toga of a grown man and the other some four years past that time. A grandson and a great-nephew. And Gemellus might have the more direct claim, but Caligula had the age, the maturity and the lineage. A sudden thrill of hope ran through me. If Caligula was to be brought into the succession, then surely the emperor meant for the security of our family, and Sejanus could not reach us here. Perhaps even Mother and Drusus could yet be saved? Whatever my brother thought, the emperor *had* delivered us.

Tiberius was studying Caligula now.

'You have grown, young Gaius. Into a clever man, I suspect, from your eyes. You are clever, and that is good, but are you wise? Wisdom is every bit as important as intelligence, strength and luck when you rule an empire. Sadly, Gemellus here, while he becomes brighter by the month, shows every sign of having avoided the fruit of the tree of wisdom entirely.' The emperor frowned. 'But he does have a point with your clothing. You are hardly dressed appropriately for the imperial court. Where is your toga, man?'

Caligula cleared his throat quietly and bowed.

'Majesty, with only grandmothers leading our family since my fourteenth birthday, no one has seen fit to arrange my taking of the toga virilis, and I still wear the bulla of childhood.'

It was said in a deferential tone, and yet carried an undercurrent of accusation, since the emperor might well be considered our de facto family head these days, and it would almost certainly have fallen to him to put Caligula in a toga. If Tiberius registered any insult, though, he failed to show it.

'Then it is time that changed, young Gaius. We shall rush the matter through and find you a toga virilis for tomorrow. Something fitting a man in the imperial line, eh?'

He chuckled, and then slipped into a coughing fit that sent jerks and spasms through him, such that he knocked the slave standing close by, and the well-groomed lad fell, his jug of wine flipping in the air. The rich, red liquid hovered oddly for a moment, like a puddle in the air, and then fell across the emperor, soaking his leg and the exquisite toga draped across it.

I saw the emperor's eyes bulge and even as he pulled himself out of his coughing fit, he cuffed the poor lad across the face, eliciting a shriek of pain.

'Fool!' the old man snapped.

He rose, shaking out the toga and watching the crimson drops spatter the floor.

'Helicon?' he said with a snarl of menace. I watched, apprehensive, waiting for the worst as the big bodyguard came around the couch and grasped the unfortunate young slave, lifting him, struggling, from his feet. Radiating fury, the emperor padded across the room, slaves and staff melting out of the way before him, and grasped one of the glazed shutters, pushing it open. The storm had finally reached the Villa Jovis, and rain lashed the glass to the left, spattering into the room as the shutter swung outwards. I realised then what was coming and I turned away as Helicon carried the poor shrieking slave towards the aperture. The boy writhed like an eel, trying to tear at his captor with desperate, delicate fingers.

'No! No, no, no, no no . . .'

Caligula suddenly whispered next to my ear.

'Straighten and watch. Gemellus and Flaccus are observing you. Do not show them a sign of weakness.'

I didn't want to straighten and watch. I'd seen death – even the death of innocents – but this was something different. This was murder. Wanton brutality. I hated even to know it was happening, let alone watch it, yet my brother was right, for I'd seen the faces of the tall man and of young Gemellus. While I think I was of little real interest to either of them in myself, a weakness in me could be used against my brother and I could not let that happen. Caligula was my last free brother, and as our family was gradually whittled down, so I came ever closer to him.

I turned and watched as the big bodyguard carried the slave to the open window, occasionally shifting his grip slightly as the lad begged and pleaded, clawed and wriggled. Helicon's face was expressionless. To him he might as well have been carrying a barrel to the stores. The emperor's expression was baleful and daemonic, his eyes gleaming malevolently as he continued to shake his toga, never taking his eyes from the slave.

'No, no, no, no . . .'

Helicon's arm was collecting scratches from the boy's fingernails and, perhaps in response, he pinned the flailing arm closer and tightened his grip around the midriff until we all heard the crack of several ribs and the whimper of agony that replaced the cries.

The bodyguard reached the window and cast his burden disdainfully out into the driving rain and the darkened sky as though he were the unwanted remnants of a meal. I heard the scream as the boy fell, and I heard the first time he hit the jagged rocks on the way down. The crunch was a sound that I will never forget, no matter how hard I try. Then the scream became a hopeless wail and there were further muted thuds. The sea was so far below that I could hear neither scream nor collision when he reached the bottom. I prayed to mighty Juno that he was already dead when he hit the water, for from that height it would have shattered every bone in his body. And then, if by some miracle he was still conscious, he would drown.

'Do not mistake this prison for a palace,' Caligula whispered, leaning close to me, 'no matter how gilded it might seem.'

There came a deafening crack of thunder and a dazzling sheet of brilliant white, and so began our time as the emperor's companions on Capri.

VII

DANGEROUS MEANING

The first year of our luxurious captivity was far from the worst, but it was probably the most tense. Getting used to our new environment and status was nerve-wracking to say the least. Gemellus proved to be everything he had initially appeared. He may not have been over-bright, and was certainly – as the emperor had noted – far from wise, but he *was* the closest blood tie to Tiberius, and so everyone on Capri barring the emperor himself was forced to defer to him. And as soon as Gemellus had realised that, he set about making my brother's life as miserable as he could. I think it infuriated the boy that Caligula managed always to maintain a loftier place than he. No matter how much the emperor's grandson taunted him or attempted to trick him into some sort of trouble, my brother always came out of their little spats seeming the better person and never – *never* – did he betray himself with misspoken words. Though he had already been careful – except in the telling case of our grandmother's funeral – the lessons of Nero and Drusus had driven that need deep.

Drusilla spent the month largely oblivious to the thorny problem of Gemellus, for she had fixed upon the absence of Lepidus and felt that loss so keenly it drove out all other problems. She simply drifted around the great halls and corridors like a lost lamb. For my part, I worried. I spent day after day half expecting Drusilla to walk off the cliff edge in a daze and plummet to her doom, shepherding her as best I could while watching Gemellus attempt to torture our brother and wondering how long we had before Caligula slipped and landed himself in the deepest of trouble. Once we had found ourselves in the company of the emperor and his sycophants, my brother had stopped his informative little whispered comments entirely lest they be seen as conspiratorial. He was ever careful.

During the preparation for the Saturnalia festival, which would be a lively but dangerous affair, Gemellus made one last move against Caligula and then finally gave up his attempts to ruin my brother. His plans had become more and more erratic and convoluted as Caligula sidestepped him at every turn. That morning, as slaves scurried around festooning the walls with decorations, my brother, Drusilla and I leaned upon a windowsill and looked down at the water far below. A slave hurried up to us, bowing obsequiously, and halted before my brother.

'My pardon, Domine,' he said in a small, nervous voice, 'but the emperor commands your presence in the baths.'

'Oh, does he?' asked my brother in a light tone. 'What is he wearing?'

'Domine?'

'You bring a message from him. Presumably you had your eyes open at the time? Was he naked? Clothed? In a towel?'

Drusilla pulled herself from her sad, self-effacing moping and her brow creased at this odd question.

'Err . . .' The slave dithered nervously.

'Or is it faintly possible,' my brother smiled, 'that Gemellus wishes me to blunder into the baths during the emperor's morning ablutions and make a total fool of myself? Honestly, the boy has moved beyond all credible plotting and now plagues me with idiotic pranks. Go back to Gemellus and tell him to pull his thumb out of his backside and put his mind to something constructive for a change.'

As the slave scurried away in a panic, knowing that he would be thrashed for his failure, Caligula shook his head at the idiocy of it all.

'It is like playing a game of *calculi* against a squirrel. I'm getting bored of him now.'

'How did you know he hadn't come from the emperor?' I asked with interest.

'Firstly, I know the emperor does not like to be interrupted when he bathes. Secondly, the slave was cool and clean, with an unstained tunic, and anyone who had been so recently in the bath suite would display sweat beneath the arms if nothing else. But mostly because I recognised him as one of Gemellus' body slaves. Our cousin really is an idiot.'

I laughed. I wouldn't have done if I'd realised what the end of his games with my brother would mean. Subsequently the young man shifted his focus from the seemingly impregnable Caligula to we two sisters. I had endured so much with the systematic destruction of my family that I was able to bear his insults and teasing without rising to them, though, and Drusilla quickly learned always to stay close to our brother for, while she was more open and fragile than I, she knew that Caligula would keep her safe. Still he tried for months to ruin us, pushing us with vicious taunts and attempting to trick us into speaking treason in order to get to our brother.

'The more laws, so Cicero says, the less justice,' Gemellus grunted on one occasion. 'What is your opinion?'

My opinion is that you cannot draw from me phrases that could attract the ire of the emperor. 'I find Cicero a bore,' I replied with a yawn.

'I saw rats fleeing the island this morning, leaping into the sea, Livilla,' Gemellus pondered another time. 'What do you think it means?'

I think it means that even they find your stench unpalatable. In answer, I simply shrugged, 'I think it means I will sleep less in fear of being bitten by rats.' In actual fact, my sleep in those days was rarely interrupted. I had never been subject to dreams, sleeping deep and untouched. Agrippina used to say that I lacked the imagination to dream, Caligula that I was far too practical for my mind to fantasise of its own volition, Mother that I did dream but simply lacked the mental discipline to recall them. All I know is that sleep for me was a refuge of untroubled time.

'My grandfather despised your mother. I wonder why that is?'

Only an idiot would rise to such obvious bait . . . 'Perhaps when you are matured you will understand your elders and betters.' That last had him stomping off, scowling.

And so it went, day in, day out, with small needling comments and poorly executed trick questions. I fear that Gemellus would have eventually escalated matters had his teasing not been brought independently to the attention of the emperor, who gave him a beating for his inappropriate behaviour towards women of the court. That ended the matter, leaving the boy impotent and able to throw at us only sour looks, which he did interminably.

Flaccus was a different matter. The courtier clearly loathed us, and he was more subtle than Gemellus. I have the feeling that there had been something in his past that had brought him into conflict with our father – just a theory gleaned from fragments of conversation I caught – and that his enmity with the long-gone Germanicus was now being redirected at us. He wasn't childishly, needlessly cruel like Gemellus, but his hostility towards us was never concealed, and he worked his rumour and spite into the emperor's ear at our expense at all times, taking every opportunity to gloat when something went awry for us.

The strain came to a head one sunny and bright summer morning, accompanied by the buzz of bees and the chirrup of carefree birds, when I went to my brother's rooms to see him and found only his empty chambers. It was early in the day and I knew that if he was not to be found in his rooms he would have gone for a walk in the grounds as was oft his habit. I was about to leave again when something odd caught my eye. On Caligula's writing table below the window lay a sheet of vellum, covered in the neat, intricate script of my brother – his handwriting was always excellent, unlike my messy scrawl. He could have written public inscriptions had he a mind to. I rounded the table to take advantage of the light from the window and began to read.

My breath caught in my throat.

O AENEAS, WHO CARRIED THE WEIGHT OF A DEAD WORLD UPON YOUR SHOULDERS
BOW NOW IN SHAME FOR WHAT YOU HAVE INADVERTENTLY WROUGHT
THE WORLD OF MEN PLAYS HOST ONCE MORE TO THE LERNAEAN HYDRA
AN ISLAND GATE TO THE WORLD BEYOND ABOVE A WINE-DARK SEA
AWAITING A NEW HERACLES

How could he leave such a work in the open?

Even as I was contemplating the dangerous meaning of the lines, I was busy rolling it up tight. It was a satire, and its subject was the most dangerous imaginable, for the Lernaean hydra which had guarded the gate to Hades and was slain by Heracles could only be meant to be Tiberius, whose word had sent so many to the underworld and who now lorded it over an island. A new Heracles? To openly compare the emperor to a monster and to advocate his slaying? How could my brother be so careless, after all he had done to guard himself?

I tucked the fine, smooth rolled vellum beneath the twin linen belts of my tunic, nestled under my breast, where no man would dare reach, and rushed out to find Caligula.

It did not take long. My brother was in the terrace garden

on the landward side of the villa. The gardens were a place of respite for us, not because we could relax our guard, of course – nowhere on the island could we do that – but there was something cloying and tomb-like about being inside that great palace with so much malice and intrigue, while at least you could breathe in the gardens and fill your lungs with the honeysuckle-scented air.

Caligula had been standing at the balustraded observation point with Drusilla and attempting to locate the other eleven imperial villas on the island by sight alone when I came scurrying across the garden to meet him, wild-eyed and out of breath.

'Do you see that hill?' he asked our sister. Drusilla squinted into the distance.

I stopped beside him and tried to interrupt, but the rush had quite winded me, and I gulped in air.

'That is the far end of the island, of course,' he continued. 'Just beyond the hill is the Villa of Diana, perched above the water like this one, but lower down. The servants tell me that there is a corridor in that villa that leads down into the earth and to a great cave full of water of the most dazzling blue that it has to be seen to be believed. And perhaps halfway to that villa, at the low point of the island and near the port, is the Villa of Neptune, with a bath suite built out into the sea itself. And . . .' He frowned at Drusilla, who was indicating me, and then turned to me, quickly realising that I was trying to get in a word. 'And on the crag above that the Villa of Mars,' he finished hurriedly. 'You seem . . . urgent, sister?'

Finally I nodded, looking around to make sure we were alone. Drusilla didn't matter. Her I could trust. I might think twice about speaking before Agrippina, but Drusilla, for all my jealousy, never showed me anything but love and trust. I don't think there was room in her soul for other emotions. Satisfied that at least no one observed us too closely, I drew the vellum from my belts and thrust it at my brother.

'For one who advocates caution, have a care where you leave such words.'

Caligula frowned at me and handled the vellum in a curious manner, as though it bore some unknown property. Waving me to calm and silence, he unfolded the sheet and scanned down it.

'Dangerous words.'

'Precisely,' I snapped as Drusilla craned to see what they were. 'You need to be more careful.'

'I?' My brother raised a quizzical brow and then cracked a smile. 'You think this was me?'

It was my turn to frown now. 'Of course . . . I . . .'

'Dear Livilla, you cannot believe, surely, that I would be so foolish. Besides, while this text is very neat, it has much more of a flourish at each "e" than my writing, and the downward extension on the "t" is overlong. And, to be frank, if I were tempted to write a dangerous satire of the emperor, I would like to think that I would be more imaginative than playing on Virgil, and certainly too subtle to compare the emperor to a monstrous guardian. This is the work of a fool who thinks he is being clever. And, Livilla, I might add how utterly foolish you are to be carrying such a thing through the villa.'

I felt a flush reach my cheeks at the truth of his words, then frowned as I wondered who could have planted such damning evidence, but before we could discuss the matter further, we both started at the sound of footsteps crunching across gravel. I felt panic close in. We were undone. We could not be found with such inflammatory words in our hands. I stared, desperate at my brother, but as always he was calm and controlled. He thrust the vellum back at me and I blanched, waving it away. I didn't want it. It was his. Even if it *wasn't* his, it was still his, for it came from his room, and only my brother with his labyrinthine mind could think his way out of this. And why me and not Drusilla? I knew the answer to that, of course.

That was one of the few, rare, days in my life where fear for my own skin overrode the imperative to preserve the family and my brother, and it still shames me to think on it. And perhaps – *just perhaps* – if I hadn't been selfish that day and sown a tiny seed of doubt into my brother, things might have turned out very different.

In the end he pushed the vellum into my resisting arms and hissed at me, 'Get this and yourself out of sight. Now!'

In possession of such a written death sentence I was still gripped by panic, but my brother, his face grave, propelled me gently into a row of shrubs behind us, bordering the viewing platform. As I struggled among the sharp, lancing undergrowth, feeling my skin acquiring scratches and bruises and my expensive tunic being torn and ruined, I suddenly marvelled at where I was. The shrubs bordered the terrace garden around three sides, punctuated by grand stairs into the other areas of the villa, but it seemed that I had found a secret world.

Behind the shrubs, hidden from the world of the villa's residents, was a concealed pathway. There were signs that it was used by gardeners – and probably slaves and servants who needed a few moments of privacy – but it was currently completely empty. I could see to the stairs that led towards the vestibule, and this secret way ran beneath them. If that was the case with all the entry stairs, then this passage ran unseen around the periphery of the entire garden. Better still, from where I now lurked, looking the other way, the passage was bounded by a wall at roughly head height, topped with various plants, some in pots, some simply growing onto the parapet. And as I stood on my toes and peeked over the top, I was rewarded with an unimpeded view of the emperor's ambulatory – a long terraced walk that ran along the cliff below the villa and ended at a precipice.

I had found refuge.

I had no time to explore then, though, for the footsteps came to a halt on the stone flags of the observation point and voices cut through the morning air, and I dared not move far for fear of being heard and attracting unwanted attention. Taking one gentle step to my left, crouching and angling my neck, I discovered that I could see through the thorns and glorious pink petals of a rose bush to where my brother stood with Drusilla, hands clasped behind his back. My heart began to race as I noted the three other men at the open arc of the observation area.

Flaccus stood before my brother with his hands on his hips, his miserable old face with the dark-rimmed eyes gleaming with malice. Behind him stood two of the Praetorian Guard. I remember being startled at the sight of them, for we rarely saw Praetorians within the bounds of the villa, which was the remit of the German bodyguard.

'You and . . . the lady Drusilla, Gaius Julius?'

My brother gave an easy smile – no simple thing when someone far beneath your station is being overfamiliar and brings the threatening presence of soldiers with him.

'You were expecting someone else?' my brother replied quietly.

I realised as I watched Flaccus' face what had happened. His expression slid through surprise, suspicion and resigned irritation. The sour-faced buzzard had *followed* me to the garden! He'd been sure to find me with my brother, and . . .

My pulse quickened again.

With the poem. He had expected to find Caligula and myself with the most treasonous document, and with the independent witness of two Praetorian soldiers. Had my brother not propelled me into the shrubbery, we would be standing before him now, condemned by our very presence. And that neatly answered the question as to who had written the damning document and left it in my brother's room. Danger had always surrounded us at the emperor's villa, but I never felt it to be more acutely present than that morning, hiding in the bushes while our enemy silently railed over his failure to catch us.

'To what do we owe this pleasure?' smiled my brother, putting the man on the spot with consummate ease. I watched Flaccus flounder and had to suppress a burst of hysterical, panicked laughter as my heart raced. He'd so expected to find us with treason in our hands that he was rattled as he searched for a legitimate reason to interrupt the emperor's heir at his morning promenade. I saw him latch on to something, and his face settled into an expression of loathsome false sympathy.

'I realise that it will be little consolation given the fates of your family thus far, but perhaps it will ease your heart a little to hear that the cause of so much disaster has finally met his end.'

Now I was interested, and I noted my brother perk up a little too. Not Drusilla. She simply stood silent and graceful.

'Your grandmother, Antonia, produced evidence of Sejanus' treachery and sent it to the emperor. The prefect has been dealt with. If reports from Rome are to be believed, he lived mere hours after his arrest before his head was hacked from his body and the whole mass thrown down the Gemonian Stairs to be torn apart by the public. And torn apart he quite literally was. My informant in Rome claims to have seen an old woman making off with an arm.'

Drusilla winced with distaste at the image.

'The Fates bring a dreadful end to those who most deserve them,' nodded Caligula, seemingly supportive and agreeing, and yet letting that pronouncement hang over Flaccus like the sword of Damocles. The awful man caught his meaning, I am sure, for I saw bitter hatred and fear in a close mix cross his face. I was sure even then that my brother had at that moment promised himself to visit just such a fate on Flaccus. And my brother never made a vow without the intent to carry it through.

My mind whirled. Sejanus was *gone*. The man who had systematically torn apart and destroyed our family as an impediment to his own advancement had gone. Somehow the presence even of the dreadful old Tiberius seemed considerably less threatening without that shadowy prefect waiting in the wings with his naked blade and leering face. Looking back, his death was a defining moment for Rome, but for us, who were now in the shadow of a different monster, it made little immediate difference for all our history.

Flaccus straightened suddenly.

'I think your time at court comes to an end, children of Germanicus. The emperor has been deciding upon a wife and husbands for you and your sister. I suspect he intends to settle you all in villas on this island with your own families. Gemellus is, after all, direct blood, and while it is useful to have a spare in the line of succession, there can be no doubt that the grandson of Tiberius will come first.'

I felt fresh panic then. A husband? What time or use did I have for a husband, busy as I was navigating the dangerous waters of the imperial court with my siblings?

'It matters not to me, anyway,' Flaccus sneered. 'The emperor has vouchsafed to me the prefecture of Aegyptus and I will soon be away from here, out from the stink of Germanicus' brood and to one of the most prestigious positions in the empire. Fare you well, Gaius *Caligula*. I pray that a life in opulent obscurity suits you. Lady Drusilla,' he added, almost as an afterthought.

With a last gloating look, Flaccus turned and strode away from the garden, back to the house, the two Praetorians at his heels. I waited for the count of fifty after they left to be sure, and then found an easier and less painful way back out of my secret world. When I reached the observation platform once more, my brother was leaning on the thick stone railing, looking out over the sea. Drusilla, shocked, had run off across the gardens as I fought my way through the plants.

'Pass me the poem,' Caligula said without turning. I stepped over beside him and handed him the offending article. He opened out the document onto the wide surface of the balustrade and removed from his belt that beautiful, jewelled silver knife Lepidus had given him all those years ago. Carefully he set to work scraping the knife across the surface of the vellum, slowly and deliberately removing the ink one scratch at a time. I had wondered for a moment why he did not simply cast it out and into the sea, but Caligula was always thorough. If the words remained, the document might always be found, but blank vellum could betray nothing. Over the work of a hundred heartbeats the treasonous satire disappeared from the vellum and with it a weight lifted from us.

Only one, though.

Another heavy weight remained, and I felt tears prick the corner of my eyes as my brother finished his work and dropped the blank vellum into a rose bed, sheathing the knife once more and looking out into the glorious morning sun.

'What will we do?' I asked through quivering lips.

'About what?'

'Gaius, we are all to be married off, it seems. You will be given some old, po-faced heifer who carries a powerful name, and Drusilla and I will be given to drooling old senators who will use us like whores and beat us as Ahenobarbus beats our sister.'

'Credit the emperor with a little more intelligence than that, dear sister. You are both prizes to him. Your matches will be costly to the coffers and has the potential to bind important men to his side. He will be most careful over your spouses, be assured of that. And my own fate should be equally comfortable, I feel. It is the uncertain role of Gemellus that concerns me. If the emperor is not preparing to marry him off, the idiot might start to see that as Tiberius placing me above him. If that happens, then Gemellus will not stop trying to ruin me.'

But on that day when my selfish side was ascendant, I was more worried for *me* . . .

'But what if I am married and sent away to an old man's

estate. I cannot bear the idea of being parted from you and Drusilla. We have already lost so much . . .'

My brother turned then and folded me into an embrace that felt warm and protective.

'You will not be sent away. *None* of us will. We are too important to the emperor, and he will want to keep us all under his nose, even you. Married you might be, but banished you will not.' His eyes rose to pick out the shape of our sister, who had come to rest by a fountain down below, where she shook with sobs. 'It is *Drusilla* for whom I really feel,' he murmured.

Thirteen years of simmering jealousy finally bubbled to the surface as I glared at him.

'Oh yes, of course. Drusilla. *Always* Drusilla. Gaius, she is *made* to be a wife. She is Vesta herself, a goddess of domesticity. All that time at Livia's villa there was no one who could match her at the art of homemaking. She will be the perfect wife, and a wife is all she ever really aspired to being!'

'Livilla . . .' he began, calmly, but I was ranting now.

'And I? I who seek nothing more than to be with my family and to remain attached only to you and my sisters? Am I to be pitied less than poor Drusilla?'

He pulled back from the embrace and fixed me with a look that silenced me utterly. He had a look that only appeared when you had gone too far. I recognised it well, and I shut my mouth tight as a clamshell for fear he was about to throw the weight of both his intellect and his anger at me.

Instead, he subsided slowly, placing his delicate hands on my shoulders – I was always a head shorter than him, even full grown.

'Do not be unkind, Livilla. Such bile does not suit you. Yes, Drusilla is made to be a wife, and she will excel at it. And I know – have always known – that you would have no husband if it were your choice. But I will change your mind over our sister's peril with one word.'

He stopped, and I tensed, waiting.

'Lepidus.'

And it struck me. Drusilla had been waiting her whole adolescent life to be promised to our childhood friend, just as he had waited at her side for years now, desperate to be her husband. Yet there was almost no chance of the emperor matching the pair together. After all, Lepidus' sister had been married to Drusus, wherever he now rotted, and to match another child of Germanicus with the house of Lepidus would be to draw too much attention to that dreadful time when our family was being systematically destroyed. No, Drusilla would be married elsewhere and she and Lepidus would be separated forever.

I felt sick, the shame of my selfishness rising to flush my cheeks. How could I be so utterly thoughtless? Here was I worrying about being separated from my family, while Drusilla faced the same threat, but also the tearing in half of her heart as she lost the man she so clearly loved.

I was chastened. All I could do was hope that the period of our betrothal would be long enough to facilitate a change somehow. In the end, those betrothals lasted a year and a half, and in that time nothing changed save the relieving absence of Flaccus, who left for Aegyptus that autumn.

The storm clouds were gathering once more over the eyrie of Tiberius.

VIII

GARLANDS AND BANNERS AND WHITE DRAPES

Almost two years passed, first under the threat of matrimony and then within its unforgiving grip. We soon learned our fates, each paired with a mate of imperial choosing, though none of us would actually meet our intended until the day we were shackled, for visitors to Capri were tightly controlled.

We had seen pictures and even painted busts of our betrothed, brought to the island for our edification. Caligula had been given Junia Claudilla, the daughter of one of Rome's most prominent and influential senators. Her bust and paintings had shown her to be a delicate thing, pretty and with a small upturned nose that gave her a quirkiness that made us smile. Drusilla had been promised to Lucius Cassius Longinus, a former consul with a distinguished family, broad cheekbones and a lantern jaw. I personally thought his bust to be rather handsome, but Drusilla, knowing that this man had forever supplanted our friend Lepidus, was less pleased. In fact, of the three of us, I clearly had come out the best, or at least I thought so at the time.

The bust of Marcus Vinicius – the consul of whom we had been reading that day Paconianus visited us on the Palatine – showed promise in every area. He was handsome enough, but not so much so that I would worry about him preening. He was mature – somewhere in his late thirties – but not seemingly old. And even on a painted bust, his eyes seemed to sparkle.

The tension among us had grown throughout the months, especially once the wedding arrangements were announced. We were to leave the island for the first time in three years, sailing as far as Antium, where the emperor had yet another well-appointed and palatial villa. There our spouses would meet us for the ceremony. The slaves of the palace had bustled around us for a month, making sure we were perfect. My brother took the fastidious attention stoically, accepting whatever was thrown at him without remark. Drusilla had sunk into a maudlin stupor, living like a docile mute, doing as she was bade without comment, but also without enthusiasm or vigour. *I* fought against every decision. The slave women were trying to turn me into some sort of painted courtier, and I have never been that – as girl or woman. In the end we reached some sort of understanding where I accepted small changes and they accepted that they had won some battles but would always lose others. I would allow them to accentuate my eyebrows and paint my lips with red ochre, but I would under no circumstances slap white lead across my face. I would wear the silk stola that was still in its thick Serican form and had not been unpicked and rewoven into a thinner material, but I would only wear it plain and without the busy, headache-inducing decorative bands at the hems. And never again in dark blue, for with my pale skin that hue made me look like a ghost – as Agrippina's wedding had taught me.

Matters came to a head with a visit from two rather stubborn hairdressers. The women took a look at my hair, which was shoulder-length and naturally curly and which I habitually wore pinned simply at the back of my head as had my mother. They tutted and fussed as I sat there, piling my hair up, twisting it and adding pins and clasps, experimenting with a gold net as they muttered about my coiffure. I simply sat silent, though I could feel my anger simmering and slowly coming to the boil, the corner of my lip starting to twitch. I was almost at breaking point when a third woman came in with a wig that looked a great deal like Agrippina's elaborate hairstyle. As she attempted to settle the hairpiece over my head, I slipped forward, ripping one of the dozen pins from my head and jabbing her in the hand with it. She yelped and dropped the wig, and I rose, defiant and seething.

'Domina, this is the latest style, and your *hair* . . .' She tailed off, making sympathetic motions to suggest that there was little that could be done to save my hair.

I took a deep breath, pulled out all the pins bar the one at the back and threw them to the floor.

'I am quite comfortable with my plain, simple hair. You are done here.'

They looked at me as though a kitten had risen up and snarled at them, unexpectedly bold.

'Domina, the men of Rome like a lady to look elegant.'

The barely concealed insult there set my teeth on edge. 'This hairstyle sufficed for my mother, and she netted one of Rome's greatest men. I am not the girl I was when I came to this place. I am fourteen and quite capable of choosing my own style. Now get out of my sight.'

It was my first true moment of empowered self-belief, and it felt refreshing and invigorating. I would no longer be a meek girl. Let Drusilla play that role. And gods help Marcus Vinicius if he displeased me . . .

The day came in early summer when all the bags were packed and a small fleet of sleek liburnian galleys wallowed on the dockside waiting for us. I remember that morning as a great up and a great down, for as I stood at the port, looking upon the vehicles that would take us from the accursed island, and at our worldly goods being loaded into them, I felt freer than

I had for many years, even with the impending threat of marriage. Then, crushing my blithe spirit, my brother brought the truth crashing back down upon me.

'Do not rejoice in freedom, for it is but an illusion,' he said quietly, and when I frowned at him, he elucidated a little. 'See how diminished are the carts since we arrived here.'

I had looked again at the baggage. The goods we were taking were definitely smaller in number than when we had come hence from Rome.

'Some of our possessions remain here for when we return,' he explained. 'This is but a jaunt, sister, not an escape.'

My brother had been correct that day we'd been told of the betrothals, then. We would remain under Tiberius' eagle eye, even married. So, with my own crest fallen, we set off across the waves, north to the ancient city of Antium, founded by the son of Odysseus and where my brother Caligula had been born some twenty-one summers ago. In fact, it had occurred to me that if the festivities dragged out, he might spend his twenty-second birthday in the city where he had spent his first.

Apparently the emperor, who was not with us, for he saw no need to leave his island just to be present at our nuptials, had sent ahead with all his plans, since the grand villa beside the sea at Antium was already decked out for the celebrations as we arrived. Garlands were strung between every column, freshly painted walls, floral arrangements and the great garden above the water all prepared for the ceremony.

I will not linger on the details of our arrival and the day we spent there in preparation for the event but to say that the villa had its own private harbour and the place was packed with over-helpful slaves, who continued the campaign of fussing, and with Praetorians, who watched the periphery carefully – as much to prevent our flight as to stop intruders, I suspect.

The morning was full of fuss and trouble. I argued and fought as usual. Caligula maintained his stoic calmness. Drusilla, who was uncharacteristically forceful and angry over the impending gulf between her and Lepidus, actually hit one of the servants. Not a ladylike slap, either, but rather a full-fist punch to the eye in the manner of a common pugilist.

Somehow, after an hour and a half of struggle, we were arrayed in our wedding clothes and led from our rooms. We three children of Germanicus met, for the first time that morning, in the atrium. Drusilla wore her white gown and red veil like a shroud. I wore mine defiantly, tugging at them and shifting them out of kilter so that they were more comfortable. I hated looking out through that flame-like diaphanous material and could hardly wait to remove it, despite the fact that that would unleash the intricate and uncomfortable ritual piling of hair atop my head, let alone the itchy marjoram wreathe around my brow to which I would later realise I was mildly allergic. Caligula was bedecked in his best toga and a *lictor* followed him, robed and with his ceremonial *fasces* – a bundle of sticks and axes – for, with his marriage, my brother had also been made a *quaestor*. It was an empty title in reality, granted to give him appropriate status at the wedding, for the emperor clearly had no plans to relinquish his grip on us and send Caligula to Rome to perform his duties.

The senior house slave who had been placed in charge of organisation led us out into the bright morning sunlight and to a small hedged garden where a fountain tinkled and burbled, three bronze nymphs pouring the water from their jugs into a circular basin. Here, in this small, secluded spot, our spouses waited.

For a moment I was shocked that we were to be wed in such privacy and with no pomp, but then I realised that this was not the wedding at all. This was the official betrothal. For while we had been promised in marriage all those months, these three had not been given permission to land on Capri, and so the traditional customs had been waved aside.

Now, on the morning of our weddings, here were our future spouses waiting to see those customs through at the very last moment.

Junia Claudilla lived up to her images. She was small and delicate and even through the red veil I could see that her porcelain skin was perfect. Longinus was a hard-looking man. Much broader and less given to humour than his bust had suggested, but Drusilla cared not. With losing Lepidus, any husband to her would be an impediment. Vinicius took me by surprise. He was thirty-eight years old – more than twenty years my senior – and yet there was a youthful energy about him that stripped him of decades and made him appear much more my own generation. I warmed to him almost immediately, not because of his apparent youthfulness, but because of the slightly apologetic, slightly mischievous smile he flashed me as I stood before him.

The senior slave passed an iron ring to Caligula, which he dutifully slid onto the finger of his intended with a ritual, largely mimed, kiss through the veil, adjusting it quickly afterwards to make sure it hung properly. Longinus must have slid the ring onto Drusilla's finger and kissed her in the same manner – I was too intent on my own match to notice. Vinicius produced his own iron ring and attempted to slide it onto my finger. It would not go on! I panicked, thinking back on the sweet things I had eaten this past month. I had watched my waist carefully, but perhaps all the fat had gone into my fingers? Likely, of course, someone had made a mistake with the ring size, but at a moment like that, all a girl can think is that she is too big for the ring, not that it might be too small for her.

As he tried once more, struggling and with an apologetic smile, I huffed and took a half step back, pulling my hand from his, the ring still on the tip of the finger. Grasping it and gritting my teeth, I pushed until the iron band slid painfully over my knuckle, scraping the skin raw as it slid into place. Vinicius seemed to take this as a sign of eagerness, for he stepped forward into me once more and, unlike the chaste actions of the others, he actually lifted my wedding veil and planted a very firm kiss on my lips beneath.

Thank all the gods that he lowered the veil quickly before the bright red flush came upon me.

The slave was staring at us, horrified, but my brother was stifling a snort of laughter, and his pretty little bride was quivering as she silently giggled beneath her veil.

That was the moment I decided that our marriages were to be good ones. Despite his forwardness and cheek, I thought that I might genuinely like the man before me, and I had instantly warmed to my brother's bride. Longinus would not please Drusilla, but then even Adonis himself would fail to please her while she pined for Lepidus.

We were led from that secluded garden to the great lawn with its floral majesty, festooned with garlands and banners and white drapes, the dazzling Italian sun shining down upon us and the brilliant blue Tyrrhenian Sea undulating beneath the low bluff.

I stood watching my husband-to-be while the pig was sacrificed by the city's most senior priest, the bread broken and shared, the fruit given in honour to Jove and the witnesses named themselves – all great men of Rome in that year, all now completely forgotten by me, bar one – Marcus Junius Silanus, the father of Caligula's new wife. Then the *auspex* – an old man with a lame foot and a decided lean – presented the three husbands with their marriage contracts and the details of the dowries that had been decided. The three couples' hands were joined and some flowery words spoken.

Finally it seemed that we were married, and in the blink of an eye all focus disappeared from Drusilla and myself, Caligula and the men becoming the centre of attention. As if a bell had been rung, with the words of congratulation from the auspex, the ceremony broke up and the various groups of witnesses and guests – those latter had remained standing further down the lawn respectfully – began to circulate. Slaves moved to clear away those things that were in the way – not me, surprisingly – while others brought out great tables and braziers and couches and the like so that within a matter of heartbeats the garden had changed from a ceremony to a grand party.

My brother was the main focus of the day. He was, after all, one of two men in line for the imperial succession, and while young Gemellus was closer in blood to Tiberius, my brother was now a man and a married one at that, with the potential for securing a dynasty. And because of that every ambitious man in the empire wanted to know him.

I stood off to one side and had all but forgotten that I was not alone until my husband took my hand and I jumped a little.

'You are not pleased with the match?'

I was dumbfounded. What could I say? If I were to be matched, Vinicius seemed a pleasant choice, but I was not made to be a wife and mother. I was made to be a child of Germanicus and nothing else. I must have floundered too long, for Vinicius smiled indulgently and turned me, taking both my hands in his.

'Rest assured that I am not a man like your sister's husband.'

My eyes flashed across to where Drusilla hung on Longinus' arm like some draped cloth, but Vinicius chuckled. 'No, not him. I meant Agrippina's husband.'

I started again, then. 'Ahenobarbus is a noble ma—'

'Ahenobarbus is an animal,' my husband interrupted, 'as anyone who has met him will attest. Your sister is strong or clever to have survived him thus far. And worry not about your other sister. She may not want this match but Longinus, for all his stern appearance, is a good man. He will look after her, as I will you.'

I don't know how it happened but, despite knowing how stupid it was and how much I needed to keep my mouth shut, a tiny fragment of honesty sneaked out.

'I am not made for marriage,' I said quietly.

'I would say otherwise,' Vinicius laughed and then peered so intently into my eyes that I flinched, wondering what he saw. 'But only to the right man. You are, I suspect, impertinent, headstrong, defiant, filled with self-belief and vim. You do not have the eyes of a pliable girl, but of a strong-willed woman. Like your grandmother, I think, for I met her more than once.' As I blinked in surprise, he flourished the contract of our marriage. 'And,' he added, 'I would no more swap you for a docile lamb of a girl than I would wish to live a drab, sedate life. You may not think it to look at me, Livilla, but I am a man of action, and I love a challenge. You, I feel, will challenge me every day.'

He kissed my hand, pulled away my veil and wreath, fussed a little with my hair and then, with a wide smile, planted another forceful kiss upon me. I was still staring in disbelief as he wandered off to circulate when another hand landed on my shoulder and I jumped yet again.

'Vinicius seems like a good man.' My brother smiled as he held me tight. Longinus was making some speech now and Caligula had used the distraction to slip away from the hungry crowd.

'I think he is,' I replied.

'Drusilla is less fortunate, sadly.'

I looked across to the miserable form of our sister, draped over her new husband's arm like the corpse of a stag brought back from a hunt. Beyond, to my surprise, I caught sight of Lepidus among the crowd, his face grey and miserable. What had started feeling like a good day plummeted once more.

'You should go to her,' Caligula said quietly. 'Wheedle her away from her husband for half an hour and try to lift her spirits.'

Another voice cut in and this time both my brother and I jumped.

'He may not be around for long.'

We turned to find Silanus, Caligula's new father-in-law, standing with his hands clasped behind his back, rocking on his toes and heels.

'I beg your pardon?' I asked quietly.

'Your sister's husband. Longinus is an ambitious man, but unimaginative. Soon he will entreat the emperor to grant him a position. He might be offered a minor administrative post, but I do not know whether he would accept that, for he has his eyes on the consulship. That being the case, he might well be given a military command and if you know his history you will see that as a tribune he had a record of making very poor military decisions. I would not be at all surprised if within a couple of years Longinus is sinking into some festering German swamp with a native blade in his gut.'

I winced at the image, but a tiny part of me wickedly wished such a fate upon him for the good of my sister.

'You speak your mind openly,' Caligula noted with interest. 'A rare quality in these days, and a dangerous one. That habit killed my brother.'

Silanus laughed. 'I fancy myself a shrewd judge of character, Gaius, and I feel certain that you are a man upon whom I can rely. Your sister here shares that look. And there is no one else close enough to bother us. I am hopeful for a long and happy marriage between you and my daughter. I have always bemoaned the fact that I had no son of my own and, while my brother's son will continue the line, I have longed for that bond. If you will grant me the courtesy of treating me with a little more friendship than is customary for our roles, I will see that you are well looked after, as though you were my own son. Not,' he added hurriedly, 'that I wish to replace your actual father, whose very name lives on as a lesson in what it is to be a true Roman.'

My brother tended to weigh up a person in the first few moments after they met. It was an abiding characteristic of his, though I might be tempted to call it a flaw. And when he did so, he had a certain way of looking at you, reminiscent of a buyer at the slave market as he has the unfortunate's mouth prised open to check the teeth. He regarded Silanus for long moments with that very look, and I have seen men shift uncomfortably under that gaze. His father-in-law broke instead into a knowing smile and I felt my brother relax as he had not done in some time.

'I may not live long enough to make a good son for you,' he said to Silanus with sharp candour.

'Oh? How so?'

'There are those at court who seem set upon destroying myself and all the children of Germanicus, even now that the dreaded Sejanus has met his just end.'

Silanus nodded slowly and smiled again. 'Do not be so sure, young Gaius. There are serpents and scorpions in the court of Tiberius, and –' his voice fell to a whisper '– the emperor himself can be more than a little dangerous too. But I have navigated the treacherous currents of the court for two decades and I am more than capable of guiding you through its dangerous eddies. I doubt there is a trick to survival at court with which I am unfamiliar, and I hear tell that you are no mean player of the game yourself. It may be that I can be of help. Come, Gaius. Let us talk.'

Silanus led my brother away. Within moments they were forced to change the subject to something harmless and banal as the hungry gathering of the ambitious flocked once more to them. I was left standing alone and contemplating the world.

We were married. Drusilla had been doomed to a relationship she did not want. My brother had acquired a pretty bride and a new would-be father. And me? I had married the pleasant, friendly, thoughtful Vinicius.

IX

A TIME OF RAVENS

I remember the following winter and spring to be a time of death and pain. A time of ravens. We had returned to Capri a week after the wedding, just before Caligula's birthday. He had brought with him his beautiful bride and her father, Silanus, being well acquainted with the emperor and one of the leading senators of Rome, came with them. Drusilla and her new husband were granted the Villa of Diana at the far end of the island and had settled in there, still imprisoned under the watchful eye of the island's Praetorians, but with the added misery of being separated from us. Longinus repeatedly lobbied the emperor for a prominent role until Tiberius tired of him and stopped admitting him to the Villa Jovis altogether.

I suppose I had been fortunate in a way. I had spent a week in Antium with my new husband, and had confirmed my opinion that he was a generous, good-natured and active man. He had not pushed to consummate our marriage on the wedding night, which was every bit his right, but had waited for me to be ready. In fact, I came to him on our second night as husband and wife and what followed held all the discomfort I had been told to expect, but also an unexpected tenderness and a deep sense of satisfaction. My journey to womanhood was complete, and I was truly grateful that it had been Marcus who had accompanied me upon it. We had coupled each night of our week in Antium, but then he had returned to Rome with a writ from the emperor himself to maintain the Palatine palaces and to clear them of the unhealthy influence of the fallen Sejanus so that they were once more fit for an emperor. I had returned to the island to live with my brother at the court just as I had done before our marriages. It was an odd wrench to learn so quickly to lean upon, and become open to, a husband, only to have him separated from you and sent elsewhere. Perhaps I learned a little of Drusilla's pain, though I knew I would see Vinicius again soon enough.

But now we had essentially lost Drusilla, who languished in separate exile at the far end of Capri. Caligula felt the absence of his favourite sister keenly and had I been a nicer person than I am, I might have felt for him and tried to console him but, as it happened, I simply relished the inevitable increase in closeness between the two of us. Now our brothers were dead or imprisoned far away and our sisters were married and parcelled off with their husbands. It was just Gaius and me.

Less than a month into the new year, as things were returning to normal and Caligula's new wife displayed the tell-tale bump of a pregnant belly – I was half expecting, and dreading, the same happening to me – the first bad news of the year came to us.

Mother had died on the island of Pandataria. She had starved in isolation – a horrible fate and one that sent me running to my chamber to cry and wail and tear at the invisible figures of the *manes* – the restless dead – in search of the one who had nurtured me. It took all my brother's silver-tongued persuasion to draw me out once more, where I fell into his arms and sought comfort amid my wracking sobs. Caligula did not cry, but I saw the hardening of his jawline and the twitch that arrived in the muscle there. The brevity of the missive informing us of her death had done nothing to soften the blow of Mother's passing. This time there was no laying of fictitious blame at the feet of a forgetful jailor. In fact there was no explanation at all, not even whether it had been deliberate execution or simply suicide. Just a brief, heartless note that she was no more. My dinners went uneaten for many days afterwards as I stared at the plate and felt traitorous for eating even a morsel while my family were starved in captivity.

We reeled over the news, but eventually the sorrow receded a little – enough to allow life back in, at least. In truth we had been expecting the news for some time, and we had almost considered her gone for five years now, though it had still come as something of a shock regardless.

The diminishing of the family of Germanicus went on, as in spring the news came that Drusus had also crossed the final river, similarly starved to death in a cell in Rome. Whether he had been held in the dreaded Tullianum prison or in a private cell on the Palatine I did not know, though if it were the latter, it is shudder-inducing to think that my husband probably passed close to his prison many a time. I spent the days following the news in a quiet stupor in my chamber, guilt-ridden over the sumptuous banquets the emperor's men lay before us while our mother and brother had starved, unable to drive from my memory that flash of my mother walking away between two Praetorians, a splash of yellow and indigo colour among their stark white tunics, her wavy hair bound tighter than Odysseus to the mast. A glory of Roman matronhood. The last time I had ever seen her.

At my birth and our arrival in Asia, my family had numbered eight. Now we were four.

Death was nothing new to me by then, and I wept just a sparse tear, I think, when the news of Drusus' passing reached us. I faintly remember wondering how long I would have before the news reached us that Agrippina had been beaten to death by her husband, and then being wracked with guilt that such a thought did not send me into a horrified catatonia.

During one of Drusilla's rare visits to the villa, I had confided in her miserably that even the passing of Drusus had barely broken through the hard shell that seemed to have formed upon me. We were the glorious children of Germanicus. I should have felt more, reacted more. Drusilla had, for once, been of enormous comfort to me. Even she, the delicate flower that she was, had greeted the news of our brother with silent, sad resignation rather than the wailing of a mourner. She believed that we had no more tears to cry, for we had shed a generation's worth within a single year. At least they died in private. Life with the emperor had taught us that things could always be worse.

Death was a constant companion on Capri.

My isolation in that villa gradually increased as spring wore on, for my brother spent ever greater periods locked away with his new wife as she neared her time, only meeting me for talks and walks in the garden when the *obstetrix* and her bevy of birthing slaves wished for privacy and a man-free environment with Claudilla.

The day when everything reached a head came in late spring, with the last of the year's three important deaths in my life. It was also the day when I realised that the emperor was not only wicked, but also insane.

I had felt pressurised by the stifling atmosphere of the villa and had fled to the gardens for a little peace and thinking time. As had become my habit, I went to that square garden and slipped into the secret and private world of the gardener's corridors behind the shrubs. There I could wander freely, unobserved by those around me. I had explored that network of earthy passages over the many months and had found that there were few places in the gardens I could not reach unseen. Moreover, there were several lesser accesses to the villa that could be reached via them unobserved. I had no real reason for such sneaking, but I filed away the information against the day that such knowledge might be important.

I had, on that morning, slid into the passage behind the hedges along that long promenade where just a railing protected the edge from a thousand-foot plummet into the sea. A slight rise in the gardens meant that my viewpoint stood above ancillary quarters and gave me a perfect, clear vista of the promenade. Though I was all but invisible in my hidden place, I had an unrivalled view of the walkway and the vista beyond. I was sitting on a warm rock, watching the sea birds wheel and dive, and eating a small bowl of cherries from an early crop that I had harvested on my way through the small orchard. I was as relaxed as I ever had been in that dreadful place, which is to say not a great deal.

My brother emerged on the walkway from some unseen doorway, clucking irritably, and his father-in-law, Silanus, appeared immediately behind him, patting him supportively on the shoulder.

'The obstetrix knows what she is doing, Gaius. The ways of women are obscure to us men at best, almost mythical in their mystery. If she does not want you there by your wife's side, there is a very good reason for it.'

My brother nodded his agreement, but he was still tense and unhappy. He strolled across to the railing, his back to me where I lurked unseen, and leaned his elbows upon it, Silanus moving next to him and mimicking the action.

'I don't care what you say,' my brother announced, picking up on an earlier, abandoned conversation, 'no prefect of the Guard can be trusted. It is a role that by its very nature entices men to treason and wickedness. Once upon a time even Sejanus had been a heroic and loyal man – the man who risked his life to save Tiberius at Sperlonga. Look how *he* turned out.'

'Macro is different,' Silanus replied quietly.

'How so?'

'He is a *good* man. Not a hero or a power-seeker, but a career soldier and a good man. I have known him for many years.

Besides, with the disastrous fall of Sejanus as an example, who would dare rise above themselves now in the role of Praetorian prefect?'

There was a short silence, and then my brother gave a sigh. 'He has to be a better influence at court than Flaccus, anyway.'

Silanus nodded emphatically, and so did I in my hidden place. Flaccus, who had made our first few years at the villa so unpleasant, now resided in Alexandria as prefect of Aegyptus, where he was no doubt skimming off more from the treasury than was customary to prepare for a retired life of rich indolence. His departure would have made Capri a happier place had life there not been so punctuated by death, either delivered by missive or witnessed in person.

They began to talk again but their speech was overridden by a series of panicked shouts further along the balcony. There, where a door led from the main imperial apartments, four of the emperor's white-plumed German Guard emerged into the sunlight, each of them gripping a limb as they bore aloft a struggling man.

Caligula and Silanus turned to watch, tense, and I repositioned myself to get a better view, the cherries forgotten. The unfortunate man was not a slave or servant, many of whom we had seen hurled from the balcony on occasion. This man was a courier with the cursus publicus – the imperial messenger service.

I felt my heart lurch.

'Mercy!' cried the man, struggling in the firm grip of the four heavyset German soldiers. 'I've done nothing. I just brought a scroll case,' he wailed. 'A *scroll*!'

I bit my lip as I watched the four men approach the end of the balcony with its waist-high balustrade. I almost looked away, but since the day we arrived here and that poor slave had been defenestrated, it had been drummed into me that looking away drew attention, and that habit is a hard one to break. Besides, this poor man deserved at least to be observed in his last few moments as some sort of testament to the evil that took him.

The four men neared the railing and shifted their grip as the man screamed and writhed, and I could see his tunic soaking through with urine, which also ran down onto the unheeding guardsmen below.

He was held there at the edge, whimpering, writhing and terrified beyond his wits. I stared in horror. The dread anticipation must be almost as bad as the act, and to drag it all out in such a way seemed inhuman. Then I realised why.

Tiberius emerged from that same door, leaning on a stick and cackling at some joke, young Gemellus at his side. The two of them turned to follow the four Germans, neither them nor the brutal guards noticing that Caligula and Silanus were present further back along the walkway, let alone me in my hidden world.

Tiberius came to a halt before the terrible scene.

'He stinks. He's urinated, the dolt.'

Gemellus chuckled at his grandfather's callousness. 'Best throw him away before he stinks out the villa.'

'No, no, no,' Tiberius snorted. 'Cut off his cock first, since it so offends us.'

Still I refused to look away. There was some difficulty and a short struggle as three of the four Germans fought to control the bucking, screaming courier while the other drew a gleaming knife from his belt. With no ceremony, the soldier lifted the courier's tunic, yanked down his underwear and set his blade at the base of the man's member. With a deft flick of his hand, he cut off the offending article and the courier issued forth a new octave of shrieking as blood fountained from his groin onto the four men holding him. My disgust and horror at such sights was steadily becoming muted by a combination of repeated exposure and nervous necessity. I bit my cheek to hold my expression steady.

At a silent nod from the emperor, the Germans took a single step forward and pitched the poor courier out into the open air, where he plummeted with an ever-diminishing scream down the thousand feet to the water, though the noise faltered perhaps halfway down as the rocks ripped and broke his body long before the sea could claim it.

I swallowed down the urge to vomit as the emperor gave a cursory command to his guards to clean up the mess, dispose of the severed manhood and wash the blood from their uniforms.

But barely had I the time to digest the unpleasantness of what had happened when events barrelled on past me. A slave came running from another door beneath me and approached my brother and his father-in-law, stopping close by and dropping to his knee. He lowered his face, but not before I registered the grey bleakness of his expression.

Caligula took a moment to realise that the fellow was there, and finally he turned with a frown. 'Stand, man. What is it?'

The slave remained in position and when his face came up there were tears in his eyes. I thought for a moment they were tears of panic, such as were unpleasantly common in the emperor's villa, but no. These were tears of sadness, and my heart hammered in my chest as I finally realised that this was one of the obstetrix's assistants.

No . . .

Caligula had immediately come to the same conclusion. He crouched.

'Tell me,' he said, stony-faced.

'The mistress did everything she could, Domine,' said the slave in a low, hollow tone.

'The baby?' My brother swallowed as he fixed the slave with a steely look.

There was an awful, leaden silence, and then the slave cleared his throat noisily.

'It never had the chance to come out.'

I felt the icy fingers of dread claw at me. If it had not been the baby . . .

'Junia Claudilla?' Caligula said, his voice cracking with emotion.

'There was difficulty. Trouble with the unborn. She was bleeding inside. We tried to save her. The obstetrix . . .' He licked nervous lips. 'She had to make a decision. We begged her to choose between the baby or the mother, but she refused. She said she would not lose either. She fought to keep the mother alive and deliver the baby both, but she could not work such miracles. They died together and are at peace.'

For the first time, I realised that not only was my brother – her husband – hearing this, but so was Silanus. Her father.

The older man was ashen-faced as he stood behind Caligula. I saw his knees give, and he would have fallen to the ground had not his grip on the railing been so white-knuckle tight. He let out a low moan.

'Both?' gasped my brother as he stared into the eyes of the slave, who nodded, mute and miserable.

'Do I hear this right?' snarled another voice, and I glanced to the side to see Tiberius and Gemellus walking towards this new tableau.

My brother stood and met the emperor's gaze.

'It would appear that the obstetrix has failed to save my wife and child,' Caligula said quietly, almost emotionless.

My eyes were drawn by a sudden movement as Helicon, the emperor's ever-present bodyguard, stepped out away from the wall where he had been lurking. The emperor snapped his fingers and then pointed at the kneeling slave. So speedily that no one would even have time to argue, the big man crossed the balcony, lifted the slave as though he weighed less than a pomegranate, and unceremoniously tipped him over the balcony.

Unlike the courier, who had been thrown bodily out into the air and fell half the distance before he met the rock, this poor slave had only been pushed over the edge and he managed to stop his fall by grasping at the foot of the railings. Gasping, he scrabbled at the ground, trying to pull himself back up. The emperor took a step towards the edge and positioned his walking stick over the grasping fingers, hammering it down so hard he broke several digits. The slave screamed twice: once at the agony in his fingers, and then again as he realised he had let go of the railing. Not having been ejected some distance, he only fell a few feet before the jagged rocks tore at him, the noises of his agony echoing across the villa's grounds as they faded. He died in some ways a much worse death than many who fell from that promenade. I later heard from the gardeners that he had caught on a particular spur of rock, half-impaled, and hung there, agonised, for half a day as birds pecked at him before a strong gust of Sorrentine wind dislodged him and dropped him to the sea.

I watched in shock through a veil of tears as my brother went inside, clutching Silanus tight to him, and the emperor stood with his grandson and his bodyguard, the reason for their cruelty apparently forgotten as they laughed about the unfortunate slave. Finally, as the jocularity faded, the old man gestured for the boy to leave him, and Gemellus scurried inside like a rodent, leaving the emperor standing, staring out to sea, leaning on his stick.

I slowly made my way through the warren of garden paths and emerged at the end of the balcony, intending to make for the door where I would find my brother, and thought the walkway to be empty until I passed a bulbous shrub and my heart faltered to see the emperor still there, leaning on the rail. I'd assumed him to have gone inside by now. I slowed and tried to pad past to the door, silent and unobserved, but Tiberius thrust out a finger in my direction without turning.

'You disapprove of me, daughter of Agrippina?'

I halted, my heart suddenly in my throat. I was alone and in the very danger I had feared since we arrived, and with no Caligula there to help guide me. I trembled as I cleared my throat.

'It is not in me to disapprove of you, Great-uncle.' It was a gamble. Not to be respectful and obedient, but to draw attention to our familial relationship. In the family of the Julii, it could tighten bonds, but it could also widen rifts. Yet somehow I felt that the emperor would see it favourably. Perhaps I was learning from my brother. The old man cackled, and I felt a frisson of fear run through me at the wickedness in the sound.

'You do disapprove of me, but I do not blame you for it, girl. You carry the blood of both Livia and Antonia and they both disapproved of me. My own mother. Your brother praised her at her funeral, I hear. Spoke as if she were divine. She was a whore and a shrew, as was your grandmother Antonia. So you see it is passed to you in the blood. You cannot help but hate me, for you are the product of two harpies. And one day you will be as awful as both of them, unless you lose your head before then.'

I felt my heart racing, my skin prickling with terror.

The emperor snorted. 'I should kill you all and be done with it. I should kill *everyone*. A man should leave his mark on the world. My mark could be painted in the blood of an empire.'

He seemed to have drifted off into some dreadful reverie then, and I wondered whether to quietly sidle away, but the wagging finger jabbed at me again.

'Run to your brother, girl. He needs you, and the presence of someone so like my mother repels me anyway. Go.'

I needed no further urging. Bowing to the emperor's back, I ran, shaking and biting my cheek.

That season of ravens I lost my mother and my brother. I lost my beautiful sister-in-law and her unborn child. And I lost the final shreds of confidence in the old monster who ruled this island and all the world around it. Tiberius was mad, and we were trapped in his lair.

X

A DISTANT SCREAM

The new Praetorian prefect presented himself to the emperor in the summer of that year. Naevius Sutorius Macro and his elegant wife, Ennia, arrived at the island's port, borne thence by a fast bireme of the Misenum fleet and escorted by half a century of his best men from the capital. It is telling, I think, of the emperor's mindset in those dark days that the prefect's men were forbidden permission to disembark, and the second most powerful man in Rome was forced to enter Capri with no guard or escort other than his wife. The Praetorians on the island, of course, had served the emperor directly for years, while soldiers freshly arrived from Rome? To a paranoid man, their loyalty may well appear suspect.

Macro was a perfectly pleasant-seeming man, short and stocky with solid aristocratic features and a soft, easy voice. He appeared surprisingly young for his age, unlined and with thick, dark hair, and he bore a scar on one cheek that spoke of a history of active military service. Ennia was graceful, almost a head taller than her husband and well-dressed, tasteful and not over-adorned. She brought home to me, with her delicate style and careful, casual opulence, the vast gulf that still lay between Rome's high-born ladies and me with my plain, almost girlish style. I was a grown woman now, but stubbornly resisted the glamour and wealth of Roman matronhood. Unlike Ennia. She also had a playful laugh and a very tactile manner. She was perfect in every way. And yet somewhere underneath the civil exterior I could picture a hungry lion on the prowl. She was altogether too good, too wholesome and pleasant to be quite true. I did not like her.

I was grateful that, as a Roman matron far from the direct line from power and with no influence of my own, I was practically invisible to the majority of the population. By rights, had I not been a ward – or more accurately a *prisoner* – of the emperor, I should now be in Vinicius' domus in Rome, managing the household like a proper wife. I was ever unsure whether that was a good thing or not. I already missed the comfort of my new husband for all the short time we had known one another, and yet I am not by nature a home-maker, and that aspect of life would have driven me mad. But I was on Capri without my husband, and because of my comparative obscurity, Macro and Ennia both looked right past or through me as we stood at the dock to welcome them.

The emperor had not come, of course. Forget the tales you hear that Tiberius never left Capri – in fact, he never left the Villa Jovis itself in all the time we were there, let alone the island. And because the emperor stayed at the villa, so did the unpleasant young Gemellus, and the murderous Helicon. And so Silanus, Caligula's father-in-law, had arranged a small party to travel to the port and welcome the new commander of the Praetorian Guard to the emperor's island. Silanus was there, his face still gaunt and drawn after three months of draining grief, but he was slowly recovering now, throwing all his fatherly concern instead into my brother. The two had become as close perhaps as Caligula and Lepidus had been in Rome, or he and Julius Agrippa at our grandmother's, and my brother was learning small matters of statecraft from the older senator along the way.

In addition to Silanus, there were Caligula and myself, of course, and Drusilla, naturally upstaging me by cleaving to my brother, who revelled in her presence. It was only to be expected that Longinus, her husband who had repeatedly been thwarted in his attempts to gain imperial favour, would seek out the arrival of the second most powerful man in the empire. I was relieved to see that while Drusilla still seemed perfectly miserable, she was clearly healthy and well looked after. Silanus had been correct in his assessment of Longinus. He might not be Lepidus, but he was no wife-beating Ahenobarbus, either. I wondered briefly what people said of my own husband. We had, after all, thus far only spent a week in each other's company, but I was already starting to miss being held when I felt nervous or cold. That single week had changed the way I viewed the world, for I was no longer a girl, and now that I knew what it felt like to lie with Marcus, I wanted more. I wondered what he was doing now, and, not for the first time, whether his remit to make the Palatine habitable once more was a signal that the emperor was starting to think about a return to Rome. With Sejanus gone, it would make sense, of course.

Apart from the five of us, a score of the island's Praetorians with a stiff, serious-looking officer stood on the dockside as the new arrivals disembarked. Macro immediately grinned, called out to Silanus and rushed over to grasp his old friend's hand. Ennia floated along behind him as though borne on a cloud, smiling warmly while her eyes searched for prey. Silanus seemed equally pleased to see the prefect and once they stepped apart again, Macro was introduced to Caligula.

'Well met, young Gaius,' he said. 'I remember your father fondly. I served with him in Pannonia before you were born. A good man, and one who influenced me in my own career in many ways. And I can only begin to express my sympathy and commiseration over what has happened to your family at the behest of my predecessor, may he rot in Tartarus.'

I watched my brother cast that appraising look at the new prefect and break out into a genuine smile. He had decided that Macro was a good man. Fortunately, his glance at the man's wife was less certain. He seemed to have picked up on her predatory aura as well as I. What was a man like Macro doing with a panther in human form like Ennia?

Drusilla and I were introduced by my brother, and we were both given polite greeting before being basically dismissed from the mind as unimportant. Longinus stood hovering, moving from foot to foot, almost vibrating with anticipation, and I wondered if he might soon explode if no one made the appropriate introductions. Fortunately, Silanus stepped in and did so. My sister's husband gushed obsequiously until Macro finally pulled back, and Silanus had to put an arm around him and guide him away to rid him of the older man's attention.

We moved to the carriages and boarded them, Silanus and the new arrivals in one, the three children of Germanicus and the edgy Longinus in the other. For almost an hour we bounced and lurched up the road to the Villa Jovis, where we alighted and entered, Macro marvelling over the incredibly bumpy journey, as did any new arrival to the palace. The major-domo greeted us at the door with a small army of slaves who were set to work carrying the new arrivals' gear, leading away carriages and beasts, taking travel cloaks and so on. He informed us that the emperor was currently occupied and could not be there to greet Macro in person but would see him at the evening meal, when he would welcome him with appropriate gusto.

Macro raised an eyebrow as he passed from the territory of the Praetorians into a palace manned by the unaffiliated Germanic bodyguard, but he brushed off any potential nerves over the lack of his men and entered the villa easily. Two Germans stood nearby, looming near the door, but they were merely in their usual post rather than actively assigned to watch the guests. The slaves scattered like the seeds of a dropped pomegranate, going about their business, and as the door closed behind us, we were all but alone once more, barring the two Germans and the major-domo who fussed around the room.

Macro threw an arm around Silanus once more and began to let loose a stream of sympathy for what had happened to the man's daughter and over his woes. My brother's father-in-law excused himself from our presence and the two old friends left the vestibule, heading for Silanus' suite to catch up. As so often in my young life, I was grateful that being a youngest daughter I was of precious little interest to most people and was largely left to go about my business. I watched the lady Ennia with interest as her gaze played around the room, her talons rapping on her hip. Just as I'd anticipated, her eyes swept over me as if I were of no more interest than a vase, and did the same to Drusilla and her husband, coming to rest on Caligula. When she smiled, I half expected to see a serpent's tongue flicker out.

'It is so stuffy inside,' she announced sweetly. 'I wonder if I might take the air. Perhaps you would show me the gardens, Gaius?'

My brother nodded graciously and escorted her from the vestibule. I waited until they had left the room, for to follow them would be impolite, despite my yearning to do so and my rather childish need to eavesdrop on their conversation. Once they had left, I excused myself from Drusilla and her husband and scurried off into the working area of the villa. The slaves and servants cast vaguely interested yet respectful looks at me, but nothing more. I was a ward of the emperor, but no empress by any stretch of the imagination. To them I was the oddly boyish young woman who was always where she shouldn't be. I'd been there so often they took it as normal. Breathlessly, I hurried out of one of the slave entrances and into the gardens, where with two sharp turns and a descent of six steps I was once more in that warren of gardener's passages through the bushes. It did not take me long to find Caligula and Ennia – they had barely left the building, I had been so quick. I watched as they moved to my brother's favourite place in the garden – the viewing platform where the whole island stretched out before the beholder. There, he began to list the interesting points of Capri to the prefect's wife as I quickly and quietly made my way around the garden to a position nearby. A lone rain cloud hung over distant Sorrento on the mainland, but the sky above Capri was clear and the island perfectly visible.

'Are we safe to talk openly?' Ennia was asking as I shuffled into place behind a rose bush with an intermittent view of them. The lady pulled her expensive blue palla mantle tighter around herself against the breeze. Autumn was in the air now, driving the warm summer from the world and here at the emperor's eyrie the winds could cut through you like a knife. My brother simply stood still and put a finger to his lips, cupping the other hand around his ear. Ennia and I both listened obediently. We were rewarded with a distant scream that trailed off into silence.

'The emperor is keeping himself busy,' my brother said with quiet disgust. 'We are as alone as it is possible to be here, but I must caution you against an unguarded tongue.'

Ennia smiled and again I imagined a serpent tongue flickering.

'You are a clever young man, Gaius Caligula. Clever, handsome, and . . . attractive in many ways.'

My brother stepped a pace away and turned, reaching out and putting his hands on her upper arms. He held her there for a moment and I had a horrible feeling that he was about to kiss her. I felt the bile rise in my throat at the thought, but instead his face became serious and he spoke in careful tones.

'You butter the wrong bread, Ennia Naeva. The only man in the empire more powerful than your husband is the emperor himself. Not I, for sure. I am no man of destiny, and your ambitious eye has misread your target.'

Ennia gave a laugh that set my teeth on edge. 'Dear Gaius, I am not seeking your attention in that manner. I am more than happy with my husband and he would deserve better than a wife who beds the powerful in an attempt to improve her standing.'

And yet she leaned forward and gave him a most improper kiss! My brother recoiled as though he had been bitten. Perhaps he had, in fact. But I know my brother well and beneath the shock and disapproval, I could see flickers of desire in his eyes. He had had a beautiful wife torn from him three months before and there was a hole in his heart that sought to be filled. Still, I was grateful when he held his desire in check and separated from her.

'But as to your value and whether you be a man of destiny,' the lady said quietly, 'I think you do yourself a disservice. I see greatness in you, Gaius – a greatness which is beginning to blossom.'

My brother shook his head. 'I share the succession with Tiberius Gemellus on equal terms.' He glanced around, aware that one was never truly alone at the Villa Jovis. His eyes lingered on the rose bushes and I suspect he knew me to be there, even if he could not see me. He went on very quietly and I had to strain to hear.

'Gemellus may not be the stuff of which great leaders are made, but he is the direct descendent of the emperor and, for all our shared status, I fear there could never be any doubt that he will follow Tiberius to the throne.'

'I am pleased to hear you make such bold and intuitive predictions. You may well be right about the succession, young Gaius. And you are most certainly correct about Gemellus. My husband believes Gemellus to be an uncouth animal and as unfit to rule Rome as any barbarian from beyond the world's edge.'

Again, Caligula looked around nervously. Though there had been no insult to the emperor yet, saying such things about Gemellus could just as easily be considered treasonable, and my brother had no interest in seeing the drop from the emperor's favourite balcony *too* closely.

'Be careful in what you say.'

She smiled and now she was no snake, but a crocodile. I shivered. 'Nevertheless, it is the truth and no matter of treason. For all Gemellus' current good luck, the emperor shunned him for many years, recognising in his grandson something ill and unpleasant. My husband remembers the boy from times in Rome and knows his lack of value. The emperor will recognise that in the end, and the succession will go to you.'

My brother opened his mouth and raised a finger to argue, but Ennia – again most improperly – placed a finger on his lips and spoke again. 'But because the Fates are capricious, son of Germanicus, it is only fitting that all Romans of good conscience help things along to their logical conclusion. My husband will spend his time on the island promoting your cause with the emperor and very carefully emphasising the faults of the boy. My husband is not the *only* one who sees you as the next emperor. Your father-in-law is another such, and you would be amazed, I think, at how many of the senate and the nobiles of Rome share their opinion. Your cause is already fought in many a corner. Do not give up and hand power to a boy who will abuse it.'

My brother simply stood, dumbfounded. I did the same. After all this time, with our family singled out by a wicked prefect and a vengeful emperor, imprisoned and killed, denigrated and torn apart, now we were to believe that a goodly portion of Rome's great were supporting Caligula and saw him as the natural heir to the elderly emperor? And at seventy-five years of age, Tiberius was now the oldest person I had ever met apart from his mother – my own great-grandmother, Livia. How much longer could he reign?

'Do not push us away, young *princeps*,' Ennia said quietly, 'for it is your future we coddle, and with it that of all Rome.'

A squawk drew their attention and in my hidden place I turned to follow the sound. I had missed the strike, but a great and glorious eagle was now swooping away towards the far end of the island, a white gull gripped tight in its talons as scattered snowy feathers fluttered towards the ground. I stared, certain that it had to be an omen of some kind. And given the conversation and the clear meaning of the eagle, it seemed natural to assume the two were connected. I had the feeling that tumultuous things were afoot both on Capri and in Rome. Not for the first time, I missed Vinicius. It is good at such times to have someone close to clutch and hug. Behind those drifting feathers and the victorious eagle with its catch, I could see how the sunlight had caught that small freak rain shower on the mainland over Sorrento and even as I watched I saw the multi-hued arch of the rainbow appear over the peninsula. Omens indeed.

After that first time, Macro's visits to the island became a regular feature. He came every two or three months and seemed to have achieved a place in the emperor's confidence. Sometimes he came with his wife, but often without. One day during late autumn the following year, he was on a visit bringing a selection of gifts for the emperor from the more influential houses in Rome, and I was standing with Caligula in his favourite spot, wondering idly whether, if we squinted hard enough, we could see signs of Drusilla at the far end of the island.

I felt my brother tense beside me and knew by that that we were not alone long before I heard or saw anyone. Caligula, in that curious way of his, spoke without ever turning or taking his eyes off the distant Villa of Diana.

'Good afternoon, Macro.'

The Praetorian prefect came to a halt a few paces away.

'Good day, Gaius. Livilla.'

'I did not picture you as a lover of gardens?'

Macro gave a light chuckle. 'Plants bore me. *People* are interesting. I am here in my less common aspect as a simple messenger.'

'Oh?' My brother turned to the prefect, and I followed suit.

The man wore an uncertain smile and there was blood on his boots, though not on his hands, and he wore no blade. Bloody boots were easy to acquire in parts of the villa.

'The emperor sends for you. He is on the ambulatory.'

My heart sank. Little good ever came out of a meeting with Tiberius these days and, even though there was still the question of the succession hanging in the balance, any such summons carried the potential of a gruesome death. Caligula nodded. 'Then I shall make haste. Thank you, Macro.'

My brother adjusted the hang of the toga he wore most days now, heedless of the weather which sometimes made the donning of such a garment a chore. Once he was satisfied with his appearance, he strode off towards the long balcony that figured so heavily in life at the villa, for good or for ill.

I watched him go, wishing I could follow him and observe, but I could hardly dip into the shrubs and my secret world beyond with the Praetorian prefect watching me. He gave me an odd smile.

'You do not like me, I think, Julia Livilla?'

His statement caught me very much off guard and I floundered for a moment, trying to find both words and the voice with which to produce them. I didn't dislike the man, did I? I hadn't been aware, but now that he mentioned it, I realised I had been frowning at him – almost scowling, in fact. Was it merely for association with Ennia that I had seemingly tarred him with the same brush? Eventually, rather weakly, I denied it.

His smile deepened rather than widened. 'Come now, let us be plain and truthful. You do not like me. And I think it stems from a lack of trust. In your position I would be exactly the same,' he said smoothly. 'You and your family have suffered long and hard through terrible times at the hands of terrible men. You do not trust easily and that is only natural. I hope to earn your trust and with it your friendship over time. I think you will see that I am nothing but a friend to your brother and the whole family of Germanicus. I wish only to see your brother secure his rightful place in the succession, and I am close to doing so.'

He sighed. 'I had thought your enmity aimed at my wife for her rather expansive and forthright charms, and so I have tried not to burden you with her presence when possible, but it is somewhat disheartening to find that I am equally disquieting to you.'

I smiled. It was not genuine. Somehow his attempt to reassure me over his motives made him now seem all the more untrustworthy, as if his protestations masked a deeper wickedness within.

'I do not wish to be so, Macro. You have my apologies, and you are correct that with what has happened to my family, I find it difficult to open myself to new people. I will attempt to put the past behind me and accept the new. And I *am* grateful for the support you show my brother.'

He reached out and clasped my shoulder sympathetically. I was proud of how I held still and managed not to recoil. A flicker of movement in the corner of my eye drew my attention, and I spotted Silanus emerging from an arch in the hedge. Macro saw my gaze flick to the side and he turned, smiling at his old friend.

'Marcus Junius Silanus, good to see you. I was just passing a happy few moments reacquainting myself with the lady Livilla here.'

Silanus inclined his head respectfully at me, then flicked his gaze back to the prefect. 'Do you have time to talk, Macro?'

The prefect nodded and turned to me. 'I beg your leave, Domina, and pray that you have a pleasant afternoon.' With that he bowed and turned to leave the garden, deep in conversation with Silanus.

I watched them go with mixed feelings. I might not trust Macro, but Silanus was almost a new father to Caligula now, and perhaps they would be good for one another, with Macro able to comfort the bereaved father and Silanus there to suppress whatever it was about the prefect that set me on edge. For a moment I considered following them and trying to listen in, but they were heading towards the villa proper and once inside I would stand little chance of being close enough to hear without being seen. Frustrated, I waited until I was alone in the garden and once more scuttled into my secret ways, navigating the passages until I came to the long, wide balcony that ran alongside the villa.

I scanned the place, thinking it empty for a moment, but then spotted the only two occupants at the end with the low balustrade, close enough to the villa wall that they were partially hidden until I craned my neck. It was an odd sight, and one that sat badly with me.

Caligula stood still, Tiberius beside him, the old man's spindly arm around my brother's shoulder despite the half-a-head difference in their height in favour of Caligula. They were deep in conversation and it looked as personal and friendly as one could ever imagine, despite the ongoing strained relationship between the two and the insanity and sheer power of the old man.

There was no one else in evidence, even the bodyguard Helicon, which was unheard of.

I strained to listen, but they were talking quietly and too far away and all I could hear was the ever-present chattering of the gulls and the general hum of life in the villa. How frustrated I was. Conspiratorial huddles between powerful men I could not follow and personal conversations between my brother and the emperor that I could not hear.

For a moment, a fanciful vision swam into my mind and I saw Caligula reach down and grasp the emperor's calf, lifting and pulling it back, unbalancing the old man and pitching him over the railing just as Tiberius had done to so many undeserving lessers. It was such a clear image that for a moment I actually thought he had done it, and I had to shake my head and refocus my eyes to see that the two men were still where they had been, close and in deep conversation.

Why did he *not* do it?

It was the solution, surely? The more important men on the island favoured my brother over the idiot Gemellus, and there could be little doubt from the furthest port in northern Gaul to the southernmost fort in Aegyptus that the emperor deserved to die. It would be a kindness now, surely?

But whatever his reason, my brother remained still, in conversation.

Then my stomach dropped and I was almost sick with panic.

The emperor's stretched arm, draped around Caligula's shoulders, was suddenly pushing forward. I saw my brother fall towards the balustrade and the dreadful, long, fatal drop beyond. I almost screamed, despite my hidden position and the danger of being discovered spying on the emperor.

I swallowed my terror in disbelieving shock as my brother's forward momentum was arrested by the emperor's other arm, seemingly much stronger than its spindly appearance suggested. The younger man was not falling to his death, but righting himself as he and the emperor roared with laughter at the sick joke. I caught a brief glance of Caligula's face as he turned and I could see plainly that he was laughing by rote and shared none of the emperor's cruel humour at the jest.

I felt sick. I wished my brother *had* pushed the old man off.

XI

WINGS OF FURIES

My brother began to visit the emperor increasingly often over the ensuing months. At first I wondered why, given the inherent peril of spending time with the dangerous old man, since more than half the time their visits seemed to be initiated by Caligula, rather than Tiberius. Gradually I realised what was happening. Rather than leave any influencing of the emperor in the hands of Macro and his friends, my brother was taking a personal interest in his own future.

Though at that point I think any designs Caligula had on the throne were the product of those around us, and he would as happily have lived out a comfortable life as a mere noble son of Germanicus, he had lately become aware that such a future was impossible for him. The emperor's naming him to the succession had removed all hope of a normal life, even had such a thing been possible before, given our tenuous family situation. He could no longer ignore the succession, since he was irrevocably part of it, and unless the emperor could be persuaded to grant precedence to one or other heir, Rome would be riven as the two fought for primacy when the time came.

And so he had begun a gentle, subtle campaign of befriending the emperor. Gemellus, seemingly blind to the game, simply sneered at my brother, feeling secure in his close blood ties. But Caligula began, with the ongoing tuition and support of his father-in-law, Silanus, to navigate the dangerous currents of the court. He began to play the emperor at strategy games, letting Tiberius win as often as seemed realistic, but claiming occasional victories for himself, all to support the lie of his inferiority. He began to discuss philosophy and politics with the emperor and as I occasionally sat in the great apsidal sunroom of the palace with them I realised that, while the old man may be dangerously deranged and paranoid, in terms of logic, debate and rhetoric, Tiberius was still as sharp as a chisel.

'The mind, like the soul, is an integral part of the human body,' the emperor stated upon one occasion, when my brother and he had watched the latest unfortunate plummet to his doom. 'If it were not, then would not the mind or soul perhaps be caught and left behind when the body departs? All parts of the body, whether physical or not, are a whole and as one. They may be separated, but only by force, as we have seen time and again. They are, by nature, a whole.'

My brother smiled. 'But as Lucretius himself said, Great-uncle, can we not divine that the parts of the body are indeed separate, for an arm may hurt while a leg on the same man is hale and well?'

The emperor cackled. 'You are sharp, Gaius, and well read, but remember that a pain in the arm is registered elsewhere. The body carries pain around. As Aristotle said, "there is nothing in the intellect that is not in the senses". If the body and spirit and mind were not a whole, why would a stubbed toe produce tears?'

I felt sure, on that occasion, that my brother's quiver of facts was far from empty, but he acknowledged the win of Tiberius graciously, and the emperor clapped him warmly on the shoulder and ordered more drinks be brought for a new discussion.

In fact, over the weeks, I started to enjoy listening to the two of them debating. I enjoyed it even more when Gemellus thought to impugn my brother and thrust an oar into the waters of discussion, only to be swiftly proved short-sighted and puerile and withdraw in a huff.

'Epicurus tells us that no pleasure is in itself wicked,' my brother intoned once, pausing to sip his wine, 'but that some pleasures carry costs heavier than the value of the pleasure itself.'

'Yet,' the emperor countered with a philosophical wag of the finger, 'Plato tells us that only the moral man can experience true happiness.'

Caligula nodded his head in acceptance of the point as I looked up from my scroll of tedious writings with a smile.

'Diogenes of Tarsus said that pleasure will end a man's life,' Gemellus put in seriously.

My brother and the emperor shared a look, and the old man rolled his eyes. 'You are speaking of Diogenes of Oenoanda, boy. And that is a misunderstanding of his point, no less. He claimed that pleasure lay at the end of a man's life, if he be virtuous enough to achieve it. A note unwittingly in support of my point, I would say.'

My brother bowed his acceptance of the loss once more, though with a quirky smile. The emperor roared with victorious laughter as Gemellus, his face pink and seething, plunged back into his seat in a fit of anger and returned his attention to his wine. I relished such exchanges.

It was sometime in early summer – Maius if I remember correctly – and we were all seated in the great glowing *aula* with the curved windows, watching a dreadful storm playing over the slopes of Mount Vesuvius and making the lives of the Pompeians miserable. By some freak of Jove's judgement, more often than not the mainland would be ravaged by seasonal storms that would completely bypass Capri and leave the sun to shine down on the Villa Jovis while those ashore were soaked.

As usual, Tiberius lounged on his gold couch, intermittently popping barely edible delicacies into his sour-twisted mouth as he propounded on the Heraclitan notion of change being the bones upon which the meat of the universe rested. I knew from previous arguments that Tiberius personally detested the idea, and somehow over half an hour of debate, my brother had cleverly turned the argument around so that the emperor was now arguing for the need for change, while my brother defended the much safer position that stability was central and change was a concept forced by man and gods. Never should an heir-in-waiting argue the need for change with their living predecessor, after all.

Helicon, the emperor's bodyguard, stood a few paces behind the couch, arms folded and face completely expressionless. Other than the three of them, the room played host to Silanus, who sat with an amused smile as he watched the debate rage back and forth, occasionally taking a sip of a wine that cost more than most town houses. Also to Gemellus, who wore an expression of boredom as he picked at the carcass of a pepper-and-liquamen-soaked hare. And finally to myself, of course, who found the theories of the ancient philosophers fascinating and silently bemoaned the fact that I had spent my earlier years studying the proper modes of dress and deportment and the management of the household rather than interesting things like history and philosophy. Such is the sad lot of women, though I found myself imagining my later years as more of a Grandmother Antonia figure than a docile wife, living in a house filled with life and fascination and far from the rigid rules of Roman civility.

My brother had just masterfully conceded a point to the emperor and I had had to force myself not to applaud, though Tiberius would undoubtedly assume I was clapping for his victory. All heads turned as the door to the great chamber opened and two of the emperor's German guardsmen entered, standing to attention to each side as the major-domo entered with a deep bow and announced that we had a visitor.

I assumed it would be the latest social call from Macro and was so surprised by the next figure who entered that I almost leapt from my seat. Julius Agrippa had changed in the half decade since we had seen him. He had grown into a man with a wide, strong face, untameable hair and deep-set, piercing eyes. Since we last met at Antonia's villa, he had had his nose broken – possibly more than once, from the new wide, flat shape. He was also considerably darker of skin from his sojourn in the east. For six years now, Agrippa had lived variously in Judea, Aegyptus and even Idumaea, reportedly taking a wife and siring children. We had heard rumours of immense debt and endless legal troubles, and yet the prince who now entered the emperor's rooms stood proud, well dressed and every bit as regal as his blood should allow. Better still, despite his royal lineage and nominal independence from Rome, he issued a deep bow to the emperor, thereby proclaiming the superiority of Tiberius, which brought forth a smile from the mad old man.

I wanted to do nothing so much as leap from my seat and welcome this old friend of the family, but even as I tensed my muscles to stand, I noted my brother's lack of movement and read in it the need to be careful. Caligula paused long enough to be sure the emperor's smile was genuine, and then flashed a friendly grin of his own.

Agrippa took several paces forward and went down to one knee perhaps ten feet from Tiberius. Helicon edged forward protectively, his eyes not on the visitor, but on the two Judean soldiers that stood close behind, their weapons absent, but still in uniform and carrying or pushing some sort of bundle.

'Divine Tiberius, Master of Rome, I bring you greetings from my uncle Antipas, Tetrarch of Galilee.' He snapped his fingers and rose, stepping to one side. The two Judean soldiers who had been behind him separated and between them was a strange lump under a purple sheet. Helicon moved to stand defensively in front of the emperor, his beautiful eagle-hilted sword rasping a hand's breadth from his scabbard's mouth. Before anything else could happen, though, Agrippa ripped the purple cloth away to reveal a dwarf, wearing a crimson tunic of linen with adornments of gold and a gilded circlet about his brow. Suddenly open to view, the dwarf thrust his arms into the air, spun twice on a heel and dropped to the ground in a pose, his legs split wide apart in the most uncomfortable-looking way. Even as Helicon accepted the lack of threat and sheathed his blade, the emperor rose from his seat in delight, clapping his hands.

'A gift,' Agrippa smiled, 'from my uncle. His name is Baratus and he is the most versatile dancer and actor at the court of Antipas, learned and lettered and familiar with the works of many playwrights of Rome and Athens.'

Tiberius continued to applaud. 'Well done, Master Baratus. And welcome, Agrippa. I am surprised to see you, given the imperial warrant seeking restitution for the funds you owe our treasury.' The old man winked. 'Be it known that the warrant is hereby served and you are forgiven your trespasses. Welcome back to our court, young Julius Agrippa. You are passing through on your way to Rome, I presume?'

Agrippa chuckled. 'My plans are carved in sand, Majesty, and the slightest breeze can alter them.'

Tiberius stepped forward, rather condescendingly patted the dwarf on the head as though he were a hound, and placed an arm around Agrippa's shoulders like a father with his son.

'Then you must stay for a while, young Julius. On my island. In my villa. I would welcome the fresh face. Perhaps you can take on the troublesome task of imparting knowledge and wisdom into my grandson. The gods know he could do with some of your grace rubbing off on him.'

My gaze flashed to Gemellus, whose face had sunk into a sour visage of disdain.

The emperor stretched. 'I am quite wearied. Gaius here has worn me out with his clever debates. I fear I must retire for a nap in order to be well rested for the evening meal. Once again, Agrippa, welcome to Capri. Gemellus will show you around the island while your retinue settles you into a suite.'

Again, Agrippa bowed to the emperor and remained motionless as Tiberius paused to examine the dwarf once more, chuckled, and retreated from the room, taking Helicon with him.

Finally, Caligula rose and approached his old friend.

'Julius, it is truly wondrous to see you. I worried that you would come to a bad end from all the tales that seep back here from the east. Are you on the run from someone there now?'

Agrippa laughed. 'No. My uncle helped me out and, though we quarrelled afterwards, we are once more friends. And my wife, Cypros, secured the patronage of Alexander of Egypt. I am, in fact, currently quite comfortably off and with no one seeking my head – well, no one of consequence. Old Flaccus, the governor, seeks me, but who gives a foetid dog fart about Flaccus, eh?' He chuckled lightly. Personally, remembering the dangerous Flaccus who had been at the court when we arrived, *I* would have worried about incurring his wrath, but Agrippa was always a little blasé over danger.

Gemellus, seemingly irritated by this exchange, rose from his couch and cleared his throat. 'My grandfather wishes me to show you around the island and, if you are to take on the role of tutoring me in matters in which I am already fully versed, we had best become acquainted, Julius Agrippa. Come.'

Without delay, Gemellus swished towards the exit, his perfectly arrayed toga covered in crumbs from his snack. He may have been seventeen summers then, but there was still the petulant adolescent about him that repelled me. Agrippa flashed a frown and a shrug at my brother, who returned the gesture, and the pair followed him out. The two Judeans and the dwarf were escorted away by the guardsmen, and, unwilling to be left idle in the great room in case the emperor returned and I found myself alone with him, I scurried after my brother. Though the emperor had foisted Gemellus on our old friend, and he himself had sought out Caligula's company, I desperately wished to catch up with Agrippa, so I tagged along.

The four of us emerged into the upper terrace, near my favourite part of the gardens, but also close to the busy ancillary buildings. At the front of our small party, Gemellus paused and turned. 'You have not been to Capri before?'

Agrippa shook his head. 'It is a little quiet and rural for my tastes. I am a man drawn by wine and song and the excitement of the city. I long to see Rome again. Especially now that *Sejanus* is gone.'

He fixed a knowing grin on the young heir and Gemellus bristled angrily. I wondered for a moment what had been said that could possibly have lowered the temperature so, but then I realised. There had been rumours. It was said that one of the reasons for Tiberius' overlooking of his most direct heir was the perpetual suspicion that his mother had lain with Sejanus and that the young man was in truth the offspring of that most hated prefect and not a blood relation of the emperor's at all.

'Sejanus is nothing to me,' Gemellus spat with the vehemence of a man who had been forced to repeat this sentiment many times over the years. 'May he rot in Tartarus for his deeds.'

'Yes,' Agrippa said with a sly grin. 'Including his habit of sleeping with other men's wives.'

Our friend might not have seen the warning look Caligula threw him, but I did. Gemellus recoiled as though he had been slapped and for once, just this once, I almost felt sorry for him, having lived all his young life with such a stigma. It went some way to explaining the embittered man he was becoming.

'I trust my cousin Gaius will keep you entertained for a moment, Agrippa?' Gemellus said coldly, gesturing to the stables nearby. 'I will secure a carriage with which to show you the island.' He disappeared into the stable complex, where two dozen horses of various types and numerous carriages and carts were stored. As soon as he was out of sight and the three of us were left in the garden alone, accompanied by the faint breeze rustling the trees and shrubs, Agrippa leaned close to my brother.

'Word is that Rome is learning to despise the emperor, you know?'

Caligula stepped aside from his old friend, his eyes wide.

'Shut up, you idiot,' he hissed.

'What?'

My brother leaned in close and pulled Agrippa to him, whispering so that only we could possibly hear, standing as I was a mere two paces away.

'Some things *cannot* be said, no matter where you are. Don't be a fool, Julius.'

Agrippa laughed a carefree laugh. 'We're alone, Gaius. Well, apart from your sister, and the lovely Livilla has nothing against me, do you, my dear?'

It was hard not to smile at his mock-worry as he pouted at me. My brother was less affected.

'You don't know this place, Julius. Keep your counsel to yourself until you leave the island altogether.'

'Pah!' Agrippa threw out his arms expansively. 'The old goat has to die soon, Gaius, and the sooner the better for everyone's sake. It's a testament to your patience that you haven't smothered him in his sleep yet.'

Even I now, wide-eyed and disbelieving, was starting to worry at such dangerous words being so blithely spoken in the open. Even poor Drusus had been more careful than this. Was this what living in the east for so long had done to our friend? Had he lost all sense of the inherent danger of Rome?

Caligula was stepping away from his friend, shaking his head, but Agrippa snorted.

'And when the emperor is gone,' he went on expansively, 'you can just do away with the little runt and all will be right. You would be a good emperor, Gaius. *Better* than an emperor. You could be a *proper* ruler. A king! A new Alexander or Xerxes, rather than these fractious emperors who rule through that gaggle of old men that calls itself the senate.'

Caligula grasped my arm and pulled me back, so that Agrippa was suddenly alone on the path. My brother was still shaking his head and mouthing 'no' at our friend.

Agrippa rolled his shoulders. 'You cannot hope to rule if you are afraid to grasp power, Gaius . . .'

I froze, my heart thundering, as Caligula's fingers dug painfully into my shoulder, for behind Agrippa the figure of Gemellus had emerged from the stables. Beyond, a carriage was being slowly trundled out by three large slaves. It was patently clear from the expression on the young heir's face that he had heard at least some of what was said. How much, I couldn't guess, but certainly enough.

Agrippa, now aware that something was wrong, turned slowly.

'Gemellus . . .'

'Shut up, Jew!' Gemellus' face was thunderous, and Agrippa turned back to us, spreading his hands wide. His face was filled with a mixture of disbelief and panic.

'It was a joke, Gaius. Tell him. You know it was a joke. In poor taste, perhaps, but a harmless jest . . .'

My brother remained stony. Gemellus' lip was twitching now.

'Traitor. Hedonist . . . corrupter . . . traitor! I will see your head removed for this,' snapped Gemellus as he waved the burly slaves forward. The three men dropped the carriage they had been manoeuvring and hurried across to Agrippa, who they grasped and held in place.

'Gaius,' pleaded our friend. 'You have to tell him it was all in jest. You *have* to!'

I could see the desperation in my brother's face. He so dearly wanted to do something.

'And you,' Gemellus barked, pointing at Caligula. 'Don't think I'm not watching you. There's every bit as much traitor's blood in you as in this one.' He turned towards the villa. 'Guards!'

The Praetorians were already running towards us all. Agrippa stared, boggling, at them. '*Gaius?*'

I tried to take a step towards our friend, but Caligula's grip on my shoulder was like a vice and I whimpered as he turned me away and walked me down into the gardens. Behind us, I could hear the sounds of men shouting and swords being drawn. I tried to turn back, my heart rending at the desperate shouts of Agrippa calling my brother's name, pleading for help, but Caligula's grip was iron and he steered me away, down to the lower terrace where he finally let go. I could feel the bruising where he had manoeuvred me.

'We could have helped him. It was only Gemellus' word against ours. Why didn't you help him?'

My brother turned to face me and there were tears in his eyes, which dried my next words in my throat.

'Have you learned nothing in your time here, sister?'

I shivered, unable to answer the question, for he was correct and I knew it.

'He doomed himself the moment he opened his mouth, Livilla. I tried to stop him, as I once tried to stop Drusus, little good it did either of them. There were others within earshot. They may only have been slaves, but if tortured, their evidence is legally viable. If I had leapt to Julius' defence, the Praetorians would even now be dragging two of us off to the emperor.'

'What can we do?' I pleaded. We had just regained an old friend and already, within the hour, he seemed lost to us.

'Nothing, Livilla. Distance yourself from the danger. Pray to the gods that Julius has sense enough to be contrite. If he is the right mix of obsequious and apologetic he might be able to blather his way out of this. Tiberius seems to hold him in esteem, after all. Perhaps his royal blood will save him yet. Perhaps he will not pay a visit to the emperor's balcony.'

After one day on the island, Julius Agrippa was whisked away to Rome, not to enjoy its life, but rather a solitary residence somewhere. I suppose I ought to have been saddened and distraught that a friend had been imprisoned, especially since imprisonment seemed to be naught but the first stage of execution-by-starvation in our family's experience. Yet I carried hope for him in my heart. After all, those who angered the emperor on Capri usually left the island much more quickly. Often vertically. Agrippa had been taken back to Rome under guard, more in the manner of a foreign hostage than a Roman prisoner.

The episode set Gemellus squarely against Caligula and therefore against me to a lesser extent, but we worried not about him. Not only did he lack the wit to do us real harm on Capri as long as we were careful, but also the emperor still saw him as a petulant young man, while he seemed to be coming to appreciate Caligula on a more equal level. Nothing had changed in the matter of the succession, of course, but at least it now *felt* as though Caligula was somehow preferred to Gemellus.

The year wore on and winter came, bringing with it the usual icy winds and snows that beset the peaks of Capri. We celebrated Saturnalia in the same muted manner as in recent years, with our small insular court and isolated surroundings.

But one other change occurred over that autumn and winter. Almost as if Agrippa's prediction that Tiberius must die soon had been some kind of trigger, the emperor fell ill and seemed unable to fully recover, moving from one bout of troubles to the next with barely room to breathe in between. By Februarius he was more often to be found in his chamber having one of his three-hour 'naps' than he was upright and involving himself in matters. And those naps gradually became more frequent and longer. Wads of phlegm, lengthy nosebleeds and crippling headaches became the norm for the ageing emperor and no matter how many physicians were brought in to help, he continued his slow and steady decline.

As I expected, Gemellus saw this as a sign that the old man was dying and set about trying to win over the support of the various people who visited, fawning and issuing promises that were not his to make. Conversely, my brother, who had more reason than most to hate the old man, spent an increasing amount of time by the emperor's side, looking after him, for he knew how to the play the game and would not plan how he would proceed with the emperor still alive, unlike his co-heir.

Rumours had begun to circulate wildly among visitors, guards, freedmen and slaves alike about the succession. Gemellus was making inroads with the island's military, using promises of financial gain and the granting of important positions when he became emperor. Never within earshot of the old man, of course, but by late winter not even Tiberius himself could have expected his reign to see another Saturnalia. He was dying. And he had not made a decision. The succession remained officially split equally between Tiberius' great-nephew and his grandson. Almost everyone believed the emperor would make a new will in the coming months before it was too late, and many maintained that he had already done so in secret and it now rested in Rome awaiting his death for it to be examined. This latter was rubbish, but it would not have been unlike Tiberius to have a new will hidden in his chamber somewhere.

Macro's visits began to come closer together, sometimes twice a month now, which meant he could hardly be spending any time in Rome. While I still did not particularly trust Macro, I relished his presence, for I knew him to be no lover of Gemellus and so while he was here, the young heir would find his hold over certain Praetorians on the island diminished to the point of non-existence. His campaign to lobby the military would be largely fruitless without the head of the German Guard and the Praetorian prefect on his side.

Over those months, my sleep pattern became erratic and, despite my stance against white lead on skin, I began to use just a little, carefully applied to conceal the dark circles that formed beneath my eyes. My appetite, never great in the first place, dwindled to almost nothing. The sheer stress of life on Capri was eating away at my health and the more I tried to fight it, the worse it became.

In late Januarius, during Macro's latest visit, the prefect had been in to see the emperor in his chambers and had been closeted away in there for two hours and, unwilling to spend time in the main rooms with the gloating figure of Gemellus, Caligula and I had wrapped up warm, braved the winter cold and stepped out onto the stone flags of the great balcony. The weather was chilly and grey with the threat of coming snow, but remained temperate enough as yet to keep the ice away. A good thing, for I would never willingly set foot on that balcony in icy conditions for fear of my life. In truth, I had only come at Caligula's bidding, for even in the best of conditions I had no wish to visit that place of death.

My brother and I were huddled tight in our woollen cloaks, leaning on the railing and looking out across the sea. From where we stood we could see the whole of the Neapolis bay. My brother talked me through the view from right to left: 'The Sorrentine peninsula, Livilla, whence we sailed to this damned island, then beautiful Stabiae. We'll try the renowned baths there one day when we're free. Thriving Pompeii, where I'll buy you fried fish – they have the best fried fish in Campania, I hear. The great cone is Vesuvius, lost in grey cloud, and beneath it is small Herculaneum nestled by the sea. They have a new theatre there, just built. The ancient Greek port of Neapolis, then the smaller gulf of Baia, surrounded by important towns.

Cumae where the Sibyl lurks in her cave – we'll visit her and learn of our futures . . . once we have one. And Misenum, home of Rome's principal fleet. And to the far left, jutting out to sea, the island of Aenaria, where we can lounge in the warm sulphur baths.'

'It looks so close,' I murmured, 'almost as if you could jump from one peninsula to the next. From Misenum to Pausylipum to Surrentum.'

Caligula chuckled. 'It might look like that from here, but even that short hop from Misenum to Pausylipum is around five miles.'

'A swim, then?' I smiled.

We never saw it coming, so intent were we on the bay. I had heard faint scrapes and shuffles behind us, but that was nothing new, with so many gardeners tending the emperor's terraces.

A blade cut through our discourse.

The gods were with Caligula that morning, for the first attacker's sword plunged deep into my brother's cloak, missing his armpit by the tiniest margin and ripping open only tunic beneath. The second blow, a fraction later, glanced off his large silver brooch as he turned in response.

I panicked. What was happening? I turned, wide-eyed at a gruff voice – a soldier's curse. Two men had come for us. One was wiry and swarthy, the other bulky and tall, both fast, and dressed in very nondescript brown tunics. Only blessed Fortuna had prevented our deaths, for both those blows should by rights have landed true and ripped the life from Caligula in moments.

My brother had undergone adequate martial training in his youth to know how to react to such a threat and in a matter of heartbeats he was facing them, his cloak ripped off and held in one hand as a paltry shield, the silver knife gifted by Lepidus fourteen years ago suddenly in his right hand, though I'd not even seen him draw it.

The two attackers did not give us time to react fully and, even as my brother was trying to wind his cloak protectively around his arm, they were on him. His speed saved him from the next blow as he ducked to the side, the gleaming iron whispering past his flesh. I saved him from another as I threw myself in a most unfeminine manner at the other man, like a wrestler in the *pancratium*. I had no skill in fighting, but I *did* have vast reserves of determination and rather sharp nails. The man might have been a gladiator, I surmised, from the criss-cross scars on his skin, but as he tried to fight me off I was like an angry cat, hissing and shrieking and scratching at his face, my nails gouging flesh and drawing blood.

He pulled back, tearing me off him and grunting in pain.

'Bitch!' he snapped in a thick accent that might have been Thracian.

Before I could attack him again, he delivered me a full-fist punch to the cheek. I heard my jaw clunk and panicked even in the flood of pain that he had broken it, though it later turned out it had only temporarily and rather painfully dislocated. I was all but knocked unconscious by that blow, my wits driven from me as I fell to the ground, crying. I desperately wanted to hit him back, but my brain seemed to be swimming around inside my head and my legs would not work. My arms felt like jelly and I could barely raise my head from the stone.

I watched through blurred eyes as my brother fought valiantly, but I knew he could not last. Luck was surrounding him like armour, but he wielded only a knife and a cloak against two men with swords. Luckily the one I had distracted – the wiry one – seemed to be the real killer of the two, and now he had to keep pausing to wipe the blood from his eyes where I had attempted to scratch them out. The other attacker was slower, but strong, and oddly familiar for some reason, though my head was swimming and vague and I couldn't place him. My brother was already wounded. I could see blood running down his arm and more from his hairline. Chopped pieces of his cloak lay scattered on the ground.

Another blow ripped through the garment's wool and Caligula was backing away towards that very railing that had seen the demise of so many innocents. My heart thundered at the realisation. Another chop and stab and more cloak fell, my brother dancing this way and that to dodge the blows, but always away – always back.

I saw him find an opening and lunge with his knife. He was good, despite the tiny weapon, and the blade tore through the flesh of an assailant's arm, sending a faint spray of crimson into the air. But the blow cost him, and he took another glancing blow across the knuckles, his hand only spared by the wrapped cloak that was now little more than a ragged net.

'Who sent you?' demanded Caligula, breathlessly.

His answer came only as a flurry of blows.

I wanted to fight so much. My legs were useless, and my brain fuzzy, but my arms seemed now to have some power to them. I used them to drag myself over to the fray even as I heard Caligula cry out in pain from some fresh wound. I miscalculated in my haze and felt one of my fingers break as the lither of the two attackers accidentally stood on my hand. I screamed and he looked down in surprise to see what he had trodden on. My scream became instantly muted as I closed my mouth on his ankle and bit into the tendon.

It was his turn to scream now, and before he fell he delivered me a powerful kick with his other foot. I felt a lancing pain across my ribs, wondering if one or more had broken, and rolled back against the wall, winded and unable to do anything other than spit out the vile blood and gag on the fleshy matter that was caught between my teeth.

I had done enough. The wiry gladiator was on the floor, bellowing in pain and clutching his ruined ankle. The bigger one was still facing my brother, but then the fight changed completely. As if from nowhere, Prefect Macro appeared, sword in hand. He hit the big assailant from behind, sending him screaming over the railing and down the thousand-foot drop to the sea. It was a poor attack, really, for it narrowly avoided carrying my brother over too, and only his quick thinking and sharp reflexes saved him.

As Caligula recovered and the floundering wounded man on the floor, desperate and regaining his wits, lunged out in a last attempt to strike my brother, Macro turned contemptuously, slamming his foot down upon the man's wrist and then punching his own *gladius* down through the man's back, beside the spine and between the fourth and fifth rib, shearing straight through his murderous black heart.

It was over.

Oddly, despite his allegiance to my brother and the coolness with which I habitually treated him, the first thing Macro did was stoop to help me to my feet. I couldn't stand. My legs wouldn't take my weight, and so my brother had to pull himself together while Macro held me up.

'A gladiator,' the prefect noted, looking down at the wiry attacker and confirming my earlier assessment. 'Probably the other was too. They could have been hired by anyone, though I suspect the prime candidate for suspicion rests not too far from here. They would need permission to dock on the island, after all. Presumably they arrived in a retinue.'

My brother nodded. 'My thoughts exactly,' he agreed, using his tattered cloak to mop the excess blood from his face and arm. 'Why did you kill him before we could ask?'

Macro shrugged. 'I was more concerned with your survival at the time. Are you wounded, or just scratched?'

'A little of both,' Caligula replied with a tired smile. 'Nothing from which I won't recover, though. Livilla?'

I tried to assure him that I was fine, but when I opened my

mouth to speak my jaw sent such unbelievable pain through my head that I almost blacked out.

'I fear she has a dislocated jaw and –' he ran his hands over my body in a swift examination '– perhaps a rib or two cracked,' Macro said quietly. 'She will be all right, but we should get a physician to look at both of you as soon as possible.'

My brother wiped his silver blade on the tatters of his cloak and sheathed it. He then came and took my other shoulder, helping Macro half-walk, half-carry me into the villa. My jaw felt oddly numb and yet at the same time agonisingly painful and I remember being strangely disappointed that the one did not cancel out the other. My brain seemed to be calming down, though I was beset by odd flashing images that went back almost a year, to Agrippa's visit.

I dragged them both to a halt as the reason for my odd mental flashes became clear. I forced myself to talk, though it must have been barely intelligible to them and it hurt like nothing I'd ever felt before to do so. Slowly, with some strain and effort, I managed to explain where I knew the other attacker from. He'd been one of the burly slaves who brought the carriage for Gemellus that day.

And that made one thing perfectly clear.

'This is it,' Macro muttered to my brother. 'The emperor is dying and men are starting to jostle for position. The only question now is whether you are happy to leave matters to chance and see if Gemellus becomes emperor and has you killed to secure his position, or whether you're willing to take your destiny into your own hands. The Praetorian Guard cannot make the move, for the emperor's Germans never leave his side now. But we can *support* a move.'

A move against Tiberius? Would my brother dare? But if he did not, how long before Gemellus took matters into his hands and did the same? And then what might the future hold for the last children of Germanicus?

*

Events snowballed after that day. The emperor's health took repeated turns for the worse and from early Februarius he never left his chamber, turning away all physicians as useless has-beens and with a predictably fiery temper. The long drop from his balcony was busier than ever, as Helicon took over the sole task of execution of those who annoyed the old man, since Tiberius could no longer leave the building to watch. Perhaps two slaves a day were thrown to their death, merely for having been in the room when the emperor happened to have an attack of whatever it was that was ailing him.

In an unexpected turn, my husband Marcus Vinicius returned to Capri at the emperor's behest, bearing news that Rome was prepared to receive an emperor once more.

'The unhealthy influence of Sejanus has been removed from the corridors of power,' my husband told the frail and wracked emperor and waited for acknowledgement. None seemed to be forthcoming, the old man far too weak, and so Vinicius continued. 'The Palatine is once more the emperor's sole domain, Majesty. The slaves are eager to welcome their true master and to wait upon him.'

I doubted this was truly the case, especially since stories must have circulated over the years of what the old buzzard did to his slaves on Capri.

'Moreover,' Vinicius announced, 'with Macro's aid, the last few seditious elements have been weeded from the Praetorians, and the *vigiles* purged of low characters too. All of Rome now displays loyalty to their emperor and spits upon the name of Sejanus. The Palatine awaits, Majesty.'

There it was. A return to Rome had to be imminent, now. The emperor would surely want to die in the great city, where his passing could be appropriately mourned and attended.

Vinicius was kept busy much of that day detailing the fruits of his labours for the emperor, with input from Macro and sporadic interruptions from the old man between explosions of coughing and shaking. I listened to them for perhaps an hour, but the minutiae were tedious, and I had preparations to make. I had not seen my husband in three years. Three years! Can you imagine such a thing? And in that time, while his absence had gone from a solid pain to a dull ache, the want for him and the desire had somehow grown, unnoticed, such that even the sight of him sent tremors of excitement through me. So I abandoned the court and rushed off to my chambers to prepare. After the evening meal, of which I took no part due to a lack of appetite – for food, anyway – Vinicius finally came to my chambers. As he shut the door behind him and dropped his writing tablets, I smiled at him.

'Gods, but I have missed you,' he said in a breathy voice, and I felt that glorious quiver again. He sat and removed his sandals before stripping off his tunic and padding across the room.

'I needed you, Marcus. So, so often. And I know you would have come if you could, and that you had your duties, but I *needed* you. I still do.'

He cast me a sad smile as he clambered onto the bed. 'And the emperor commands me to leave once more. In the morning I am bound for Rome, but soon you will come. You will be with me, and all will be right. I have prepared our house with every bit as much care as I have prepared the emperor's palace. But let us not talk of tomorrow. We have only one night, and I have no wish to waste it.'

The few hours we spent as the winds buffeted Capri, the candles and lamps guttered and the braziers glowed and spat, were among the happiest of my life, and all too soon it was morning. We'd snatched only moments of sleep, yet were as content and invigorated as if we'd dozed a month or more. That single night took me another step above our first distant week together and changed us, bringing us closer together than we imagined possible, curse the Fates.

The next morning Vinicius was sent back to pave the way for a glorious return. I moped for a few days after that but, sure enough, the emperor soon announced that, since he knew the final boatman to be hungry for his coin and the plains of Elysium awaited, he would return to the city to die. He had been born in Rome during the aftermath of the death of Caesar, and he would die in the great city of his birth, as an emperor should.

Tiberius intended to reach Rome as quickly as he could, though he knew the journey would be slow by necessity, due to his weak condition. He was not convinced he would live to see Aprilis.

The fuss and busyness was unprecedented. I had never seen the imperial court on the move, and I was astounded at just how vast a task it seemed to be. Apart from a few lesser slaves and servants, the Villa Jovis was stripped bare of occupation and goods. For three days before the ides, wagons had taken crate after crate and bag after bag down to the port, where they were loaded onto ships and transported to Misenum across the bay, and then gathered and organised into the enormous caravan that would snake slowly up Italia to Rome, for the emperor's condition precluded potentially rough spring sea travel up the coast.

The Praetorians were mustered and shipped to Misenum. The German Guard, barring a few who stayed with Tiberius, were taken ashore ready. Endless scribes, administrators, officials and faceless toadies crawled out of the woodwork of Capri to be added to the huge mobile court. I'd had no idea there had been so many of these people on the island. The denizens of the island's other eleven villas, mostly Tiberius' lesser cronies, were brought to the mainland.

And once everything had been made ready, on the morning of the Ides of Martius – not an auspicious time for the family of the Julii – the final three wagons bounced down the bumpy road to the port. Actually, now that I think back on it, it was two wagons, containing Caligula, Drusilla and myself, Gemellus, Silanus and Longinus. The emperor himself was carried on a litter by four enormous brutes of Numidian origin, for there was every chance that a rickety, bone-jarring ride down that road could be the end of him. Escorting the column came the last of the German Guard.

At the port below, Macro awaited with a small detachment that were the last of the Praetorians on the island. Tiberius might favour his Germans, but the emperor's security was the concern of the Praetorian Guard and no amount of northern hirelings would change that. The last bireme departed Capri bearing the emperor, two groups of bodyguards who eyed one another warily, Helicon, the last family of Germanicus, Silanus, Longinus and Gemellus, as well as a few of the emperor's surviving personal slaves.

A leather awning erected at the rear of the ship near the steering oars sheltered Tiberius and a few guards and slaves, while the rest of us stood and took in the bracing sea air with its salty tang of freedom. We were leaving the island at last.

Of course, that might be no real cause for celebration. We might be exchanging virtual imprisonment on delightful Capri for the same situation in the stifling environment of the Palatine in Rome, with a hot, dusty city summer on the horizon. Or worse still, if the emperor died without solving the succession issue, there could be a short, very dangerous time in which my brother would be forced to murder Gemellus, while the oily little rat tried everything he could to remove Caligula and our whole family from the scene.

Still, despite our uncertain future, we were all pleased to be leaving Capri. It felt like a new tale was opening in the collection of our lives, and sometimes uncertainty can only be better than certainty.

The sea voyage to Misenum is something like twenty miles and took almost five hours in that season, given the lack of prevailing winds and the difficult currents that are the product of so many headlands and islands channelling the sea around the mouth of the Bay of Neapolis. The water there is the most excellent blue, unlike anything I have seen near Rome or further north. That is one thing I missed about leaving Capri – the sea.

Throughout the trip I tried to strike up conversations with my brother, but he was uncharacteristically reticent, not even stooping to small talk. In fact, he seemed distracted and far away, spending the entire journey leaning on the same section of rail at the front of the ship while the rest of the luminaries on board stuck close to the imperial awning in case they were required or there was some way to gain from proximity.

I tried to speak to Drusilla, but the disapproving glare of her husband Longinus – who seemed to consider me an aberration due to my relative freedom and the permanent absence of my husband – soon put me off. Shame, for I had seen little of her in our time on Capri despite her geographical proximity, and the age-old jealousy I'd always borne for her had diminished somewhat with her sad situation. But she was unreachable past Longinus. I had no interest in speaking to Gemellus, and Silanus was busy with Macro, so I spent most of the voyage watching the landscape slide by and the choppy waters at the outer periphery of the bay, hoping to see the dolphins that often followed ships in this region but failing even to pass the time with *them*.

In the end, I leaned on the fore rail close to my brother and observed in silence.

We watched as Cape Misenum approached, a brown rock of impressive size rising from the blue. Atop it were watchtowers and various military structures, and within it the great cisterns that supplied fresh water to the largest of the Roman fleets. The cape slid by on our left like some jagged sleeping turtle. We were said to be sailing to Misenum, but in truth we were making for the Portus Iulius, the great home harbour of the Misenum fleet that sat within the shelter of the bay a further two or three miles beyond the projecting cape.

The port was enormous, purpose-built half a century ago to house the fleet, and dozens of powerful triremes sat at ease within, bobbing gently on the calm waters of the harbour. The nearest jetty had been left clear for this, the most important vessel, due to its most precious cargo.

Our ship, the *Agathopus*, slid easily between the towers at the ends of the twin breakwaters that created the safe harbour and began to slow and turn, making for the empty jetty to the right. That anchorage lay close to the main land exit of the installation from which the road ran south through Puteoli, or north through Cumae and Formiae and eventually to Rome. I could see, as we began the delicate task of manoeuvring within the port, a full century of Praetorians standing at attention on the jetty, with more beyond on the dock, awaiting the arrival of their emperor.

I stood at the front rail along with my brother. Drusilla was further back, obediently close to her husband, and everyone else towards the rear, where the emperor's awning stood and the business of steering and commanding the ship was carried out.

Everyone except Prefect Macro it seemed, for the officer, his gleaming salt-marked helmet tucked under his arm, was strolling down the walkway between the oarsmen towards us. As the ship turned, preparing for the final approach to that jetty, Macro strode across to the rail and leaned next to my brother. When he spoke, it was so quietly that I hardly heard.

'The emperor has summoned Gemellus to him. Not you. You know what that means?'

We glanced back to see that indeed Gemellus was gone from the small group who had stood close to the awning throughout the trip. He was inside the makeshift room with the emperor, his body slaves and his few German guards. I felt my heart flutter. Surely that could not be good.

'It means nothing,' my brother replied calmly. Macro's face suggested otherwise.

'It *means* that the rumours were true. He will make a new will in favour of Gemellus, if he has not already done so. If that document makes it into the light of day, it will also serve as your execution warrant – you know that.'

Caligula nodded slowly, still seemingly unconcerned. 'The will has not yet been produced, and there is no time left to do so, for I hear the beating of the wings of Furies even now. My great-uncle breathes his last, Macro.'

The prefect put on a weary, disapproving look. 'You've spent the whole journey here at the rail. You cannot be sure of that.'

'Yes, I can,' my brother replied with a tone of leaden certainty that sent a shiver through me.

Macro's expression slid into a frown that hung somewhere between surprise and suspicion. I opened my mouth to question my brother's calmness over such an important subject, but my words were drowned out by a scream from the rear of the ship, which swiftly became a commotion of angry, panicked voices and disharmonic wailing, all slightly muted by the leather of the imperial awning. Amid the cacophony one could hear the word '*Imperator*' here and there.

Macro's face was a picture. Had not the fate of the whole world rested on the events taking place on that single ship as it slid towards the jetty, slowing as it went, I might have laughed at it. The prefect glanced back at the awning – as did I – to see the turmoil surrounding it. German guards, sailors, slaves, even Silanus, all milling about, as well as the *trierarch* of the ship and his first officer. Even Drusilla's husband was running for the awning now, dragging my sister along in his wake.

Yet my brother stood at the rail as though contemplating what to order for a meal, his expression serene. I boggled at him, but Macro's face, utterly astonished, was all the more impressive as he turned back to my implacable brother, perhaps torn, wondering whether to stay with Caligula or run to the emperor's side. Of course, there was every chance Tiberius' Germans would not let him through the tent flap. In the end the prefect simply stared at my brother.

'What has happened?' he asked breathlessly.

My brother slowly lifted his hand from the rail. I hadn't realised that he had been clutching something in it as his other gripped the timber. That folded hand came up to head height and he half turned so that it was in front of Macro's furrowed brow. His fingers unfolded, and within his palm sat three small items. Seeds or beans, by the look of them, one end black and shiny as the eye of Hades, the rest gleaming bright red. Macro continued to stare, though now at the small items in my brother's hand rather than his calm face. Suspicion was still evident in his expression, though dread had now taken the place of surprise in the mix.

'A blade may not be able to pass the German Guard,' my brother murmured quietly to the odd background noise of an imperial demise, 'but a blade is the least subtle of weapons. An abrus berry from the lands beyond Arabia,' he explained, nodding at the red items in his palm. 'Too rare for anyone – even the terminally paranoid – to reasonably have built up a resistance. Sometimes the Furies need to be nudged along.'

I was utterly dumbfounded. Questions sprang into my head.

How long had he been poisoning the old man?

How had he delivered the poison with so many careful guards around Tiberius?

How in the name of the twelve gods of Olympus had he managed to acquire such an incredibly rare poison within the close confines of the island?

How had he so neatly timed the emperor's demise?

I found a sudden new respect for my brother's determination

and strength, though for the first time in my life it was threaded with a trace of fear. I had known my brother for a purposeful man and a careful one, and to suffer occasional fraying of the temper, but never before had I thought him capable of such a thing as calculated murder.

Of course, all this passed in mere moments, leaving stoic acceptance. He had done what he had to do for his own survival, and for that of the rest of us. He had done it for Rome and for the good of the world. And the act of murder and the decision to undertake it must have burned in his soul for some time, as he kept everything to himself.

But the fact remained that all he had done was prevent the confirmation of Gemellus as primary successor. We were now back to the very position we had dreaded for months – years, even. The emperor was dead and the succession undecided.

Civil war was nothing new to Rome but had to be avoided at all costs. Yet my brother remained calm, as though everything were unfolding according to some hidden plan.

'The emperor was never going to reach Rome,' breathed Macro.

'The emperor was never going to reach *Misenum*,' corrected Caligula.

Behind us, along the deck, the clamour was ongoing. The German Guard were milling about uselessly. They could protect Tiberius from swords and fists, but this was, as far as anyone could see, the final product of his long illness, taking him before he managed to complete his last journey. And while they could continue to protect his lifeless body, they suddenly had no idea to whose authority they should now submit. Similarly, the small detachment of Praetorians, who remained at the ship's edge in order to prevent accidentally starting a scuffle with the Germans, waited to see what they were ordered to do. Slaves were tearing at their hair and wailing, though I could see that for the show it was. No one had liked the old man, least of all the slaves who lived in daily danger of displeasing him and making a personal visit to his high railing.

Gemellus emerged from the awning, ashen-faced. I wondered whether he'd been told he was to be the next emperor before the old man died, or whether he'd entered anticipating the good news, only to watch his grandfather die first. Behind him came Helicon, the emperor's bodyguard, whose expression was dark. He could hardly protect his master from illness, and he was bright enough to realise that over the last few years he had heartlessly murdered an endless stream of people on his master's word, so he was unlikely to be very popular now.

There was a brief clash of steel at the stern, where a confused German had traded insults with a Praetorian and the two had gone for one another. Their officers pulled them apart angrily as chaos reigned.

It helped in no way that the ship chose that moment to bump against the jetty and slide to a halt, sending several arguing or panicking people stumbling and collapsing to the timbers of the deck. Uncertain of what they should be doing, the sailors went about their business as if all were normal, tying up the ship and preparing the ramp for disembarkation.

Macro and I had our wild-eyed attention drawn back as my brother spoke quietly and with great purpose.

'Time to decide, Macro. Gemellus may be over a hundred miles from Rome, but he is one short step from the throne, as am I. There could be war. There could be murder and treachery and death. Rome could descend into chaos as it did in the aftermath of Caesar . . .'

I remembered as he spoke of divine Caesar that today was the Ides of Martius. How the Fates love to play with the lives of mortals. But then this had not been the Fates, had it? I wondered madly whether my brother had planned it so carefully that he'd even selected a meaningful date.

Macro was still lost for words, staring at the commotion to the rear.

My brother cleared his throat, drawing the prefect's attention once more.

'The support of the Guard means everything now, Macro. Time to decide.'

I swallowed my nerves. There was always something odd about the prefect that precluded any possibility of me trusting him, and yet he had unswervingly supported my brother thus far over the idiot Gemellus.

The world held its breath.

Great Jove on Olympus readied his thunderbolt.

Macro turned and looked up at the Praetorian centurion on the jetty at the head of his column, whose face was full of concern and confusion, suspecting something of what had occurred on board but as yet with no confirmation. The centurion realised his commander was looking at him and straightened.

'Form up the men, Centurion. Divine Tiberius is no more. Hail the new emperor of Rome. Hail Gaius Julius Caesar!'

The irony of the name and date together was not lost on me, nor apparently on Gemellus, whose jaw dropped, leaving him gape-mouthed and astonished. There was a moment of tension – just the blink of an eye, as the commander of the German Guard dithered, looking down at the slack-jawed youth, before forming up his men and marching them along the ship's central walkway, stopping a respectful distance from my brother and dropping to a knee. My brother smiled as he cast the three red berries surreptitiously into the swirling dark waters below the rail. I wondered whether he had kept them in hand for a sure death should the Praetorians decide against him. It would not surprise me. Caligula rarely left matters to chance.

It was decided. Nothing Gemellus could do now would change anything.

The family of Germanicus had arrived in Rome eighteen years

ago, noble and honoured, but endangered. We had watched our family riven and torn, arrested and executed. We had lived under the vile persecution of the traitorous prefect Sejanus. We had survived six years of imprisonment in the deadly court of Tiberius.

It was over.

Caligula was the new emperor of Rome.

The Ides of Martius would finally lose their dreadful stigma, for a new golden age would descend upon the empire.

PART THREE

THE REIGN OF THE GOLDEN PRINCE

'By thus gaining the throne he fulfilled the highest hopes of the Roman people, or I may say of all mankind . . .'

– *Suetonius:* Life of Caligula

XII

A GOLDEN AGE

Oddly, the second time I entered Rome from a far-flung home, a rainbow hung over the city once again. It may have been a trick of the eye, given the glory in which we returned, that the arch seemed so much higher, brighter and more vivid on this occasion.

This time we were no oppressed noble family in mourning, bearing the ashes of our dead with an eye on an uncertain future. This time I was no babe, carried in the arms of my nurse. This time, my brother was the most powerful man in the world and we were the honoured imperial family. During our journey north from Misenum, carrying the decomposing body of old Tiberius with us, the slaves of the imperial household, eager to impress their new master, carefully tried to preen and dress Caligula so that he looked the part. I have to say, the transformation was impressive. My brother was ever shrewd and he forbade the worst excesses they attempted to heap upon him, trying to maintain a sober appearance, and the result was excellent work. He appeared handsome, regal and impressive, while in essence seeming at the same time little more than a toga-clad noble of senatorial rank.

Certainly the population of Rome lapped it up as we entered in triumph. It is somewhat telling of the reputation of the late emperor that there was no hint of mourning among the crowds gathered, only of celebration at the arrival of their new ruler, for this was a child of Germanicus, the great general beloved of Rome, and a golden age seemed to be anticipated in the lee of Tiberius' exiled wickedness.

My memories of that return are somewhat vague, as it was so unutterably busy and clamorous. I remember bits and pieces. The rainbow that caught my eye and drew me rather sadly back to my first day in Rome and the family I had lost, the ceremonies at the Capitol, the sacrifices, the speeches – all of it comes in flashes interspersed with endless shouting and colour and light.

One of the things I remember most clearly is Gemellus, who had languished in one of the wagons for the return to Rome under the watchful eye of a small party of Praetorians. And while we drank in the acclaim in the forum, I watched out of the corner of my eye as, unseen by the crowd, Gemellus was led by half a dozen Praetorians to the Tullianum, the stinking pit that served to hold Rome's political prisoners while they awaited sentencing. The greatest enemies of Rome had been kept here, from the Numidian king Jugurtha to the Gaulish rebel Vercingetorix. And now Gemellus, the grandson of Tiberius, joined that dreadful inventory. I was somewhat disappointed at my brother for that. Silanus and Macro had both urged him to put Gemellus to death to remove a potential thorn in the side, and, while I was uncertain of what I wanted for him, languishing in a pit in his own filth was not it. But my brother merely told us that he thought Gemellus might yet have a use. And, after all, he *was* a political prisoner.

I remember too the return of Agrippina. We had not seen my oldest sister for some time, and the ever-present background worry about her husband made me truly grateful to see her in full health and unharmed. Indeed, there was a glow about her that I could not quite put my finger upon, for the blessing – or perhaps curse – of motherhood was still unknown to me. I tried as we walked to persuade her to petition our brother for a divorce from Ahenobarbus, for he had the power for that and more, but she would hear nothing of it. Whatever her reasons, she was committed to her marriage and had no intention of letting Caligula separate them. Perhaps it was the knowledge of what they had created together.

'You owe him nothing,' I said as we passed along the Via Sacra. 'You are the emperor's sister!'

'It is not a matter of debts owed,' Agrippina hissed as she waved absently to the crowd. 'It is a matter of eggs unhatched. All things in due time.'

Clearly she had some plan laid out, for there was ever a scheme behind anything she did. I disagreed with her, no matter what plan she was working, but my pleas fell upon deaf ears.

'You have all the power you can desire now,' I blurted, rather bluntly referencing her habitual playing of power games with those around her. She snapped a sharp glare at me, but I was unapologetic. 'You are the imperial family. *We* are the imperial family. We will have honour, and peace, and even glory, perhaps. Your sons will be princes of Rome!' That last said still oblivious to the life within that had given her the healthy glow she wore like a cloak.

'You know nothing, Livilla,' Agrippina said with a barbed tone that shocked me. 'You live in your happy little shell, believing in the value of our father's blood. It is not about what you can see and who you know and can manipulate in the now. You will never learn, sister. It is about suffering whatever the now throws at you while you position your pieces for the future. It is of no value to maintain a comfortable lead when the goal is to win the game. Now speak no more of this.'

Whatever her design, seemingly occasional beatings were worth enduring. And the way she spoke to me put me off any further attempt to help, anyway. She had always been cold and clever, but I fear that marriage to her brute of a husband had also brought out a vicious streak in her.

I turned my attention back to our glorious return.

After a while the fuss died down and we made our way up to the Palatine, where the great palace of Tiberius – the palace of Gaius now, I suppose – awaited. And with it waited my husband. He was greeted by Caligula as a close friend and brother-in-law and the two laughed and smiled as Vinicius showed him around the palace, noting how parts had been changed at the last moment to remove not only Sejanus' mark but also the less healthy aspects of its previous owner. Tiberius, it seemed, had had some odd – one might say dark – tastes and habits.

I was not sure what to expect from a reunion with a husband of four years who I had only seen twice and for less than two weeks in total. I was surprised to find him cheerful, loving and passionate, and those first few days in Rome passed in a whirlwind for me. Vinicius had a house on the Esquiline, but he had been living in the house on the Palatine that had once belonged to the emperor Augustus, and when my brother heard this he expansively gave the place to us. In our pleasant little home we became man and wife once more and I recalled our first days together and why I cared so much for him. Indeed, while I was always more than a little cynical when it came to love, I realised that what we shared had grown beyond respect and friendship to include something primal and passionate.

We lived for a few weeks in the warm glow of reunited lovers in the shadow of my brother's palace while he set about making changes, securing the loyalty of the Praetorians and the military with a healthy donative of coin, appointing those deserving to lucrative and powerful positions and those he considered untrustworthy to distant and low-grade, uninfluential postings.

My brother gave the dwarf Baratus his manumission and granted him permission to return to Capri and occupy one of the old imperial villas as his own. Such generosity was typical of Caligula when he was in a good mood. Indeed, the scarred

Helicon who had served the brutality of Tiberius so well was given a role as a chamberlain to the imperial household, despite Macro's urging to the contrary. Few could match my brother in his munificence, though his fury, when provoked, was similarly great. I had thought his quick anger from the days of our youth gone, for it was not something we had seen in our time on Capri. I think it had always been there, but Caligula had been clever enough to keep it concealed and controlled in such a dangerous place.

The first event that I really paid any attention to after our return was the special session in the senate. It was perhaps three weeks after our arrival, and finally my brother felt settled and comfortable enough to meet with the senate of Rome. And in that time, those more aged senators who had been away for the colder months flocked back to the city in preparation. One might rather uncharitably suggest that the returning nobles might be men who had fallen foul of Tiberius' temper and had been avoiding any chance contact with the court or the Praetorians, and that now they felt my brother might waive their indiscretions and treat them anew. They were *almost* right.

Due to the grand nature of his first session, where every senator would attend rather than the usual fifty per cent, as well as the public interest in his new reign, he decided to call the session in the large Basilica Aemilia. Here there was adequate room not only for the full senate to meet, but also for the public to gather at the periphery and observe the session – the curia was much too small for such a grand meeting. This, of course, meant that women were given unprecedented access to the business of the senate. Drusilla, Agrippina and myself were shown to seats with an excellent view of proceedings, while our husbands were all among the toga-clad ranks of the senators attending, along with Silanus. Needless to say, a number of guards from our brother's own units surrounded the three of us and kept us from harm, maintaining a cordon to protect us from the throng.

It was the first time I could remember that the three of us women had been together without old Tiberius, violent Ahenobarbus or stifling Longinus, and while the crowds thronged and the general hum of conversation reigned, we talked like the sisters of old.

'Vinicius brought home a slave yesterday with the oddest look,' I said. 'A boy from the north-east, who came through the slavers of Byzantium. He has skin like tanned leather, a moon face and the narrowest eyes and he speaks with a peculiar accent. I have never seen anything quite like him.'

'Longinus has twin Numidians who dance like snakes coiling. It sends a shiver up my spine to watch them,' Drusilla said with no trace of humour.

Agrippina snorted. 'My husband has taken to buying whatever girl takes his fancy, then discarding her when she is broken.'

I sighed and prepared myself once more for verbal war with my eldest sister. 'Gaius will sort everything out, if you would but ask him.'

'For the last time, sister,' snapped Agrippina, 'I am where I wish to be. When I need things to change, they will change, but for now keep your nose from my business and let me live my life.'

I leaned back away from the force of her words, but her eyes narrowed and she leaned towards me. 'Drusilla is a fragile butterfly, flitting about the world wishing she could be more colourful. *I* know what I want and how to achieve it. You, Livilla? You drift through great matters as though you were a wart on our brother's backside. Before you start telling us how to live our lives, perhaps you should work more on your own. You have a husband you never see, seemingly no hope of birthing children, the least feminine look I have ever come across, no direction, no goal and just a strange need to hang around our brother as though you were his puppy, not his sister. What is it that you want, Julia Livilla?'

I was shocked at the venom of her words and from the corner of my eye I saw Drusilla's dismay at this drab portrait painted of her too. But the problem was that I didn't really know how to answer the question. What *did* I want? Throughout our youth in the various villas of Rome and then on the island of Capri, the question had never occurred to me. What I had wanted was to survive, and for my family to survive. But we had done just that, and now we were in Rome and safe. So what *did* I want? It took me some time to work through that, and it was in the hours of a sleepless night some days later that I realised what I wanted was simply for my family to go on. We were the glorious children of Germanicus, but only one male heir remained to carry on the line. I wanted my brother to thrive; to create a dynasty that would brush aside the cruelty of Tiberius and create a new golden Rome. Grand dreams, I know, though they should not have been beyond our reach. But that was later.

At that senate meeting I was frowning and fretting at the question so much that I actually missed my brother's opening words, though I caught much of his address and appreciated how carefully he had tailored his speech and had worked on his oratorical skills for the event. The public were impressed and cheering, the senate undecided, but hopeful.

I listened as Caligula expounded on the virtues of the senate as an institution and the special relationship that existed between the emperor and the senate courtesy of the wisdom of the great Octavian Augustus. That went down well enough, as did a number of concessions he announced, which stood to make a number of rich men richer and the powerful even more so. His largesse was impressive and I could picture the coin counters of the treasury wincing at his decisions as they desperately tried to work out whether there would be enough money in the coffers.

He announced that he would take on the consulate – that was expected, of course – and singled out a figure in the crowd of senators, bidding him rise. I frowned for a moment, but as the man turned to bow to the masses I recognised the slightly lumpy, unlovely face of our uncle Claudius. A lame-footed stammerer, he had been the butt of every joke for two generations of emperors, shunned and snubbed into virtual isolation. His resentment at forty years of mistreatment by first his step-grandfather Augustus and then his uncle Tiberius emanated from his very form, and his expression made clear his scepticism at the possibility of any improvement under his nephew.

Claudius, my brother announced, would join him as co-consul for the year. Very political. Claudius would be feeling a little put out that the succession had been decided without even consideration for him. After all, he was Tiberius' nephew, while Caligula was only a great-nephew. The consulship might mollify the sour-looking old goat to some extent, and it would make him appear valued while granting him very little actual power or influence. He was bright enough to know that, though, of course.

Caligula's next order of business took me as much by surprise as it did everyone else, but made me chuckle to myself for reasons that no other could comprehend. The senators had an air of expectancy about them as though they were waiting for something to be said that had as yet been unheard and, despite the various great promises of my brother, they felt undecided.

'Senators of Rome,' he said, gesturing oratorically with an extended arm while gripping the hem of his toga with the other hand, 'who have been to me in times of hardship and danger as a father to a son, I thank you for your support and loyalty.'

Support and loyalty that had yet to be fully secured, as some of the hard faces in the crowd suggested. The dangerous and unpredictable reign of Tiberius has made trust between emperor and senate a tenuous and fragile thing.

'Conscript Fathers, I recognise here many faces that have spent some time away from the court. Faces that fell foul of Tiberius' temper or were denounced by neighbours and enemies under the lex maiestatis during the dreadful time of the prefect Sejanus.'

There was a tangible increase in tension as those men who had thus far scraped through without quite meeting trials for treason bit their lips in hopeful strain.

'Senators, I ask you to look to my right.'

In confusion, the crowd did so, not at all sure what they were looking for.

'Look out of the basilica,' Caligula urged them, 'and across the square, past the Basilica Iulia, towards the slave markets.'

The confusion grew and with it came an air of faint irritation. My brother was playing with them and his playfulness was missing the mark slightly – a habit that came back to haunt him time and again. His humour had been forced down convoluted and oblique alleys in our time on Capri, and it did not appeal to everyone.

'What do you see?' he asked, slight exasperation creeping into his tone.

There was a long silence until someone suddenly, breathlessly, called, 'Smoke!'

A clamour broke out as people began to suggest that the Velabrum region beyond the forum was aflame. The city was on fire. Rome was burning, and fire in the city could be more dangerous than a thousand barbarians. A single spark among the dry wooden *insulae* of Rome could lead swiftly to the destruction of whole districts.

My brother frowned and, quickly realising what was happening, waved the crowd into silence with a laugh. 'The city is *fine*, my friends. The smoke you see rising from the Velabrum is caused by a small army of slaves from the Palatine, along with a unit of Praetorians, burning the old emperor's records of trials, accusations and other misdeeds. My time as princeps will start afresh without the fear that accompanied my great-uncle. There shall be an end to the trials under the lex maiestatis. All outstanding matters are hereby nullified and all records expunged. You are proud senators of Rome once more.'

He fell silent and waited. There was a long pause – longer than he expected and I could see him start to feel the faintest irritation again at the lack of recognition of the great deed he had just performed.

As the crowd began finally to react, cheering and calling his name, he drank in the acclaim and I chuckled, quietly at first and then louder, until Drusilla stared at me and asked me what was so funny. I waved aside her question and sobered myself, though inside I could still only laugh. For only I of everyone in that great basilica had seen my brother's clerks at work for over a week, copying in precise detail every word of those transcripts such that an identical set of records now existed secretly within Caligula's palace on the hill. Generous, he might seem. Foolish, he was not.

But as far as the senate were concerned, he had just won a great political battle. The tension relaxed somewhat, though there were still unsettled faces.

'The fires that consume those records will burn day and night beyond the basilica until the accounts are all gone. I invite you all to visit the pyre of my predecessor's despotism and watch it burn.'

It was well done. It was *very* well done. And had there not been one more matter playing on the minds of the senate that first session would have been an unqualified success. My brother had made his announcements and given his address. Now would come the meat of the session, as the leading men of Rome put to him questions for resolution.

It was the hawk-nosed, white-haired figure of a senator by the name of Gaius Calvisius Sabinus who soured proceedings. Sabinus was already prominent in the city, having held the consulship a decade ago, and had been the subject of one of the most prominent cases of maiestasis under Tiberius. The records of his trial might be currently charring beyond the forum, but all present would remember the high-profile case that had almost cost Sabinus and his family their lives.

The white-haired ex-consul stood and as he did so a hush spread across the crowd, rippling out from him to silence the jubilation.

'Sabinus,' my brother acknowledged with a nod of his head. Of those involved in the proceedings, they were the only two standing.

'Imperator,' nodded the old man, 'nothing has been said, in this session or before it to my knowledge, of the fate of Tiberius.' No acknowledgement there of the old emperor's rank or titles. We knew he had been hated, of course, but to not even offer the customary respect due a deceased noble of Rome was unseemly.

'The emperor passed in Misenum of a long-term illness,' Caligula reminded the man in a flat voice, puzzling over the statement.

'And what does the *future* hold for him?' asked Sabinus archly.

My brother was frowning deeply now. 'His ashes rest in an urn awaiting the appropriate ceremonies. It is fitting to deal with the more urgent matters of succession and the governance of the empire before such issues are dealt with.'

And, of course, organising the weeks of games and races, the funerary rites and so on for an emperor was a massive undertaking. Already, a small army of clerks and officials were busy arranging parts of it. Once the senate's session was ended and my brother's announcements made, more attention could be paid to it.

Sabinus folded his arms over his toga front. 'It is the considered opinion of an influential and powerful element of this senate that Tiberius represented the very worst of Roman power. That he was a detestable and vile creature. That he played off brother against brother to execute those he did not like and steal their households for himself. That he abandoned Rome to play god on his little island and left the good folk of the empire to suffer under the wicked hand of Sejanus. No good came of the reign of Tiberius and it seems ill fitting to us that he be remembered as an emperor of Rome. I would see him suffer *abolitio nominis*, his name and images erased, the very memory of him damned.'

My breath caught in my throat at the request.

Damnatio.

To be reviled as an enemy of Rome, as a man of no honour, who had brought shame on himself and the empire by his actions. To be expunged from history entirely, his name struck from every inscription, his busts and statues smashed and broken, his buildings rededicated, his coins melted down and reworked. His remains discarded in the gravel pits above the Esquiline where the poor, the beggars and the homeless lay decomposing. It was an unbelievable thing to ask.

My brother stood silent and still, perhaps shocked by the notion. To damn Tiberius in such a way *did* carry a certain logic, and in other circumstances my brother might well have seconded that very proposal. But imperial succession was a delicate thing. There had been difficulties over the succession of Tiberius from Augustus, and it would take only a slight nudge for the great and the powerful to begin to question the legitimacy of my brother, regardless of the Praetorians' support. To damn Tiberius would be to cast doubt upon all those who bore his blood, including my brother. The damage to his credibility could be vast. We knew that Caligula could not damn Tiberius without endangering himself.

Sabinus waited, impatient, his arms folded. Others were nodding their agreement, and the mood was beginning to spread. I willed my brother to act – to do something to put things right.

Finally, Caligula squared his shoulders and threw out an

oratorical arm. 'Would you heap blame upon great Jove when your loved ones are taken from you, just because his brother Pluto is master of the underworld? Of course you would not. Nor should you transfer to my predecessor the guilt for the trials and crimes and deaths committed by Sejanus. That monstrous prefect, you must remember, was put to death – and therefore removed from your lives – by the order of the very Tiberius you seek to damn.'

The public leapt upon this and I smiled at the cleverness of my brother. He had not defended Tiberius against any accusations levelled at him, but had neatly used the name of the reviled Praetorian prefect to shift the focus of the crowd's hate. Sejanus had already suffered a dreadful end, and no one could defend him.

'I cannot in conscience agree to the *damnatio memoriae* of Tiberius,' my brother announced finally and, as Sabinus opened his mouth to argue angrily, he held out a restraining hand and spoke once more. 'Do not press me, for I will not agree upon it, but I *will* grant this concession to those of you who continue to feel the affront my predecessor caused you: he will be buried with a family funeral only in the tomb of his ancestors, but in the memory of all those ruined and executed in his name, there will be no funeral games and no decree of apotheosis. None shall say that Tiberius resides among the gods or enjoys the divinity granted to Augustus. There shall be no temple raised to him. This I decree.'

There was a long pause once more. The senators around Sabinus were nodding approval, or at least acceptance, of the emperor's decision. Sabinus himself appeared unconvinced and unsatisfied, but with support melting away in the face of adequate compromise, he nodded his grudging acceptance. My brother and he continued to glare at each other for a while, until a brave soul called out, asking what would happen with respect to the will of Tiberius.

Ten heartbeats it took Caligula to tear his gaze from the stony figure of Sabinus, who remained standing in a sea of seated senators.

'The last will of the old emperor is rather sparse,' my brother announced. 'However, he had promised bequests in earlier wills, and in the spirit of benevolence I will see that those legacies are met, along with other gifts granted in the will of the great lady Livia, whose legacies have been jealously held back following her death. Both wills and all bequests made by the two will be published in the *tabularium* for the viewing of the public. Livia promised three hundred sesterces to the pater familias of every citizen household of the empire, and Tiberius, in his halcyon days of power, had promised a total of forty-five million sesterces to the people of Rome.'

There was a collective intake of breath at the staggering sums of which he spoke and once more I could imagine the money counters in the treasury sweating blood at the announcement. For while Livia's bequest would come entirely from her own considerable fortune, Tiberius' will had been changed and any funding to cover it would have to be drawn from public moneys, or from other sources.

'The treasury cannot fund such a payout,' snapped Sabinus, still standing and glaring at my brother. Caligula's gaze fell once more upon the man, his lip twitching enough that I noticed it even at a distance, his fingers digging so tight into the hem of his toga that his knuckles were the same colour as the material. At times in our youth I had seen him like that just before he exploded at Drusus in fraternal argument.

'The treasury, as Senator Calvisius Sabinus so kindly points out, is not capable of meeting such amounts, at least until the next year's tax has been gathered. And so any shortfall will be met from my personal funds.'

There was an impressed silence. Such beneficence was the

stuff of legend and would lift my brother's reputation in almost every quarter.

'And thus does the new emperor purchase loyalty,' sneered Sabinus.

I stopped breathing altogether for a moment. The colour had drained from my brother's face and silence fell like a thick blanket upon the basilica. I waited for an explosion of temper but instead my brother merely cast a sharp glance to one side, to some unseen personage, and a moment later men stepped forward from the watching crowd, almost encircling the senate. They wore togas of white just like the majority of the other citizens in the crowd, but those of us who had spent time in the imperial court or on the Palatine could spot the tell-tale lump beneath the right armpit that spoke of a concealed sword and declared those who had stepped forward to be men of the Praetorian Guard.

Silence continued to reign, though recognition of the nature of these new, standing, implacable observers filtered quickly through the seated senators and Sabinus was, within heartbeats, standing at the centre of a widening circle. Still he appeared unappeased, but his support among his peers had entirely vanished. For good or for ill, my brother had made it clear that he would not be weak.

'I suddenly find the air in here unpalatable,' my brother announced with a sour expression, his eyes still boring into Sabinus. 'Good day.'

Without further ado, he turned and, grasping his toga tight, walked away from the basilica, through the colonnade. Out of the corner of my eye I saw Silanus in conversation with Macro where the gathered Praetorians had encircled the senate. Without waiting for Drusilla or Agrippina or my husband, I rose from my chair. The men guarding us were uncertain whether to follow and protect me or attempt to *prevent* my leaving. In the end, four of them accompanied me through the crowd as I made to intercept my brother, who was now emerging into the forum with eight Praetorians at his shoulder.

By the time I reached him, he was striding purposefully and angrily between the Temple of the Dioscuri and the fountain of Iuterna, making for the hillside, the guards spreading out to open up a space around him and keep the public at bay. I fell in alongside him, having to scurry at a most undignified pace to keep up with him, with my considerably shorter legs.

'I will see Sabinus ruined for that little display,' my brother grunted as he realised I was with him.

'Don't do anything precipitous.'

'I *had* them,' he snapped. 'The senate, I mean. I had them in the palm of my hand for the mere matter of a few coins. And that rat of a senator kept testing me.'

He stopped suddenly, and I had moved on several paces before I realised and hurried back to join him.

'He broke my composure, Livilla, and for that I am more angry with myself than with him. I had believed that once we were free of Sejanus and Tiberius and I was master of Rome I no longer had to guard my tongue. Now I see that I am wrong. I must continue to play the game, but this time with my lessers. Damn the man for goading me. I never intended to lose my temper, but he *would not stop!* It was just like the old arguments I had with Drusus when he wouldn't listen. Those Praetorians were present only for protection, not to be used as a threat. Damn Sabinus for driving me to that.'

I looked around to be sure that he and I were speaking privately. We were now in the Via Nova, the street that ran from the lower forum up the side of the Palatine to emerge near the great palace's entrance.

'This walk is interminable,' grumbled my brother. 'I need to construct a stairway from the forum to the palace to save me this hike, *if* I lower myself to visiting the accursed senate again at all, that is.'

I watched him go, the Praetorians gathering closer to him as they went, the four that had accompanied me closing in once more. I was beginning to see why Tiberius had put such stock in his German guards. Praetorians had stolen most of my family from me over the years, and the presence of the four soldiers around me did not fill me with confidence.

XIII
A THUNDER OF HOOVES

Caligula was Rome's golden prince. In three months in the city, he won over the military and the people. Some will tell you that his support from the legions, the Guard and the navy was born solely of coin, but they are lying, or mistaken at least. Oh, the very healthy donatives to the troops certainly pleased them, but it was more than that. Caligula was *their* emperor. Augustus had carried out a civil war and won great victories, but those victories belonged as much to his generals, and once he had secured power, that first emperor remained in Rome while his officers prosecuted his wars for him. And Tiberius? Well, Tiberius had certainly been a great general in his day but, again, to the common soldier he had been little more than a name and a figure in white on a horse behind the army during battle.

Gaius Julius Caesar – my brother, that is – had, like his revered namesake, marched alongside the men when our father campaigned. Indeed, our father's popularity owed something to his closeness to his men. After all, my brother's famous nickname – 'Little Boots' – derived from his marching with the army, so over those three months the sobriquet, which had clung to him on and off throughout our childhood, became a common moniker. To his face he was Emperor Gaius Julius Caesar, but when speaking *of* him everyone, even down to the Praetorian prefect and his own father-in-law, began to call him Caligula. Yes, the military loved him for more than his coin.

And the people of Rome? Well, it takes only spectacle and a little comfort to earn their love. Caligula made sure the money from the wills of Tiberius and Livia, augmented with his own funds, went to every appropriate household, and, in a move that was clearly more philanthropic than calculating, increased the accessibility and quantity of the grain dole – only a little, but to those who have nothing a little is important. Thus he won over even those who had no voice in the politics of the city. And where Tiberius had languished on Capri and left the city to sweat under prefects and senators who were not over-forthcoming with public largesse, my brother spent money like water from a cascade, funding plays, games, races and other spectacles to keep the population entertained.

And Caligula was self-effacing almost to the point of depredation. He was consul, and allowed himself to be called *princeps civitatis* – first citizen, as the great Augustus had been known – but eschewed the jewelled glory and pomp and superiority that had been Tiberius' wont. Caligula had in fact dedicated a temple to his great-grandfather, the first emperor, and yet had refused to let anyone raise a temple, a building or even a statue to himself. After his predecessor he must have felt like a breath of fresh air to the ordinary people.

Of course, the senate was another matter. There was still a strain between Caligula and the senators. Many were supportive of him, it's true, singing his praises and making noises about how he needed to attend more meetings, but that one small group of senators who rallied around the bitter Sabinus had rather soured the experience for my brother. I once pressed him on the need to interact more with his senate.

'They need your presence, and you need their support, Gaius,' I had urged.

'They need to accept that they are not the steering oars of

the ship of state that they were in the Republic,' he had replied acidly. 'They are a tool of governance, not rulers in themselves. This is not Athens of old, and this is not a democracy.'

I swallowed nervously. I knew what my brother could be like when driven to unleash his anger. 'But, Gaius, they still represent all the powerful families of Rome. You ignore them at your peril.'

'I have no wish to involve myself in discussions with a gaggle of old women who fail to recognise the hand that feeds them,' he snapped, that ire rising slowly but surely.

I backed down. Better to plant the seed and let it germinate than to overwater and drown it. Despite his vehemence on the subject, I could see through the anger. I knew my brother well, and what I saw inside was fear. Fear of himself and of his reactions. He had approached the senate once with nothing in mind but munificence and brotherhood, and they had rebuffed him. He could have recovered from that, but they had driven him to extreme measures and he had rediscovered a side of himself that he did not like very much. Whatever he might say, the true reason he avoided further senatorial sessions in those days was his fear of what had been unleashed within him, and what he might be pushed into doing again.

You see, he had spent eight years wearing a mask of silent, stoic humility in order to survive in a world of wicked and dangerous masters. And throughout that time he had been forced to suppress joy, anger, fear, or any other emotion that might invite trouble. I think that even though he was now past those days of constant fear and peril he had become so used to donning that mask on waking that he'd forgotten how to deal with emotions when they manifested without it.

There would be time to heal rifts with the senate, though, and for now he had the support and love of the army and the people. And the people were loving his games.

One day in the month of Julius, during the Ludi Victoriae

Caesaris games in memory of great Caesar, Drusilla and I were seated in the *pulvinar* – the imperial box – of the Circus alongside our brother, with my husband and Lepidus also in attendance. Julius Agrippa, freshly returned from his exile on Lipari, was there too. I was twitchy and uncomfortable. It was against all custom and law for women to sit here, but Gaius had been insistent, and so here we were. The notion did not seem to bother Drusilla, but then she was, I think, revelling in being granted unprecedented freedom.

Her husband Longinus had been appointed a commissioner of drainage in Rome. It might not sound a high-profile position, but one has to bear in mind the value of good drainage to a city of a million people built mostly upon hills and reclaimed swamp. In actual fact, Longinus claimed that Tiberius had appointed him to the position on his deathbed, and my brother, too caught up in the real problems of government, had not the energy to argue with the man and had simply acquiesced. Consequently, Longinus had thrown himself into his work, hoping to excel enough that Caligula would notice and grant him a more important position in due course. This, of course, freed Drusilla to spend time with her family.

Agrippina was not there, though, remaining in Antium with her husband. She had announced just the previous week that she was pregnant, and in fact had been for several months. Our brother sent her his hearty congratulations along with a cartful of lavish gifts. I sent the gods an urgent wish that her unborn child be safe from its monstrous father.

The sound of the opening ceremony finishing drew me back to the games I was here to attend. I shuffled uncomfortably, sure that people were staring at me. Our brother laughed at my discomfort and leaned closer as some officious toady below made a number of announcements to the crowd.

'I have already set the rules in ink and had them lodged in the tabularium,' Gaius said. 'My sisters are no common women of

Rome. You shall henceforth have the right to sit in the imperial box with or without me. You have the right to attend meetings of the senate, too, should you have not suffered enough on any particular occasion and feel the need to burden yourself with their very special brand of misery. You have new rights, and many of them – I will show you the list later. For now, you will have to simply enjoy sitting in the best seats in the Circus and watching the most highly anticipated races of the season.'

I was agog, but was not afforded time to digest these tidings adequately. There was a great energy about Caligula that morning and he waved aside my questions as the droning official neared the end of his monologue.

A slave appeared from somewhere with a plate of hot delicacies for us, and my brother nodded to one of the guards, who gestured in turn to a man standing high up in the seating nearby. That man passed on the gesture, and a moment later a fanfare began from the musicians above the imperial box. It was so loud that not only did it silence the crowd, but it left my ears hissing for precious moments afterwards.

As the last ringing notes died away and I wondered whether my hearing would ever be quite the same again, my brother rose and approached the box's front ledge with his hands raised.

I will not bore you with his rhetoric, for it would be endlessly time-consuming. My brother was always an expert at speaking and for all that he occasionally missed the mark with his wry humour, he knew how to play a crowd. A quarter of an hour later if he had given the mob an order to march into the Tiber, a tenth of the city's population would have drowned.

He then went on to make his announcements – announcements that would traditionally have been given to the senate, and to the rich and powerful that formed that body, first, in acknowledgement of their precedence, even if they required no senatorial confirmation. These were Caligula's decisions and his alone, ratified by no one and announced for their first time to the hungry populace of Rome, both high-born and low, with no distinction.

His first announcement shocked the crowd – in a good way, I suppose. It shocked Drusilla and I a great deal more, and as soon as the races began I quizzed him over it at length.

He would adopt Tiberius Gemellus as his heir.

Can you believe it? After all that time on Capri where the dangerous, oily, childish little man had vied with Caligula for the succession, and now my brother would adopt him?

'Why?' I demanded half an hour later as the chariots thundered around the circuit mercilessly, risking life and limb with every turn.

'Why?' my brother replied. 'Because I will not suffer the same to happen under me as did under Tiberius. There must be a succession always planned and ready in effect, to provide stability to a reign, and it must be unquestioned. It must have the support of all involved. Gemellus has languished long enough. You didn't want him killed. What did you want, then, if not this?'

'But he will kill you to take the throne.'

'No, Livilla, he will not.' He sounded so *sure*.

'Why?'

'Because he does not need to. I have no other heir – I have no wife, remember. He stands to succeed. If I sire a son, he might start to think otherwise, and then I will reconsider the matter. But for now, he has nothing to gain and everything to lose by attempting a coup, for if he fails he will die the worst death imaginable. It is the sensible thing to do, sister, and after that unpleasant time with the senate I need to *heal* rifts, not *create* them. Gemellus still has a small but vocal group of supporters. With him in the succession, those supporters become my allies too.'

I will not say I agreed with him but I said no more on the point, for my brother was decided and his mind was always difficult to change in that mood.

Other announcements he made that morning were more sensible and were well received by all concerned, myself and Drusilla included. Especially the latter, in fact, for his next proclamation was that of an imperial edict ordering the divorce of Longinus and Drusilla. The noble drainage manager was to be granted the role of Governor of Sardinia and would be leaving forthwith. Even as the words left his mouth and I realised what he'd done, I glanced across at Drusilla and watched a new day dawn upon her face, full of hope and joy. A light entered her eyes – a light which I had last seen almost a decade ago in the house of our grandmother. She had revelled in the freedom to come to the Circus with her family, but that freedom had just expanded beyond any horizon.

I wondered, as I watched her almost explode with delight, whether Longinus had been told anything about any of this beforehand, or was he perhaps sitting somewhere in that crowd below us, eager for the races and suddenly discovering that he was no longer married and was about to take ship for a new land. I could imagine him wrestling with the idea, disappointed to be removed from the imperial family, but excited to be made a governor. Likely his ambition would win out.

Whatever the case, it meant that Drusilla was free. I suddenly realised what that meant for our friend Lepidus and turned to see a smile of satisfaction spreading across his face as he glanced across at the woman he loved. It was a moment of true warmth and love, and I have always treasured it. I felt eyes on me as I watched the pair of them and turned to a similar smile from Vinicius. I had a husband that I felt was a good choice and, if I cannot say that I was as hopelessly lost to love with him as that other couple beside us, I certainly cherished him, and could have done a lot worse. I sometimes wonder what true love is like. Are fondness, comfort and desire the same thing? If so, perhaps I *did* truly love him.

Caligula's third announcement came as a surprise also. His

great friend Agrippa was to be made a king – a client king of Rome, of course – and to rule various territories in the east that had been parts of Judea and the province of Syria. I wondered whether he would return there or whether the titles were to be just that, so that he could remain by Caligula's side in Rome.

Finally, my brother himself would be departing the city the next day, with only a small Praetorian escort. He would travel to the islands of Pandataria and Pontia, where the ashes of our mother and eldest brother remained, and would return them to Rome in honour, to be interred with the rest of the family. I felt a small canker burning in my soul that they would share the great mausoleum with Tiberius on whose authority they had died, but it was not my place to argue, and at least we would be able to celebrate Parentalia properly. Moreover, he would issue the edicts having them declared divine – a privilege denied Tiberius. That went some way to mollifying me over their sharing a tomb with him, for while he languished in the dark, they would rise to take their places with the gods.

His grand announcements over, Caligula received the customary adoration of the crowd and then sank back into his cushioned seat to watch the main event. The Circus was a sea of faces. It seats a hundred and fifty thousand and that morning the famous Pyrrhus of Rhodos was racing, as well as a new unknown named Arpinax, from Saguntum in Hispania, who had accrued a fearsome reputation in the provinces and seemed a fitting challenger for Rome's champion driver. Consequently, the public was in a festive mood and the stadium filled to capacity, with those who failed to get a seat forced to find the best available positions high on the Palatine or Aventine hill to view the action from a great distance.

The noise was immense, drowning out all other sounds in the city. The colour in evidence was impressive, many of the spectators wearing blue or green, white or red to favour whichever team they supported, and the atmosphere was positive and eager.

There were five races that morning, with another seven scheduled for the afternoon. I cheered on all five, throwing my fickle support behind whichever driver thrilled me most at the time. I have never been a lover of games, and chariots were to me generally things of mundane transport, but even I found that morning exciting. By the time the Circus took a break for lunch, I was tingling. At noon, while the masses bought food at the many stalls built into the outer arches of the Circus and then returned to their seats eagerly, we lofty nobles left the pulvinar and sought grander sustenance. Drusilla and I returned to my house across the Palatine while Caligula, accompanied by his friends, was drawn by affairs of state.

I forget what distracted us so during our sojourn in my triclinium but we only realised that we had overrun lunch when we heard the clamour from the stadium as the next race started. Worrying that Caligula would be angry with us for our tardiness, we hurried across the Palatine once more with our guards and attendants and made for the Circus, listening to the surge and roar of the crowd appreciating the race we were missing.

At our approach, the Praetorians opened the door and admitted us to the pulvinar, our escort settling in to wait for us outside. I stepped across to my seat – *my seat, in the imperial box* – and looked around. My husband was there, and Lepidus, and Agrippa too, but I could see no sign of my brother.

'Sit, my love,' Vinicius smiled. 'You're distracting us.'

'Where is my brother?' I asked in confusion. Julius Agrippa's smile widened and he pointed past me.

I turned to look at the track. Of the eight chariots that must have started the current race, five were still running, the wreckage of three having been dragged to the edge and removed from the race area as quickly as possible. The poor horses were evident, only four of which had survived of the twelve involved in the wrecks.

I was utterly confused, and then suddenly realisation thrilled through me and brought with it terrible, dreadful concern.

'There?' I whispered in disbelief.

'In the red,' Lepidus grinned.

'*In the red*?' I repeated, still incredulous. I turned to peer at the driver of the Red chariot. It was impossible to make out much of the driver, given the distance and the chariot's speed, but it certainly had Caligula's colouring.

'Surely he wouldn't?' I gasped, though clearly he had. The others nodded. Chariot racing is, in case you've not seen it close up, one of the most dangerous pastimes in the world. Baiting bears or fighting gladiatorial bouts is safer. Hades, walking up to a Suebi tribesman and calling his mother a whore would be safer. One in every five charioteers lived long enough to retire well, and a single race without a death or a crippling injury was a noteworthy event.

'A wager,' my husband said, as though that justified the whole thing.

'What?' My voice had risen an octave, I suspect, and it came out close to a shriek.

'There was a good-natured argument between two men in the row below the imperial box during the last race. Some fellow aired the opinion that the Reds were incapable of winning, it had been so long since they had taken home a wreath. The argument spread until dozens of men were cheerfully calling each other names. Your brother leapt up, leaned over the railing and bet them en masse that a Red would be placed in the next race.'

'The idiot,' I hissed, watching with a thrill of alarm as the Red chariot cornered so sharply it almost fell on its side, one wheel coming off the ground by several feet. As it thudded back down to the sand and my brother urged his steeds on to the straight, I was shaking my head.

'A wager?'

Lepidus nodded. 'He will pay each of the men below five thousand sesterces if he is not placed.'

'And if he is?'

'He gets their shoes.'

'Their *shoes*?' This time it definitely came out as a screech. I must have sounded like a harpy, but I simply could not believe the idiocy of my brother. 'They will let him win, though,' I reminded myself out loud. 'No charioteer would be stupid enough to beat him at a race. They'll let him win, because he is their emperor.'

'None of the racers know,' Vinicius replied, 'apart from the Red who relinquished his chariot. He's wearing a leather helmet and a cloth over his mouth, and the uniform of the Reds. He's just another racer to them.'

I felt panic settle over me again and now I sat, for I wasn't sure how long my legs would continue to hold me up. Of the seven bronze eggs and the seven bronze dolphins that announce the lap count, four had gone already. Three laps to go, then. I wondered if I could contain my fear that long. Even as I panicked, I saw the fifth dolphin and egg tip.

The Whites had gone from the race, as had one of the Reds. No shock to see that both Blues and both Greens – the main contenders for any title at the Circus – were still running. What *was* a surprise was that, as I actually started to pay attention to the race, only two chariots were ahead of my brother, one Blue and one Green.

'The green one is the upstart from Hispania,' Vinicius said quietly beside me. 'He's good, and he's very lucky, but he's also a little unpredictable and makes plays that could go either way.'

Fabulous. A dangerous driver too.

The rear Blue and Green were pushing on along the straight, trying to catch my brother, desperate not to lose to the Red, which would see them ridiculed by their team and supporters.

My eyes moved back to the Red chariot and its four grey-white horses with the skew-whiff, bedraggled crimson plumes. Caligula was forced to dip towards the centre of the track as he passed one of the chariots' wreckage and I panicked as he came close to the stonework of the *spina*, though he managed to keep it straight, at least.

'What's he doing?' Vinicius fretted.

'What?' I was no great watcher of the races. I knew the basics, but the strategy often eluded me. I preferred my books and poetry or a good comedy at the theatre.

'He's too close to the spina. He'll not have room to turn. He'll *over*turn!'

I watched, sweat beading on my brow that had nothing to do with the bright sun above. My brother was approaching the turn. The dangerous foreign Green was out front, already in that turn. The lead Blue was only just in front of Caligula, though more sensibly further out in the middle of the track to allow for an easy turn.

Then I watched my brother perform the impossible. Or at least, the impossibly dangerous. Just a breath short of the turn, Caligula slapped the reins on the horses, coaxing an extra burst of speed from them, and shot forward, edging out from the spina even as he closed on the turn. He was going entirely the wrong way, veering right into a left-hand turn. The wheels and hooves threw up dirt in a choking cloud as he slewed across the track. I closed my eyes involuntarily. He was heading for the stands and the solid wall that shored them up.

But he was also veering towards the Blue and, given the extra turn of speed he managed, he was actually ahead now, cutting across *in front* of that other chariot.

The driver of the Blue panicked. He was left with no sensible option. If he pulled left, he would be too close to the spina to execute a good turn and he was done for. If he went right, he would never make the turn and would more than likely plough into the stands. Yet if he went straight, he would thunder directly into the Red chariot, and there was little likelihood of anyone leaving that collision alive, man or horse. The Blue veered right – his direction, I presume, chosen at random in that moment of blind panic.

The two vehicles pulled apart again. As the Blue ploughed on towards the wall, my brother, realising he had achieved his goal, swerved back to the left, throwing all his weight with the turn to try and make it. He might have had to throw himself into a left turn from a right, which is problematic to say the least, but at least he had now acquired space to make the attempt, and removed an opponent in the process. It was fascinating in its horror. I tried to watch both vehicles and therefore caught only moments of both.

The Blue, unable to do anything, found that he was hurtling to an inevitable death on the Circus wall, so yanked his knife free and began to cut through the reins bound around his wrist. He threw himself clear of the chariot just before the collision, which made a mess of the horses and kindling of the vehicle. The driver bounced four times and rolled to a halt, leaving a spattered trail of blood in the dust. Men rushed out into the thunder of hooves with a stretcher and gathered him up, hurrying him back out of the arena.

At the same time, my brother essayed the tightest, most unbelievable turn you could ever have seen. I heard it said afterwards that the paint had been stripped from the outside of the wheel spokes, which showed what an angle he achieved and how close he came to complete disaster. My heart was thundering, keeping pace with the hooves as his wheel came down and the chariot bounced twice before settling into the straight. As he hurtled into the second turn at a much more sensible angle and I watched the next dolphin and egg fall, I realised that the race was done, even with one lap to go. The rear Blue and Green were too far back now to harbour any hope of catching my brother, but the lead Green, that dangerous Hispanic, was now too far ahead for Caligula to catch. The drivers had all seemingly reached the same conclusion and, while they kept up the pace, they had clearly settled into merely surviving the race.

Next to me, my husband whistled through his teeth. 'I thought he was gone then, you know?'

I shook my head, still in shock. When did my brother learn to drive a chariot like that? It was typical of Caligula – he never tried to do anything by half measures. It was always all or nothing.

'He's saved his purse,' Lepidus laughed, 'and won a hundred shoes. He'll be placed second, and he only promised to be placed.'

That collection of shoes is still in a box on the Palatine. The oddest trophy ever won, but treasured more than any victory wreath.

XIV

BLOOD

October should have been the best month imaginable in our family. Drusilla was preparing for her wedding to Lepidus in a few weeks, which would see the two of them finally together after two decades of working to that end, and Caligula was riding high on a wave of popularity. Agrippina was nearing her time down in Antium and her husband had magnanimously stopped his regular beatings of her for fear of harming an heir. My husband and I were living well together and growing ever closer the more time we spent in each other's company.

But a cloud descended that month over the Palatine, for early one morning, not long after the kalends of the month, it was reported to me by a white-faced, wild-eyed Praetorian that the emperor was dying.

Vinicius and I rushed from our house across to the palace, where we were ushered inside to meet Macro, the Praetorian prefect, and Silanus, Caligula's father-in-law. The pair were grave, and neither of them could confirm any actual details. With little resistance from anyone, I hurried to my brother's bedside.

He was so pale as to be almost grey and his face had a waxy sheen, his hair soaked through with sweat. His lips were blue-ish, and his eyes yellow. In short, the report that he was dying did not seem remotely far-fetched. I tried to talk to Caligula to ask him how he was feeling, but he seemed unable to form words, merely making burbling, grunting noises and drooling uncontrollably.

I hurried back out to the main hall to rejoin my husband just as Drusilla and Lepidus arrived. My sister's terrified eyes met mine and with added urgency she hurried in to our brother's side.

'Tell me,' I said, aiming my question this time not at the unhelpful pair at the heart of the room, but at a panicked-looking slave loitering in the corner. The young man held a damp cloth and a sodden loincloth and I had immediately surmised that this was one of my brother's personal body slaves and had probably been with him earlier. Often, if you want to know things, speak to a slave. They are far better informed than their masters.

The slave filled in the details in a nervous, extremely deferential tone.

'The emperor retired early last night, Domina,' he said, head lowered, eyes downcast.

I snapped my fingers and his gaze came up to meet mine, then dropped again immediately, the requirements of a slave's manner drilled into him long ago in the palace. 'Go on.'

'The master spoke of an upset stomach. He appeared extremely ill even then, Domina, but he would not allow me to send for a physician. I worried.'

'Apparently correctly so. Your concern does you credit. What happened?'

The slave faltered, shaking slightly in fear. 'Domina, I went into the emperor's chamber during the night.'

He flinched at his own words, and I could understand why. Slaves were absolutely forbidden to enter their master's chambers while they slept, for very clear reasons. The boy had risked flogging at least, or far worse, in doing so. And in admitting it to me, he was admitting his trespass. Needless to say, I was less than concerned with that at the time.

'What did you find?'

'The emperor was lying on the floor, face down, Domina. He was unconscious, but breathing. I could tell from the rising and falling of his back. I . . . I turned him over.'

So he had touched the emperor's person unbidden, too. I could see Silanus' disapproving gaze on the boy, and Macro was furious, his hand on the hilt of his sword.

'Go on,' I urged the slave.

'He had vomited, Domina, when he fell, and he was suffocating in it. It took me some time, but I managed to get him back up onto a couch and then went to get cloths and water to clean him up once I was certain he was breathing again.' He looked terrified. 'I know I should have found a guardsman or a *medicus*, Domina, but there was no time.'

I nodded. 'Fear not, boy. I believe you saved the emperor's life. No man shall take a rod to your back for that.'

Somewhat reassured, the boy spilled the rest of the details as I asked, the tale supplemented by additions from Macro. The emperor had vomited and coughed up yellow matter from deep inside. He could not swallow easily and the slave had had to stick his finger into Caligula's throat to allow water to pass inside. The most distressing thing, as far as the slave was concerned, had been when he went to change the emperor's fouled underwear and discovered a surprising quantity of blood among the mess. No wonder Caligula had gone grey.

Had a physician seen him?

Yes, the court medicus now had done so and pronounced it 'the Syrian Flux'. No one else seemed to have heard of this disease though, overhearing the discussion, Macro confirmed that he had seen it cut through an army in the east some years earlier.

I ordered other physicians sent for, including a renowned Jew who worked out of a small shop in the stands below the Circus. The fact that we had watched the great Livia slowly decline partially because she would see only Roman doctors had reinforced my opinion that only Greek and Judean doctors were truly worth their fee. I had certainly eschewed all Roman physicians when I had minor ailments, placing my well-being in the hands of more knowledgeable foreigners.

Over the next day, as the medics came and went, we were offered a dozen different diagnoses, none of which seemed to quite fit, but were all close enough to represent possibilities. Drusilla and I visited my brother almost on the hour, every hour, though he never seemed to change. The slave who had helped him was given unprecedented access and authority in reward for his solicitude and quick thinking, and some time later he was freed and made a ward of the imperial court for his efforts.

Our brother lay sweating and bleeding and vomiting in that bed for days thereafter, with no appreciable change. Two things came to my attention over the three days I flitted to and from Caligula's bedside, all else failing to penetrate the shell of worry and sleepless desperation that surrounded me.

Firstly, it became quite clear how respected and loved my brother was. It was almost impossible to get from the Palatine to other parts of the city, for the population of Rome stood a vigil for the emperor, gathering shoulder-deep in the forum and the Velabrum and the valley of the Circus and even in the streets of the Palatine hill itself, except where the Praetorians kept it clear for us. The people of Rome held their breath, praying to numerous gods that their emperor would survive this dreadful illness that seemed to have claimed him so soon after his ascension.

The second thing was that Gemellus seemed to have crawled back out of whatever pit he'd been hiding in these past months. Since my brother had released and adopted him, he had wisely kept well away from the centre of power, probably in his father's old town house on the Viminalis. But suddenly, after months of keeping his profile as low as possible, the squat, miserable little runt seemed to be everywhere. One might have thought him wracked with concern for my brother, especially with the way he lauded Caligula as he addressed the gathered crowds of citizenry. But those of us who knew Gemellus for what he was could see him trying to work the crowd and shuffle into position ready to succeed my brother.

On the third day, when I was on the way to visit my brother and see if I could get through to him, I pulled myself up short as I spotted Gemellus standing in the entry hall of the palace, deep in discussion with both Macro and Silanus. It was a fact that Gemellus was now the heir to my brother and, realistically, given the state Caligula was in, no one would be surprised that he was lobbying for attention. And given that, along with the fact that Macro and Silanus were so closely tied to my brother and to the succession, it should hardly be cause for comment to see the three of them together.

Yet there is a certain shiftiness of the posture which, when combined with furtive looks and gestures, labels conspirators more clearly than any written sign. The moment I saw the three of them together, I knew they were working their underhand magic. And because of that, I took the logical mental step to deciding that my brother's illness was not natural.

I needed to speak to Caligula. I needed to arrest what was seemingly destined to be a steady decline into death. And I needed those three men out of the way to do it. In the end I brought in Drusilla. Of the women in our family, I was the middle ground. Agrippina was scheming and wily and far more dangerous than we gave her credit for. I am crafty in my own way and not afraid to push for something if it be required. Drusilla is . . . well, Drusilla is one of those women who never did anyone any harm and never had designs beyond the acceptable. She is an open scroll to be read without confusion. And because of that, no one ever suspected Drusilla of anything.

I explained as much as I dare and set her to work. She approached Macro, claiming that Lepidus had been struck down with the same dreadful illness that had befallen our brother. If I'd needed any evidence that the prefect was responsible it would have come then, as I saw his face crease into perplexity. After all, if he had poisoned Caligula, how could Lepidus also be suffering from the same malady?

Sure enough, Macro and Silanus hurried off to visit Lepidus and clear up the mystery. Lepidus, of course, would fake some unpleasant stomach upset, and Macro would be relieved and irritated at the same time. Most importantly, though, he and Silanus would be out of the way. Better still, with the pair of them gone, Gemellus also left the palace and went back to work appealing to the crowd . . . if Gemellus could ever be called appealing.

Knowing now that my brother was no longer watched over by that wicked triumvirate, I rushed into the palace again and grabbed that Jewish physician from the hallway, where he was poring over his books and trying to figure out my brother's ailment. It made me twitch to put my trust in a man of whom I knew so little, but then it had been I who brought him to the palace, so he likely had no connection to Macro, and my brother's very life was worth whatever risks I had to face.

I all but hauled him to Caligula's bedside and pointed.

'What did you think was wrong with him?'

'An illness of the bowel, similar to some that have been noted by those living near the swamps in middle Aegyptus.'

'And you've been treating him for that?' I prompted.

'Yes.'

'With any appreciable success?'

He looked abashed and lowered his eyes. 'I am afraid not, Domina.'

'That is because it is not the illness you describe. If I were to suggest that it is not an illness at all, but the effects of poison, how would you alter your ministrations?'

The physician frowned. 'I would approach the situation a *great deal* differently, Domina.'

'Good,' I said flatly. 'Do it. Don't mention this to anyone else. Just change your approach and see if things begin to improve.'

I left him there and was in the street outside speaking to my husband when Macro came stomping back irritably, accompanied by Silanus. He ranted for a short time about being distracted from important matters by attention-seeking hypochondriacs. I cared not. I had achieved my goal.

I left then and went back to my house. Sometime late that evening a messenger arrived at my door from the palace, sent by that Jewish physician. I probed the visitor for information as I quickly threw on my cloak and hurried out into the dark, taking my muscular doorman with me for protection. There was no need for further escort, to my mind, for it was less than two hundred paces between my door and my brother's, where his German Guard stood. Indeed, the big hairy guardsmen could see my front door from their posts. I was not accosted on the journey.

To my great relief, Macro, Silanus and Gemellus were all absent from the palace when I arrived. The prefect had given his men orders not to let anyone disturb the emperor, except his medicus, and I was almost at the point of launching myself physically at the Praetorian who denied me access when a thin, reedy voice from within called my name.

My brother spoke . . .

No matter what Macro might order, no Praetorian was about to refuse the emperor and as that Jewish fellow with the long ringletted hair appeared in the doorway and informed the guards that the emperor would like to see his sister, the defiance in the soldier before me melted away and he stepped back into a corner. In my brother's name, I ordered all the Praetorians out of the entire suite, telling them they could guard him just as well from the atrium. They seemed disinclined to argue and I was shooing them from the suite as Drusilla arrived, breathless, with Lepidus in her wake. It seemed likely, despite the fact that their nuptials were still weeks away, that they had been together at night when news of our brother had reached her, but I had enough on my mind at that point without chastising her over the niceties of society. He'd probably been bedding her for months, anyway.

She persuaded Lepidus to stay outside in case Macro or Silanus should return, and she and I entered our brother's room and hurried to his bedside. He looked much the same – pale grey, sweating and weak – but there were two notable differences: his eyes seemed to be a more normal colour, and his mouth was no longer hanging open and drooling. Hope coursing through me, I looked across at the physician.

'Will he recover?'

The man made a non-committal gesture. 'I would like to say yes, Domina, but there is no certainty at this point. I believe he has ridden through the worst point of the toxin and I wonder at his fortitude, since most strong men, even those with seemingly greater constitutions than his, would have passed on by now. He is a remarkable man, I think. We should know by noon tomorrow. If there is no more blood in his stools, then recovery is likely. With God's help, he will make it.'

'The *gods'* help,' I corrected him, absently, though there were more important matters at hand than arguing religion with a Jew, and he gave me an indulgent smile in response, as though he knew something I didn't.

There was a croaking sound and I leaned close. Caligula was speaking.

'What is it, Gaius?'

He shuddered, tried to shuffle slightly higher on his pillows, gritted his teeth, and spoke in a hiss as though he had to expel the words on a painful breath.

'I . . . might not survive.'

'The gods will not let another son of Germanicus die,' I replied defiantly, and he smiled weakly.

'I need to do things, in case . . . you understand?'

I shook my head. 'Gaius, you *have* to recover. Macro and Silanus are up to something. They are parading Gemellus around as though he's already succeeding you. The idiot is trying to make appeals to the people, preparing for his accession. I think Macro is behind your illness. Probably Silanus too.'

I prepared for the argument, but to my surprise our brother nodded with an odd, curious smile. 'Macro used to complain to me, Livilla, that you didn't like him. It made me think, and I have been watching him, even before this happened . . .'

He paused for an awful wracking coughing fit, expectorated something offensive into a cloth, and sagged before trying to go on.

'I've seen something coming. Tiberius was a dreadful old man, but he taught me one life lesson for which I am now grateful.' I frowned, and he chuckled painfully. 'Since coming to Rome, I have been steadily poisoning myself with tiny doses of various toxins, increasing my immunity. Fortunately for me, I also took a lesson from my own actions and have been using a tincture from the abrus berry. All this is the effects of that same red poison, of that I am certain.'

I rocked back a pace, my eyes widening.

'Yes,' he smiled. 'I introduced Macro to the abrus poison, and in gratitude he used it upon me. But I have hardened myself to its effects over the months, and so I may survive, which Macro could not possibly have counted upon.'

I rolled my eyes. 'You have been taking poisons? You're mad!'

'But alive,' he sighed. 'Though there is still a chance I may not make it through. I want you to send me a scribe, and to have the Praetorians ejected from the building. From now on, the German Guard will take on protection of the palace.' I shivered as my mind drew a worrying parallel between my hoarse, sweating brother and the old tyrant he had replaced. The poison. The Germans. The Praetorian traitor.

'A scribe?' Drusilla asked.

'Yes. Against the possibility of my death, I need to make a new will. I am leaving my entire estate to you, Drusilla.'

My sister boggled at the news, and I fought valiantly against bitter jealousy that Caligula's favourite sister would be the recipient of everything, and I of nothing. Yet his next words clarified his reason, and I could not argue with them.

'Gemellus will be struck from the succession and will have to be dealt with in due course, but a solid succession must continue for the stability of the empire. Through you, Drusilla, Lepidus will become my heir, and if I die here, in this bed, a man I have always trusted will follow me.'

Lepidus. Of course. That was why it had to be Drusilla. Our childhood friend was the nearest thing to a son of Germanicus, and as a great-grandson of Augustus, he too carried the blood of the Julii. There would be no argument and no crisis – just a smooth succession.

'If I die tonight or tomorrow with that document lodged and sealed, Gemellus will get nothing and all my sisters will be safe.'

Drusilla nodded, leaned forward and kissed him on the forehead. 'It is a burden I accept reluctantly, Gaius. But one I will give you back when you recover.'

I nodded. 'You need to rest, so that your chances of recovery improve. What will you do about Macro and Silanus?' I added as an afterthought.

My brother's expression darkened. 'Silanus I will think upon. He is my father-in-law and my friend, and I find it unfathomable that he could be part of my poisoning. But Macro? Flaccus has gone to Syria, and his former position is as yet unfilled, so I will make Macro Prefect of Aegyptus.'

I blinked in utter astonishment. '*What*?'

Caligula fixed me with a calculating, predatory look that actually made me flinch, and I realised then just how angry my brother truly was. 'Here, Macro is surrounded by men who obey his orders. Once he is Prefect of Aegyptus and not the Guard, he is alone. You cannot kill a lion so easily among his own pride, Livilla. First we cut him off from his pride, and *then* we hunt him.'

XV

A THING OF CRIMSON DARKNESS

My brother's survival was a gods-born thing. What followed was born only of vengeance. A thing of crimson darkness.

I was bustling around my house, preparing. In two days' time my sister Drusilla would marry Lepidus, sealing a bond that had begun as children, and there was so much to get ready. While the ceremony was to be a fairly quiet and small family affair, given the circumstances, Lepidus had been determined to give her the best wedding she could have. I tried not to fall foul of the sparks of jealousy once more. I failed. Weddings are the province of the fathers, who decide on the details of the ceremony and the banquet – whether there will *be* a ceremony or banquet, even. The bride chooses nothing. It is her lot to be bought and sold. And yet somehow, because Lepidus so adored her and our brother doted on her, Drusilla would get anything she wanted.

But I bit down on the memory of my own wedding, part of that triple affair planned by the emperor Tiberius to showcase his stock, and began to focus on helping everyone make Drusilla's second marriage a special occasion. It is not often we women get to marry for love, after all.

I remember arguing with my seamstress over the hem of my stola when my doorman answered a knock and hurried to inform me that the emperor was at our threshold. Such a thing would stop the heart of many a matron of Rome, but I remember waving at him and asking him to tell my brother that I would be just a moment, and then going on to detail what I wanted with the seamstress before I rose and made my way to the door.

Caligula stood outside with his entourage. By rights, even over such a short distance he should be carried in a litter or carriage for the look of things – he was the emperor, after all. But he did not acquire the nickname 'Little Boots' from sitting in carriages. He was dressed in a plain white toga and were it not for the twelve *lictors* that stood in two lines behind him denoting his rank, he could easily have been any senator or citizen of the city. The lictors and his guards, at least.

I was rather surprised to see that the party was escorted by the German Guard, their plain, undyed wool tunics and furs and basic mail shirts matched by dirty off-white plumes and brown unpainted shields. They bore heavy, very un-Roman swords and wore beards that, frankly, made me shudder with revulsion. No Praetorians were in evidence, but then Caligula had rather eschewed their presence since his near-death at the hands of their commander.

He still looked drawn and pale now, almost a month after his near demise, and he still tired quickly. His appetite remained small, and he drank his wine less watered than he really should. But given what he'd been through, he was lucky to be walking at all, let alone in good health, and he was steadily improving. Our new favourite Jewish physician assured us that by Saturnalia he would be back to his old self entirely. *Physically*, that would be the case, anyway.

Certainly that morning he seemed more full of energy than I had noted thus far. Not *positive* energy, mind. There was a fierceness about his eyes, a determination that boded ill for someone. As I walked across to his side, I spotted his carriage arriving a few dozen paces away.

'Good morning, Gaius.'

'Good day, sister. I would appreciate your company on a small task or two. Is your husband about?'

I shook my head. 'He was gone at dawn for an early visit to the baths. He has a busy day ahead, meeting with the masters of the cursus publicus.'

My brother nodded his understanding. He himself had appointed Vinicius as a *praetor* and set him in control of the imperial courier system and all government communications. There had been disturbing reports recently of bandit activity in the mountains waylaying couriers, and missives failing to reach their destination, and Vinicius was determined to solve the problem and boost his reputation rather than see it suffer as a failure in his role.

'Then steel yourself, Livilla, and join me in the carriage.'

As he began to walk, me scurrying along to keep up, I frowned. 'Where are we going?'

'To settle a few outstanding debts. Today the new prefect of Aegyptus leaves for his posting.'

My heart skipped as I realised what we were doing. Macro had spent the past few weeks delaying his departure for his new command as much as he could. Leaving Rome meant abandoning whatever conspiracies he was involved in and essentially giving up any hope of a role in the succession and at court. But he'd not been able to delay forever, and eventually Caligula had insisted that a ship be made ready for him. It seemed we would arrest him before he boarded it, then. And as I have already mentioned, my brother always paid his debts.

'We don't have to be present, Gaius,' I said, trembling. 'Even *you* don't have to be present. You're still weak . . .'

'No, Livilla,' he retorted quietly as he climbed into the carriage. 'You're wrong. I'm strong now. I may *look* pale and thin, but be assured that I am stronger than I have ever been. And I will never be weak again. Never. Not in front of anyone.'

He reached out for me to help me board the vehicle, and as I entered and the horses clipped and shuffled in anticipation of the off, I realised we were not alone. The carriage already held two occupants, both wearing the Praetorian colours beneath their togas, both were suntanned and scarred, and neither was a young man.

'Livilla, allow me to introduce the new prefects of the Praetorian Guard: Lucius Arruntius Stella and Marcus Arrecinus Clemens.'

The two men bowed as neatly as the confined space allowed, and both murmured greetings. Shrewd at investigation and quick appraisal from those dangerous years on Capri, I noticed several details at once. Clemens had a northern accent, very rustic and with poor pronunciation. Stella's accent was decidedly Gallic in its tone. Both wore white military Praetorian tunics with a narrow red stripe visible on the shoulder. They were members of the equestrian order, knights of Rome drawn from the lower ranks, and their colouring, scars and accents put them as minor ones, plucked from relative obscurity on the periphery of things. My brother was rebuilding the Praetorians as a force he could trust and I had heard from my husband that since Macro had left their ranks there had been a great deal of thinning out. Caligula had ordered transfers to and from legions, sending those men who had been too close to Macro to less important postings near the frontiers and drawing veterans who belonged to legions with a historic link to Germanicus to take their place.

I realised in a snap where he had found Clemens and Stella, and the reason for their appearance. They had clearly been career officers in the military, and I would have bet my house and all my slaves that if I examined their history, they had both served with our father in Pannonia and had accompanied him to Syria where he died. Two decades under the Syrian sun had changed their skin, but not their hearts. They were Germanicus' men, and that meant they were ours.

I really didn't want to speak openly or appear weak in front of these men, but as the carriage began to move off, I was left with little choice. 'I don't see why you want me there.'

My brother turned an appraising gaze on me. 'I trust your opinions, sister. I trust your judgement. After all, the first time you saw Macro and Ennia you knew something was wrong with them. Yes, you pinned it to Ennia, but the fact is something alerted you to a problem. If I had noted your discomfort earlier, or had been more alert myself, I would have been more careful around them and never have suffered as I did. I want you with me as I finish this, for I want your wisdom and your shrewd eyes. And you are often a calming influence. I have learned of late that certain types can push me to losing my temper no matter how restrained I try to be. Perhaps you will keep me settled in the face of ire.'

Wisdom? Instinct, perhaps, but I had never thought of myself as wise. I still do not.

I sat, brooding on what was coming and wondering what use I could possibly be, as we rattled on through the city. Down the hill from the Palatine, through the forum, where I was aware through the carriage's curtains of the cheering crowd. An emperor cannot do anything without raising a fuss, you see. We rumbled on past the Basilica Iulia and through the Velabrum, where the streets became steadily bumpier and the noise more insistent. We passed close to the markets – the animal, flower and vegetable ones – and the smell of dung and pollen mixed created a strange, cloying aroma. I was pleased when we came to the river and moved west along the bank, breathing in the cold November air and cleansing our lungs of those lingering smells.

It was a silent journey. I was anticipating the task ahead with due dread. The two new prefects were respectfully silent, and my brother was inscrutable, sitting looking out of his window as we approached our destination. We arrived at the navalia shortly afterwards, and the guards around us came to a halt. I steeled myself as someone opened the vehicle's door for me. I had visited the navalia twice in living memory – once when my brother and mother had been arrested by the agents of Sejanus, and once when we were whisked away from our settled life with Antonia to the emperor's side at Capri. The place felt unlucky for me, and I couldn't shake the feeling of dread as I disembarked the carriage. I looked in vain hope for my lucky rainbow. I could not see one, but the sun, gleaming between high buildings, created an odd, red-gold corona when I looked towards it, and that I could hardly see as a good omen.

Praetorians were everywhere, armoured and without their togas.

We were outside the pomerium here, and the carrying of weapons of war was permitted. Just in that first sweep of my eyes I could see five groups of eight Praetorians, geared as if for war. My brother and the two prefects followed me out of the carriage, and I stood, testing my feet for cramp after the journey, as I spotted Macro.

He looked different somehow. He was dressed in his toga, as usual, but there was something different about the way he moved, like a mouse who knows a cat lives in the same house. Ennia, his graceful wife, alighted from another carriage not far behind him, leading two children close to taking the man's toga. They had a small army of slaves with them, carrying all their gear for stowing on board for the journey.

Macro spotted my brother and his face went through half a dozen expressions before settling on something I can describe only as warm, friendly panic. His eyes were pleasant, but his eyelid twitched and his mouth kept straightening and curving, straightening and curving, as though he didn't know what to do.

'Darling, the emperor himself has come to bid us farewell,' I heard Ennia smile to her husband.

Odd. I had remembered her from our few encounters on Capri being a devious and cunning creature. Was she really dim enough not to have noticed the presence of so many armed men and put one and one together? From the faltering step of Macro, he clearly had.

'Majesty, it is a great pleasure and a great honour to see you here,' Macro managed.

'Stella? Clemens?' my brother said, simply.

Suddenly those numerous groups of Praetorians flooded forward and surrounded the meeting. The two new prefects stepped out in front of us and stood to either side of Macro, facing him.

'Quintus Naevius Cordus Sutorius Macro, you are charged with treason against the state and against the person of the emperor.'

Macro's smile never slipped, but his eyes changed. 'A ridiculous notion.'

My brother stepped a pace forward then, urging me to join him.

'The question of your guilt has never been in doubt, Macro. Nor that of your accomplices. There shall be no tiring and lengthy public trial, and the only reason your head did not bounce down the Gemonian Stairs on the first day of my recovery was that I needed to remove your influence from the Guard first. My sister's husband, Vinicius, has been very helpful in that matter, since he had achieved that task once already with your predecessor.'

'I assure you, Gaius, that anything I have ever done was all for the good of the throne.'

My brother didn't even blink at such a disrespectful use of his given name. Instead, he folded his arms. 'In a short time as prefect, Macro, you seem to have acquired a reasonable fortune in money and estates. You have a very comfortable household, a fine wife and . . . two sons, is it not?'

The colour drained from Macro's face.

'I shall offer you a boon, Macro,' Caligula went on. 'Tell me why, and I will make your death fast and allow your wife and children here to take ship with their honour and fortune intact. Dissemble, and I shall see that you are taken to the Tullianum, where you will remain until the truth is dragged from you, when you and your entire family will be put to death in public for your crime. Decide now.'

I swallowed nervously. I had seen enough blood shed on this cobbled landing when my brother and mother had been arrested. No matter how much I disliked Macro and his over-elegant wife, I did not wish to see a repeat performance. I turned to my brother to protest, but when I saw his face, I quailed and fell silent.

Macro must have been studying my brother's expression too, for he slumped.

'Simple greed, Gaius,' he said finally. 'Nothing more.' When my brother remained implacable and silent, Macro sighed. 'My son would have been Gemellus' heir. Who plays the *maker* of kings when there is a chance to be the *father* of one? If it is any consolation, I am sorry.'

My brother turned to me and looked into my eyes. Whatever he saw there decided the matter for him, and he nodded twice – once in acknowledgement of Macro's words, and once to the two prefects. Clemens made a small gesture and a Praetorian stepped forward from the gradually tightening circle around us. Ennia, her face white and eyes wide, made to join her husband, a whimper escaping her lips, but two of the Guard grabbed her and held her back, where she crouched and hugged her two boys tight.

Macro held his chin high, proud to the last. The soldier stepped behind him and raised his blade to plunge in for the killing blow. My brother coughed, and Clemens made another gesture to the soldier. In response, the Praetorian lowered his arm.

The former prefect, expecting a swift death in the manner of a military execution, gasped in shock and pain as the point of the guardsman's gladius emerged through his gut, a torrent of crimson pouring from his belly and forming a blossoming rose on his white toga. Horrified, the prefect pulled aside the folds of his garment to stare at the blood-slicked steel protruding from his gut. Blood oozed and spurted around the blade. He looked up at my brother in shock. 'Gaius?'

'Traitor,' grunted Caligula, and turned his back on Macro, just as the guardsman twisted his sword, opening up new dimensions of injury and agony in the man's middle and making the damage utterly irreparable. I understood as I saw my brother's face. Whatever he promised Macro, this man had put Caligula through weeks of writhing, excruciating agony, and my brother was determined to repay him for his care. I shuddered. A gut wound could take days to kill a man. I had heard of soldiers lasting over a week in unbelievable pain as their belly rotted around the wound. And it was always – *always* – fatal.

The guilty prefect had paid the price for his ambition. And my brother had paid another debt.

Caligula climbed back into the carriage, ignoring the figure of Macro. The guardsman withdrew his blade and cleaned it on the fallen prefect's toga as Macro collapsed to his knees, holding in a coil of his gut and gasping in pain and disbelief. Ennia ran over to him, but the new prefect Arruntius Stella stopped her with a raised arm.

'The emperor's goodwill stretches only so far with traitors, Domina. Board that ship with your children and never come back, lest you follow your husband to the grave.'

What happened to them, I do not know. Perhaps Ennia still lives in Alexandria with her children. I had heard that a message followed swiftly after bearing an order to commit suicide, but that does not sound likely to me. My brother had dealt with Macro and now he was moving on to his next prey. I understand that Macro himself lingered for three days, never leaving the bank of the Tiber. If the rumours are to believed, in the end his throat was cut by robbers and he was rolled into the river, where he disappeared.

We left the Praetorians there, at the navalia, with both their new prefects, while we rattled back through the city. We were silent all the way, and even as we alighted once more on the Palatine, with the lictors and the German Guard around us, neither Caligula nor I spoke. In fact, it was only as I made to return to my home that he addressed me.

'It is not over. Come, Livilla.'

I was already feeling sick at the brutal end of the former prefect and had no wish to witness any more, but my brother still wore that same expression that had so startled Macro, and there was simply no refusing him that day. Swallowing my fear and distaste, I followed him in through the door of his palace. His *aula regia* – his great room for public sessions – was empty, but a seat had been placed close to his for me, and as my brother sat, so did I. The German Guard took up their accustomed places and slaves entered to attend upon us. Wine was brought, and trays of rich morsels. I took a small cup of wine, watered very heavily. My brother took a great swig of his wine before adding just a splash of cold water. Neither of us touched the food. My brother's appetite had not fully recovered from his illness, and mine had fled in that square as Macro sank to the ground in a pool of his own blood.

'What are we waiting for?' I asked quietly.

'There are two men waiting in the hall outside,' he replied, and I had no time to ask him who they were before the doors opened once more and the German Guard escorted in two figures. One – no surprise at all – was Caligula's father-in-law,

Silanus. The other I didn't know, but he wore the tunic and satchel of a member of the courier service – I knew them well, for I had seen plenty of them since my husband had become responsible for them.

'Majesty,' the courier said, bowing low, a good ten paces from my brother, and proffering a scroll case. A slave appeared seemingly from nowhere and collected the case, carrying it to my brother. Silanus also bowed. His face was grave. There was no sign of fear there, but upon catching his expression, I think he had no doubt as to what was coming. He made no sound, waiting patiently as Caligula split the dark wax seal on the case and slid out the scroll.

'There was more to Gemellus than I expected,' my brother said finally as he let the scroll furl once more. I frowned and he turned to me. 'Gemellus seems to have received word of the arrest warrant before it arrived. My men found him dead in his house. He had taken his own life like a true Roman. I would never have believed he had the courage for such a thing.'

I shivered, thinking of the bully who had always seemed so childish and bitter in our time on Capri. I had hated him every day I had known him, yet I had lobbied for his survival when we left the island, and had argued against his incarceration in the Tullianum. I had no love for him, but somehow an odd strand of sympathy crept into me again as I thought of him, devoid of both family and friends, sitting alone in the house of his dead father as he lifted a blade and made to end his own life. I had lost brothers and a mother, but he had lost everything. In his place I might have been sharpening my own knife.

'And are you a coward, too?' asked my brother suddenly. I started from my thoughts and realised he was talking to his father-in-law.

'You know me, Gaius.'

'Do I? I thought I did. I thought we were friends. How was I so wrong?'

Silanus straightened. 'What I did, I did for the good of the empire, Gaius.'

My brother lifted an eyebrow. 'How so?'

'Can you not see the corruption endemic in this dynasty? The gods do their best to kill off every heir, do they not? Caesar himself failed to have a male child to carry on his despotism. Augustus, who claimed the Republic as his own property, also sired only a girl and watched as his chosen heirs both died young. Tiberius, a sick, twisted monster who allowed other monsters like Sejanus to rise, watched his only son die. Gemellus would have died before he could become emperor, you see, for the gods curse the line of Caesar.'

My brother was visibly taken aback by this stark appraisal of his lineage and, I have to admit, it shocked me also with its revelations. Silanus' face became hard, his lip lifting to a sneer.

'I gave you my daughter. My beautiful child. My innocent, noble girl. In the hope that you and she could change things. I saw *possibility* in you, that you could change Rome forever and make her great again. But no. The sickness of the Julii lives in you, too. The gods would no more give you an heir than any of your family. And in refusing you a boy child, they tore apart my daughter.'

I blinked in shock. Could he really think that the gods so despised our family that they killed his daughter to prevent the child being born? And we might have carried the blood of the Julii but we were the children of Germanicus – the loved and the blessed.

'I tried to remove you, yes,' Silanus said defiantly. 'And Gemellus would have gone soon after, for he was as sick and depraved as all of the get of Caesar.'

My brother's brow lowered suspiciously.

'And you would have put Macro on the throne? Or yourself? Who?'

Silanus threw out his arms. 'Who *cares*? So long as your dynasty is not involved, it matters not. *Anyone.* The lowest beggar in the street has as much right as the Julii to command an empire. Why not a republic once more? Why not put power back in the hands of the senate? They ruled Rome well for hundreds of years before your clutch took control.'

My brother was speechless. So was I. I just had no idea how to reply to such a statement.

Caligula made a subtle gesture, and one of the Germans nearby drew his weapon and tossed it forward. The heavy northern sword clattered across the marble floor and slid to a halt in front of Silanus. Still silent, my brother waited, glaring at his father-in-law.

Silanus bent and picked up the sword, testing its weight and frowning at the unfamiliar, long blade. 'I go to Elysium knowing that I did what I could, and I will find my daughter there. I go, happy to leave this stinking, rot-infested place behind.'

With a deep breath, he reversed the sword, grasping the blade a little over halfway along and wedging it in the gentle hollow between two ribs. Then, with no ceremony and apparently no fear, he fell forward onto the marble in front of us. I heard the crunch as the sword punched through bone and muscle and organ, and I saw the odd lump as the man's toga at the back jerked upwards, lifted by the blade-tip beneath. The body twitched a few times, but Silanus' aim had been true and his fall straight. The sword had sheared his heart every bit as much as the loss of his daughter, and he was gone in mere moments, sagging with a last exhaled sigh. I watched with numb horror the pool of blood spreading out from him, saturating his toga.

'Now it is done,' my brother said firmly, his voice oddly emotional.

'I hope so,' I snapped. 'I have seen enough blood this morning to last me a lifetime. If you are quite done turning the city into one giant arena, I shall return to my house, douse myself and try to wash away all memories of this as I prepare for our sister's wedding.'

I rose without waiting for permission and went to leave the room angrily, skirting widely around the bloody heap on the floor and the wide-eyed, terrified courier. As I left, I saw out of the corner of my eye my brother rise from his chair, close on Silanus and crouch, slipping a coin into his mouth to pay the boatman – a last gesture of respect for a man he had loved as a father for a short time.

I spent that night in Vinicius' arms, shuddering at the memories of what I had seen that day. My husband consoled me and held me tight, but while I murmured at the savagery my brother had displayed, Vinicius seemed untouched by the events, telling me that the emperor had done what he had to and what was best for both him and the empire. It had not felt like what was best to me and, for all his words, I was sure I could see a fragment of uncertainty in my husband's eyes, too.

XVI

SIGNS

Over the two months following the death of Gemellus, my brother gradually returned to full health, though his pallor remained evermore. And as his body recovered, he began to fret over the matter of succession. He had supplanted Gemellus as heir with our childhood friend Lepidus, who was now our brother-in-law and was present at every court and family gathering. And he loved Lepidus as a brother – always had, long before they had become related – but he soon came to the conclusion that as long as the succession fell to an indirect relation there would always be a question over its validity. Whatever the truth of that, it is what he believed. And it drove him to the inevitable decision that he must sire an heir for the good of the empire.

I personally believe that Silanus' accusatory summation of a curse upon the Julii had more than a small part in this new desire to sire a boy, but whatever the case, I considered it a good decision, for to sire a boy meant he would have to remarry, and he needed to do just that to soften him around the edges where he was beginning to become sharp, and to disperse the spectres of Silanus and his daughter, which still haunted Caligula, though he would never have admitted it.

Agrippina had not helped the matter. Down in Antium in mid December, she had given her husband a healthy, chubby, smiling little son, whom his father had named Lucius Domitius

Ahenobarbus, overriding his mother's favoured choice of Nero, after her brother. This happy, portly baby gave extra impetus to our brother's desire to produce an heir. After all, if our oldest sister could produce such a content child with a wife-beating dissolute, what could Rome's golden prince produce?

I had been surprised, in truth, that the half year I had spent in Rome with my husband had not left me with child, for we lay together regularly. I was grateful indeed that Marcus never railed and ranted at me about his lack of an heir, which is oft the all-consuming need for any new-married husband, regardless of dynastic successions. In all honesty, I was rather glad that it had not happened, for my marriage was convenient in that it consumed remarkably little of my time and energy and left plenty of both for my family. Vinicius had proved to be better than any husband I could have hoped for since he was always there for me when I needed him, to hold me tight and drive away the demons, and yet the lack of demands he placed upon me granted unparalleled freedom for a Roman matron. As soon as Saturnalia was over, my husband was whisked off again, anyway, precluding the further possibility of children.

The east was troubled. Not the Jewish regions, oddly, which were always difficult in some way, but the more settled provinces of Aegyptus and Asia. The governor of Asia had been mismanaging the economy there and skimming considerably more from the top than was acceptable, leaving Asia a borderline financially viable region. And in Aegyptus, which was vital to Rome's supply of both bread and gold, the detestable old Flaccus, who had so inflamed our early days on Capri, had managed to sink the capital, Alexandria, into a Jewish revolt that had all but halted the flow of goods and had endangered Roman rule. Consequently, my brother had sent the capable Gaius Asinius Pollio out to replace the governor of Asia, and was waiting until Flaccus had contained the revolt in Aegyptus before replacing him. But my husband, known to Caligula for his success in putting Rome and the Praetorians in order twice and repairing the failing courier system, had been sent east to aid Pollio, where he would very likely remain as a governor. I had begun to pack for a sojourn in the east, but my brother persuaded Vinicius that I would be safer with the family in Rome than in that troubled region, and so in Rome I stayed. I was torn, for while I would miss my husband, I had no wish to leave my family and take up residence in some provincial palace with slaves with painted eyes and false beards.

In mid Januarius, my brother visited a well-known and respected *augur* on the Esquiline. The old man, who was among the most expensive of such professionals to be found in the city, had observed signs and omens for some of the most influential people in Rome and had had his advice proved efficacious.

I have never been able to make head nor tail of augury, but then I am no augur, and perhaps this is why women are not allowed to learn their secrets. The old man, said to be from ancient Etruria – the home of all augury and divination – was blind in one eye, and looking at that filmy, rheumy blue orb made my own eyes water. He was also lame, walking with the aid of a crutch. But for all his infirmity, he was clearly well off. His house was as well appointed as any noble town house in the city, not part of any shaky, crumbling insula. More impressive still, it had a plain wall facing the street – an extremely rare sight, given that every scurrilous landlord across the city made the most of their street frontage by renting it out to shopkeepers.

We were led into a comfortable room, where I was told to wait. Apparently I was not only barred from learning augury, but I was not even to see it in action. I did then have to chuckle to myself as the old man and his young boy slave herded a dozen chickens from some other room past me, through the atrium and out into whatever space in which he performed his duties. I waited perhaps for a quarter of an hour, hearing only occasional shouts that made no sense to me, and then the boy went back past, herding the chickens whence they came.

There are many ways augurs seek divine wisdom. Why this old man chose *ex tripudiis*, which somehow involved dancing chickens, I have no idea. Certainly his floor must have taken a great deal of cleaning afterwards.

My brother appeared, grinning with satisfaction, paid the man a healthy donative on top of the requested fee, and led me out of the house. Outside, a detachment of Praetorians in their white togas waited for us. Caligula, suddenly full of energy and good humour, told his litter bearers to return to the palace. We would take a stroll through the forum. The guardsmen disapproved. You could see it somehow in an aura around them, but Caligula was in a good mood and cared not.

'What did the old man say?' I enquired as we descended to the heart of the city.

My brother smiled. 'He told me that if I wished to found a dynasty like my forebears, then I should take my cues from the great Augustus. By following his example, I shall follow in his tracks.'

I pried no further. I just enjoyed the new positive feel to the day, and I hummed an old happy tune as we descended into the forum. There, despite the Praetorians surrounding us, we were almost incognito, since our escort were all toga-clad, much like the rest of the forum's population. The citizens repeatedly pulled each other aside in amazement as we were spotted, and I kept hearing the words 'it's the emperor!' in surprised tones. We stopped at several stalls, where my brother examined trinkets for sale and gave his patronage to a few, our escort paying his dues to startled, overwhelmed stallholders. It was one of the most enjoyable afternoons I have ever spent and gave me a curious, tantalising insight into how pleasant it might be to be ordinary.

It was as we passed between a stall selling phallus charms

and a stall selling curse tablets – that in itself should have been a warning, now I think upon it – that my brother's tendency to form immediate judgements, and not always for the better, once more reared its ugly head.

A man with the most extraordinary nose was examining a table full of bronze figures of the household gods with a view to purchasing them for his home. He was being referred to as Senator Piso by the stallholder, and his wife and two hirelings hovered nearby. His spouse was olive-skinned and pretty, with lustrous black hair that reminded me of Drusilla's. I saw my brother's eyes all over her and rolled my own. No matter what the situation, men's gazes will always dance across a pretty woman. It is rarely with any real interest, I have noted, but more of an automatic, natural imperative.

But at the very moment we passed, Senator Piso turned and consulted with his wife on the figures, and something occurred that changed everything: he called her Livia.

My brother stopped still in the road, his mouth working silently. Piso and his wife had not seen us or our Praetorian escort. He purchased two of the handsome bronze lares, then the pair turned and strode away from us, chatting as they went, the two burly guards trotting on close behind.

'The gods send me signs now without the need for a room full of chickens,' my brother said breathlessly.

'What?'

Caligula gestured after the retreating couple. 'The example of Augustus is laid at my feet. Can you not see?'

'Gaius . . .' I began, holding out a warning hand, but he was enlivened and full of purpose suddenly.

'Augustus fell in love with a Livia, and he had to force her husband – our own great-grandfather – to divorce her so that he could have her. Can you not see? I must have this Livia. I must persuade Piso to divorce her so I can have her. She will give me a dynasty. She will be a new matron of Rome.'

I watched the couple retreat across the forum, her hand delicate on his arm as he patted her fingers and pointed out items of interest, and it became obvious to me from their stance and behaviour that they were that rarest of things in Rome, a married couple still in the hopeless throes of love.

'Do not rush into anything so precipitously,' I warned my brother, but I might as well have been trying to talk a dog out of a bowl of meat.

I watched as he bristled with anticipation, and I knew that this wouldn't end well.

XVII

THE SEED OF THE JULII

By the kalends of Aprilis it had become apparent to all that my brother had made a mistake. His new empress drifted around the echoing halls of the imperial palace like a lost pet looking for its owner. She smiled rather mechanically when required to do so at important functions, and performed her wifely duties with efficiency and little in the way of interest. She did not love Caligula and, in that rather obsessive way of his, the more it became apparent that that was the case, the more he tried to force things to become what they were not.

For my part I had made small overtures of friendship to her, but I found it difficult to carry on even a modicum of conversation. She was lost and uninterested and hard work, to say the least. It was much easier to leave her alone than to attempt to draw her out.

My brother's great plan for a dynasty was further challenged by the fact that no matter how often he lay with Livia Orestilla, she remained steadfastly un-pregnant and, while that had been a boon for me, it was a curse for my brother. He had her consult the best physicians in the city – not, I might note, any official *obstetrices*, since he still blamed them for the death of his first wife. Each and every one pronounced her healthy and more than capable of bearing children, and it was simply bad luck that she had yet to become pregnant. Caligula took this as well as could be expected, trying not to attribute such a failure to the will of gods who had cursed the seed of the Julii.

Lepidus' solution was unconventional to say the least, but had the merit of a good record of success in other cases. One night when he and Caligula were in their cups after a day at the games, Lepidus had pointed out how many of Rome's children had been, in fact, the unwanted by-product of a night of drink and overindulgence, which can lead to heightened amorousness even in those generally disinclined. My brother congratulated Lepidus on his idea and would try it forthwith.

And that was one reason for the banquet.

Other than Caligula's private hope to see Livia inebriated into pregnancy, he was also cresting a wave of popularity unprecedented in recent months, and capitalising on good feeling is a must for any political animal.

The regular games, the peace that had settled across the empire, the restoration of the abundant grain from Aegyptus, full coffers and the regular good publicity of the court had seen the public of Rome fall in love with my brother as they had once done with our father. The revolt had ended in Alexandria and Flaccus had been removed, tried and sent into exile on Andros, where he would be expected to take his own life in due course. Pollio had consulted with the emperor and had taken on the prefecture of Aegyptus in order to repair the damage done, while my husband, Vinicius, had been made governor of Asia to put things right there. Wherever there had been small fires, capable men were sent to put them out and rebuild.

The military was content too, for there were no wars and no troubles with arrogant barbarian tribes, and their time in garrison in the winter had involved no marches and battles in the snow, ice and rain. Plus their pay had increased a little, and many were still basking in the glow of the gold they had received upon my brother's accession.

Even the senate, with which my brother had experienced a strained relationship at best this past year, began to ease their disapproval of him, and many senators began to visit him as clients to a patron. Caligula had been shrewd, upon realising that any dynasty he wished to found would rest at least partially on the goodwill of the empire, and so he had instituted a number of measures to please the senate; nothing that gave them any real power or diminished his own in any way, of course, but enough to mollify the bulk of the dissenters and to calm relations. He had even attended a senate session briefly the previous month, which I saw as a huge step towards reconciliation.

He still did not trust his temper enough to stay long in their presence.

The support of the great families of Rome was the other major reason for the banquet.

That and the Dies Natalis Romae, anyway.

In late Aprilis the festival of the founding of Rome is always one of the great events of the calendar year, but *this* year my brother had poured attention, effort, and money – chests and chests and chests of gold, in fact – into making the festival the best in memory. And it truly was.

The sacrifices had been auspicious, formed of a pregnant cow, and of the self-same racing horse that had been Caligula's lead beast in his now famous race. There were races and fights and beast hunts and plays, and even the lowest figure attending the festival wore a crown like a king. In a previously unseen addition to the proceedings, Caligula had the one true *ancile* – the golden shield of the god Mars – carried by singing priests to the Capitol where the public would sigh in amazement and remember how the gods favoured their city. More food and drink had been made available for the people than anyone could remember being donated by a single benefactor. It was a time when the people of Rome gloried in who they were and where they lived.

Late in the afternoon, once the last of the races was done with and that upstart from Saguntum had been dragged half-dead from the kindling of his chariot, the great and the rich of Rome had descended upon the palace of my brother for a banquet.

And like the rest of the festival, no expense had been spared. In some ways, it was *too* much, which was another of my brother's less proper habits. He could go too far a little too easily, with gestures just as much as with his rather dry and acerbic humour. A stuffed she-wolf – some thought that in itself a little in poor taste – formed something of a centrepiece in the atrium. The wolf itself was relatively ordinary, though, compared to the fact that its teats supplied wine from some hidden source, and two great decorative *kraters* – formed in the shape of Romulus and Remus – stood underneath to collect the wine and mix with water.

Wall hangings had come from the east, shipped at the expense of Pollio, formed of linen and silk, of Tyrian purple and Aegyptian gold. Carpets had come from Syria and Parthia, through my husband's province, to warm the colder areas of the floor. Incense from Arabia that cost a soldier's yearly wage for one small pouch burned in braziers all evening, giving the palace a spicy, sweet scent. Wrestlers spent the entire evening oiled and grunting, in bout after bout for the entertainment of all present, while the best musicians, acrobats and singers plied their trade around the halls. The Praetorian Guard were nowhere to be seen, though the two new prefects were present, enjoying themselves. They were never far from Caligula and were hanging on his every word. It seems he had made a good choice with Stella and Clemens, for they owed everything to him, and appeared to be extremely loyal.

Instead of Praetorians, the German Guard hovered around the palace, mostly clustered near wherever the emperor could be found, and while the banquet flowed and ebbed, not one of the soldiers took part, each remaining professional and alert.

The main space for the banquet had been set out in an open courtyard of enormous size that had only recently been finished.

My brother had begun to extend the palace of his predecessor towards the forum and the Capitol, intending to create a new vestibule with stairs that would eventually rise beside the Temple of Castor and Pollux to provide more convenient access to the palace. By that Aprilis the work was perhaps half complete, but the great open courtyard was in place and the tables, fountains, couches and endless decorations filled the square, where a balmy spring evening greeted the guests. Once the main meal itself was over, much of the palace would be available to wander, for most of its rooms contained some form of entertainment for the guests. My brother spent a fortune on that event.

There had been some speculation among the upper echelons of society as to who would be chosen to recline in the most honoured spot by the emperor's left hand, and my brother surprised everyone – and insulted a few hopefuls too – by placing his bored-looking, uninterested new wife in that coveted position. The place usually reserved for the host's wife, by his right, was given to Drusilla, myself, and Agrippina, in that order. The arrangement shocked the more rigid of Rome's social elite and surprised everyone else. Lepidus occupied the next highest section of seating along with Agrippa, who had been in the east for several months but had recently resurfaced in Rome, among those most honoured by the host. Many faces new to me, but ones well-known in senatorial circles, were present in that area, too, including a young fellow with a rather uncultured rural tone named Vespasian, the son of the governor of Asia by the name of Aulus Vitellius, who had become something of a friend to my brother through their mutual love of the races. And the current consuls, of course, Aquila and Nonnius. Even that self-righteous senator Sabinus who had so angered my brother the previous year sat among the honoured couches close to the imperial family, though he continued to make snide remarks throughout, just within hearing of my brother.

Throughout the opening declarations, speeches and trays of appetisers, one particular attendee fixed Caligula and the rest of us in the family with the most hate-filled, baleful look: our uncle Claudius, who, since laying down his consulship at the start of the year, had once again sunk into miserable obscurity. Claudius had arrived at the feast all pomposity and self-grandeur, dragging his lame leg and stuttering at the most influential men of Rome to get out of his way, for he was family to the emperor. And then, once into the main banqueting courtyard, he had discovered that no place had been assigned for him with the imperial family, or even in the seats of the honoured guests. In the end, he had found himself a couch between a thickly accented notable from Corinth and an old senator with a lazy eye and the most extreme deafness, which led him to shout constantly. If it were possible to wither a man's flesh with a gaze alone, our uncle would have murdered Caligula with his eyes.

As guests took their seats and all was made ready, I tried to start up conversations with my sisters, with little success. Drusilla was at best half-listening, her defocused gaze turned inwards to dreamy ponderings of Lepidus. Agrippina, whose husband was seated among the honoured guests, was busy peering intently into the faces of the great and powerful and when I spoke she irritably waved me into silence. I did note, following her gaze, that her husband was sitting with General Corbulo, recently returned from the east, and Sanquinius Maximus, a notable senator said to be destined for high office. There was something in their manner that made me uneasy.

Once everyone was settled, a signal was given and the doors to the new wing of the palace opened. A fanfare blared out, startling the assembled diners, and a man in a plain green tunic stepped into the midst of a sea of expensive white togas and richly coloured stolas. He wore leather sandals that had been chosen for comfort and not appearance, and he appeared to be injured, from the way he limped slightly. Then I saw his head and spotted the golden laurels resting amid the curly black hair. A charioteer. I might have known.

His identity quickly filtered through the guests and came as a great relief, for there was talk of a fever running through the slums of the city, and a weary, injured, lower-class visitor would not be welcome for fear that he brought the illness with him. In truth, such a man would not have been welcome at the best of times among such a crowd, but *especially* not then.

The racer, it seemed, was the new hero of Rome: a local boy who had risen in a single year from relative obscurity to take the title from that once lucky Hispanic driver. His name was Eutychus, and his rugged charm quickly warmed the rest of the guests towards him. My brother congratulated him on his phenomenal win and his clear ability, commiserated with him that he should receive such a paltry prize as a simple piece of floral headgear for his great win, and announced that he had an extra gift for the driver that more suited his victory. The rest of the gathering watched, dumbstruck, as sixteen of the German Guard entered, wheeling eight chests on low carts. As they were lined up in front of the puzzled sportsman, the two leading guards jerked one open.

A collective sigh susurrated through the palace as the crowd of fascinated attendees gazed upon the heaps of shining coins within. *Eight chests?* The mind boggled at the amount of coin they must contain. Our curiosity was quickly sated.

'Two million sesterces, Eutychus,' my brother announced. 'A more fitting prize for the bravery and skill you displayed today than a simple wreath.'

The charioteer was so stunned that he actually staggered a little. He spent the entire evening wide-eyed and flabbergasted. He was not the only one. The coins were taken away and delivered to the stables of the Greens, and the charioteer was granted a seat with the honoured guests – further inflaming our uncle Claudius.

Throughout the meal, my brother spent much of his time in close discussion with Lepidus and Agrippa, his two closest friends, the two Romans listening with fascination as their eastern friend regaled them with accounts of the rather un-Roman lavishness he had encountered in the courts of the various eastern client kings and satraps. Antiochus of Commagene – who we had once known in the house of Antonia – was said to have had a slave with saffron skin and unusual eyes brought all the way from distant, exotic Serica purely to oil his feet. Caligula had chuckled at the idea and pointed out that a Roman who tried such a thing would be laughed out of the city. And yet I could see his and Lepidus' captivated expressions as Antiochus continued his tale. They were periodically interrupted by Vespasian, who took every opportunity to approach my brother on the flimsiest of contexts to seek his advice or judgement, or to offer a gift or some titbit of news he felt might be important. I could see ambition in that one, for a barely Romanised provincial.

The banquet was well received and a sociable occasion, though the sky began to cloud over as the night's shadows drew in, and the temperature started to drop slowly. Still, the weather was not of prime concern to me and nor was it, it became apparent, to my brother. Once the food was consumed and all that was left were myriad trays of sweets and desserts, the guests began to move around and mix a little. My brother continued to chat half-heartedly with his friends, but seemed distracted. At first I thought Caligula had lost something, then I realised that his wife was no longer beside him. I began to frown and look around for her myself. She appeared from some corner at last, stately and calm, and I began to grow suspicious immediately. My brother's face exhibited the same distrust, and we watched her intently for some time.

At length, while Vespasian was telling some dreadfully crude and off-colour joke about a legionary in the Alpes and a lonely goat, the empress Livia Orestilla made an excuse about womanly troubles and left the gathering once more. My brother's eyes narrowed, but he nodded. It was not seemly for a man to pry into such matters, after all.

Me, though? I would have been willing to put a chest of sesterces on a wager that she lied. Everything about her demeanour cried it out. I caught Caligula's eyes and there was a question in them. I nodded slowly.

Then, suddenly, as though it had somehow been triggered by our exchange, a flash of dazzling white filled the sky above Rome as Jove tested his first thunderbolt. A few moments later a low boom rolled across the city from the direction of Tibur and the mountains. Vespasian, still in the throes of ribald humour, stopped dead and frowned up at the sky. A moment later another dazzling flash filled the dark void, and I could see him counting. The crash of Vulcan's hammer came quickly, and young Vespasian cleared his throat.

'Majesty, the storm hangs over Gabii, but within one quarter of an hour it will be here.'

Trust a country provincial to have such a trick as predicting weather. Still, his warning was timely and well received. My brother nodded his thanks at the young man and rose to stand amid the reclining guests. With one hand on his hip, he smiled and thrust his other finger accusingly into the sky, declaiming, 'Lift me, Jove, or I will lift thee!' The crowd frowned in confusion, and my brother's triumphant grin faltered. There was an awkward pause, and Caligula defused the increasing tension with a chuckle. 'And I thought my guests were learned men and women. *Homer!*' he laughed. 'I misquote Homer with a challenge to Jove. But I jest poorly. Come, let us rush inside before Jove takes me up on my challenge, for we have wrestlers inside and they would be better to watch than I.'

This time his humour hit the mark, and he was rewarded with laughs from many of those assembled. The slaves scurried round madly, trying to gather everything up to ferry indoors without inconveniencing the guests in any way.

Politely, the entire gathering waited for my brother to make the first move, and Caligula swept up his cup in one hand, grasped the hem of his toga with the other, and hurried inside.

I was moments behind him, as was Drusilla. Agrippina lagged a little, still recovering physically from her childbirth four months earlier, and keeping her eyes on her husband and his companions. Thus it was that my brother was flanked by two of his sisters as he entered a wide, sculpture-lined vestibule on the way to the largest of the dining halls in the palace. Crowds came behind, with Lepidus and Agrippa closest.

We all saw it at the same time.

Unaware of what had happened outside, Livia Orestilla was emerging from a side door into the vestibule, hair in disarray, sandals unfastened. It came as no surprise at all when, as she stumbled, shocked, to a halt, her ex-husband, the senator Piso, appeared from the same room, his toga askew.

We stopped in an instant, staring at the pair of them, and I could see my brother's knuckles whiten as he gripped his toga so tightly he almost tore through it.

'Whore!' he bellowed, hurling his half-filled cup. The bronze goblet struck Livia on the forehead, coating her face and chest in dark wine and sending her staggering back into her former husband, whose face had drained of all colour.

'Whore!' Caligula repeated, jabbing a finger angrily at her. 'Adulteress!'

Many of the most important people of Rome were now in the vestibule behind us, the German Guard hemming them in. Shock and fascination rippling through the crowd.

'M-M-Majesty . . .' began Piso with a stutter.

'Cease to speak, Piso, lest you cease to breathe.'

The man fell silent. Caligula was almost vibrating with fury. I could see him trying to frame the words he needed through all-consuming ire, and I could see the tell-tale signs of that same anger that had so struck him in the senate. I felt a sick wave of dread wash through me at what was to come. Livia and Piso were a half step from being beheaded, and we all knew it. We were on the very shore of a bloodbath I had no wish to witness. Perhaps there was an alternative? Leaning close I whispered, such that only my brother would hear.

'You are under the scrutiny of all Rome.'

He frowned, his eyes still on the adulterous pair. Without turning his head, he whispered back, 'Clemency?'

I nodded. 'Better than a tyrant's reaction.'

There was a long pause.

'Begone from Rome on the morning tide, the pair of you. Find an island somewhere, for another sunset in Rome will bring with it a trip to the *carcer* and the Gemonian Stairs.'

And there it was. Clemency. Banishment. With the added threat of ignominious execution.

So it was that on a night when storms wracked Rome and fevers plagued its streets, my brother ended his second marriage.

XVIII
THE SUBJECT OF HIS VENOM

There was a general feeling of unhappiness across Pompey's great theatre on that warm summer evening, for a troupe of actors from Leptis Magna in Africa were performing their acclaimed version of Aristophanes' *Lysistrata*, and things were not going well. Rumour had filtered through the crowd that the actors playing both Stratyllis and Lysistrata herself had succumbed to the fevers that still stalked the streets of the city, and the two strutting across the stage now were desperate, last-moment stand-ins from the company.

It showed.

One of them spoke Greek – the play was performed in the original Greek for the best effect – with such a horrible thick African accent that he sounded more like a Persian trying to swallow a cat than a refined Greek wife seeking to use her wiles to end a war. The other, who at least had a good Greek speaking voice, was utterly useless in every other way. He had so far fallen over three times and forgotten his lines so often that I had lost count. And he came out once without his mask, too.

My brother was twitching in his seat. He had initially found it quite amusing, though that had faded quickly and it irritated him to see such a poor performance after all the excitement and publicity that had followed the troupe from Africa.

In truth, it was Drusilla that was truly preying on his mind, his eyes repeatedly straying to the empty seat beside him.

Agrippina's chair was also empty, but she was hale and hearty and busy with her young son elsewhere.

Drusilla had fallen ill after the banquet at the festival. She had had a little too much to drink, which was very unusual for Drusilla, and then gallivanted off across the Palatine with Lepidus in the torrential rain in the middle of the night. She had come down with an easily anticipated chill within days. Unfortunately that chill lingered, and even as it finally relinquished its grip on our more delicate sister, her weakened state left her open to other illnesses. She immediately contracted a strain of the fever sickness that seemed to be everywhere in the city.

Fortunately, the city's physicians seemed to have mastered whatever was causing the illness, and fewer and fewer people were now dying. In fact, from a point a month earlier when it had been a veritable death sentence, now if victims saw a physician soon enough, nine of every ten were making a good recovery. My initial fears for my sister were abating as the city-wide epidemic was rapidly brought under control.

And no one had better care than the emperor's sister. Alongside numerous physicians, including my favourite, the Jew who had so helped my brother, Caligula had been by her side for weeks and had wept with relief when, the previous day, she had started to show signs of improvement. He had been very vocal in his intention to miss the play so as not to leave Drusilla, but this morning, as she had finally sat up in bed, smiled, and taken a little water and bread, she had rolled her eyes and told him not to be such an idiot. Lepidus was with her, after all, her husband having been as ever-present as her brother.

Yet Caligula could not truly concentrate on the play, for his thoughts were still with Drusilla – the innocent, fragile sister of whom he had always been so protective. The knowledge she was so unwell and there was nothing he could do to stop it was eating at him.

He knew *Lysistrata* as well as any actor. It was one of the old Greek works that he had read time and again in Tiberius' library on Capri when trying to escape the cloying world in which we lived.

I glanced sidelong at him, to see his lips moving in time with the words.

'Disgraceful, women venturing to prate
in public over affairs of state.
They even – men would not be so naïve –
the blandishments of Sparta's wolves believe . . .'

At least the leader of the chorus seemed to have a good working knowledge of Greek inflection and a pleasant, sonorous tone. I sat back, enjoying his voice as well as those of his fellow chorus members. If they were an indication of the quality the troupe usually enjoyed, then we had to make an effort to see them perform when their two missing members were returned to health.

I closed my eyes and nodded gently along to the rhythm of the words until suddenly I was startled from my pleasant daze by an angry grunt from my brother.

I was aware that his fingers had begun to drum on the seat beside him, which was certainly a sign that his temper was fraying, and his breathing was becoming faster. He was getting angry – his temper had flared more often and more violently since his divorce. I clung to the belief that once he was truly over her he would return to the more clement brother I remembered, and in the meantime I would do what I could to keep him temperate. I opened my eyes with the full intent to talk quietly to him and calm his blood, but even as I turned to him, he rose to his feet, drawing the attention of the entire audience.

'*Cinesias*, you dolt!' snapped my brother loudly.

The play stopped in an instant, the actors looking up in stunned disbelief at the figure standing on the seat of honour at the front-centre of the *cavea*. My brother was waving an angry finger at Lysistrata.

'What have you to say for yourself?'

The actor stood in panicked silence. I saw his masked face turn once, then twice, to seek the support of his fellows, but he was rewarded with only heightened panic as the others backed away from him.

'Nothing?' Caligula demanded angrily. 'You have *nothing* to say? Perhaps that is an improvement. I think the entire audience would have been grateful if you'd had nothing to say for the past hour. For if, like myself, they are waiting to hear the wondrous and eloquent words of Aristophanes, then they are probably as disappointed as I to hear those words skinned, butchered, and hung to cure in the meat shop of your play. Never before have I seen an actor fail so dismally to put any feeling into words that seem to me to carry feeling naturally. And I could forgive the mangling of one of my favourite plays if you could *damn well remember even half the words!*'

By the time he shouted the last of his tirade, Caligula was red-faced and shaking. Though the mask hid the subject of his venom, the actor also was shaking, and I could imagine was more white-faced than red.

'Say it again!' Caligula demanded.

There was a terrible silence.

'Speak your line once more, imbecile.'

The poor actor, shaking uncontrollably, stuttered and slurred out his words: 'Cintesius. The name we know well.'

My brother pinched the bridge of his nose. 'Who?'

'Cintesius?' hazarded the actor again, his voice trembling.

'Cinesias!' bellowed Caligula. 'He's supposed to be your husband. His name is hardly unheard throughout the play. Everyone else around you has been saying it correctly, and yet you mispronounce and mangle his name every . . . single . . . time!'

'I . . .' the man began, but trailed off swiftly into trembling silence.

'I am in half a mind to have you flogged,' my brother

snapped angrily. 'In fact, I will. I see that the musicians in the background have good, long, *tibia* pipes. You can stand in a small room with one of my Praetorians and repeat the name a thousand times. And every time you get it wrong, he will hit you with your friends' pipes around the ear or the face. By the end of your time there, you will either be able to say Cinesias any time you are asked, or you will be disfigured and unable to say anything much through your fat, useless lips!'

He'd gone too far. I baulked at the thought of the poor fool battered beyond recognition simply for failing to live up to expectations.

The actor collapsed, whimpering, on the stage, and the audience was as silent as the tomb as they looked back and forth as one between the emperor and the stricken thespian.

'Gaius . . .' I began, hoping to calm him and overturn his initial judgement, but my eyes fell upon the only other upright figure in the audience, and I fell silent again. Prefect Clemens was shuffling through a crowd of seated senators until he reached the open steps and then hurried down them towards us. My stomach churned. There could be no good reason for the Praetorian prefect to interrupt matters, and he had not been in attendance, claiming an utter disregard for Greek comedy.

As Clemens approached, I caught a good look at his face and shivered at the bleak sombreness of his expression. I knew what was coming even as he slowed and bowed his head, hurriedly.

Caligula turned to his prefect, the anger draining from him as he stared.

'Drusilla?'

Clemens nodded, his eyes downcast.

'Is she . . . ?'

'The lady is deathly ill again. She struggles for breath, suddenly. Marcus Aemilius Lepidus sent me to find you at once.'

Caligula was moving immediately. I followed in his wake, Clemens going ahead to make sure the way was clear. Four of the German bodyguards who had been present for my brother's protection came with us, but found themselves outnumbered by the score of Praetorians that Clemens had brought with him. We cared not. Out of the stands we went, through the corridors of the theatre, down the zigzagging steps and out into the early evening. The sun had just set and Rome was lit by that strange, otherworldly dark sapphire sky that heralds the end of a true summer's day.

Clemens led us to a carriage, while he himself clambered up onto a horse, and then we rattled off through the city, making for the house of Lepidus and our sister, the Praetorians and Germans pounding along the streets to keep up. Lepidus' security opened the door of the house at the sight of our approach, and my brother didn't even wait for the carriage to stop. He jumped from the door and staggered, righting himself as the vehicle finally pulled up, and Clemens came hurrying round to help me down.

We two ran into the house mere moments after Caligula. Wordless slaves pointed the way, and in heartbeats we were in Drusilla's chamber.

My heart was torn from my breast at the sight that awaited us.

Drusilla lay still and peaceful in her bed, paler even than usual, a single trickle of blood from the corner of her mouth the only sign that anything was amiss and that she wasn't merely sleeping. Lepidus knelt at her side, clasping one of her hands in his, his face drawn, tears fresh on his cheeks.

Our brother stood at the other side, his mouth slightly open, breathing heavily as he looked down at her.

'What happened?' I asked quietly. 'She was improving.'

Lepidus looked up at me. 'The medicus said that sometimes they seem to improve towards the end. They accept what is happening to them and because they are not fighting the illness any more, they seem to be easier. Drusilla seemed to have understood that she was going. In her last moments she told me not to worry and to look after you two.'

I felt the tears start then. I don't cry often – when you have lived through the abject horror, misery and fear that was the norm for our youth, tears are too precious to waste on the unimportant. But for Drusilla I cried. And for Lepidus, who had lost her for so long and found her suddenly in unexpected joy only to lose her again almost immediately, I cried. But most of all, for my brother I cried.

Gaius Julius Caesar, who was called Caligula, had a heart in four pieces. One was his own. One belonged to Rome. One was for his family. The other was for Drusilla alone – his delicate songbird whom he had sheltered and cared for as long as I had known him. And that evening a quarter of my brother's heart shrivelled and died.

We had lost Nero and Drusus and our mother to the wily machinations of wicked men. And, if my mother's conspiratorial whisperings were to believed, our father also had died of a poison sent by Tiberius. It had become the norm over the years to have the outspoken and defiant in our family torn from us by enemies.

But Drusilla *had* no enemies. She was a quiet, harmless darling of a girl who had never wished ill upon anyone. And no evil man had taken her from us, but a chance illness – or perhaps the malevolent designs of the gods. I felt the odd pangs of envy I had felt for my brother's favourite throughout my life crumble and fade in the face of our loss.

So it was not the same. And that was just for me. For Caligula, who had been close to her all his life, it was the end of a world. I stood in silence, sobbing. Lepidus, past his first veil of tears now, rose from his wife's side and came to me, clutching me as I shook, holding me tight.

Caligula stood and stared.

And stared.

Then he bent, to where a solid Samian-ware jug sat on the table by her bed, holding her water. He gripped it tight and rose once more.

'Curse you, bastard gods,' he snarled and threw the heavy jug across the room. His aim was precise and the container smashed into the small altar to the household gods, sending the figures of the spirits crashing to the floor.

'Curse you, Aesculapius,' he growled, picking up her cup and hurling it against the wall, where it smashed to small pieces.

'Curse you, Hermes.' The table shattered against the same wall.

'Curse you, Jove. Curse you *all*, for this!'

He staggered, his fingers twitching, looking for something else to throw, to add to the wreckage, but there was nothing easily to hand. He floundered for a moment and then collapsed at Drusilla's side and clutched at her hand as Lepidus had done.

'You *cannot* leave,' he said quietly. 'I will not allow it. They say we are divine, you know? The family of Caesar, I mean. They say we will be gods when we die, like Augustus is. Well, if I am to be a god, then let the others bow to me now and give you back. *I will not let you go.* I will not give you a coin for the boatman. Let Charon turn his back on you, so that you *must* come back.'

I fought through the tears. These were mad, dangerous words. 'Brother . . .'

Lepidus straightened a little. 'I placed the coin in her mouth immediately. She will have crossed to the realms beyond by now.'

Caligula rose and turned to us, his eyes blazing.

'No. You should not have done that. She is your wife of months, but she was my sister all her life.'

He advanced angrily on us, and I saw his hand rip something from his belt. A knife came up and the way he held it made it clear that he intended to use it on Lepidus. But at the last moment a curious thing happened to him. He saw the knife in his hand – the beautiful, jewelled silver knife that had been a childhood gift from the very man he was about to use it upon. I saw the anger drain once more from his face, to be replaced by a bleak hopelessness, and he turned, gripping the knife in both hands such that the blade dug deep into his palm. Dripping blood, he stormed to the wall where he had broken the cup and slammed the blade so deep that it jammed in the plaster, quivering slightly. Then he began to pound the wall with his fists, bloodying his knuckles more and more, all the time wailing like some animal caught in a trap. It was an appalling thing to watch, and the horror of it dried my tears.

Lepidus held me tight and leaned in close.

'Remember that it was this very grief over the loss of a son that drove Tiberius mad. Watch your brother in the coming days, Livilla. Watch him closely.'

And had I had the chance, I would have.

Caligula disappeared from Rome the day after Drusilla's death. He left various instructions with the new Praetorian prefects, Stella and Clemens, took his personal slaves and fled to one of the more obscure imperial properties in the Alban hills some fifteen miles south of Rome.

It took me several weeks to discover where he had gone. Rome, of course, was in turmoil. While no official announcement of the emperor's movements had been made, just that he was in private mourning for the lady Drusilla, rumour was rife that the emperor had withdrawn into retirement.

And so we were left to pick up the pieces – I, who suffered every bit as much of a loss as my brother and yet was given no time to grieve while he sank into a rather selfish pit of despair. Caligula had told Clemens and Stella to 'see to her funeral and burial'. No expense was to be spared. Clemens had been a little concerned at that, but the emperor had been insistent that

Drusilla receive such funeral games as had never before been seen in Rome, and that the prefects had his permission to drain the treasury dry if they needed to. There would always be new lands to conquer and new loot to take, my brother had told them tersely, but Drusilla could only die once. They had tried to persuade him to stay in the city using every means at their disposal, but he would have none of it. He would not even be at the funeral to give the oration, claiming that, as her husband, that was Lepidus' right and duty. In truth, I knew that, while he had given a rousing, if dangerous, oration at Livia's funeral, he would be unable to deliver such a speech for Drusilla without collapsing in public, which would be unacceptable.

In fact, the main reason he had withdrawn from Rome was to work through his grief without such public displays. We had all learned, in our time at Tiberius' eyrie, to keep our emotions to ourselves and to display a public façade of calm and obedience. This was no different, and he would not repeat his anguished violence at Drusilla's deathbed in front of the people of Rome.

I helped Lepidus with the funeral rites and aided the two prefects where I could in organising everything. Agrippina wished to stay and help too, but her husband dragged her away to his seaside villa at Pyrgi in the north, claiming that their baby was becoming difficult and did nothing but cry and act up when it was in close proximity to Rome and our family. And so I went on alone – for Lepidus was not often approachable at that time, and all my family were absent.

I wished time and again that my husband was with me and not in some gilded palace in Asia, imposing the emperor's peace on that province. If ever there was a time in my life when I needed him, it was then, for I was forced to be the rock upon which everyone anchored while they dealt with Drusilla's death and the endless troubles it brought. And when the nights rolled in and the work of the day was done, I had no one to console me as I sat in my lonely bed and cried myself to sleep.

*

Finally, as mid Iulius came around and the games for Drusilla had truly ended, everything in Rome began to return to normal, and I managed to persuade Prefect Stella to tell me where Caligula had gone. It then took me another week to drag Lepidus out of his darkened chambers and into the light and persuade him to come with me to visit him. He needed it, to be honest. Lepidus was a sensible and practical man, but Drusilla's death had hit him hard, and I could almost feel the exposure to the world doing him good as we rattled south in our carriage, a small group of slaves following on behind, all escorted by a detachment of Praetorians. Clemens had insisted he join us, and while I still sensed no ill will from either Praetorian commander and trusted them both, I refused. They had enough on their hands keeping Rome running as smoothly as it was, and I was not sure how Lepidus and I would be received by my brother, let alone a Praetorian prefect.

The villa in the hills was a sprawling affair, but old and very out of date. The gardens had not been tended since the days of Augustus, his successor preferring the sea and the island of Capri. As we turned off the main road and began to angle down towards the small but beautiful Nemorensis lake, we caught our first sight of the villa. Though it had been in the hands of the extended family since the days of the great Julius Caesar, his namesake, my brother had never previously visited it. I saw at once, though, how it would be the perfect place for complete solitude. The high hillsides around the lake hid the nearby towns from view and muffled all sound. The villa itself sat on the western shore of the lake and was long and low, stretched along the waterfront. The only other real sign of occupation in sight was the great temple complex of Diana on the far shore. The villa was surrounded by an extensive overgrown garden and park. The place might almost have been made to accommodate a grieving individual.

I somehow felt comforted now that I had seen the place. It was easier than simply knowing that my brother was to the south somewhere. The sight had the opposite effect on Lepidus, who shook his head and called for the carriage to pause.

He looked down the slope at the villa and turned to me.

'This is not right, Livilla.'

'What?'

'This place. It is unhealthy for him.'

It looked perfectly peaceful and pleasant to me. 'How so?' I asked.

'History is repeating itself, Livilla. Tiberius' son died and he languished in a grief that claimed him so utterly he gave up all interest in the ruling of Rome and fled to Capri to live in seclusion. Look what happened to him there. He went mad and became twisted and evil. And while he wallowed in his pit, he left Rome to suffer under the whims of the Praetorian monster Sejanus.'

'My brother is not mad like Tiberius,' I replied quietly, though my memory furnished me with images of him throwing things in Drusilla's room, and advancing angrily on Lepidus with a knife. 'And the new Praetorian prefects are good men, not power-seeking animals like Sejanus.'

Lepidus simply breathed slowly and shook his head. 'Tiberius was not mad to begin with either. And Sejanus was once an efficient officer of the Guard. Things change. We have to get your brother out of here and back into the world before he becomes a shadow of Tiberius. Rome needs to know its emperor is looking after things.'

'Stella and Clemens . . .' I began, but Lepidus held up a hand.

'And don't forget your uncle. Claudius has been prowling around the Palatine for a month now, sniffing out possibilities and speaking to people in what he clearly thinks is a secretive manner. Even if you trust the new prefects, do you trust Claudius?'

No. No, I did not. In fact, since the deaths of Silanus and Macro there was no one in Rome I trusted less than our club-footed, stammering uncle. I tried to find another argument, but there wasn't one. For all the pleasant solitude of this villa, Lepidus was correct. Caligula had to be brought away from it.

At a gesture from Lepidus, the carriage rolled on down to the gravel drive behind the villa, and we had all disembarked and prepared ourselves before a harassed-looking slave appeared from a door and shook his head.

'No visitors, Domina. The emperor does not wish to be disturbed.'

I was so taken aback at being spoken to thus by a slave that I almost complied, but the man was terrified, and I realised that this was Caligula speaking, not the poor wretch before me.

'I am not seeking permission to visit my brother. I do not *need* that. Get out of my way.'

As if on cue, the detachment of Praetorians came forward and fell into lines, the centurion in command stepping forward to my side, where he loomed menacingly. Lepidus flanked me on the other arm, and the slave shrank out of the way as I began to walk forward. I would have walked through or over him if he hadn't moved.

We entered the villa and passed through a gloomy atrium with a non-functional fountain. The windows were all covered with drapes and shutters, and the place was unheated. It felt more like a mausoleum than a home. Lepidus had been right: this was not healthy. We searched several rooms and found no one. Were there servants and slaves here? Surely my brother had not been living for a month with just one slave to help him?

No. We found another haggard-looking wretch in a triclinium, exhausted and sitting on the steps by a window.

'You. Where is my brother?' I demanded, Lepidus and the centurion providing added persuasion.

The slave rose and peered myopically at me in the most

arrogant manner. I almost beat him, and I do not readily beat slaves – even the bad ones. Instead I bit down on my anger and gestured at him with a pointed finger.

'My brother. I wish to see him. And you need to clean up this villa, open the windows and light the furnaces.'

'I like it cold and dark, Livilla,' the wretch replied, and I suddenly found my heart in my throat as the truth hit me. This was no slave, standing in the dark and the chill in a stained tunic and with wild, unwashed hair. This was the emperor of Rome. I was struck at once by a mix of striking compassion and downright disbelief.

Caligula was so pale as to be almost translucent, except beneath the eyes, where his cheeks sagged under great purple-black circles. His hair had not been washed in some weeks, and had not seen a comb, I thought, since leaving Rome. He had a beard of several weeks' growth that stuck out at odd angles and contained scraps of food. His body had lost much of its tone, becoming spindly and unhealthy-looking.

And his eyes . . .

I flinched as I looked into them, and then turned away.

'Go away, Livilla. And you, Lepidus. I wish to be left alone.'

'The funeral was well organised and most seemly,' I said, by way of reply. 'It was attended by everyone from the lowest to the highest. And the games went well. Your pet charioteer won two races. Rome celebrates your largesse, but they still worry, for their emperor is not among them. And there are still honours to be given to Drusilla, not the least of which is a visit from her brother.'

'I cannot go.'

'You must,' I urged.

'No. But . . . but . . . do you have a scribe with you?'

I frowned, but next to me Lepidus cleared his throat. 'I have no scribe, Gaius, but I have a neat hand and a tablet at my belt. What do you wish?'

Suddenly the tired wretch that was my brother became frantic, rattling out words faster than Lepidus could get them down, listing the endless honours he wished to heap on Drusilla. For a quarter of an hour, he itemised the decrees with barely a breath, until Lepidus was squeezing in tiny notes along the margins of his tablet. Finally, my brother seemed to run out of energy and subsided, instantly becoming the sad, silent creature we had initially found.

'You are repeating the failures of the past, Gaius,' I said finally, trying to sound firm. He simply looked blankly at me, so I sighed. 'You have left Rome for seclusion as Tiberius did. How long will it be before you are laughing at murders and drowning slaves in the lake for spilling your wine?' I had expected that to draw an angry retort. Nothing. 'You leave the city in the hands of Praetorian prefects, despite the fact that you have said to me time and again how no commander of the Guard can be trusted. How long before Clemens and Stella turn into Sejanus and Macro, Gaius?'

Again, silence.

'Talk to me!'

My brother simply stared. It was time to use the one angle I felt sure would produce a reaction, though I'd been avoiding it for it could go badly just as easily as well.

'Drusilla would be horrified if she could see what you were doing,' I whispered.

He focused on me and his fists gripped and un-gripped. Anger flashed through his eyes and while that was not the emotion I had been hoping for, it was better than nothing. No luck with the Tiberius comparison or the Praetorian angle, and not enough of a reaction to Drusilla's name either. Perhaps I could go deeper into the heart of a matter unconnected to Drusilla and his current despair and drag him over to think about that? A change of subject.

'If you wish to avoid a repeat of the dark days of Tiberius, you need to clarify the succession,' I said, trying a new tack. 'You need an heir, and to have an heir you need another wife. And to have another wife, you need to stop looking like a dishevelled bear and surface into the light of day.' Perhaps not an *entirely* new angle, though . . . 'Drusilla would have told you the same thing, and you know it.'

Twin-pronged attacks are a classic strategy of the legions, as my brother was fond of telling me during our youthful games, and here I had trapped him between the fear of repeating Tiberius' succession crisis and the name of his beloved sister. I saw conflict in his eyes, and grasped on to the hope it created.

'Come. Come back with us.'

'No. I cannot.'

I caught an odd look from Lepidus at my side, and he stepped forward. 'There are half a dozen beauties at the court these days,' he said quickly, 'all of whom would love you and all of whom should be able to bear you children.' When my brother did not simply argue, Lepidus smiled and took that for encouragement. 'There's Julia Drusi Caesaris?'

'A cousin,' Caligula grunted. 'A close one, too. We are not the Ptolemies. We like our cousins distant among the Julii.'

I couldn't tell whether it had been an intentional joke, or just the off-colour wit to which my brother was so prone. Either way, it sounded good to hear him speak even remotely normally. Lepidus seemed to think so too, for he smiled. 'Aemilia Sextia, then? She's not related at all, and she has a smile that melts the knees of strong men.'

Caligula snorted derisively.

'Well what about Servilia Sorana? Two husbands so far, with a get of seven children off them, and looking for love once more, so they say? Or Marcia Barbatia? Or Lollia Paulina? Now *there's* a possibility. She's a beauty beyond compare, is Lollia Paulina. Yes, she's married to the governor of Macedonia, but word is that she hates him and would be grateful to be freed of his yoke, and he likes his whores, so I doubt he'd take much persuading.'

Caligula finally stepped forward.

'Stop, Lepidus, I implore you, before you begin to suggest that I marry Livilla here. I care not who runs my house. You seem to know the women of the court better than anyone. Just pick one and send her to me. If she can live in a place like this, she can stay.'

I opened my mouth to argue, but Lepidus was shaking his head, and he was right. I could see that the discussion was over. My brother had retreated into himself once more, and a single tear on his cheek announced that he had returned to silent mourning.

'Then we will stay a few hours, open up the curtains and shutters, have the furnaces lit and the floors warmed through. And while we are here, I shall send some of our slaves to Albanum to the market to fill your larder with fresh, good food. If you must languish here in solitude, then you will do it healthily, in the sunlight and the warmth.'

Caligula looked as though he might argue for a moment, but simply spun and walked away into a different room. I turned to Lepidus and began to list the things I wanted to see put right before we left. And one slave was not good enough. I would find out later that the constant sobbing and the awfulness of the situation had driven the other few slaves to take their chances on the run. With only a maudlin master and no guards on the estate, who was to stop them?

My retinue put the house in order that afternoon and restocked it with food. We even tidied a little of the nearest gardens. During the whole time we saw no sign of Caligula, who had fled the enforced activity to mope somewhere quiet. By the time the sun began to descend, the place was at least liveable. I left half my slaves to help maintain the place and gave them a stern order that they would be expected to do as I told them and not my brother. I left Caligula's one remaining slave in charge. He had stayed when all the others left, and that had proved his worth to me.

I also left half the detachment of Praetorians to guard the villa and estate. They were given instructions to keep working on the grounds any time they were not otherwise occupied. And with an hour left till dark, we found my brother in the boathouse and bade him farewell, warning him that we would return in a few days.

We lurched and bounced back up the hill to the main road, and I looked across at Lepidus as we swung north once more for Rome.

'What was the idea of that list of women?' I asked, frowning, wondering at that odd look I'd caught back in the villa.

'Just jumping on your idea and trotting out a few suggestions,' he replied casually. 'You are right. We want to find him a wife, but it should be a suitable wife, given his last two disastrous marriages.'

'And so I ask again what the idea was of that list? Close family? Sluts? Hard-hearted women? And why Lollia Paulina especially? I had not heard she was dissatisfied with her husband. Why not leave *him* to select a wife?'

Lepidus shrugged. 'Your brother is lost in himself and cares little about such matters. He could no more choose an appropriate wife than he could hold a cup without shaking. Come, Livilla, let us return to Rome and begin the process of helping him heal. I will try and find him a wife, and you can put his household in order and make sure he begins to act human once more.'

I nodded my agreement, but I couldn't shake the feeling that there was something he wasn't telling me.

The next month was a busy time for Lepidus and myself. For *everyone* connected with my brother, in fact. Slowly, over the next two weeks, we encouraged him back to a semblance of humanity. By our third visit we had him shaved and trimmed, bathed and reclothed. By the fifth, he was eating meals with us and discussing small matters. By the seventh, he had signed the appropriate contracts to marry Lollia Paulina, agreeing a handsome little payment to her husband to free her of her current matrimony. While the couple did not seem to be as bitter and unhappy as Lepidus had intimated, there was none of the closeness of heart and misery at parting that I had seen with Piso and Livia, so at least I had hope that this woman might make my brother happy.

All our visits and our gradual edging of Caligula back into the world of men was extremely hard work and very trying. And as often as not when we left, he would backslide into misery. It was a laborious process and one I would never wish to repeat.

The wedding ceremony was held at the Alban villa, out of the public eye and with little in the way of celebration. And when we left him after our eighth visit, she stayed at the villa, and they began their journey as man and wife.

It was another half a month before we saw them again, just after the kalends of September. We had left plenty of time for their nuptials before we visited, but the summer was now coming to a close and Lepidus and I both had the feeling that a cold, miserable winter in this place might well undo all our hard work, and so we had come up with an idea. We put it to him on our ninth and final visit to the villa. Sitting at an evening meal with the emperor and his new wife, I studied the pair of them.

Caligula was starting to look more like his old self, though his earlier exuberance had gone, and he was much less given to smiles and humour than before. It seemed, from passing comments, that he and Lollia had involved themselves in the appropriate husbandly and wifely duties, but from what I could see before me there could not have been a great deal of enthusiasm to it. Lollia was pretty, certainly, and deferential and pleasant. There was just something indefinably . . . off . . . about her. I could not tell you what it was, but something was wrong. Something stood like a stone barrier within their relationship, and I did not think it was entirely Drusilla's shade.

'Come to Sicilia,' I said, suddenly, as though it were a thought I'd plucked from the air, and not the entire reason for our visit.

Lollia seemed to cheer at the idea, and I began to wonder if this miserable villa was the impediment ruining the relationship between them. Possibly. It would certainly ruin any relationship for me.

Caligula merely furrowed his brow as he nibbled on the pork in apple and *garum*.

'The procurator of Sicilia has been sending missives to Rome,' I added, 'seeking aid on matters of finance and organisation. It seems he came from a posting in Cisalpine Gaul and believes Sicilia to be backwards compared with his former province. The senate have been debating whether to send someone to oversee things, and our uncle Claudius is considering the matter. Why not you instead, brother? Vinicius would have done the job well, but he is still in Asia, and what better to relieve a struggling province's tensions than a visit from their emperor?'

I sat back, having lit the kindling, and watched the flames race through the beacon of Caligula's spirit. I have absolutely no doubt that he would have refused to go, even to leave the villa at all. He had no special love for Sicilia, and there were bound to be better men for the task than he. There was no reason he should agree . . . except for the idea that the senate were considering sending our unsavoury uncle Claudius. I knew that even through grief and ennui *that* would grab him.

Lollia Paulina almost jumped when Caligula clapped his hands together and agreed. He made no mention of Claudius or the senate, though I was well aware that they were what had decided him.

'A splendid notion,' he said, rubbing his hands together. 'A little sea air and travel will do us all good. And it will be seemly for Lollia and I to be seen together in public.' There was a strangely optimistic excitement to his actions that Lepidus took at face value. Me? I ignored the talk and the hands and watched his eyes. Whatever positivity he exuded did not touch them, and I saw in him largely a façade of acceptance covering his broken heart for the benefit of his family.

The spell was broken as we left the villa. There *had* been changes in Caligula – deep, heart-searing changes. Drusilla's death would never leave him and he would never again be entirely free of grief, but he was regaining his energy, as well as his determination to return to his empire. In wearing that positive mask, some of that optimism began to seep into the man beneath. So no matter what else came of it all, at least he avoided turning into another Tiberius.

It was mid September before we arrived in the harbour of Syracusae. We were on Sicilia for six days, and initially I thought we might have made a mistake when Caligula's first act upon arriving at this southern metropolis was to arrange grand and expensive funeral games there in honour of Drusilla, and to devote a new temple to her.

As the games were organised, the days passed by, Caligula still unable to become truly enthused with anything as the memory of our sister continued to plague him. Then, on the third day, something happened.

We were standing on the top of the seating stands of the small theatre by the impressive gymnasium, where some of the preparations for the funeral games were being made. Lollia and Lepidus were deep in discussion over some trivial matter, and I stood with my brother looking out over the great harbour below us. Three members of the *ordo* – the council of the city – were standing with us, albeit a respectable distance away, waiting to be of use, and members of the German Guard along with a full detachment of Praetorians stood in position around the complex.

'Busy port,' I noted. 'Much busier than Ostia.'

My brother nodded, and I saw his brow furrow as he paid attention to the great harbour below us, where once upon a time the famous Archimedes had employed an ingenious claw mechanism to destroy the attacking ships of the Republic. When the city had fallen, it had been a turning point in the wars with Carthage.

'It *is* busy,' he replied. 'Rather ridiculously so, in fact.'

We watched for a while as huge merchant vessels queued in the narrow harbour entrance, waiting for the previous ships to unload. A military trireme sat impatiently within the break-waters, oars idle as its trierarch yelled angrily at the merchant vessels preventing him from putting to sea. But those ships waiting in the entrance could no more move aside than they could climb over the stone moles to either flank, for many more awaited a berthing space as they sat outside in the choppy waters. I counted. Thirteen ships were waiting for a chance to enter the harbour and, unless something was done, they'd be there all night, for the arriving queue had snarled things up so thoroughly that no ships were able to depart the harbour and make room. It was almost farcical. I could imagine the officials of the port tearing at their hair in exasperation as they tried to sort things out.

'There are over a hundred ships in the harbour,' my brother said in disbelief. 'And only a few of those are actually loading or unloading. Most of them are jostling about waiting for a jetty or trying to leave. What in the name of unforgiving Neptune is happening here?'

We watched as the trireme actually began to move forward threateningly, as though it were planning to ram the side of the merchant blocking its way. I had the distinct feeling that the ship's trierarch might very well do just that if something didn't move soon.

It took me a moment to realise that something *had* changed. After two days of essentially playing the role of smiling emperor, nodding appreciatively as the local officials showed him things of interest but all the time really brooding on Drusilla and thinking about the games for her, suddenly, something had changed. The mask had slipped, but the face beneath was no longer grief-ridden and sour.

Caligula was *interested*.

'There's going to be a ship sunk down there soon,' I noted, gesturing at the trireme.

'Indeed. And I'm not sure I would blame him.'

My brother turned to the three councillors nearby and waved them over. They approached bowing, so that they resembled hunchbacked old men, and stood nearby in respectful silence.

'What is going on at the harbour? This cannot all be because of the games, surely?'

One of the ordo members peered over the wall, frowning in confusion. 'Majesty?'

'The harbour. The mess it's in?'

The councillor shrugged helplessly. 'It is a busy day. No, Majesty, this is not for the games. This is normal, if a tiny bit busier than usual. It is . . . what, the third day after the ides, Majesty? Then we are two days away from the city market, and that's when we get both the weekly Aegyptian grain ships in and the ones from Carthage, as well as the copper deliveries from the east and the lead from Mauretania on every fifth week. We're a busy harbour.'

My brother stared and scratched his head. 'It's *always* like this?'

'Weeeeeell,' drawled the councillor, 'some days it's better. Some it's worse.'

'Worse? *How*?'

'Well, if there's any kind of military operation going on in Africa or the east, we see endless resupply visits from the Misenum fleet plying to and fro. And on days when the big Italian cities are holding festivals, we see five or six extra cargo vessels full of animals every day. Some days it can be chaos. This is acceptable.'

Caligula stared at the man as though his head were spinning.

'This is *insane*. No harbour can operate effectively like that.'

'I'm afraid I'm told it has to, Majesty. Nine in every ten ships of goods delivered here goes off onto the Italian mainland and all the city gains is the harbour fees.'

'So most of this isn't even for your city?'

'For Syracusae, Majesty? Jove, no. Very little stays on Sicilia at all, but the extra journey around the west of the island to put into any Italian port drives up the price of transport by an extra day or two, so most merchants won't do it. And the currents in the straits between here and Rhegium are brutal. Only the military really uses the straits, apart from the braver of merchants. So all goods come ashore here and are taken to Messana in the north by cart, then ferried across the narrowest part of the strait. It's fair chaos up there, too, since neither Messana nor the villages opposite have the port facilities to handle it. Often the roads on this side of the island aren't much better than the port.'

Caligula was still rubbing his head and frowning. It was nice to see him actually concentrate on something, I have to say, after so long simply moping.

'So you gain very little from having everything so constricted?'

'Hardly anything, Majesty.'

'Can the harbour not be extended?'

The man shrugged nervously. 'We have asked the procurators before now, but the rocky shoreline makes everything difficult, and with Syracusae being one of the best defensive ports in the world, neither the governors nor the various naval commanders who have become involved have wished to see the place open up.'

The emperor nodded, and even I could appreciate the good sense in not ruining the world's most defensive port just to ease traffic.

'Then a new port must be built.'

'Majesty?'

Caligula reached out and grasped a piece of fallen limestone and used a corner of his toga to wipe the top of the wall clean – a desecration of the garment the great Augustus would have been horrified to witness. When the wall was clear and smooth, he began to draw a map of the region from memory.

'Here we are at Syracusae,' he noted, tapping a circle with his piece of chalk. 'This is the strait, narrowing as it goes. But shipping from the east and south could approach the coast of Italia without getting too close to the currents, if they made for, say, Rhegium.'

'But, Majesty, Rhegium has an insufficient port.'

'As I said, my dear fellow, a new port must be built. The coastline flanking Rhegium in both directions is flat and giving. Rhegium can be expanded to become a major port. It could take a great deal of pressure off Syracusae without endangering the precious loads. Perhaps we might even open up larger harbours in Puteoli and Ostia to allow for more transport, given the pitiful landings they currently bear.'

The three men from the ordo smiled slowly.

'It would be a great relief to all concerned, Majesty.'

'Good,' Caligula smiled. 'Before I head north once more I shall have the appropriate orders sent out. By next summer I want this situation resolved.'

'Thank you, Majesty.'

As my brother went back to looking at the harbour, I shuffled closer and leaned on the wall next to him.

'Rome needs similar attention, brother. Did you realise that?'

He turned to me with an expression of curiosity.

'Well,' I mused, 'the water supply is becoming woefully inadequate in places, or so I am told. It would benefit from the same kind of imperial attention you have lavished upon Syracusae.'

He narrowed his eyes with a mysterious smile.

'So, Livilla. You are not content to marry me off, drag me from my villa and parade me in public, but you would also pull me all the way back to Rome? I always had you marked as the independent one, and Agrippina as the manipulative one, but I suspect you have been taking lessons from 'Pina, yes?'

'That villa has served its purpose, Gaius. It is now haunted by the memories you took there. Leave it to be the tomb you made of it, and come back to the world. You have a wife, a purpose and an empire to rule. I could not let you follow Tiberius into his own little Tartarus.'

He laughed.

'Very well, Livilla. Once the games are done and I pay a short visit to Messana and Rhegium to confirm my plans, we shall return to Rome and you can hold me up to the public and make me rule again. Happy?'

For the first time since the day Drusilla died, I was.

XIX

THE CLEANSING FIRE

I shivered and pulled my thick wool cloak tighter, glancing up at the sky and expecting the first flake of a blizzard to strike me in the eye. Caligula, next to me, grunted distractedly. We stood near the crest of the Esquiline Hill, surrounded as usual by Praetorians but granted space to ourselves and positioned on a podium constructed hastily for the occasion.

The area was a vast construction site now. Gone were the many rickety wooden insulae, which housed the poor and rose into the air like timber fingers daring the gods to send the single spark that would ignite the entire city. Gone were the few larger houses with their extensive gardens. Oh, it had filled my brother with glee to discover that one such house that had been required to be purchased and demolished for the works belonged to the ever-difficult Senator Sabinus. He had been all the more gleeful that he himself had had nothing to do with the planning of the route, and that Sabinus had seen his house purchased out from under him – at a sadly deflated price – and demolished by designs of an engineer and by the order of the very senate of which he was a part.

We could all imagine Sabinus – currently serving as governor of Pannonia – hammering his fists on the walls of the governor's palace, raging over the unfairness of the matter and wishing beyond all else that he could lay the blame for his woes squarely at the feet of my brother. But he couldn't. Caligula may have set the overview, goals and rough plan of the project, but the details had come from engineers and administrators.

I peered into the dismal grey that threatened snow and made it difficult to see any real distance at all. Atop the rise, perhaps a hundred paces away, vast stone bridges carried into the city the water that kept Rome alive. The Julian, Marcian and Tepulan aqueducts rode one atop the other along one such great span of arches that marched for miles out of the city towards their pulsing sources. And now another bridge, grander even than the first, would file in from a similar direction, meeting the three ancient waterways, and then angling off towards where we stood. The Aqua Augusta would bring water from several powerful springs located high up in the Anio valley beyond Tibur. And the Anio Novus aqueduct would draw water directly from the Anio River itself downstream from there. The two would meet somewhere near the city and combine to travel along the same bridge, one atop the other to the spot at which I now stared.

From there the new aqueducts would pass through the scar in the city, where all the housing had been taken down and the ground scraped to bare rock, towards the grand cistern that was rising behind us, the height of ten men and constructed of five immense chambers. There, the water could be channelled off to increase the pressure in other, failing aqueducts. A vast improvement in water pressure would bring great relief to the city. It was ingenious, really.

You won't know it as the Aqua Augusta now, of course, but one must brush aside the name of the club-footed villain who eventually inaugurated it and remember that he merely stole the glory from my brother, whose sharp mind and generous soul began it in the first place.

It would be many years before the water flowed through those channels to relieve the citizens of Rome, but it was exciting to think that at that very moment, forty or fifty miles away, remarkable engineers from the legions were busy damming and channelling waters that would in time rush and gurgle down pipes with the gentlest decline imaginable to pour into the basins of the city. And all along that course, men were busy hollowing out the channels where they ran underground, carving tunnels through rock and preparing great soaring bridges to allow the water to cross valleys and dips.

All to bring it here.

And already more engineers were at work preparing the ground across the Esquiline for the last stretch of those arches. As I blinked in the cold grey, wondering how it all really worked, a soldier walked towards us with a *groma* – a surveying instrument the engineers use in working out their nuances. The man spoke to the Praetorians surrounding us and was quickly escorted into the emperor's presence. The legionary bowed deeply as he came to a halt a few paces away, two guardsmen standing at his shoulders looking fierce and suspicious. Caligula chewed on his lip for a moment and then jumped down from the podium and strode across to the soldier. Much to the surprise – and disapproval – of the Praetorians, he waved them away and gestured to the legionary.

'The work goes well?'

The soldier grinned with no sign of nerves, which surprised me. 'That it does, Majesty. Respectfully, I was about to make the last sighting before the lines are all in place, but I wondered if, this being mighty Caesar's project, he would wish the honour of making the final call before we begin work on the bridge.'

My brother's face split into a broad grin and he reached out, placing an arm around the legionary's shoulders. Despite the apparent lack of nerves in his voice, the man flinched at the emperor's touch and anxiety sprang into his expression. My brother, though, was already steering the soldier back whence he had come, walking with him and muttering about sighting lines and foundations. The Praetorians stepped respectfully aside, and my brother and his new friend stopped at the correct spot. The soldier passed his groma – a staff with a cross atop it that sports hanging lead weights from each arm, allowing lines to be sighted with accuracy – to the emperor, who took it, positioning it carefully at the last marked spot. Though I'd not heard him discuss what was needed with the soldier, and I certainly couldn't think of any time in my brother's past in which he might have learned the proper use of the groma, Caligula turned and sighted towards the new construction – the reservoir – and then trotted a few paces that way and turned, looking back the way he'd come, lining up the lead weights to his satisfaction. With a quick gesture, he told the engineer at the cistern site to move two paces to his left. Happy that things were in position, he nodded, and that indicated man drove his painted post into the ground to mark the final turning point of the aqueducts into the huge structure.

My brother sauntered back to the soldier who'd approached him, thanked him, and handed back the surveying tool, before unclasping the fibula brooch that kept his scarf fastened and giving it to the man with a smile. The soldier looked stunned, bowed deeply, and scuttled off to his next chore. Caligula strolled back to the podium and stepped up next to me again.

'Where did you learn how to use an engineer's tools?' I muttered.

'You would perhaps be surprised at how much spare time I created last year by not attending endless argumentative meetings of the senate,' he grinned.

'You'll have less time now you have a wife again,' I chuckled, somewhat brazenly, I admit.

I was surprised as my brother's expression darkened immediately.

'Is something wrong?' I asked quietly.

Caligula looked around as though making sure we were

alone. We were not, of course. We were in the middle of a busy construction site full of engineers and labourers, with a circle of Praetorians surrounding us. But the ambient noise was such that low conversation would be private anyway. Even Lepidus, who since Drusilla's death seemed once more to spend much of his time with us, was a dozen paces or more away, talking to a centurion. My brother leaned in closer.

'Lollia remains childless. I have done all I can, and I have come to the conclusion that she is infertile and totally incapable of giving me an heir. I am going to have her see the best physicians in the city, and I intend to visit the augurs to see what they say, but unless they somehow persuade me that I am mistaken, I intend to divorce her forthwith. She was the product of Lepidus' desperate need to drag me away from that villa anyway, not a serious choice in which I had had my say, and I feel she has been something of a mistake.'

'Are you sure?' I asked quietly.

'Yes. I am positive the augurs and the physicians will echo my own sentiments. Within the month she will be gone, back to her former husband if she so wishes.'

'And you?'

'I . . .' He drifted into silence for a moment, and I saw the old pain cross his expression once more. 'I shall be fine. The succession is still in place with Lepidus, despite Drusilla's passing. There will be time in future to find a wife who is suitable. But not now. This is not the time. I have been absent for some months, and now I need to spend time throwing myself into the role of emperor once more.'

'I agree. And it is good to see you back where you should be.'

My brother smiled, and I decided to leave him to it, descending the podium and making my way between the Praetorians to where Lepidus was waving off the centurion.

'Will you walk with me?' I asked as I turned back towards our carriage. Our old friend smiled and nodded, falling into step alongside me as we strolled. I wrestled with the decision over the privacy of my brother's words, and came to the conclusion that Lepidus would be among those in whom Caligula would confide.

'Gaius is going to divorce Lollia Paulina. He is convinced that she is infertile.'

Lepidus gave me an odd look that I couldn't quite work out, as though he were at once surprised and awkwardly unmasked.

'She *is*, isn't she?' I said. 'She *is* infertile.'

He had the grace to look uncomfortable, and not a little guilty into the bargain. Still he said nothing.

'She is infertile,' I repeated, 'and you knew about it. Have you found out but recently, or have you known all along?'

'I found out a matter of days ago,' Lepidus replied with a weary sadness that somehow came across as blasé, 'through chance conversation with her ex-husband's brother, who is a senator in the city.'

But I was shaking my head. I had known Lepidus a long time and I could read past that open expression to the locked vault of his mind behind. He was lying, and we both knew it.

'You *always* knew,' I said accusingly. 'You foisted off on my brother a woman you knew would never bear him children. I am so utterly stunned that you would do such a thing when you know how close the subject of a son is to his heart.'

'He needed harmless fun to pull him out of his misery, Livilla, and that's what Lollia is. She cannot bear him a child, but she is pretty, young and . . . energetic. I knew she would do him good, and she has. You can't deny that. I was not thinking of children at the time, but of the urgent necessity to pull my friend out of his self-destructive grief and get him back into the world. I would do it again.'

It was a persuasive argument. I wasn't sure how I felt about it. But whatever the case, whether it had been right to wed my brother to an infertile plaything rather than a future empress, my brother had been correct. The time had come to send Lollia away and move on. I would have to see what I could do in terms of a better choice of wife.

I still felt strange making use of the honours my brother had done us. I was slowly becoming accustomed to sitting in the imperial box at the races, often without the emperor himself, but some places seemed sacrosanct, to invade them somehow wrong. To be a woman, no matter how noble, no matter how strong, in a place of honour among a sea of men was jarring.

The curia – the senate house of Rome – is often thought of as a single great chamber where old men argue out the minutiae of our lives, but that most important of all public structures is in truth a complex of three such places linked by a decorative veranda across their frontages. To the right is the hall of seats where the senate discusses the public matters. To the left is the records office where the minutes of every session are kept. And tucked between the two is the atrium of Minerva, a wide decorative courtyard surrounded by a roofed portico, where the senators can work through private matters out of the eye and earshot of both the public and their fellow politicians.

And I was strolling towards it in the wake of my brother.

In truth, I was making for the meeting chamber, rather than the atrium. I didn't really want to attend, though I have to admit to a certain curiosity as to how relations between the senate and my brother had progressed since he had been attending sessions regularly once more. But the main reason I was here was for support. Caligula had long since commanded three seats be set beside his own, one for each of his sisters, beneath the altar of Victory facing the rows of chairs that would seat the senate. This had been instituted upon his initial proclamation of our new rights, but we had never occupied them, for Caligula himself had almost immediately withdrawn from senate business.

Now, with Agrippina closeted away with her boor of a husband and her new child, and with Drusilla among the honoured dead in the great mausoleum, I felt the need to occupy at least one of those chairs today, as my brother intended to announce the initial preparations for a new campaign to subdue and Romanise those troublesome German tribes beyond the Rhenus that our father had once so valiantly fought. It was a grand announcement to make on the second anniversary of his accession.

The crowd cheered as we crossed the open space of the forum, past the fig, vine and olive trees and towards that veranda. My brother still rode high in public opinion, the Roman people throwing flowers and praise at his passing. Caligula was preceded by his lictors with their ceremonial stick bundles, and I followed on close behind, a detachment of Praetorians in their white togas trooping to either side of us to keep the crowd away from their master. It was a bright blue day, with a touch of frost in the air, but the sun had already burned off the white and left a chilly yet beautiful world.

Despite the oddness of what I was doing, everything felt good. The people were in love with their emperor, the army adored him and would relish his announcement for the potential spoils and glory it promised, and even the senate was once more in communication with him as he returned to the sessions. I should have taken my warning from that. In my life's experience, one thing I have learned is that when everything feels most settled and happy, *that* is the time to be watchful for disaster.

We reached the veranda and the lictors peeled off to the side, collecting in a small group, for they had no place in the senate's buildings proper. The Praetorians similarly would take up positions outside the complex, waiting for my brother to reappear, when they would escort him to his palace in preparation for the great anniversary celebrations that would follow.

The senators were busily filing into their chamber on the

right in preparation for the session, and I started to make my way there, but faltered as my brother made instead for the adjoining courtyard.

'Go on,' he urged me. 'I will attend in a few moments. I am required for a number of minor matters first.'

I nodded as the Praetorians began to take up position a respectable distance from the doors, while four of them escorted me to the main chamber's entrance.

I paused before entering, some preternatural sense warning me, though I wasn't sure what about. Senators bumbled past me, nodding their heads respectfully to the emperor's sister. The Praetorians waited impatiently, wanting me to enter so they could move into their assigned positions.

Something was wrong.

I had even turned back from the door before the shout came.

My brother's voice. A cry of alarm.

I was moving before the soldiers who accompanied me, but I was hampered by my stola and palla, as well as my shorter stature, so in the thirty paces it took to reach the doorway to the atrium of Minerva, all four men had passed me, joined by six more from their positions nearby. All the Praetorians and lictors had reacted immediately, though most had drawn a protective line around the veranda, aware of the potential for overcrowding in the doorway.

I reached the corner and turned to look inside and my heart froze.

As a young girl of the house of Germanicus, with the blood of the Caesars flowing through my veins, I had heard time and again the tale of my great forebear's demise. Of that dreadful moment when the deluded republicans fell upon their dictator and sheathed their blades in his flesh twenty-three times as he attended the senate.

Today was the second anniversary of my brother's accession.

It was the Ides of March. What was unfolding in the courtyard could not possibly be coincidence.

My brother was struggling in the centre of the open space with three men, all wielding knives. He was fighting valiantly, for Caligula was no slugabed and had trained in the arts of the soldier, but even then, with three opponents, he was hopelessly outmatched. He was managing to hold two off well enough, but as they kept him defending himself, the third would repeatedly try and place a blow, and only the favour of the gods had kept my brother alive thus far. He had taken cuts to his arms and shoulders and one to the neck that, had it been any deeper, would probably have been lethal.

He wouldn't be able to hold them off much longer.

Eight other assassins were facing off against the approaching Praetorians, buying their comrades enough time to kill my brother.

I watched in horror as a knife was plunged towards Caligula's eye. He ducked just enough to take a long scrape of the blade along his hairline. My brother yelped, but his searching hands found the arm wielding the knife and with some instinct born of Mars he grabbed it and rammed it down against a knee that he brought up, snapping the wrist.

I lost sight of him then as the Praetorians engaged the other assassins, desperately fighting their way to their master. I moved back along the wall to one of the high windows into the atrium and pulled myself up until I could rest my elbows on the stonework to hold my weight, peering inside with dreadful tension tugging at my heart.

The Praetorians were making quick work of the knife-wielding senators in front of me, their longer swords giving them an unmistakable advantage. Caligula, beyond them, took another blow to the forearm and a glistening red line sliced through the folds of his toga. But although he was becoming fatigued with the constant effort in his heavy toga, he was now facing only two men as the third edged away across the courtyard in tears, clutching his shattered wrist.

There was a rear door to the atrium, though it was traditionally kept locked. It was open now, and Praetorians were pouring in through it, circumventing the delaying assassins as they ran to the emperor's aid. The man with the broken wrist died almost instantly, three swords ripping out his life through his chest, his armpit and his face as he stared in shock at the soldiers blocking his escape.

The fight was over in moments. The newly arrived guards butchered one of the men fighting my brother, and the other, realising that their plot had failed, pulled back, stumbling away from the scuffle, his face snapping this way and that looking for a way out. There was no such thing. Both doors were disgorging furious armed Praetorians, and the last of his companions in the doorway had just fallen.

Realising he was alone, the man stood straight and proud, Roman to the last, and plunged his blade into his own neck, yanking it in agony across his throat, sealing his fate and saving him from the inevitable interrogators.

Caligula stood at the centre of the atrium, shaking with exertion and with ire. Not, I think, with fear. That moment had passed. I saw his eyes, and there was no room for fear in them, filled as they were with an unassuageable anger. Suddenly, despite his wounds and breathlessness, my brother was all business. He turned to one of the soldiers – presumably an officer, though I have never understood how one could know when they were all attired in similar togas.

'Collect the knives.'

'Sir?' the officer frowned in confusion.

My brother's composure was close to cracking. I could see him struggling not to shout, and his voice came out of thin lips in a low, menacing hiss.

'Collect the knives. Count them. There were more than this.'

I looked across the courtyard. I had not seen any more, but then, while the fight first raged, my view had been blocked by the secondary scuffle just inside. And the rear door had been open, hadn't it?

As Praetorians moved to block off the doors once more and I shifted into a more comfortable position, seated on the windowsill, the officer and two of his men began to gather up the weapons of the assassins. Caligula had two more of the men line up the bodies to one side of the courtyard, their faces on show. I recognised several by sight, if not by name. Senators and nobiles of Rome: new would-be *liberators* murdering a tyrant.

As my brother walked along the line of the eleven men, the three Praetorians approached him with armfuls of blades.

'How many?'

'Sixteen, Domine,' the officer confirmed and my brother nodded, counting again the bodies on the ground. 'Five escaped.' He reached out and picked up one of the blades in the pile in the officer's arms. Longer than the rest, it was a gladius rather than a knife – a weapon of war expressly forbidden within the sacred bounds of the city. But it was not *that* which had singled it out for my brother. The sharp, gleaming blade of a soldier, the hilt of this sword was formed of ivory in the shape of an eagle. I remembered such a blade on Capri two years earlier, hanging at the side of Helicon, the old emperor's bodyguard who had served as a chamberlain these past two years with no real distinction to his credit or detriment.

'Come with me,' Caligula rumbled.

As he and the Praetorians strode with dreadful purpose towards the rear door of the atrium, I realised what was coming and dropped from the windowsill, scurrying along the veranda and into the senate hall.

The curia was abuzz with murmured rumour and talk. Many senators were on their feet, gesticulating as they wondered what all the commotion was about. Almost the entire senate was in session. That is unusual at any time. Five long rows of chairs sat on ascending steps to each side of the central space, and most chairs were occupied, suggesting perhaps two hundred and fifty members present.

My speedy move was fortuitous, for I entered the great chamber just as the Praetorians behind me sealed the entrance, shutting the great bronze doors with a deep booming clang. The room dimmed and it took moments for my eyes to adjust, though there was plenty of light pouring in from the large, high windows.

At the rear of the curia, to either side of the altar of Victory, were twin doors that led to various ancillary structures. Two Praetorians appeared through the one on the right and slammed it shut behind them. The one at the left remained open until my brother appeared in it, his bearing regal, his toga ruined. There was a collective intake of breath at the sight of the wounded emperor, his toga soaked with blood, fire in his eyes. He walked with slow purpose through the hall to his seat, but he did not sit.

All murmuring stopped and you could have heard a feather fall to the floor in that dreadful silence. I swallowed nervously and willed my brother to rein in his temper. If being blatantly insulted in the senate had sent him off into a year of poor relations and petty revenge, what might an attempted murder bring? Caligula was always generous to a fault and the most loving and protective brother a sister could desire, but his temper was as hot as his smile was warm. Visions of a bloodbath floated through my mind. I could imagine a sanguine lake spreading across the floor, flowing down those stepped seats in endless cascades, bodies piling up and two and a half hundred heads mounted on spears around the building.

I willed as hard as I could for common sense and mercy.

I got it. After a fashion, anyway.

'Stand up!' Caligula said, his voice quietly threatening though carrying like a cry through the absolute silence. There was palpable confusion and concern, and none of the assembled senators rose, though a few were already on their feet.

'*Stand*,' my brother said once more, and this time the sheer menace in his tone was unmistakable. The entire room rose to their feet nervously.

Behind Caligula, Praetorians began to emerge into the room until an entire detachment of them were with us, following which the door was shut, sealing us all in. Suddenly the huge room felt a great deal more enclosed and suffocating, and unpleasantly like a tomb, albeit a crowded one.

'Search them for blood,' my brother growled, and the soldiers began to filter along the lines, looking each senator up and down for tell-tale crimson spots on their pristine white togas.

Slowly, the tension heightening with each terse examination, four men were singled out by the Praetorians and hustled from the rows out to the central floor. My brother stepped forward, wiping the blood from his face with the white toga on his arm. Trickles immediately ran back down from the wound on his scalp.

'Four of you.' His face twisted into a sneer. 'And unlike your traitorous co-conspirators who at least had the courage to stand their ground and die like men, you fled to preserve your skin. For your cowardice I will see to it that each man who lies in the atrium next door is given appropriate rites and a coin for the ferryman. You four, however, shall be taken before nightfall to the Gemonian Stairs and executed like the uncommon criminals you are, so that the loyal people of Rome can tear apart your bodies and take your bones for souvenirs.'

The four men began to shout desperately, pleading for their lives, but the Praetorians were there immediately, forcing the conspirators to one of the rear doors and out of the chamber, the heavy wooden portal crashing shut behind them.

'Is it coincidence, perhaps,' Caligula said in the uncomfortable silence that followed, 'that my dear uncle Claudius is not among your revered number today?'

I started and a chill ran through me. Claudius was not there? I could hardly countenance the notion that our own uncle would have been one of the conspirators. Yet that sword of Helicon's was unaccounted for, and the former bodyguard would have no right to be in this room. So if not Helicon, who had wielded a blade in memory of Tiberius?

There was no evidence, of course. Claudius, if he was guilty, would weasel out of any accusation – he was an expert survivor, second only to my brother. And Helicon, for all his brutality, was not subtle or clever enough to have planned or even helped plan something like this, and would not have had access to the curia anyway.

'It occurs to me,' my brother went on in a low tone, slowly turning to take in the assembled nobility of Rome, 'that if a man wanted to examine the strata and ranks of villainy in the world, he could do no better than peer around the assembled faces of this august body.'

There was a moment of shock. Despite the arrest of four of their number, the others here had felt safe in the knowledge that they were not suspected of being part of the conspiracy. But being innocent of that one plot clearly was not enough to save them from my brother's disgust.

'Villains. Each and every one. You sit here, fat and purulent, living well off the backs of the soldiers who protect you, the citizens who bake your bread, the boys who massage your feet and the freedmen who administer your lands and affairs. And you vie and plot and seethe and conspire like children playing a foul game.'

The senate were staring at him now, to a man, not used to being insulted by anyone, let alone a man as powerful as this. Many were staring nervously at the soldiers who kept them shut in this increasingly tomb-like chamber.

'And most of the time it does little harm to Rome, for you plot against one another, wheedling out imperial favour in support of your case against a peer who you dislike enough to sleep with his wife and steal his house. And that affects only your own houses and your own honour. It matters not to the man who bakes your bread, or the soldier who protects your lands, or the freedman who does your accounts. And it matters not to me.'

He took a step towards the nearest row of standing senators and one of them flinched, stepping back and becoming entangled with his chair. In better times, as he fell in a muddle, there would have been a chorus of hooted laughter. Not so that day.

'But something like *this* changes everything. This body is sick. It festers with discord and greed and malice and wickedness. And a sick body needs the physician's knife. It needs to be bled.'

That vision of a room of bodies and a lake of blood swept into my thoughts again.

'I shall purge this senate; heal the body of the sickness. No more will the most degenerate and malevolent of all Rome's populace make its laws and sit in hallowed comfort.'

He turned and pointed at a senator, who recoiled as though a snake had been thrown at him.

'Those of you who mismanaged the public roads? Yes, I know who you are. Vinicius' investigations into the cursus publicus a year ago turned up some interesting information. Those of you I know to be guilty will pay back every denarius the city lost through your embezzlement and poor handling, and a further ten per cent on top of that to be spent upon the public works of the city.' The man at whom he was pointing started flapping his mouth soundlessly, but my brother glared at him. 'Be grateful you are paying for your greed in coin and not blood, and silence those lips before I change my mind.'

He turned, singling out another face.

'Gaius Calvisius Sabinus . . .'

It came as no shock to hear the name of Sabinus, so long my brother's nemesis in the senate. The man who had decried my brother's munificence so often simply stood rigid and cold.

'Sabinus, who rushed back to Rome the moment his governorship of Pannonia was up, determined to make his presence felt in the senate once more. But I have had a quaestor in Pannonia with you. No, you didn't know that, did you? And you did not know that I was aware of your corruption and extreme embezzlement of that most important province, which holds back the tide of the barbarian world. And you would be surprised at the things I have come to learn about your wife's subtle and uncivic crimes. Between the pair of you, I make the total count of fallen heads to be seven and the sums owed the treasury in the hundreds of thousands, without even listing your crimes under the morality laws of my esteemed predecessor Augustus. I suggest that when I open that door you scurry home, sell everything you have and donate heavily to the treasury before you flee the city, for when I come looking for you I will show no mercy – you who have denounced me and held yourself as a paragon of virtue while you undermine everything we do.'

I could see the truth of my brother's words in the look that slid across Sabinus' face. Exile was his only true hope, though I doubted, with my brother in his current mood, whether he would even reach a ship. I remembered Macro at the navalia, falling to his knees in a torrent of blood. No, Sabinus' future was bleak and brief, I was sure.

'Junius Priscus!' he barked, spinning to single out another man, who blanched. 'The catalogue of your transgressions is simply too long to list here, but I think it would behove you well to take your own life as a good Roman before I release the details to at least four other men standing in this very room who would tear you apart for your crimes against them.'

Priscus was already forgotten as Caligula gestured again.

'Gnaeus Domitius Afer! Your proposal of an inscription in my honour is heart-warming. Or at least, it would be, were it not for the fact that I know it for an attempt to mollify me now that the details of your illegal land acquisitions are a matter of record.'

'Seneca?'

The saggy orator and writer stepped forward with a frown, clearly unaware that he had done anything wrong.

'I am aware of your speaking against me among your peers. It may not be a crime, and you will leave here a free man, but be aware that I am watching you, and my men will uncover any wrongdoings on your part.'

He stepped back to his chair and gestured expansively at the room as a whole.

'Those proscriptory records collected by my predecessor that were so publicly burned in the Velabrum two years ago? I'm sure you all remember it well, given how many of your names appeared on those dangerous records. Let it be known that another copy of those documents exists within the imperial archive. I shall set good, incorruptible men to looking over those records, and any wrongdoing that proves to be more than mere internecine squabbling will be dealt with as it should have at the time. Upon my accession I sought a new age of trust and I washed aside your transgressions in the belief that they were a symptom of Tiberius' wickedness. Now I see that your transgressions were more a symptom of the corruption of the senate and that I was foolish to give such a dishonest and unscrupulous body of children any level of trust. I shall not make that mistake again. This session of the senate is cancelled and before a new one is called its body shall be weeded of vice.'

The main doors were thrown open. Nobody moved. The hypocrisy of my brother's accusations of untrustworthiness while he had kept a copy of the records was not lost on me, nor I suspect on anyone else present, but the emperor was on the warpath and it would be a foolish man who drew attention to himself that day.

'Go!' shouted my brother. 'Run to your homes and prepare, for the cleansing fire is coming.'

The senate fled.

XX

WIDENING THE RIFT

Everything had changed once more on the Ides of Martius, that most portentous of dates. The world felt different. The golden glow had gone. The polish had worn off. The people still loved my brother. Jove, they probably loved him more than ever, for he played to their desires. The man in the street knows the senate only as a distant bunch of fat old oligarchs who lord it over common folk, and seeing them put in their place for the attempted murder of the emperor? Well, that went over surprisingly well with them. And it did little harm to his standing with the army, though a few senior commanders of senatorial rank had to be recalled from key positions, of course. But the common soldier held the emperor in high esteem, and the senate in little.

In the row that followed the events of Martius, senators seemed to fall every day, proscriptions became the norm and the bulk of those accusations that had been levelled in the time of Tiberius were carried through mercilessly to their invariably unpleasant ends. By the closing days of Maius, when the senate sat, just twenty-one members attended. The pressure placed upon the nobility of Rome was immense and the senate reeled. Yet who could blame Caligula? Was it revenge? To some extent, of course it was, but it was also self-preservation. We had learned harsh lessons in the houses of Livia and Antonia and the palace of Tiberius, and my brother had finally decided to rid himself of any malicious individual who intended him harm, which was, of course, an increasing number with every death announced.

I and others, such as Lepidus and Vinicius – who had returned from Asia the following month – tried to persuade him towards leniency as often as we could, but my brother's blood was up, and so the blood of others would flow. Having spent two years showing his generous side, the depth of his anger was suddenly revealed. I would stress again, though, that this was directed solely at the senatorial class, and munificence and love was still lavished upon the common people and the military.

My husband, with whom I enjoyed a somewhat muted reunion given the strain and gloom-laden mood of the city, clearly feared for my brother. He worried that in ever widening the rift with the senate and picking off their numbers daily he would turn the most powerful in Rome against him, and I could see in his eyes his disapproval of Caligula's violent means, no matter what he actually said.

'Herennius Pollio?' Lepidus said on one occasion, his eyes sliding down that day's trials.

My brother simply grunted in reply as he perused yet more of the deadly documents in his possession.

'Pollio is a poor choice, Gaius,' my husband said quietly.

Caligula looked up sharply. Few people would dare address him without title or honorific. Both these two men were those who could generally do so safely, and my brother waved the comment aside dismissively.

'He is popular and largely harmless, a writer and orator with no designs on higher power and no known argument with you,' Lepidus put in.

'Moreover,' Vinicius added, 'he is one of the few senators who has actually supported your cleansing of the body. Would it not be politic to ignore his minor misdemeanours in favour of retaining the support of him and his friends?'

Caligula looked up once more and reached out, snatching the document from my husband's hand, none too gently. A quick scan of the words and he thrust it back to Vinicius.

'They are minor misdemeanours, and his punishment is correspondingly minor. There will be no blood, but I will cut out every hint of the canker from the senate, whether they call me friend or foe.'

Lepidus and Vinicius exchanged helpless looks. 'If you ruin him, as this is sure to do, it will only make you more enemies,' Lepidus said with a sigh.

'I no longer make enemies,' Caligula grunted. 'I simply reveal them, for they lurk behind every curtain in this pox-ridden city.'

My husband and our old friend both turned to me where I sat reading, and I simply shrugged. There was nothing I could do. I no longer had that kind of influence over my brother and, if I had, I knew that even the gods could not change his mind now.

Pollio did not die, and in the event he proved to be hardy enough to weather that storm. But in that courtroom, his support for my brother crumbled to dust.

Even beyond the senate, those who had achieved positions of prominence at court were removed, with notable exceptions such as my husband and our old friend Lepidus, as well as a few others like Vitellius and Vespasian who cleaved to my brother's side and helped him wreak havoc through the ranks of the senators. Those positions important to the running of the empire left vacant were given to freedmen who would be forever loyal to my brother, grateful for their elevation. Indeed, old Helicon, the former bodyguard, who had been cleared of all involvement in the plot due to his sword having been stolen and holding a more than sufficient alibi, retained his position as chamberlain. One such new freedman, Callistus, swiftly became an important figure in the court. To this day I could not tell you what precise position he held, but he was rarely far from my brother, toadying and wringing his hands gleefully like a moneylender counting his dues. Callistus I immediately took a dislike to in the same manner as I'd felt with Ennia. I tried to tell my brother, but he was in no mood to listen, especially as Callistus was instrumental in every new attack on the senate my brother made.

I was sickened by the reaction of the senators to my brother's change in policy. To some extent it validated his depiction of that once august body as obsequious, self-defeating, honourless and cowardly. By Jove, that was how they began to seem. There was little sign of a backbone among them, and I suddenly found a grudging respect for the late Sabinus who had at least stood his ground and argued with the emperor. There was no longer such strength in evidence. The ranks of the senate were neatly divided into three. One group fawned over and supplicated the emperor, acting like eastern catamites or little more than slaves in their desperation to stay off the proscription lists. Another group fled the capital in the hope that distance and obscurity would save their necks, retiring to country estates and keeping their heads down. And the third? Men like Vitellius and Vespasian, wielding the blades that filleted the senate for Caligula. In essence there was little value to any meeting of that once-august body now.

Still Vinicius, Lepidus and I continued attempting to steer my brother towards a course of resolution rather than conflict. Not that we disagreed with his general stance, mind you, just his rather indiscriminate methods. The senatorial class had tried to kill him and had proved to be every bit as corrupt and cowardly as he had intimated. But despite that, the danger of alienating the entire elite of Rome struck some of us as too important to overlook. If one pushes a flexible object hard enough, eventually it will bounce back. Caligula disagreed – egged on by the powerful freedman Callistus and those few vicious senators who surrounded him – stating in confidence that the people and the army would provide ample support and that the senate could go drown for all he cared.

With the advent of Junius, the proscriptions were more or less done with. All the records from the days of Tiberius had been worked through and those senators who wished to sell out their peers for a hint of imperial favour had done so. Little more than a quarter of the original senate remained. According to the records in the tabularium, when my brother came to power the senatorial rolls had counted among them five hundred and seventeen names. By Junius, they held less than two hundred, and many of those were absentees, cowering in their rural villas.

I had half expected my brother's anger to diminish then, with the Ides of Junius, and so many of his potential enemies, gone. But what had begun as burning rage had now become cold determination. What had started as a conflagration tearing through the ranks of senators had turned into a calculated campaign to ruin the survivors' lives.

Once again we argued for a path of reconciliation, especially Vinicius, who seemed almost desperate to recreate the Caligula of two years earlier, full of hope and benevolence. Once again, Caligula was adamant. And if we argued too hard, he took us to the Temple of the Divine Caesar in the forum, where he had kept the shredded, bloody toga he had worn that fateful day on which he had almost followed our illustrious ancestor to Elysium. As long as that bloodied toga remained in the temple as a reminder of what the senators had tried to do, his revenge would never be complete.

A few days into Junius, my brother announced a gladiator auction to be held at the amphitheatre of Statilius Taurus on the Campus Martius. Invitations had been sent out and Vinicius had shown me the list with a sense of dread: twenty names, each of them belonging to the loudest remaining voices in the senate, each of them the pater familias of one of the great families of Rome and each rich by anyone's standards. We had decided to attend against the faint possibility that we might prevent the bloodbath we all feared. After all, the unprecedented rights given me by my brother allowed me a place at the amphitheatre, and my husband remained one of Caligula's favourites.

The public were not granted access, and the twenty senators were shown to seats at the lowest tier surrounding the arena. My brother eschewed the imperial box, choosing to seat himself close to the action, and Vinicius and I joined him, sitting on the other side of him to his escort – the oily Callistus and our old friend Lepidus.

There was none of the general chatter that such an event might be expected to spawn. None of the senators present were here by choice. Invitations they may have been, but in the current climate of Rome, a senator would be extremely foolish to turn down the emperor's invitation. And so twenty men, most of them of advanced years, sat silent and nervous, wondering what fresh hell the emperor had cooked up for them.

I have to admit that I was rather surprised myself when an auctioneer came out and gladiators were trooped out one after another to display to the buyers. I had expected some wicked trick, not a genuine auction.

Then, as the sale began, my brother's purpose gradually became clear. A *retiarius* from Bithynia with his trident and net was first on the block. He was a minor champion from some provincial hole out east and had survived three fights thus far in Rome.

The bidding began at a thousand sesterces – a steal even for an untried, freshly trained fighter. Several of the senators began to perk up. It looked as though this might be a good day after all. The sale moved on moment by moment as three of the attendees vied with one another until the price reached eighteen thousand sesterces, when a wide-faced fellow by the name of

Cornelius Cotta announced that the bids were too rich for him and sat back. The remaining two bid for a few more heartbeats, pushing the price to twenty thousand, and it looked as though the older man with the wispy hair had won.

'Twenty-one thousand,' my brother called.

The two senators who had been vying looked up at Caligula in surprise. The emperor was the man *selling* the gladiators, after all. It took a moment for them to realise their trouble. Watching my brother nervously, the old man croaked, 'Twenty-two.'

The other man, brave as he was, sat back.

'Twenty-three,' Caligula said.

The old senator, crestfallen and sick with the realisation of what was happening, croaked out, 'Twenty-four.'

'Thirty-four,' Caligula said.

The old senator's eyes widened. 'Majesty . . .'

'The bid is to you, Valerius.'

The old man sagged. He was going to lose to my brother, because he was going to win the retiarius. The alternative was unthinkable.

'Thirty-five.'

'You spend thirty-five on oils for your fat backside, Valerius,' my brother snorted derisively. 'Forty-one.'

I lowered my eyes. He was toying with the man. I heard Valerius in hopeless tones offer forty-two. Fifty from my brother. Fifty-one from Valerius. I couldn't watch. Caligula let the old senator off the hook at eighty-five thousand sesterces. It was not that the man couldn't afford it – there was no doubt in my mind that any of the attendees could have spent that on every lot going and still walked home to a comfortably full coffer – but it was the cruelly toying with them for no reason other than to humiliate them that unsettled me.

And I cared not whether they were humiliated, really. But again and again I came back to the idea of what happens when you push something to breaking point. Would the senate break, or would they rebound with equal force? Caligula had embarked upon a dangerous course, and he seemed intent on steering directly into the maelstrom. Vinicius' face as he squeezed my hand was full of concern. My brother was going too far again, and we all knew it.

The morning progressed in much the same manner, the senators present paying well over the odds for each lot, the imperial treasury becoming healthier by the moment. When I looked up here and there through proceedings, I could see hopelessness, embarrassment and disappointment in the assembled faces. But I could also see resentment. I had to bite my tongue not to shout out and try to draw an end to the auction.

And then the worst thing possible happened. An old man – Saturninus, one of the more venerable and respected of the remaining senatorial class – fell asleep. A half-dozen expressions passed across my brother's face. He wasn't quite sure what to make of this insult. My breath caught in my throat as his cycle of expressions stopped on malicious glee. Saturninus was a close friend of two of the senators who had met their end in a bloody heap in the atrium of Minerva, and I could see my brother's thoughts tentatively connecting the old man to the conspiracy. I felt a cold sickness deep in my soul at the leering malice on my brother's face. This was not the sudden flashes of ire to which he had always been prey, but something new. Something dreadfully unsettling.

'Sit still, all of you,' Caligula hissed across the arena. Reluctantly, obediently, all did just that. The *lanista* announced the next lot – a *scissores* gladiator from Gaul. He was a big man with flame-red hair and his smooth gleaming helmet tucked beneath an arm laden with enormous muscles and a network of scars. This Vetrius, as he was seemingly called, was some sort of hero from Narbo and was already impressing the crowds in the capital.

'Do I hear ten thousand?' asked the auctioneer.

Silence reigned until my brother frowned earnestly and cleared his throat.

'Did you not note Saturninus' nod?' Caligula prompted the man on the sand. The auctioneer's brow furrowed and he glanced up at the snoozing senator. The old man's head was lolling with every deep breath. He cleared his throat nervously. 'Ten thousand to Senator Saturninus.'

'Fifteen,' my brother called.

Silence fell once more. The auctioneer paused uncertainly but, catching sight of the look on my brother's face, waited for Saturninus' head to dip once more and announced, 'Twenty to the senator.'

I felt queasy again. This was ridiculous – which was, of course, the point.

I listened. 'Twenty-five.'

A nod. 'Thirty.'

'Fifty.'

A nod. 'Sixty.'

'Seventy.'

A nodded eighty.

Time passed in that sizzling arena, the sun beating down and baking those present as Saturninus unwittingly spent his fortune on a red-headed Gaul. Finally, as we neared time for a break and were all beginning to feel pangs of hunger, one of the other senators near Saturninus took his life in his hands and surreptitiously nudged the old man, stirring him and bringing him from his sleep.

'Ah, a final bid,' my brother chuckled.

'The bid stands with Senator Saturninus at nine million, two hundred and twenty thousand sesterces,' the auctioneer said, his voice cracking with a combination of embarrassment and sympathy.

The old man blinked awake, murmuring in confusion. The man who'd woken him leaned forward and whispered in his ear.

Saturninus fainted.

The rest of the proceedings were tame by comparison and not long after noon the auction ended, a group of very unhappy senators trudging out to their litters and guards, Saturninus supported by two of his friends, his knees seemingly unable to support him.

Four days passed in which I remained tense, half expecting some sort of backlash from his treatment of the senators. Once again, his depiction of them as self-serving cowards seemed to have hit the mark, for all they did was cower and mutter as they paid their enormous dues. Saturninus, it seemed, had taken to his bed ill, leaving a son of the same name to head the family from a secondary property out of the city.

Things took another step into the bizarre a few days later.

I was returning from a jaunt into the countryside with Vinicius on an afternoon in which the heat was already stifling and the perpetual dust cloud that engulfs the city in the summer was choking. We, along with a few muscular hirelings to ward off potential bandits, had been travelling the Cremera valley up towards Veii, me in an open carriage with my body slave attending, Vinicius on horseback beside us. We had eaten a small meal on a grassy sward and returned to the city reluctantly after sampling the fresh country air to the north.

Our house was far from small, but it was not equipped with all the facilities of an estate, and so our carriages and horses were stabled with Caligula's blessing in the large imperial palace.

As we rattled in through the arch and I came to a halt and dismounted, I was surprised to see Caligula there, tying ribbons in the mane of his favourite midnight black stallion, Incitatus. It was not entirely an unusual thing to find him doing, for my brother loved his horses, and Incitatus in particular was close to his heart. He was often to be found doing a stable-hand's job, brushing the beast down or feeding him treats. But that was usually early in the morning or late in the afternoon. At the height of a Roman summer day, those in the city with money were uniformly to be found in gardens or in the baths, relaxing away from the heat and the dust. Or these days, in my brother's case, tormenting senators to the applause of the common folk.

'Dear sister,' my brother smiled, 'and friend Vinicius. Welcome back. I had not expected you to return yet, though your arrival is fortunate. Perhaps you will accompany me on a short errand. Lepidus is coming too, but his mood is foul this afternoon.'

Lepidus emerged from the stables, a groom leading his chestnut mare. His face did indeed appear sour. I resolved to enquire as to why later, for now Caligula was already gesturing for the stable hands to turn my carriage around. Moments later we were leaving the palace once more, my brother on his favourite horse, Lepidus and Vinicius on their own steeds, my carriage rattling along behind and two dozen Praetorian cavalrymen keeping pace with us.

Down the hill we clattered, making for the eastern end of the forum – the new vestibule my brother had built linking his palace to the western forum was almost complete but not yet viable for leading horses and carriages down. We passed the pond and the market below the Temple of Venus and Rome and began to ascend the Esquiline Hill. I had no idea where we were going and, indeed, had no idea where we were when we seemingly arrived.

A large domus on the hill fronted onto the street directly with no shops built into the façade – the mark of a very wealthy owner who values his privacy. The wall that encompassed a clearly sizeable garden marched off to both sides, encircling an oasis of green amid the civic sprawl. A man with a pronounced nose and receding hair, wearing an expensive toga, was sitting on the edge of a decorative stone fountain opposite, a dozen slaves crowding around him. He looked distraught, and I felt myself becoming slightly on edge at the sight.

'Do you know Proculus?' Caligula asked conversationally as he and the others dismounted. Vinicius crossed to help me down from the carriage and I stammered out a negative, uncertain what was going on here, but sure that it boded ill for someone.

'Gnaeus Acerronius Proculus,' Caligula explained, gesturing to the distressed man at the fountain, who was swatting away slaves as they tried to help. 'He was the last consul Tiberius appointed. A true follower of the old bastard. He's been conveniently absent from senatorial proceedings ever since, hiding in some rat hole in Sardinia. But he had the good fortune to return to Rome just as I was weighed down with excess money and looking for property.'

My mind raced and I stared at the domus.

'You bought this house?'

'Indeed,' Caligula smiled. 'I happened to have just over nine million sesterces lying around, you see. Oh, I didn't pay *that* much. In fact, I think I got it at rather a steal. In confidence, I'm not entirely sure Proculus really wanted to sell it, but his final price was just too low for me to refuse.'

'So you bought his house cheap?' Lepidus grunted. I read the undercurrent in his words. The house had been taken more or less by force and meagre coin given in compensation. This was little more than punishment of an opposed senator in the form of forced land purchase. And Proculus was looking almost sick with the deal.

'What do you need another house for, Gaius?' I asked, half bitterly, half in genuine interest. My brother rarely did anything without there being a good – if sometimes warped – reason behind it.

Caligula turned a smile on me.

'Oh it's not for me. You know how I so enjoy lavishing gifts upon those who deserve them.'

As I stared in confusion, the dreadful ever-present Callistus emerged from the house.

'It's ready, Domine.'

Grinning, Caligula handed the reins of Incitatus to the freedman, who led the tall black beast in through the atrium, his hooves clopping on the priceless marble threshold and the intricate mosaics within. I continued to stare.

'What is happening, Gaius?'

'The stables on the Palatine are full, Livilla. And Lepidus just bought a new horse for me, so I have to make room. Incitatus deserves the best, and Proculus has prime grazing land, once the fountains and gardens are ripped out.'

'You're turning it into a *stable*?' I stared in disbelief. He may not have paid nine million sesterces for the place, but it seemed unlikely he had paid less than a hundred thousand at least. For a *stable*. Of course, this was not about housing his favourite horse so much as utterly humiliating one of the few remaining influential senators.

'Of course,' he laughed. 'Given the record in office of that old debaucher on the fountain over there, I'm thinking of naming Incitatus to the consulate next year. He will probably do at least as well, and he has almost the same sized nose, though perhaps a little bit *too much* sense.'

Caligula cackled at his own joke and Lepidus snorted. Vinicius shot me a helpless look and I shrugged. How far would my brother go? Soon there would be no senate, for those who were still healthy would have been financially reduced to the point where they no longer met the criteria to be viable for the body that had once ruled Rome unopposed. What would happen when the last chair in the curia was emptied? Could Rome exist without a senate?

I thought back to the many times my brother and I had

listened to the tales of Julius Agrippa, Antiochus of Commagene and Ptolemy of Mauretania. Rulers of the east and the south in the old mould of the Macedonian kings. *Absolute* rulers. Divine kings. Yes, a land and its people could be ruled without a senate. But could *Rome*?

'And now,' my brother said, dusting his hands together and turning from the domus, 'I have a mind to turn to matrimony. Heirs do not sire themselves, after all.'

I blinked at the sudden change in subject. Perhaps a wife would help tame him, though. And time had marched on since his last disastrous escapade into marriage. I nodded, hoping that this new pursuit would leave him with no time to petrify and torment the senate.

I barely noticed the sour look on Lepidus' face deepen.

XXI

TREACHERY AND SECRECY

The brides of Caligula had come and they had gone. Junia Claudilla, a woman for whom my brother had felt genuine affection, if not love, had been torn from him through dreadful chance in childbirth – or perhaps through the curse of the Julii, if her father had the truth of it. Livia Orestilla had been an unwise second choice, born of augury and the desperate need to prove the notion of a curse wrong. She and her husband now languished, probably blissfully happy, in exile on some distant island. Lollia Paulina, more or less foisted upon him by our friend Lepidus, had played the part of empress well, and had even helped drag my brother from his deep melancholy. But her apparent inability to give him a child had led to swift divorce.

While my brother could be impetuous, especially in the matter of his spouses, I have to say that the case of Milonia Caesonia showed no such impulsiveness. It seems that, although none of us knew of it at the time, Caligula had already been involved in a very private little dalliance with the lady Milonia for some time. He had been bedding her since early Iunius at least, and probably a month before that. So when he had announced his intention to seek a new bride on that same day we watched his horse acquire a palace and almost a consulate, he was in reality just announcing to us the next step in a relationship that was already burgeoning.

Milonia Caesonia was . . . well, it seems malicious of me to speak such, especially since I liked her a lot, but she was not a *pretty* woman. In fact, standing alongside some of the men of the Praetorian Guard in their togas it would be hard to say who was less feminine. She made me, with my plain dress and hair and boyish habits, seem the epitome of femininity. Her family were of modest origins and given very much to the martial pursuits, and that blood flowed in the female line as strongly as in the male. Her more senatorial half-brother, Corbulo, was already a celebrated military officer, whom I had last seen consorting with Agrippina's husband at that dreadful banquet on the Palatine. Milonia had a plain face and hair that remained unruly and untameable no matter what her slaves tried. Broad-shouldered and thick-limbed, her hips were narrow and her breast large, much the contrary to the shape of a good Roman matron, and a form that should bode poorly for childbearing.

But she had been married before to a praetor who had died the previous year, and had given her former husband three children, all of whom were strong and hearty. If ever there was a woman selected for her ability to produce an heir, it was Milonia.

But the thing was that for all her manly looks and forthright manner, she was one of the most engaging and pleasant people I have ever met. Ten heartbeats into any conversation with her, and none of her physical shortcomings made any difference. She was a plain body containing a beautiful soul. And even more spectacularly, it became obvious to all of us that she was utterly smitten with my brother. Her half-brother had come back from Dalmatia where he had been governing early in the summer, had seen what was happening in the senate and had done the most astoundingly brave thing. He had visited the emperor and spoken to him man to man, noting that he approved of a cleansing of the senate, which had been over-corrupt and oligarchical, but warned him to take it no further. The emperor had incised the wound and removed the rot. To continue to cut away good flesh could only harm Rome. He vowed his loyalty to the emperor, but with the reservation that he would never act against the good of Rome on behalf of its master. When I'd heard this, I feared Corbulo had been parted from his head and sent down the Gemonian Stairs. Conversely, his straight talk had impressed my brother, who had apparently said that 'if Rome had five hundred Corbulos in its senate there would be no need for an emperor'. The war hero was made consul the next month.

Thus was the family of Milonia raised from relative obscurity to become a leading family in the empire. It also heralded, at Corbulo's suggestion, a cessation of the systematic destruction of the senate, at least for a while.

A second thing became clear as the end of the month of Augustus and the festivities for the wedding of the emperor approached: Milonia was pregnant. Moreover, the bump that had begun to show on her proclaimed the child to have been conceived not only before the marriage, but some *four months* before. While that evidence made their secret trysting public knowledge, my brother did nothing to hide the fact from the world. While such a thing was commonly a matter for embarrassment, the wife usually sent off to deliver in a secret place with a distant relative, my brother was so clearly thrilled at the prospect of a child that he showed Milonia and her burgeoning bump off to everyone he found. And the prospect of an heir and a settled succession brushed aside concerns of customary etiquette among those who might more vocally disapprove.

The wedding was held in the palace, which was lavishly decorated in preparation. Each of my brother's weddings had been very different. His first: a public affair tailored by Tiberius and shared by his sisters. His second had been swift and laden with prophetic images, attended by the very best of Rome's upper circle. The third had been a rather private affair during those dark days following Drusilla's death. But this fourth was perhaps the oddest.

It had every aspect one would expect from a society wedding at the highest levels. Except the guests. A few of those senators who had cleaved to Caligula as those instruments of terror he had wielded against their fellows were present. And Corbulo and the rest of Milonia's family, of course. And that was the sum total of the patrician guests. In fact, there were not enough of that senatorial rank to fill the standard ten witnesses, and the two Praetorian prefects were required to join them to make up the numbers.

The palace seemed to be filled with freedmen. Well-dressed figures who had almost all been slaves less than a handful of years ago were now celebrating with the emperor, toasting him with raised cups and drinking among their betters as though there was nothing odd or socially unusual about it.

It irked me to see that unpleasant Callistus at the heart of matters, but my brother found him effective and useful and the freedman had his hand in every pot of honey from the Aventine to the Campus Martius. So much authority and responsibility had been heaped upon him, in fact, that a second freedman by the name of Protogenes had become his sidekick, forever under our feet. I wasn't yet sure what to make of Protogenes, though while I would never say I trusted him, he did not immediately repel me the way his superior had.

One interesting figure included was Helicon. In the aftermath of the senatorial plot against my brother, the former bodyguard who had so faithfully served Tiberius had been cleared of all involvement, but his unhappiness and embarrassment that his famous blade had so found its way into the hands of a would-be murderer was such that he took a vow on the altar of Apollo to protect Caligula, and he now stood as proud behind my brother as he had behind Tiberius, playing his old role once more, though without a high window and a parade of victims.

At the ceremony itself, I stood beaming with pleasure to see my brother and his new bride so clearly happy at their mutual lot. It seemed a good end to a long, hard matrimonial road for both of them. My eyes occasionally slid to other guests as the auspex felled the ewe and began the grisly business of examining the whim of gods within the gut – I am far from squeamish, after what I have seen in my eventful life, but I have never relished watching the evisceration of animals in this manner. I occasionally glanced at Lepidus, whose expression flipped back and forth between rigid, forced joy and dark brooding. At other times, I would peer across to Agrippina and her pig of a husband, Ahenobarbus, who had relented and allowed his wife the freedom to attend her brother's wedding, fearing the wrath of the emperor if he refused. Agrippina held her one-and-a-half year old with her left arm and occasionally lifted him to her chin and coddled him when he began to stir and become unsettled – which seemed to be often. Her right arm, I noted, was not used in any of this and when she shifted slightly at one point and her sleeve rucked up, I spotted with sour anger the purple-grey bruising that seemed to coat it. Her husband truly was loathsome. I resolved to once more ask Caligula to do something about it, though I knew he was powerless to do so, for he had offered before to annul their marriage, and Agrippina had refused. Few people could refuse my brother, but headstrong Agrippina remained one of them.

Vinicius squeezed my hand and my attention was drawn back to the ceremony itself as the auspex pronounced what he found to be good and that the gods would bless the union – a relief to my brother, who put great stock in such things. I could never truly imagine great Jove stooping to the unpleasant task of making his will known in the slippery, sticky entrails of an animal. Why would the great god who had through his infinite power aided Regulus and the army of the Republic in so easily destroying the Samnites not find a less messy way of making his will known?

'*Ubi tu Gaius, ego Gaia*,' Milonia breathed happily, signifying the end of the ceremony proper.

As you are Gaius, so am I Gaia.

Ancient words spoken in formula, but rarely so meant as that day.

'*Feliciter*!' shouted the auspex, and the call was taken up by the assembled attendees.

Half a hundred heartbeats later we were in that grand courtyard where that party had taken place a year and a half – and two empresses – earlier. Much like that previous occasion, when my brother had challenged Jove in a somewhat obscure Homeric joke, the afternoon was balmy and dry and it was with a touch of trepidation that I stepped into the square, aware of how quickly storms can pull across Latium.

The banquet and entertainment began and the guests, highborn and low, began to enjoy themselves. One odd consequence I might note at the increased elevation and responsibility of freedmen was that the slaves of the imperial household seemed greatly happier and worked harder than ever to please their master and his guests. After all, some of those they were serving had been their equals not so long ago, and each slave in the palace saw his potential future in the cups they filled.

Vinicius kissed me on the hand as we passed through into the courtyard, promising to return shortly, but hurrying off to speak to Lepidus on some matter of business or other. I was left on my own, which suited me. I was often on my own, and I was most comfortable there. While I loved my family and being close to them, and I had even come to realise through our growing passion and closeness that I had come to truly love my husband, it is only when one is alone that one can think objectively.

I spent some time watching the happy couple. They did, indeed, seem to be happy. And the various freedmen fawned about them until my brother chuckled and playfully swatted them away as though they were flies buzzing around him. I watched the freedmen for a while, trying to weigh them up, but they all seemed rather miscellaneous except for Callistus, who I still disliked intensely.

And because I was alone and my view objective, I picked up on something that I don't think anyone else present could have done. As I scanned the crowd, my sister had sought out Lepidus, pressuring he and my husband to end a heated discussion. While Vinicius stalked away, Lepidus seemed shadowed and resentful, his face twisted into a scowl. Agrippina was unreadable. She was ever an able player of roles, and her mask only came off when she decreed it. But her innocuous placidity was one thing that sparked interest in me that day. It was simply *too* innocent. Agrippina was always at her most dangerous when she appeared least so.

My curiosity piqued, I kept my eye on them over the next hour of the banquet. Even as people moved about and viewed entertainment, spoke to the emperor and his new wife, and even as Vinicius returned to my side and chatted away about this and that, I watched the figures of Agrippina and Lepidus.

If I hadn't known better, I would have thought the pair of them were having an affair.

Lepidus had been devoted to Drusilla his whole thinking life, though, and in the year since her passing, he had not once looked at another woman. It seemed his desire for matrimony had died with his wife. And Agrippina was too clever by a mile to cuckold her brute of a husband, especially when my brother had offered her a divorce from the man and she had refused. She would use him and eventually throw him away once she had wrung from him every bit of title, deed and inheritance for her son – for I had concluded that this must be her plan.

So why the strange, almost flirtatious looks the pair were sharing?

I failed to enjoy the rest of the day.

It was pure chance that I happened across a scene that changed my life utterly. I was in the palace on the Palatine on a breezy autumnal morning. Vinicius was off with Vespasian, who was trying to divine the secrets of my husband's administrative successes to apply to his own position as *aedile* in charge of street cleaning, and I was looking for my brother. The Praetorians I had questioned at the entrance had told me he was inspecting his new annexe, and I'd decided to find my way there and see the latest work for myself, but the additions were unknown to me and I was easily turned about. I soon found myself in an unfamiliar part of the palace – an area more for slaves and workers than for the imperial family. I'd been there once, during one of the soirées my brother had held in the palace, but it was still unfamiliar territory, and oddly uncluttered with life that morning.

I was strolling down a corridor that was painted masterfully to resemble an arbour full of vines and birds when I heard the voice. Oddly, the first thing that struck me was the silence through which the voice cut. The palace was *never* silent. Even if you found a secluded spot, the background hum of life in the building was always there. But not on that morning. For some reason I had stumbled upon a spot with no guards and no slaves.

Just that voice.

Agrippina's voice.

You might ask why it was a surprise to hear her there. After all, we were in the emperor's palace, and she, like me, was the emperor's sister. I frowned as I worked out the timings, but I was right.

It had been a little over two weeks since the wedding of

Milonia and Caligula, and my brother had urged Ahenobarbus to stay so that Agrippina could enjoy some time with the family. That mean bastard of a brother-in-law stayed for as long as he deemed politic, but as soon as he felt able to scurry off without incurring the emperor's wrath, he did so. That had been four days earlier, and Ahenobarbus had returned to one of his favourite villas at Tarracina. As he left, he had relented to my brother's polite 'request' and allowed Agrippina and her son to stay a few more days, citing a need to tend to business interests as a reason for his own leaving. Our sister was permitted to stay, but he wanted her back at Tarracina by *comitialis* day, and Tarracina was a two-day journey by carriage. That meant that in order to return to her husband on time, Agrippina should have been well on the road by this morning. In fact, she should have been somewhere around Lanuvium on the Via Appia, many miles to the south. We had bade her farewell the previous night so that she could get an early start.

And yet here we were, in the late morning, and I could hear her voice, clear as a bell, if rather quiet, susurrating through these lonely chambers.

Something was definitely out of place, and my instincts told me to keep quiet. I paused in that beautiful corridor and listened. I could not quite make out her words, for she spoke in soft tones, and her speech was further confused by the burbling and chattering of young Lucius Domitius – her son, who we girls had nicknamed Nero after our lost brother, whom he was already beginning to resemble. There was also the occasional murmur of a male voice, so low as to be barely audible.

There is a moment when you know something is wrong and before you can even identify or define the problem, your senses know of it. Your skin chills slightly, your heart and stomach flutter, your mind races, and the fine hairs at the nape of your neck and along your arms rise to the breeze. It is the gods' way of warning you to pay attention, or so Drusus used to tell me when we were young. If only *he* had listened to the warning. Perhaps things might have been better had I not done so, but I doubt it.

I reached down and quietly removed my soft leather sandals, holding them together in one hand by the rear strap and gathering up the loose folds of my stola with the other. Thus prepared, I padded almost silently along the corridor, following the sound of my sister's voice.

The whispers became louder as I slowly turned a corner, peeking one eye around the stonework first to check the passage was clear. I crept quietly towards the sound and the hairs on my neck, which had begun to lie flat once more, suddenly leapt to the alert again, for that second voice spoke, slightly louder, and this time I recognised it as that of Lepidus. A few moments later, I approached a side door carefully. I gripped my shoes and stola and risked a momentary peek around the corner.

The room was some sort of storeroom for furnishings. Half a dozen couches were stacked to one side, as well as numerous chairs, a few low tables, cupboards, chests and the like. I recognised much of the room's contents as the extra furniture brought out for the various great occasions. I had probably reclined on one of those couches and placed my cup on one of those tables at more than one banquet within these halls. The room smelled musty and unused, as is common in storerooms that are only emptied on rare occasions. The idle qualities of the chamber and similar surrounding ones contributed clearly to the silence and emptiness of this part of the palace.

Agrippina and Lepidus stood in the room's centre, little Lucius Domitius scurrying around under chairs and among the stacked furnishings, giggling and clattering about. As luck, good or ill, would have it, I happened to peek at the room's clandestine occupants at the very moment that Agrippina and Lepidus closed in a tight embrace.

My eyes widened as I drank in the awful scene, and then quickly ducked back in case they saw me. I wanted to scream.

What were they doing?

I tried to tell myself the whole scene was perfectly innocent. There had been no kiss to the embrace and both of them were fully clothed, after all. They were brother-in-law and sister-in-law. They were family. Is it so unseemly to embrace family? Even secretly? In hidden places? When one party is by rights supposed to be some twenty miles away by now?

I could no more convince myself of their innocence than I could kiss Lepidus myself.

But then, there had been no kiss.

Lepidus did not love Agrippina. That I would stake my life upon. He had only ever loved Drusilla, and we all knew it. And Agrippina was not foolish enough to dally with Lepidus unless she had the best of reasons. Neither of them would tryst together for simple romance. So what was this about?

Their words began again as I listened, and each one thudded into me like an arrow to my heart.

'What would the public think of the wedding, though?' Lepidus said quietly. 'It would appear that we were making your husband a cuckolded fool.'

'Ahenobarbus is less popular than the Syrian flux,' Agrippina snapped nastily. 'No one, from the senate to the cleaners of the *Cloaca Maxima* would give a fig for his happiness. I have what I want from him now, and he can rot for all I care.'

Somehow, without any confirmation, my instincts – honed by those years of treachery and secrecy on Capri – told me that the consuls Maximus and Corbulo, who I had seen with both her and Ahenobarbus, were what she wanted. I shivered. Damn, she was clever.

'And Milonia?' Lepidus retorted. 'She *is* popular.'

'Accidents happen all the time, brother. You would be surprised how easily a wife can pass from the world, especially in the difficult later stages of pregnancy.'

My eyes widened. How could Agrippina be so callous? I had always known her for a schemer, but this was something wholly different.

'She will have to go at the same time as your brother. If there is any delay, then her sons could be proclaimed to the purple by the senate, and once that is done, we will find it very difficult to put forth our own case for succession. Timing is crucial.'

I could hear the nerves in his tone, but Agrippina was cold, cool, confident.

'Get a grip on yourself, brother.'

'Stop calling me brother!'

'Until such time as you become husband, I will call you brother, for I always have and it is safer and more sensible to maintain the façade until the very last moment. Our union is the stuff of dynasties. You bring legitimacy and prestige as the extant heir of Gaius. I bring a boy of imperial blood to secure an ongoing succession. The family of the Julii will not be tainted by the low, peasant blood of that woman.'

I was reeling.

Agrippina and Lepidus, conspiring to kill our own brother, who had so looked after us all. Who had freed Drusilla from her unhappy marriage so that Lepidus could have her at last. Who had made Lepidus his de facto heir. Who had granted Agrippina, along with Drusilla and I, rights previously undreamed of for the imperial women. And they would repay him with an assassin's blade?

I fought against believing it.

Lepidus was our friend. Perhaps the closest friend Caligula had ever had. Closer even than Julius Agrippa. Second only to his poor beloved Drusilla. And Agrippina? She was our *sister*. Had she not suffered alongside the rest of the children of Germanicus?

How cold was her blood? I could see how it had happened in those moments, though. How Lepidus, suddenly faced with being ousted from the dynasty and cut out of the line, having already lost his love, had been adrift and angry and in the darkest of places. And how Agrippina, scheming for the future security of her infant son, had persuaded the lost Lepidus towards this most despicable of plans.

My attention was drawn back at the sound of names.

'. . . because the consuls will be with us. The senate will side with the consuls when they support us.'

Maximus I knew little of, so I could hardly say what I thought of his motives. But his co-consul, Corbulo? The general was a staunch supporter of my brother, and an outspoken, forthright man. He was the sort of man to openly challenge an opponent over his beliefs, not to sneak around in the dark and stab them in the back. Moreover, the emperor's wife was his half-sister. She was family, and it was said that their family was as close as our own.

'As close as our own'. *There* was bitter food for thought, given the morning's revelations.

I heard another name as my mind churned: Gaetulicus. It was a familiar name, from long ago, and it took me a moment in my horrified, fuddled state to place it. A close friend and associate of the dreaded Praetorian prefect Sejanus, who had barely escaped the proscriptions following his death. An untrustworthy name if ever there was one.

What should I do? I could stand and listen longer – perhaps more detail would be revealed. Perhaps I would learn something even worse? But, no. There was only one door to the room, and sooner or later the occupants would leave. And if they caught me listening in at the door . . .

I shuddered and turned to pad off as quietly as I could, but Fortuna was not with me.

As I turned, the sandals in my hand slapped very gently against the wall. It was not a loud noise – barely audible at all under normal circumstances, but then these were *not* normal circumstances. The voices in the room fell silent, and for a moment the only sound at all was the burbling of young Lucius Domitius as he played among the chairs.

Then a hissed exchange, and footsteps.

I ran.

Heedless of sound, I ran back along the corridor.

In my panic to get away, since Lepidus would be faster than me given his longer legs and less restrictive clothing, I took the wrong turning at the end and found myself in an area I had not previously visited on my wanderings. I contemplated running back to the corner and righting my course, but Lepidus' footsteps had become a run now, and he was close. I could hardly turn and go back, for I would run straight into his arms, and if Lepidus could contemplate the death of his oldest friend, of what value was *my* life?

I ran on through unfamiliar rooms and corridors, my bare feet slapping the marble of the floor.

I was panicking, and I knew it. I was working on pure instinct and reaction and without a conscious plan, I would inevitably end up in disastrous trouble. Lepidus was gaining on me. His footsteps were louder than ever as he pounded across the marble, aware that his deadly secret had been revealed to someone, though not yet who that someone was.

I had to find my way back to an area that I knew. I had gradually curved to the right as I ran, so I should now be heading in the direction of the Capitol or the Velabrum. A strange scent of resin and timber and fresh paint greeted me, and I realised I was close to the new work area, with the vestibule that descended to the forum.

I could follow the smell and it would bring me to the more inhabited area of the palace.

But would I manage before Lepidus caught up with me? He was so close!

I turned a corner and almost fainted on the spot as I ran full pelt into a figure, knocking him back against the wall. My heart pounding, I stared, wild-eyed and panicked.

Callistus. That unpleasant freedman who served my brother was pressed against the wall with a frown of concern. He opened his mouth to ask a question, but I got my words out first. Through heaving breaths, I managed to stutter, 'Danger . . . escape . . . brother . . .'

He seemed to understand and, despite the bizarreness of our meeting, he grasped my wrist in a vice-like grip and ran, dragging me along the corridor. Two turns later, he ducked into a side room, yanking me in behind him and closing the door quietly. I tried to breathe another question, but he put his finger to his lips to silence me. We huddled like lovers in a dim, windowless room as we listened to Lepidus' pounding feet pass the door and pause at the end of the vestibule for a moment before turning and disappearing off into the distance. Once I could hear only silence, I pulled myself from Callistus' grasp and turned. I did not like the man, but he had almost certainly just saved my life.

'Domina,' he whispered. 'Who was that?'

'A usurper. My brother is in danger. Can you take me to the emperor?'

Less than a quarter of an hour later, Callistus showed me into a grand chamber. My brother was standing at a wide window in his new complex, looking down upon the busy life of the forum.

'Dear Livilla, you look a fright,' he smiled, turning as we entered.

My heart was thundering, and I realised in that moment that I had a decision to make. Could I so easily condemn my sister and our oldest friend to a traitor's grisly demise? There was certainly an argument that they deserved it, but perhaps there was still a way . . . Maybe I could speak to them, persuade them from their chosen course. If I could buy them time, they could repent of their decision. But how could I?

The consuls. And the old friend of Sejanus. I would sacrifice them to buy a second chance for my family.

'A plot, Gaius,' I rushed out, and then fell into a chair, breathing heavily. My brother's smile slid from his face as he realised how serious I was. He glanced at Callistus, who nodded gravely. For a moment I felt ashamed of the way I had condemned the freedman simply because I did not like him. He had saved my life and now, with no true evidence to support my accusations, he was backing me as I spoke to my brother.

'A plot?'

'I overheard conspiracy,' I managed, my breathing still laboured. 'A blade for your back.'

Caligula's brow knitted and he sniffed loudly. 'The senate? They wouldn't dare after last time.'

'Not the senate,' I replied, breathlessly. 'The consuls.'

'Maximus? *Corbulo*? You are mistaken, or perhaps imagining it.'

'No, brother. It's true. And old Gaetulicus. That friend of Sejanus? I heard his name too.'

'It's beyond credibility,' Caligula frowned. 'Corbulo? I'm married to his *sister*. His family will inherit the purple because of me. And he is a man of honour. I cannot credit this as being truth.'

'She *was* being chased, Domine,' Callistus put in. 'And she was in fear of her life. I am inclined to believe her.'

'But these are not fat old senators with a grudge,' Caligula murmured. 'These are men who have shown me their utmost support, who owe their very positions to me. How could they be so foolish?'

'Foolish or not,' I hissed, 'it is the truth, on the name of Minerva I swear it.'

Not the *whole* truth, but a part of it, certainly. If those three fell then the plot would presumably fail. Perhaps Lepidus and Agrippina could be saved.

'I still cannot believe it,' my brother said.

Callistus cleared his throat. 'You have nothing to lose in detaining them, Domine. There are experts in the Guard who could extract the truth from them.'

'Torture my brother-in-law?' Caligula barked out a hard laugh. 'My wife, I think, might be a little put out.'

'Then Maximus at least, Domine.'

'And this Gaetulicus,' I added. 'A friend of Sejanus could never be trusted.'

'Gaetulicus is in Germania,' my brother replied with a frown. 'I cannot simply have him rounded up. He is governor there, with command over the most battle-hardened legions in the empire.' As if some great plan had been revealed to him, one eyebrow cocked as he started to pace, tapping a finger in the palm of his other hand. 'He controls the strongest contingent of all Rome's military. Moreover, they are the legions upon whom I would naturally count in times of trouble. They were the men of our father, and their love of Germanicus has always made them most loyal. If Gaetulicus has swept them out from under me . . .'

He turned to Callistus, suddenly business-like.

'Send for the Praetorian prefects and tell them I want Maximus and Corbulo arrested immediately, and have word sent to the ex-consul Galba. He has been assisting me in early preparations for my planned campaign across the Rhenus. I fear we will be marching for Germania ahead of schedule.'

As Callistus nodded a bow and hurried off, my brother turned to me.

'Thank you for your warning, Livilla. Senators and generals and consuls and praetors might conspire against me, but family is the most sacred of bonds, is it not?'

I simply could not answer that. Not with the fresh memory of Agrippina and Lepidus in that room. If he knew who was truly behind this new threat, the knowledge might just break him.

XXII

DISGRACED

The following two weeks were among the most uncomfortable in my life. The consuls had been rounded up that very afternoon. Corbulo had not denied his involvement, though he had informed my brother in his most regretful tone that he had not been party to plans of murder, especially of his sister and brother-in-law, but he *had* been party to some conspiracy to secure the succession, not wishing to see the children of Milonia's first husband on the throne, for he believed the man to have been a scoundrel. Despite everything, there was something about his honest-appearing confession that led my brother to mercy and, since Milonia so begged for clemency for her brother, Caligula brushed aside his anger and the plan of execution, instead removing Corbulo from office and sending him into retirement. Maximus barricaded the doors of his chamber as the Praetorian Guard came for him and, seeing no hope, threw himself upon his sword. Thus did the two consuls pay for their parts in the matter.

It quickly became clear, though, that they were at best peripheral to the plot, and not central. My brother plied me for information as to whom I had heard, but I claimed not to have seen anyone – just to have heard voices I could not identify. He was frustrated with me, but could do little to press the matter. He was certain someone else was behind the plot and almost had Corbulo tortured to reveal more, until his wife begged him tearfully not to do so.

That left Gaetulicus as the only man who could reveal more, and who had not yet answered for his part in the plot. Caligula had Corbulo's sword – a priceless blade granted him as a prize by Tiberius – torn from him and put in the Temple of Mars Ultor. It was joined by the still-bloodied blade of Maximus, pulled from the consul's own gut. Vinicius had noted rather tastelessly that soon every temple in Rome would house a relic of a plot against my brother, remembering the bloody toga in the Temple of the Divine Caesar. But the swords given as an offering to Mars 'the avenger' were a statement to the world, as was my brother's vow to add Gaetulicus' blade to the pair.

And so we set off for Germania to bring to justice the third of the triad responsible for the plot, or so my brother believed. It cankered my soul to know that in the carriage that followed his horse two more of his would-be assassins travelled in state luxury. Caligula had insisted on taking his family and his close court with him. Helicon, Callistus and Protogenes travelled north, as well as Vinicius and myself, Lepidus and Agrippina, along with the two Praetorian prefects, Stella and Clemens, the old soldier Galba and a unit of cavalry. We moved north as fast as any army ever travelled, our force consisting of the bulk of the Praetorian Guard and a unit of regular cavalry. The Praetorians travelled light, leaving their campaign gear in Rome.

Throughout the two-week journey Lepidus and Agrippina, sharing the carriage with Vinicius and myself, continued to flick careful, calculating glances at me and spoke guardedly. Word had spread in the court that the plot had been uncovered because I had overheard unnamed conspirators talking, and the two such plotters in the carriage regarded me somewhat carefully all the way north. I had, in the intervening time in Rome, approached the door of either my sister or my brother-in-law more than a dozen times, thinking to reveal my knowledge of their plot and beg them to step away and deny any involvement. That I never once actually knocked or spoke was born partially from a total inability to see how to approach the subject but mostly, in truth, through the fear that they would do away with me as a potential witness to their evil. And so I sat, tense, through that long journey.

We travelled along the coast of Italia and then inland, heading for the great peaks of the Alpes and the high passes that led through Raetia towards the great River Rhenus and Germania beyond. Wherever we went, surprised councillors tried to welcome us to their towns, the unexpected imperial visits a great honour. And we left them all unfulfilled as we hurried on north into Raetian mountain lands that no sensible merchant leads a caravan through so late in the year.

Beyond the Alpes, at Argentorate, the fast-moving column, which had travelled so quickly that harassed slaves had to be sent ahead each night with barrels of water to wet the road and suppress the cloying dust, met with part of my brother's still-assembling northern campaign force. We passed through Mogontiacum, where the governor's palace was, only to learn that Gaetulicus was further north, consolidating his forces. We travelled on.

We arrived at Ara Ubiorum at the end of September and with a force numbering perhaps ten thousand. It must have been odd on several counts for my sister, since she was coming to confront her co-conspirator alongside the man she had planned to kill, and oddly this was the very city of her birth in the days when our father had campaigned in these lands. A quarter of a century ago these hard northern legions had revolted, trying to put Germanicus on the throne when old Augustus died, but our father had remained loyal and talked the army down from their mutiny. Now, it seemed all too possible they were repeating their actions against that man's own son.

There was no sign of resistance as we reached that northern

frontier fortress. The Fourteenth Gemina legion was encamped within the walls, while the Sixteenth Gallica and the Ninth Hispania lay camped outside. It was a sight to behold, I have to say. As a woman, war is not my place, and I had never seen such a vast array of men and horses, weapons and tents. Added to the ten thousand we brought with us, Germania became a sea of armoured figures to my eyes.

Whatever Gaetulicus was doing, or had intended to do, it seemed that his legions were not prepared for our arrival, or perhaps were, but were unwilling to stand against us. Our column halted outside the open gates of Ara Ubiorum and the duty centurion approached the emperor and bowed deeply. He seemed nervous and deferential, which sat at odds with his scarred, grizzled appearance. He welcomed the emperor to Germania and to Ara Ubiorum and regretted that the senior commanders and the governor were not present. Had they been aware of the emperor's imminent arrival . . .

My brother interrupted the man, business-like and military all of a sudden.

'Good man. See that appropriate camping land is marked out for the Guard and the cohorts I have brought north. Please inform the senior officers of the legions present that they now answer to Servius Sulpicius Galba.' Here, he indicated on a horse beside him a tall man with a long face, long nose and pronounced cheekbones. 'Galba is hereby made *Legatus Augusti pro praetore*, governor of Germania. I shall want to inspect the men first thing in the morning. In the meantime, be so good as to tell me where I can find *ex*-governor Gaetulicus.'

The centurion frowned. No surprise, I noted, so the legions here must have been aware of at least *some* wrongdoing on the part of their governor. 'Yes, Domine.' He bowed to the emperor and then to Galba. 'The gove— Gaetulicus is in the headquarters building, Imperator.'

Caligula nodded, gave a half-salute to the man and turned

to Galba. 'Have the cohorts and cavalry settled in, as well as the bulk of the Praetorians. Make your presence felt among the three legions here and make it damned clear that they are now your men and that if a single one of them denies you he will be hanging from a cross on this road by nightfall.'

Galba nodded, saluted, and began to issue orders to the various officers riding along with us. As the majority of our force peeled off and Galba went to secure the German legions for the emperor, my brother led what was left of the column – the civilians and one cohort of Praetorians commanded by their prefects – into the fortress.

Ara Ubiorum was no civil sprawl like Mogontiacum to the south. This was a stark, grey military fortress with a burgeoning civilian support settlement a respectable distance from its walls. Father had based himself here in his time in Germania, and Agrippina had been born in the very headquarters building for which we were now making.

I was beginning to feel nervous. What had seemed like a perfectly sensible idea in Rome was starting to appear utterly ludicrous now. How could I preserve the anonymity of my sister and friend? Unless Gaetulicus could conveniently and helpfully fall on his sword before we arrived, my brother would have him tortured to reveal other names. Lepidus and Agrippina would be implicated. And there was, therefore, every chance that the city of my sister's birth would now also become the city of her death.

And what would my brother do to me when he found out that I had hidden the identity of his would-be assassins from him?

What had seemed such a peaceful seizure of control at the gate proved to be less simple within. An alarm was raised as we moved up the street towards the headquarters building at the fortress centre, and the men of the Fourteenth Gemina began to fall in. The Praetorian prefects exchanged quick words with the emperor, and the Guard split into two groups and then into further units, flooding the fortress and ordering the legionaries to stand down, at sword point in many cases.

The Praetorians were moving with a steady, implacable rhythm and we civilians behind were able to take in our surroundings. Here and there the ring of sword on steel and the clonk of shields taking blows rang out between the ordered rows of barracks. Cries of anger and desperation and agony rose in a subdued din around the walls and streets of the fortress. As I passed one side street with a sign pointing to the bathhouse and crudely painted graffiti labelling someone called Laetius a whore, I glanced to the side at a sudden increase in the noise. I watched with horror as two legionaries fought off a Praetorian, hacking him down to the cobbled ground only to themselves be felled an instant later by half a century of the Guard. Praetorian blades rose and fell, accompanied by the screams of the German legions.

Something must have happened in the main street for, as I shuffled on, shaking, my sandal slipped in something wet and when I looked down I was leaving sticky red prints on the ground. Here and there, rivulets of crimson trickled between the stones. We passed three ironclad bodies a moment later, the Praetorians of our escort veering off around them and then closing once more.

As we approached the central core of the fortress with one century of Praetorians remaining in our company, soldiers poured from the headquarters doorway and began to seal off the street. The Praetorian centurion with us turned to look at the emperor and coughed. 'Sir?'

Caligula regarded the soldiers, and muttered, '*Singulares* – Gaetulicus' bodyguard.' Raising his voice, he shouted, 'You are in violation of your oath to your emperor. Stand down and no charges will be levelled. You are the glorious Fourteenth – sons of Germanicus, as am I. We are brothers, not enemies.'

There was an uncomfortable pause. The bodyguard unit did not move, but they looked less than happy. Their centurion and his *optio* – second in command – moved along the line, ordering them to stay in place and brace to meet the enemy.

'Try to kill the officers, then the men's resistance will collapse,' my brother said to the centurion by his side. The Praetorian officer gave orders to his standard bearer and musician and the *signum* dipped in time to the horn calls. The century of the Guard poured forward in unison, falling in at the head of the column. They were an odd contrast to the soldiers they faced. The Praetorians may be slightly dusty and travel-worn, but they still gleamed. Their equipment was the best money could buy and their tunics the purest white wool. They arrayed like some display team, looking immaculate and efficient. The legionaries facing them were grizzled veterans, having spent decades in Germania. Their armour was dulled, slightly pitted and showing signs of polished-out rust. Their tunics were drab and thick, their shields scarred and battered. They were bearded like the Germans, rather than clean-shaven like Romans. The two units were almost perfectly matched in numbers.

I held my breath as the Praetorians charged.

The serried ranks of the Guard hit the disgraced governor's veteran singulares at a run, maintaining their line. The northern legionaries saw the charge coming and began to extend their line, leaving gaps between shields. As the Praetorians hit them, the soldiers braced behind those great curved boards, taking the force of the impact and using it against their enemy, turning with their shields so that the attackers bounced off and rolled past, through the gaps. Several Praetorians took well-placed blades to the back or side as they passed, while only one of the bearded legionaries fell. I was no student of military matters, so I know not whether this was a standard tactic or some odd development of the northern forces, but it was extremely effective.

As the butchery began the Praetorian centurion, taken by surprise, tried to rein in his men and reform the unit, but now all was chaos. I watched nervously from the vantage point of the carriage. The Praetorians were coming off worse in the engagement, that much was clear. They may be better equipped, but they rarely saw true warfare, while their opponents seldom passed a month without facing howling barbarians across some soggy field.

Things may well have gone very differently for us had not one enterprising guardsman, who found himself through the enemy and at the far side unharmed, spotted the optio who was bullying the soldiers and barged him to the ground. As that second officer of the enemy unit hit the dusty ground, the Praetorian's sword rose and then came down. I did not see the blow itself, but there was a fine, dark spray, and when the Praetorian stood once more, he threw the optio's head into the midst of the legionaries.

Resistance collapsed in moments. The shock of their officer's head bouncing among them sent half the men running for cover. The rest began to reform, looking pale and a little panicked. Then, at the final breaking point, one of the enemy turned on his own centurion, plunging his sword into the officer's back. The tip of the blade burst from the gasping centurion's chest and in moments he was mobbed by his own soldiers, hacking and beating at him. The officer disappeared under a flurry of blows.

By the time the remaining fifty or so men of the Praetorian century had reformed, the survivors of the bodyguard had dropped their swords and were kneeling before the emperor.

Caligula looked them over.

'You are all docked one month's pay. Pick up your swords and get yourselves to the hospital or barracks as required.'

The soldiers blinked at the unexpectedly generous conclusion to their resistance. My brother gestured with a waving, dismissing hand. 'And do something with the bodies!'

As the legionaries scuttled around, clearing away the dead and collecting their weapons, Caligula leaned towards the Praetorian centurion.

'Let's find the former governor.'

We were told to dismount, and with the Praetorians and the three freedmen accompanying my brother, we passed through the arch and into the headquarters building. My brother was at the front of the group as we crossed the great basilica and entered the office of the commander.

Gaetulicus was not expecting us, or at least not so swiftly. A brazier in the corner was busy roaring away with incriminating parchments and vellum hastily burned. The governor had his sword in his hand, but the only other occupants of his office were two unarmed clerks who were busy grabbing piles of documents.

'You are under arrest for conspiracy to commit treason against the person of the emperor,' the Praetorian centurion announced, entering the room. Gaetulicus spun and his wide eyes took in the new arrivals, including the emperor in the fore. Without warning, the governor leapt forward, sword swinging, in an attempt to gut my brother, but Helicon, true to his vow, was there immediately. As Caligula stood impassive, eyeing the blade swinging in to kill him, Helicon's arm swept past him, his own blade catching the governor's sword and flicking it to the side. Before the nobleman could recover, the bodyguard smashed the pommel of his eagle-hilted sword down on Gaetulicus' wrist with an audible crack. The man's sword fell from spasming fingers and he grabbed his ruined wrist, whimpering.

The two clerks scurried away into a corner, cowering.

As the governor backed away, Caligula bent and gathered up the fallen sword, passing it to the Praetorian centurion. 'See that this reaches the Temple of Mars Ultor with the others.'

The officer nodded and took the sword as Caligula turned back to the governor.

'Have you anything to say for yourself?' my brother asked wearily. 'And please do not insult me with pleas of innocence.'

Gaetulicus had been wild-eyed, but now his brow furrowed as he hugged his wrist to his chest.

'If I help you, you will let me die like a Roman, not like some traitor, tortured to death?'

I felt sick, for I thought I knew what was coming.

'If I believe you,' my brother replied, matter-of-factly. 'Dissemble, though, and I will have you peeled until you reveal the truth.'

Gaetulicus nodded.

'I am but a tool in this matter, Domine. The northern hammer to crush military opposition. A safeguard within the army.'

Caligula cleared his throat. 'Please do not try to blame the consuls, for they have fallen already.'

'The *consuls*?' Gaetulicus snorted. 'Mere padding for the comfort of the senators. Look closer to your breast for the snake that bites you, son of Germanicus.'

Caligula frowned. *This* was not something he was expecting to hear. I felt icy fingers probe my spine. The noose was tightening on Agrippina now, and I was inadvertently implicit in the entire business. What could I say that might turn aside the blade of accusation? I coughed desperately over words that would not come.

'Go on . . .' my brother urged the governor.

'The lady Agrippina seeks your throne for her boy child. And your friend Marcus Aemilius Lepidus wields the knife, for it's he who first sought my aid in this.'

I felt cold. Like ice. Everything I had tried to avoid was falling into place despite my best efforts. There would be no saving my sister or our friend now. Gaetulicus had sold them to save his honour.

'I do not believe you,' Caligula said quietly, his tone shocked, hollow. He took a step back, and then another on quivering legs, staring first at Gaetulicus and then Agrippina and Lepidus, whose expressions might have carried a look of disdainful denial had I not known the truth. By the gods, my sister was cold, but she was good at it. Lepidus I had never imagined to be so cunning. Our brother found himself backed against the wall, his eyes wide, face paler than I had ever seen it, even during those weeks of poisoned illness. Tears dripped from his face. No, not tears. Sweat. No tears, for he was in disbelief.

Gaetulicus snapped his fingers and gestured to one of the clerks, who scurried across. The governor leafed through the documents in the man's arms and pulled one from the pile, proffering it to the emperor. 'See for yourself, Imperator.'

Even from my place a few paces back I could see the document, and I recognised Agrippina's writing. There may be no incriminating seal, but I knew her pen, and so did my brother. Caligula stared at the document, reached for it but flinched away from actually touching the vellum.

'Kill the governor,' my brother said in a hoarse voice, stepping away from the wall once more and past me. 'Cleanly.'

Helicon stepped forward, and Gaetulicus braced himself, flicking one last meaningful look at Agrippina. The bodyguard's glorious blade plunged into the former governor's chest, impaling his heart and then bursting from his back. As a torrent began from the wound between his ribs, so a gobbet of red also burst from his mouth. Helicon twisted his blade and pulled, drawing it out with ease. The sword was followed by a fountain of crimson that poured to the floor. Gaetulicus sighed and fell to his knees in the growing pool before slumping to the ground, where he shuddered a few times and then lay still.

I dared not look at Lepidus or Agrippina now. And I could not see my brother's face, for he was in front and staring ahead. The world seemed to teeter on a knifepoint. Jove rolled his die.

My brother turned.

I had expected fury, now the shock had passed. I had seen his reaction to betrayal before and it was far from pretty, and that had been a betrayal of lessers. This was *family*. I had expected anger on an unprecedented scale, giving way to a bloodthirsty vengeance. Instead, all I could see was hopeless disbelief, Caligula's eyes welling with the tears I thought I had seen moments ago.

'How can this be so?'

Agrippina snorted, standing haughty and proud, every bit the princess of Rome, her eyes flashing with dangerous possibility. 'This piece of filth would say anything. And those words have been forged to incriminate me, Gaius. *I* would use my seal.'

My brother's face was stricken, disbelieving. 'It was you. You and Lepidus that Livilla heard in the palace, wasn't it?'

'Gaius,' Agrippina said, starting to sound desperate, 'I'm your *sister*. You *know* me.'

'I do,' said our brother in heavy tones.

'Don't snivel, Agrippina,' Lepidus said in a dead tone. 'He knows the truth. Be proud.' Our old friend turned to our brother with a sad expression. 'You are not what you were, Gaius. You're not that golden prince – my friend who came from Germanicus' house. You've become something twisted and dark. You're a proper son of the Julii now. Rome needs new blood if it is to thrive, not the tired and corrupt red of Caesar's line.'

My brother stared at his oldest friend. I could see through his eyes and into his heart. That day, at the end of September in a fortress at the edge of the world, my brother's heart broke. It had cracked and corroded with the loss of Drusilla, but the sudden revelation that there was no one in the world he could trust – even the family he had coddled and preserved through the worst of times – finished the destruction.

There was no fury in Caligula's eyes, but the tears had dried once more. When he turned again, he was naught but a shell of a man. He reached down into his pouch at his belt and drew the small, glorious silver knife that Lepidus had given him sixteen years ago, when the world was a different place. Agrippina was shaking, looking this way and that for an exit, but the Praetorians with us had them surrounded, and Helicon was at my brother's side for protection, along with the Praetorian centurion holding Gaetulicus' sword. There was no escape.

My brother took a single pace forward, reaching up with his empty hand almost in supplication to Lepidus. 'You are my *friend*. My *oldest* friend. We have been *closer* than brothers.'

'Then you are the most foolish of fools,' Lepidus snapped, though there was a crack in his voice that suggested just how hard it had been for him to say. I was shaking. That Agrippina could be cold enough to use her husband to make a son and then position him with land and power, and even challenge our brother to put the boy on the throne? Despite the closeness of our family, I could almost believe that of my dangerous sister. But that our oldest friend would wield the knife against Caligula simply because he stood to be cut from the succession? That was not the Lepidus I had always known.

Our old friend blinked in surprise as my brother's other hand lashed out and that glorious silver knife sliced open his throat from side to side. He wheezed for a moment and pink bloody bubbles emerged from the slit before the vital fluid started to pour. He tried to say something, but blood dripped from his lips instead of words.

'If Rome needs new blood,' Caligula snarled, 'then let her have it.'

Agrippina stared from the whitening, shocked face of Lepidus to the still, bloodied heap of Gaetulicus. Her eyes bulged. 'Do not do anything rash, Gaius. Whatever these two have done, you know I am not part of it. I am your *sister*!'

'I have long known you for a dangerous woman, Agrippina,

and for a cunning one. But I could never have foreseen this.'

He held up the silver blade of Lepidus' gift and watched the blood run down the gleaming edge with silent fascination.

'The letter was written by Livilla!' my sister blurted suddenly. I turned, astonished, to stare at her. So did Caligula.

'What?'

'The letter there. Her writing is so like mine. We learned from the same tutor. I used to hand in her study work as my own, we were so alike. *Livilla* wrote the letter. I didn't want any part of this, but she and Lepidus, they dragged me in – dragged me deep – so deep I couldn't get out. They threatened young Lucius. I can't bear it any more!'

She collapsed in a shuddering heap of tears and I could do nothing but stare at her.

Suddenly, I felt eyes on me and I turned to see Caligula looking at me in disbelief.

'She lies,' I said simply.

'She said we needed to cut the dead weight,' Agrippina grunted through her fake sobs. 'She said we couldn't trust Corbulo or Gaetulicus. So she came to see you. Sold them out to preserve the rest of us. She's wicked, Gaius, wicked!'

I turned my dumbfounded gaze to my sister again. How could this be happening?

'Both of you?' Caligula said quietly. '*Both*?'

'Gaius . . .' I started.

'What happened to my sisters who lived with their grandmother?' my brother wheezed in shock. 'The sisters who watched the vultures of Rome pick and tear at our brothers and parents? Who cleaved together through the worst days of the empire and became closer than close? What happened to our family? To the glorious children of Germanicus? When did we turn into the very people we used to fear?'

'Gaius?' I tried again, but it was hard to be heard above the overdramatic wailing of Agrippina.

I felt strong, hairy hands grasp my shoulders and I was suddenly pulled backwards.

'Take them away,' growled my brother under his breath.

No, I thought as I was hauled from the room. *I'm no traitor. I'm no enemy. I* am *a child of Germanicus. I am loyal.* Always *loyal.*

Gaius?

PART FOUR

THE FALL OF EMPERORS

'Thus Gaius, after doing in three years, nine months, and twenty-eight days all that has been related, learned by actual experience that he was not a god'

– *Cassius Dio:* Histories

XXIII

STEEL, FIRE AND BLOOD

I suspect that the world considered me lucky. After all, despite what had happened to Maximus, Gaetulicus and Lepidus for their part in the plot, *I* had walked away from the affair with my life. How could one argue with that? Apart, of course, from the fact that I, unlike them, had been innocent of all wrongdoings.

I had been dragged from the headquarters of the fortress protesting my innocence, my wicked sister hauled away beside me, weeping and wailing that I was the heart of all the troubles, the evil bitch. Even in my youth when I had watched her playing her games and getting that poor slave girl beaten and sold for the want of a brush she never looked at thereafter, I had always thought the bond between we siblings unbreakable. I had believed that the world arrayed troubles against us, but that we were fated to stand together against them. I had even tried to make her life easier, constantly lobbying to remove her pig of a husband. I had put my family above everything, even above the growing bond with my husband and, in the end, Agrippina had betrayed me every bit as much as she had betrayed our brother. She had torn the children of Germanicus apart where even Sejanus and Tiberius had failed. Three of us had survived murder and illness, and now Caligula would not look at either of us, and my sister and I experienced a level of seething separation I could not have anticipated at any time in my life.

Caligula had pondered on our fates for three days at Ara

Ubiorum while Agrippina and I languished in a cell. The first night I did not sleep, sitting cold and hollow until the squeaking of bats around the rafters ended and the song of larks began. Agrippina and I had not spoken a word since the door had closed on us.

That first dawn after the world ended, we spoke finally, and perhaps we should not have.

'Why?' I said, eventually, once I had distilled everything down to one word.

Agrippina simply opened one eye from where she had probably been feigning sleep and glared at me with that single malicious orb.

'Tell me why,' I repeated, quietly. My voice was as dead as I expected us soon to be.

'Self-preservation,' she said, simply.

'What?' I spat the word.

'For a moment, I had him sold on the notion that you had masterminded everything. I could see it in his eyes. For the briefest of moments, I almost walked away from this, leaving you in my place. But Gaius is clever. In fact, after me, he was always the cleverest.'

'Why would you sell out your family?' I pressed. 'I have never done you any harm, or borne you any ill will. We were sisters. Family.'

'We still are,' shrugged Agrippina. 'But family is not the bond you think it is, Livilla. Our family has been falling apart for years. Ever since the death of our father, the bonds have rotted and frayed. Sometimes that's still enough. Sometimes it isn't. I have a new family now, and that takes precedence over all.'

I frowned. 'Your husband is an animal.'

My sister laughed then. A cold, unpleasant laugh.

'Ahenobarbus? He is a fool. An idiot. And his time and usefulness are almost past. I talk of my son. My little Nero.'

'Your little Ahenobarbus,' I corrected, thinking of the happy, gurgling boy who had remained in Tarracina with his nurse during our journey to the north.

'Nero,' she said in an odd tone. 'I will never call him by his birth name. He is my little Nero. And he is my reason. He is my family. And I will sell out my siblings and murder my husband and tear down the gods if I need to in order to put my boy in that purple cloak.'

I shivered. 'There could have been other ways.'

'No,' Agrippina said. 'No. There is no other way. And you have no son, so you cannot see that. You are as barren as that heifer Lollia, and without children of your own, you could never understand the all-consuming need to shelter and enrich your offspring. Loss of children sent both Augustus and Tiberius mad, and on Capri it almost did the same to our brother. *That* is how much it means to a parent. And you can flatter yourself in your simple way that family is all, but not in the face of parenthood. I would sell you again and again, and drain the last drops of blood from you and our brother, if it secured young Nero his future.'

'And now there is no future,' I replied, hollow.

'Do not be so naïve,' Agrippina spat. 'You are simple and plain-thinking. You will suffer Caligula's wrath for what we have done, and so shall I. But I am clever. I shall bide my time and, mark my words, this is not the end for me and my boy. As long as I draw breath, I shall continue to build my son's future. And when I am finally free of this taint somehow, I will retrieve him from his nurse and coddle him once more.'

I fell silent then, mulling over her words, finding them hard to believe, and yet hard to deny. I gave serious consideration to clawing out her eyes and ripping out her lying tongue in that tiny space, but despite my wrath I knew that 'Pina was stronger than I, and more devious. Even had I the strength to overcome her, she would have turned it to her advantage somehow, and the guards would probably beat me for it. So the two of us sat in opposite corners of the room in silence for the next three days, glaring at one another. We were released from the cell only to use the latrines, for which I was grateful I suppose, and we were fed regularly and well. But after a lifetime free of the disturbance of dreams, my nightmares began that evening. Dreams that made me sick and wake in a dreadful sweat.

Blinding, eye-searing flashes of red and white, which gradually resolve into a canopy of crimson with the brilliant sunlight of a Roman summer slashing through like a blade. And the world below is a dreadful crimson, battered and stabbed by those sharp beams of light.

They never left me again, becoming my constant night-time companions. Horrible and jarring and robbing me of restful sleep, and yet still far more welcome than my cellmate.

From what I hear, as we had been marched away my brother was already calling for the headsman, but Vinicius, who had managed by some fluke of Fortuna's whim to avoid any taint of treason and remained close to Caligula, somehow succeeded in persuading him away from such a brutal and final course. My brother had been so shattered by the revelations that he had raged and rampaged like a trapped beast and had needed to be talked down from having us beheaded. The emperor's temper that had begun in his youth as a fiery staccato, and had blossomed with his reign into a dangerous and twisted thing, had finally developed into unrestrained violent fury and only gods-blessed Vinicius managed somehow to draw him back from the edge and commute our sentences.

The emperor had us brought before him one cold morning. It was the first time I witnessed Caligula as an ordinary subject, and it felt odd and disturbing. There was a distance between us that had never existed before. Had I any more tears to shed, that might have brought them forth, but I'd been bled dry of sorrow long ago.

As we stood before our brother, shaking and exhausted, a soldier stepped forward at the emperor's gesture. He carried a heavy stone urn, and he proffered it to Agrippina. She stared at it.

'It is Lepidus. Your *lover*,' my brother spat as though the word left a sour taste in his mouth.

Still Agrippina stared.

'Take it.'

Slowly, she reached out and did as she was bidden. I saw how heavy it must have been from the sagging of my sister as she strained to hold it until she found a more comfortable position.

'You will carry him with you, and if the urn falls to the ground even once, you will join him in it. Do you understand?'

'Gaius . . .'

She stuttered to a halt with that one word under our brother's awful gaze. 'You will address me with appropriate respect and titles,' he hissed angrily, 'or I shall have that traitorous tongue torn from you.

'I have matters to attend to here in the wider reaches of the empire,' he went on in frosty tones, 'and cannot afford to simply drop them and return to Rome, and so nor shall you. The pair of you shall travel with my entourage under the close guard of my Praetorians. You shall have neither comfort nor luxury, for I have lavished them both upon my sisters since the day I donned the purple, and my largesse seems to have done little other than turn your poisonous hearts against me. So you shall live like the poor – like a soldier. You too shall be *little boots*. Agrippina will carry Lepidus, and you will both carry the weight of shame in the knowledge that you had the highest honours an emperor could grant, and you cast them into the flames in your spiteful game.'

Agrippina glared sullenly at our brother. I opened my mouth

to say something but could find neither words nor the voice with which to say them, for Agrippina had damned me and nothing would rebuild the trust she had demolished. Caligula looked broken. Lost. Beyond mere sadness. Gone was the glorious boy who had carried little Drusilla beneath that first rainbow in Rome. Gone was the shrewd brother who had navigated his sisters through those dangerous days on Capri. Gone was the young god who had entered Rome less than three years ago to the roar of a loving crowd. All that I could now see was a shell of a man living out the final stages of a betrayal that had taken his last refuge from him.

'I have not yet settled upon your punishment,' he said quietly, with no small hint of menace, too. 'Some here still urge a traitor's death, while others – Vinicius, for example – counsel leniency. I will make my decision upon our return to Rome. Until then you will stay under guard and out of my presence, lest I lean towards the former counsel at the mere sight of you.'

I shivered as I lowered my face from his gaze. Perhaps in time, maybe by the day we reached Rome, Caligula's wrath would fade and he might be persuaded to the truth, but that was a day yet to come. Now, we had to meekly accept whatever scraps he would throw our way.

At first we were confined to that same barrack block in Ara Ubiorum with the same squad of Praetorians for company while Caligula dealt with the army of Germania. I spoke only infrequently to Agrippina and each time it ended in violent argument. By our seventh day we were so heartily sick of each other's company that we hung a mouldering blanket across the middle of the cold, timber room to hide from each other's sight. It stopped most of the arguments, but one day not long after – by which time I had totally lost track of the days – Agrippina said something in her solitude that goaded me once more into argument.

'Had you one iota of sense, sister, you would have taken the opportunity to name names when Gaius turned on you.'

'When *Gaius* turned on me?' I started in disbelief.

Agrippina brushed it off as meaningless. 'We are of the Julian blood,' she said, as though that were more important than being the family of Germanicus. 'If there is one thing our kin have learned it is that survival is about cultivating the right friends and removing the right enemies. You could have sent each of your enemies to the grave with just a name given in that moment.'

I stared at her. 'Until that day, I did not know who my true enemies *were*.'

'You are a fool, Julia Livilla. I was not your enemy. Nor was Lepidus. In fact, until you went to our brother with your mouth running like a public fountain, we might just have been your greatest *allies*. Gaius is your enemy, for he stands between you and power – between you and security.'

I simply stared in angry disbelief at her vile pronouncements, but she was not yet done.

'And even he would have turned on you eventually. They all do. Tiberius, Ahenobarbus, now Gaius. Men are to be used to position ourselves properly, and then discarded before they fall into someone else's hands. If I believed for even a moment that you were not destined to rot in a pit, I would advise you to rid yourself of Vinicius before he disappoints you.'

How dare she? She could impugn the vile old Tiberius and her own sickening husband all she liked, but to paint our brother the same? My husband? Something inside me snapped. I tore aside the filthy blanket and threw myself at her, fingernails raking, teeth snapping like some wild animal released from a cage. It was only as the Praetorians entered and separated us forcefully that I realised I had scratched her badly and she had not fought back at all. In fact, she had a wicked smile. The witch had even planned the argument and my response. She was taken from the room and treated by the fortress medicus, then moved to a new cell, with more homely comforts, leaving me languishing in our dank barrack room.

I was in two minds how I felt about it. To have been used so once more for her own comfort rankled, but it was almost worth it to be alone and rid of her.

Over the ensuing days and weeks of my incarceration, I heard in small snatches what happened in the outside world. Caligula cleaved through the northern legions like a hot blade through butter. Anyone deemed to have links that suggested they might be untrustworthy, or with an uncertain history, was removed from position and replaced with someone in whom Caligula had faith. The army was rebuilt.

Then, he led campaigns across the River Rhenus. It could have been glorious: the son of Germanicus imposing the might of Rome upon those foetid barbarians on the far bank of the river. Just as our father had done decades ago, earning his name, and with the same legions, no less. But Caligula was now savage. That was the impression I received from the snippets I heard, anyway. Where our father had been vengeful but precise, Caligula had been like a wildfire, destroying everything in his path indiscriminately. And that was not like him. That was not the Gaius with whom we had grown up. This was a *new* Gaius, unrestrained and furious – a man of steel, fire and blood.

I could picture it from my incarceration. Caligula sitting astride Incitatus, his pampered steed, a cavalry long-sword in his hand as he leans low in the saddle and swipes. A German head rolling free of its neck with a brief spout of crimson. Behind him, the German bodyguard struggling to protect their violent, headstrong emperor who leads from the front, a boy who grew up marching alongside these very legions. Blood, mud and death. And my brother's face displaying no anger or joy or satisfaction. Just that same hollow, broken expression he left me with at Ara Ubiorum. Such imaginings only fed my nightmares.

Blinding, eye-searing flashes of red and white, which gradually resolve into a canopy of crimson with the brilliant sunlight of a Roman summer slashing through like a blade. The world below is a dreadful crimson, battered and stabbed by those sharp beams of light.

The roar of a crowd is still audible as a din in the background.

I am moving, walking casually, calmly.

I am filled with a strange ennui, though that itself is just a boat of emotion bobbing upon a sea of despair that has always been there, dark and immense, threatening to engulf me. But now that is changing. The untroubled nature of my mind is cut through with new emotions . . . stark, terrifying ones.

The army finally returned after two brief campaigns into Germania, though no one came to see me. I was beginning to lose the power of speech, I think, for there was no one in my prison to talk to but the Praetorians who brought my food and escorted me to the latrines when required, and they were hardly forthcoming. I lived in silence for weeks in Ara Ubiorum, until my brother decided to move on.

Once more, Agrippina and I were reunited, drawn from our individual prisons and thrown together. I found now that every last trace of sisterly concern had gone and all I harboured in my heart for her was hatred. It was an odd and unwelcome feeling for me. In my life I had feared and mistrusted people, but I wasn't sure how much I had ever really hated someone. Even Sejanus and Tiberius had been more figures of dread. But I hated Agrippina. And it made me queasy to realise that I did so. I was dirty and dishevelled, despite having had a weekly escorted visit to the fort commander's baths. I was in desperate need of grooming and fresh clothes. It irked me further to see that Agrippina seemed to have been less neglected than me, her hair neatly combed and a clean, pressed stola and palla covering her. By comparison I must have looked like one of those beggars who crowd around the Circus Maximus on a race day. One of the Praetorians threw fresh clothes to me and launched a comb, which I caught with difficulty. I changed behind a hastily raised blanket and raked my tangles loose. The result would not be a stylish matron of Rome, but at least might look less like a Germanic fishwife.

We travelled then, for days, for weeks. Leaving the bulk of the army in Lower Germania, my brother took his Praetorians, the German bodyguard and a single legion with him to the south to winter somewhere more suitable. The nobiles of my brother's entourage rode in fine carriages, and the military men, Caligula included, upon horses at the head of the army. Agrippina and I were relegated to a rickety wagon in the endless baggage train of animals and vehicles that followed the legion. I had never travelled with the army like my brother, barring that fated ride north to confront Gaetulicus. I had no idea how unpleasant the rear of a marching column is.

The wagons are jolting and uncomfortable and often stained and pitted with unpleasant substances, smelling of old vegetables and the like. But that odour is well masked by the constant aroma of beasts: oxen and donkeys, horses and pigs. Animals for transport and for food. And each one defecates on the move, adding to the cloying smell. There is a constant haze of dust from the thousands of feet and hooves that have stirred it up ahead, and the cavalry have dropped endless swathes of horse dung that the carters seem determined to drive through, releasing fresh waves of nausea.

I had tried to start up conversations more than once during that awful journey, with either the driver or his mate, or one of the eight Praetorians who escorted us. No one would speak to us. The emperor had forbidden it. Stinking, uncomfortable silence for hundreds of miles. And all this with the ashes of Lepidus and my bitter, treacherous sister for company, and the knowledge that even at the end of it all an uncertain fate still awaited us.

I saw Caligula once during the journey. Only once, when he was required to ride back along the column and speak to the camp prefect on some logistical matter. He never turned his head to look at us on the way past. What he believed we had both done – what Hades-born Agrippina *had* done – had severed the sibling ties between us, seemingly for good.

We arrived in Lugdunum in southern Gaul just before the winter weather hit. In Lugdunum this meant mostly sporadic rain and damp winds that rushed down the valley, carrying dirt and mists, while in Germania, where we had so recently been, they would have suffered through snow and sleet. Not that it mattered to the two disgraced sisters of the emperor, who once more languished in an unlit hovel with only dour Praetorians for company. I could see Agrippina spoiling for yet another fight in our time there, no doubt planning to get herself removed to more comfortable quarters. While I loathed sharing my cell with her, I put up with every barbed insult and every inflammatory, provocative phrase without the reactions she sought. I felt sick just being near her, but I was damned if I was going to let her goad me into a fight that would send her once more into luxury while I languished in dank timber quarters. And while my nightmares had become less troublesome during our journey, now that we were once more confined in the dark in Lugdunum, they returned in force, leaving me sweating and thrashing in the night and drawn and pale and trembling in the morning.

That winter brought one small relief in our endless shadowy prison. Somehow my husband had managed to persuade the emperor to let him visit me. Caligula must have been caught in an unusually light mood at the time, but sure enough Vinicius began to visit me sporadically. And being loyal as always, he brought me news but spoke not one word to Agrippina. In return, she had nothing but spiteful glares for him as she sat beside the jar that contained the remains of our friend.

Rome had been told of the plot and its failure, Vinicius informed me. Of the death of Gaetulicus and the recreation of the army of Germania. The traitors' swords had been delivered to the temple as Caligula had ordered. The senate had given thanks that the emperor was saved and the plot prevented, though I could imagine how many sour faces greeted the news in truth. Seemingly our names – Agrippina, Lepidus and myself – had not been made public as part of the plot. Rome was unaware of our role and our fate, perhaps because my brother had not yet decided what to do with us in the end.

The news my husband brought was rarely good. It began well enough, though. Vinicius came with a report that Milonia Caesonia had given birth to a girl. My brother finally had an heir, even if it was not a boy. She had been named Julia Drusilla, which thrilled and saddened me in equal parts.

Worse news was to come, though. It transpired as the winter wore on that my brother's new favourite attack dog, Vespasian, dealt with matters in Rome for him. Fifteen senators somehow implicated in the plot met a grisly end, and in the process they named others, who named others, who named others. If the conspiracy to kill my brother had truly involved every name that came under accusation that winter, they could have simply marched on the city and killed him openly, for they surely would have vastly outnumbered the Praetorians.

Vespasian reaped a bloody harvest in Rome that winter, and my husband was vivid with detail.

'They are not even spending a night in the carcer now. When a name is torn from the tortured tongue of a *conspirator*,

Vespasian has them brought to the Palatine and cut and burned until they in turn scream a name. Then they are taken down to the forum, hacked to pieces in front of a baying crowd and then heaped into carts and wheeled out of the city to the far heights beyond the Esquiline Hill, where they are dumped for carrion eaters. It is worse than the days of Sejanus, for no one is safe and even the dead are mutilated and left dishonoured and unburied.'

'My brother *condones* this behaviour?' I remembered how Tiberius had been all but oblivious to the vicious excesses of Sejanus. Was history repeating itself?

'I don't think he cares. He has changed, Livilla. What Agrippina and Lepidus –' a quick pause to throw a look filled with disgust at my sister and her jar '– did has broken him. He has given Vespasian free rein, and the butcher of the Palatine is dealing with things in the way he thinks Caligula would want it done. He will not stop until your brother tells him to, and your brother won't lift a finger to save a member of the senatorial class these days, so the killing goes on.'

I felt shocked and sickened at the thought of our city. The fair streets and columns and steps of the forum soaked in the blood of . . . well, not the innocent, per se. One could never accuse the senatorial class of innocence with a straight face. But they did not deserve to be hacked apart by Vespasian and his animals for something they did not do. In a way, just briefly, I was suddenly grateful for continued silent incarceration in this provincial hole.

'And what of Corbulo?' I asked, for that former consul was the emperor's brother-in-law and *had* been part of the conspiracy, yet had escaped punishment entirely while half of Rome's nobility paid the price.

'He has taken oaths to your brother and aids Vespasian in his work. And the empress, still in the city in your brother's absence, does nothing to halt the excesses either, for she must condemn the actions of the conspirators lest she appear on that list herself. After all, your brother has forbidden any honours to be granted to the entire imperial family. He is starting to see you all as enemies, and with some justification, I might add.'

The Saturnalia passed. We could hear the joy of the people of Lugdunum, favoured by the presence of their emperor, out in the streets beyond our prison, but we celebrated nothing.

Vinicius visited again at the beginning of Januarius with more news of what was happening in the world outside. 'Your brother lavishes funds on Lugdunum like a waterfall of gold, turning it into a city of marble and monuments. His agents are bleeding the treasury dry in the capital. He's had all your estates and houses – those of Agrippina too – auctioned off. All your possessions as well, except what you had with you. And all the heirlooms of Tiberius have gone to the auctioneers. It's as if he strips Rome of any memory of his family, which is, I suspect, exactly what he is doing. And those memories are paying to rebuild Lugdunum as a city to rival Rome.' He sighed. 'He rules the empire from Gaul. He keeps court here as though it's a new Rome, but a Rome without a senate, which suits him very well.'

I pictured my brother sitting on a throne in this provincial city, alone and all-powerful, like some wicked despot.

'He rules alone? As an old-fashioned tyrant?'

Vinicius shrugged again. 'Not quite. More like an eastern king. When we first marched south for Lugdunum, he sent out letters summoning old friends, and they have arrived over the past few weeks. His court is a glittering, golden, lavish one, filled with exotic figures. Julius Agrippa is here with him now, and Antiochus of Commagene. Ptolemy of Mauretania came too, though Callistus came across a document incriminating the African prince in yet another plot, and the man left Lugdunum in a jar two days after he arrived.' Another sickened glance here at Agrippina and her own funerary urn companion. 'Still, there are others of a similar ilk, and it is a court of client kings and sycophantic freedmen now. With no senate, I think your brother is beginning to think like Agrippa or Antiochus. Like an eastern king – an absolute monarch. Things are changing, Livilla, and eventually his new court and the old senate in Rome will come into conflict . . . if there are any senators *left* after Vespasian finishes with them, anyway.'

I was fretting now. I didn't like what I was hearing about my brother. It didn't sound like the Gaius Caligula I knew. On his current path, the only destination could be destruction.

'In an attempt to put an end to the culling of the senate,' my husband told me sadly, 'your uncle Claudius brought a deputation from Rome to the gates of Lugdunum, but Caligula publicly insulted and threatened your uncle and then sent the entire deputation back to Rome without even allowing them a change of horses or a night's rest. I saw your uncle's face. I truly thought he was going to explode. With his dreadful stammer, he was perhaps an unwise spokesman, even given his blood ties, but your brother was merciless in his mockery. I know your uncle and the three of you have never seen particularly eye to eye, but I think Claudius now plots and conspires against the emperor.'

'That is nothing new,' I said.

Vinicius was shaking his head. 'Your family have broken Gaius, I think. He survived plots by prefects and senators and came out strong, but the loss of Drusilla and then the betrayal of his siblings changed everything. The senate and your brother are on a war footing, or fast approaching it. The empire teeters on a knife-edge, my love, and the day Caligula sets foot in Rome, I fear the world will be cleaved in half.'

XXIV

A LEGION OF OATH-BREAKERS

Spring came exceedingly slowly to we prisoners in our dingy room. I was not coping well. Agrippina remained strong, like some statue of a harpy or Fury in the shadows, seemingly certain that this dank containment was merely a temporary setback in her rise. Me? I was suffering appallingly. It was not the solitude, though that certainly played a part, snatching away words from my vocabulary and stealing my ability to form a coherent chain of thought. And it was not the presence of Agrippina, though it felt like sharing a chamber with a scorpion, waiting for the inevitable sting. It was not even the heartbreak of the descent and fracture of our family.

No. It was the nightmares.

Blinding, eye-searing flashes of red and white, which gradually resolve into a canopy of crimson with the brilliant sunlight of a Roman summer slashing through like a blade. The world below that shelter is a dreadful scarlet, battered and stabbed by those sharp beams of light.

The roar of a crowd is still audible as a din in the background.

I am moving, walking casually, calmly.

I am filled with a strange ennui, though that itself is just a boat of emotion bobbing upon a sea of despair that has always been there, dark and immense, threatening to engulf me. But now that is changing. The untroubled nature of my mind is cut through with new emotions . . . stark, terrifying ones.

The unexpected. A shock. Horror, even. How can this be?

My hand goes out to ward off the unseen threat. No! I am surrounded only by the trusted. This cannot happen. Such threat is the province of enemies, not friends.

After a life free of nightmares, I had now spent months beleaguered by a constant barrage of night-time images of death and horror. Some nights it drove me from sleep to wake shrieking and sweating until Agrippina threw some piece of detritus at me and snapped at me to go to sleep. Other nights the images would replay over and over without waking me and I would suffer till dawn, waking more tired than I had been before sleep. I was starting to feel weak in both body and mind from the never-ending assault.

Vinicius continued to bring us news in short visits. I had begun to beg him to stay beyond the delivery of such tidings, if only to provide company less loathsome than my sister and her jar, but whether he wished to or not, he had been forbidden. The emperor still held my husband in high enough esteem that he was permitted to visit his wife for short snatches, but nothing more.

Things had not improved between Rome and my brother over the close of winter. The senate waited much of Januarius for the emperor's decision over consulships for the year. It was twelve days before they got their word, and that word was that Caligula didn't care. He'd resigned his consulship and called it a worthless thing. *Almost as worthless as the senate*, he'd added, according to Vinicius. The emperor had dismissively given them the responsibility for settling on the consuls themselves. They had argued over it vehemently.

Vinicius told me at length how he had debated with my

brother's friends over the importance of this move. The consuls, he had pointed out, were the centre of political life in Rome and always had been. Agrippa had been scornful. 'Why would the senate be so concerned over such a redundant office as the consulate,' he had scoffed.

'Redundant?' Vinicius had replied. 'The consulate? It's been the heart of Rome since the days of the kings.'

'And it is entirely unnecessary,' Agrippa announced in bored tones. 'The consuls and the senate, the tribunates, the assemblies . . . it's all utterly meaningless when an emperor sits on the throne. Caligula is starting to see that, and I think Rome is, too.'

Vinicius felt less sure, and certainly less confident.

'If your brother is truly beginning to envisage a Rome without a senate, ruled by a king, he will be placing himself in great danger,' he said on one of his visits.

I huffed uncertainly. In my seclusion, my cares for the institutions of Rome were minimal, but noting interest crossing the face of my wicked sister over in the other corner, I forced myself to become involved in the conversation, lest Vinicius turn to her. Unlikely, but she was ever a smooth talker.

'His position will always be strong,' I replied. 'The army and the people still love him.'

'The military and the mob might still love him,' Vinicius sighed, 'but Rome's bones are the patrician and equestrian classes, and their reaction to such change would make or break things. How much did the army and the mob save him against the plot of the senators, or the consuls . . . or his *sisters*?' he added archly, looking over his shoulder at Agrippina, who sneered in reply.

Rome expelled its last king – Tarquinius Superbus – over five centuries ago. Since that day and the founding of the Republic, Rome had steadfastly refused even the notion of a return to monarchy. It was unthinkable. That was what the Republic had been instituted to prevent. Two consuls so that no one man could ever be supremely powerful. Of course, there was a solid argument that the emperors had been just that over the past seventy years, but great Augustus and even wicked Tiberius had been very careful to couch their reign in terms that denied the possibility of monarchy, styling themselves princeps civitatis – first among equals.

'A move to true sole rule would be dangerous and would meet stiff opposition,' Vinicius muttered, and from his tone of disapproval, I wondered if one of those voices of opposition might even be my good, loyal husband. There are limits to every man's devotion, after all.

'Is my brother strong enough to win such a challenge?' I asked absently, and Vinicius' bleak expression clearly stated his thoughts on that matter.

I spent the whole of the month of Martius waiting for more news, wondering where Vinicius had got to. There can be little doubt that I had started to go slightly peculiar by that time, and the visits of Vinicius were probably the only thing that kept me marginally sane. The nightmares continued to rage nightly, bringing scenes of blood and death, exacerbated by my imaginings of what had happened under Vespasian in the streets of Rome as well as what had happened to both Roman and barbarian in the German campaigns.

I had my next visitor on the kalends of Aprilis, and it was not Vinicius, but some tribune of the Praetorian Guard come to inform us that we were departing Lugdunum. I felt my pulse quicken. *We were finally returning to Rome*. Admittedly, there was as much chance of a blade waiting there for my neck as there was of any kind of freedom, but this dingy confinement with Agrippina had become a waking nightmare to complement my sleeping ones and any change now had to be for the better, or so I thought.

But we were not bound for Rome. We were once more to

endure the bone-shaking wagon of the army's baggage train as we marched north. On the twenty-third day of the month just past, the festival of Tubilustrium had been held in Lugdunum rather than Rome, marking the start of the campaigning season. My brother had abandoned his work with Germania, perhaps content that he had suppressed their ever-present urge to raid Roman lands. Certainly a Germania that had seethed with anti-Roman tribal feeling and had been policed by an army led by a traitor was now quiet and settled and occupied by legions with new, loyal commanders. Of course, if might be said that any cemetery would be quiet and settled – my brother's rage had left in his wake a sea of German bodies. *Pax Romana* had become the peace of the grave in the northern lands.

Regardless, other events had led him to set his sights on a new land. A prince from the soggy and distant island of Britannia had petitioned the emperor for aid against a neighbour, and so the army was to cross that awful northern sea and visit that northern island.

I emerged blinking into the light of a spring day in Lugdunum as the army made ready to march. Agrippina, still clutching that now filthy urn and glaring daggers at me as usual, pushed past as though this were some queue to a performance at the theatre and not just another mobile prison, and clambered up into our wagon amid the sacks of turnips that were to be our cushions for the journey.

I let her have the pick of positions. None would be comfortable anyway. By the time the sun was high enough to see over the roofs of the city, we were gone, bouncing and rattling our way north along the Rhodanus valley. Even given my own predicament, I felt nervousness at the thought of our destination: an island that had seen off two expeditions from Caesar himself.

It was said that both Augustus and Tiberius had coveted the place and secretly desired to conquer the island and make their name with it. Britannicus, they would have been. But neither had done so in the end and so my brother, it seemed, would be the first to dare to cross that sea and try to succeed where even mighty Caesar had failed.

Despite the fact that spring was now in full bloom, the weather began to turn as we travelled. It is ever colder and wetter in the north, and while Lugdunum, and most certainly Rome, would be feeling the change in the season and the gradual warming of the land, we were treated to regular impromptu downpours in our uncomfortable, stinking cart as we slowly rattled north.

The journey seemed to last forever, but eventually the legion and the emperor's entourage managed to reach the north coast of Gaul, where it rendezvoused with a grand force he had ordered hither from Germania – his newly trustworthy legions.

We made camp within sight of the coast and on the second day, while I was escorted from my prison tent to the hastily built latrines, we happened to cross a rise in the ground. I could see, amazingly, through the blue sky of an unusually clear day, a thin grey line across the sea that had to be the fabled isle of Britannia.

Britannia: home of swamps and monsters and tribes who had defied the greatest general in Rome's history.

I noticed the problem before, apparently, my brother and his people. On my visits to the latrine and the few occasions I managed to poke my head out from the tent, I quickly became aware of the mood in the huge camp. The legions were not happy. We were kept in a tent between the First and Twentieth legions, and more than once I heard the soldiers, when their officers were out of earshot, grumbling nervously about how any campaign across the grey roiling ocean into that isle of terrors was doomed to fail. Superstition was beginning to rule among the men during the twelve days we waited for the last units to arrive and the ships to come down the coast from Germania.

In fairness, I cannot say that I myself was thrilled with the idea of crossing that ocean, but then I was living a life beyond my assigned end now, anyway. Death could come any day at any time on the whim of my brother. The fact that it hadn't suggested to me that in the presence of his eastern friends he had almost forgotten Agrippina and I existed. The soldiers in the nearby tents knew well that we were there, though, given the blood-curdling shrieks that issued from my tent during the night when the imagined blades cut down into my dreaming form and drew illusionary blood, driving me to wake, writhing and sweating.

Blinding, eye-searing flashes of red and white, which gradually resolve into a canopy of crimson with the brilliant sunlight of a Roman summer slashing through like a blade. The world below that shelter is a dreadful scarlet, battered and stabbed by those sharp beams of light.

The roar of a crowd is still audible as a din in the background.

I am moving, walking casually, calmly.

I am filled with a strange ennui, though that itself is just a boat of emotion bobbing upon a sea of despair that has always been there, dark and immense, threatening to engulf me. But now that is changing. The untroubled nature of my mind is cut through with new emotions . . . stark, terrifying ones.

The unexpected. A shock. Horror, even. How can this be?

My hand goes out to ward off the unseen threat. No! I am surrounded only by the trusted. This cannot happen. Such threat is the province of enemies, not friends.

Gleaming metal – blue Noric steel shining with that sickly all-pervading red glow – lances towards me. I lurch away and the blade that seeks my heart instead cuts through flesh and grinds against bone.

Agony. Flashes of agony and panic. Disbelief and horror.

Vinicius visited us on the twelfth day, the first time since Lugdunum. I asked, rather hurt and desperately I fear, where he had been. He had picked up a rather haunted look that worried me, and his own eyes were slung with bags, suggesting that he had been sleeping almost as badly as I. He apologised profusely, but warned me that his visits would continue to be rarities. He spent every hour the gods gave him now with my brother, trying to steer him on a path of which our father would be proud and in defiance of the eastern monarchs who constantly nudged him in the direction of a whole new kind of empire.

Vinicius told us about the situation, though, oddly, I believe it was I who told him more things of import when I passed on what I had seen of the army's mood.

Two more days passed in tense silence as I listened to the increasing disaffection in the camp around us, when the wind carried the whispers further than it should. Every few hours a new snatch of restless unhappiness.

'—and the centurions went to see the pissing *tribune!*'

'—see if we can delay till it's too late to sail.'

'—was caught vowing an altar to Neptune if the emperor's ship sank. It's the end for him, the poor bastard.'

'—think it's time we stood up for our rights.'

Then, as the sun rose that morning and the dew burned from the earth in wispy clouds, I saw Caligula again.

I happened to be at the door of our prison tent asking the Praetorians to refill our water bowl when the emperor rode into view. From the door flap we could see down a short alleyway of identical tents to the muster ground of those two legions, near their officers' quarters. Caligula was on Incitatus, and Vinicius and Agrippa were by his side, as were Galba, with whom we had ridden into Ara Ubiorum the previous year, and two more legates. Behind him were a century of Praetorians and a smaller, yet no less impressive, unit of his German Guard. They looked not so much like an emperor and his court as a war party.

'Where are your leading centurions?' my brother roared at the tents around him. I was shocked at the fury and violence in his voice. Had he changed so much in half a year? He bore precious little resemblance to the brother I had once known, his face pale, his eyes flashing dangerously.

Clearly surprised by this impromptu imperial visit, a number of officers poured from the tents of the First and the Twentieth, saluting and standing straight with their expressions carefully neutral. I stood watching, grateful that the Praetorian had not shoved me back inside, since he too was rapt at this development.

'Imperator,' coughed a man with a feathered crest, presumably the senior centurion of one of those legions. 'We—'

'There will be no talk of mutiny,' my brother roared. The centurions almost recoiled before him, and Caligula thrust out a finger at them. As he did so, the German bodyguards threw something, and two heads bounced across the turf, coming to rest before the man who had addressed him. I felt sick at the sight, even at this distance.

My brother, the head-taker!

'The legate and senior tribune of the Fourteenth legion,' Caligula announced, pointing at the heads. 'It has been brought to my attention that there is disaffection among the First and the Twentieth: a mood of rebellion at the thought of crossing that sea into a new land. And where a good legate should be stamping down such mutinous talk and making examples, I find instead that your officers had made the decision to defy imperial orders and planned to march away with their men. Moreover, I learn that they have been spreading their seditious talk among their peers. The legate of the loyal Fifth Alaudae was not so easily turned by treachery, unlike the commanders of the Fourteenth. Your own legates and tribunes have been taken into custody, awaiting my decision as to their fate. What of the centurions of these two troublesome legions? Do they share their commanders' disloyalty or, when they took their oath before their legion's eagle and standard to serve faithfully Rome, their commanders, and their emperor, did they consider it a binding truth?'

There was an uncomfortable silence.

'What is it? A legion of oath-breakers or a loyal army of Rome?'

'Imperator,' said another impressive-looking centurion, once the emperor had fallen silent again, 'I can assure you that even were our commanders to turn upon you, our legions would not walk away, and our men hold true to their oaths.'

It was well and bravely said, though I couldn't help but replay in my head the many whispered dissenting words I had heard among the legions.

Caligula snorted. 'Your very legions are the ones who mutinied against Tiberius when he took the throne. The very legions my father brought back into the fold. You served the traitor Gaetulicus. What sensible emperor could trust the loyalty of such units now? I am of a mind to be strict. I had even considered decimation . . .'

I stared in horror.

Decimation – a punishment from the days of old. The practice of randomly selecting every tenth man to be beaten to death by the other nine. The most brutal and humiliating punishment a legion can be given. From the cold silence, I could tell that the centurions were as shocked as I.

'Fortunately for you all, Vinicius here has a glib tongue and a soft heart. He has persuaded me that to punish you so harshly for the sins of your commanders would be unworthy. But the fact remains that you mutter of mutiny, for all your denials. You have been heard doing so, and I must respond in some way, lest

I be seen as weak and such insurrection spread throughout the army.'

'Majesty,' said a centurion, clearly a man of unsurpassed bravery, 'this sea cost Caesar forty ships. Storms are common. And the tribes on the island are—'

'The tribes of Britannia are no different to their Gaulish cousins!' Caligula snapped. 'And Caesar's ships were poorly moored during a storm, not crossing the sea. I am half persuaded to send the centurions of your two legions for a swim to see how many make it to Britannia. Caesar's standard bearer took the fight to the enemy and leapt from the ship into the water, urging the Tenth legion on, and here you are, two veteran legions, cowering in your tents. Shame on you all. Fortunate are you that during our enforced delay here the circumstances surrounding our friend, Prince Adminius, have changed, and we are no longer required in Britannia. The army will shortly be returning to its winter quarters.'

There was a sigh of relief from somewhere. I waited, tense. I knew my brother well enough even now to know that this was far from the end.

'Not these two legions,' he barked, angrily. 'Of all those assembled on this coast, only the First and the Twentieth had the temerity to speak openly of mutiny. Your legions need a lesson in humility and loyalty, I feel. Every centurion will see to it that his men gather up shells and stones and sand equal to the weight of their campaign gear. They will then march back to Rome with us, carrying both this new weight *and* their full marching pack. They shall do it quietly, accepting their lot with the stoicism that won Rome an empire. Any man heard complaining about their treatment will be removed from the lists of the legions and summarily dismissed without pay or pension. I will *not* have mutinous talk. The legions are the pride of Rome, her spine and her spirit. The eagle is feared by our enemies in every quarter. What do you think the Parthians or the Sarmatians would say if they discovered two legions that were afraid of crossing thirty miles of water? I am appalled. You and your men will suffer this punishment with humility and silence, and when I allow them finally to unburden themselves of this weight, the matter of their insubordination will be forgotten and never spoken of again, their honour restored. Do you understand?'

There was a barked chorus of affirmatives. My eyes were still on those two heads, though. My brother had been at odds with the senate since the day we left Capri, but he had never had trouble with the people or the army. They were his, and they always had been. Was I seeing a new fracture developing here? I hoped not. Despite what he had done to me, I still loved my golden brother, and the last thing I wanted was to see him beset from all sides.

I engineered a fake latrine break that afternoon and my Praetorian escort walked me over that rise, where we all slowed to watch in fascination ten thousand men gathering detritus from the seashore and slipping it into sacks, some carrying helmets full of shells and others using their cloaks as makeshift bags. And while the First and Twentieth legions gathered shame to carry all the way to Rome, their sister legions, who had seemingly remained loyal in both word and deed, gathered around the small lighthouse that had been constructed on a headland there to watch their emperor board a trireme and escort a prince of the Britons back out across the water towards his home. He only went a mile or two, I think, but the fact that he had done unthinkingly what the legions had so worried about was not lost upon anyone.

We set off south the next day, with the two punished legions slogging away under the most torturous weight, men falling out of line and collapsing under the pressure. The arrested tribunes, legates and prefects of the guilty legions had been stripped of their commands and now rode in disgrace with the baggage train, little more than prisoners, facing as uncertain a future as I. The breaking of the *sacramentum* – the military oath – was an offence that could be punished by death and their long faces, when I saw them as we mounted, suggested that was exactly what they now expected. The standards of the two legions had also been stowed away from them, partially in disgrace, but also to allow the standard bearers free hands with which to carry the same burden as their compatriots.

I settled in against a lumpy bag of something in the wagon for our return journey the length of Gaul. It was a slow, interminable business. Every day saw the two struggling legions reduced. Vinicius reported from time to time how many men had collapsed of exhaustion, their sacks of shells and pebbles falling away, and how many soldiers, unable to stand any longer the strain and the shame, had simply slipped away in the night – a dangerous choice carrying a fatal penalty. Every morning the names of any man who hadn't mustered were added to the list for the removal of pensions and benefits and would henceforth face the death penalty if found. Inexorably we moved south. Oddly, the mood among the soldiers gradually lightened. Despite the horrible burdens of the two legions with their punishment, by the time we passed into the lands of the famous Aedui in the heart of Gaul, only the strong and the determined remained. Perhaps a tenth of each legion had fallen or fled, but those who now marched south were steadfast and proud, shouldering their burdens heartily, looking ahead to the time their weight would be removed and their standards returned. They knew they had done wrong by their emperor, and they were fast on the way to retrieving their honour.

On one rainy, warm day when the world steamed, we passed by Lugdunum, though this time we did not stop. We moved into Cisalpine Gaul and then down into Italia proper. While the army was camped fifty miles north of Rome, near Cosa, Vinicius vouchsafed to me that a senate embassy had come to the emperor to welcome him back, which was something of a surprise, given their frosty relationship. Vinicius suspected that Vespasian had been the guiding hand in that, and he may have been right. Certainly, given the number of noble bodies that man had sent to the burial pits, no senator in his right mind was going to ignore one of Vespasian's suggestions. Whatever the case, my brother had told the deputation that he would need time to prepare his legions and entourage for the triumph.

The senators had frowned. 'Triumph?'

'Yes,' Caligula had said, now wearing a frown of his own. He had suppressed the German threat once more, personally, wetting his own blade with German blood, and had carried out the most successful campaign beyond the river since the days of his father, when the lost eagles of Varus' legions had been recovered. Moreover, he had done so with an army that had, until his arrival, been opposed to him and led by a traitor. He was due a triumph, and that was no petty boast. He had every right to expect one for what he had done.

The senators had shrugged. No such motion had come before the senate, and none would do so, they could assure him. They were here to welcome the emperor to Rome and invite him to the next sitting of the senate in the curia. I could imagine my brother's face at that invitation.

Vinicius sighed. 'There is an impasse now. The senate have no intention of voting your brother a triumph, though certainly there have been men who have enjoyed that honour for less than Caligula's achievements. But your brother *needs* that triumph. His reputation has been repeatedly tarnished by the tales of the senate and the knowledge that he has been forced to secure rebellious legions. He needs the triumph to rebuild his reputation. He will not enter Rome without the triumph he feels he deserves, and the senate will not grant him one.'

I frowned. 'Could he not just grant himself the triumph?' I

asked. 'After all, if he has the power to change the law and grant his sisters the same seating rights as he at the games, surely he could simply decide upon a triumph?'

Vinicius shook his head. 'His eastern friends have been urging just that. When they want something like that, they take it, regardless of what their lessers think. But that is not how Rome works, I reminded him. The emperor is not an autocrat. He is the first citizen, but not a divine king. The senate granting him a triumph would be seen as support from the elite of the city and would heal some of the rifts that are opening up, but to grant himself one would drive another wedge between your brother and the people. He cannot afford to do so.'

I shook my head.

'What will he do, then?'

'What *can* he do?' My husband shrugged. 'We will march to Rome, he will unburden the legions and heal *that* division, and then he will settle in and wait for the senate to change their mind.'

'And if they don't?' I prompted.

'Then I can see only two ways to proceed. Either he abandons Rome – perhaps sets himself up at Lugdunum again – or he marches into Rome with sharp steel leading the way like a Sulla of old.'

'Neither option will improve his lot,' I mused.

'Let him march on Rome,' snarled Agrippina. I blinked in surprise. They were the first words she had spoken to me in nearly a year other than accusation and name-calling.

'What?' Vinicius replied sharply.

'*Let* him march on Rome. There are plenty there who will wipe the smug victorious grin from his face. Sulla marched on Rome and he was dead five years later. Caesar marched on Rome and was dead six years later. Let us wager on how long dear little Gaius lasts before the senate's knives are sheathed in his back.'

There was cold silence for just two heartbeats before my fingers were clawing for my sister's throat, seeking to silence the bitch forever. Even strong, dangerous Agrippina would have ended her days there and then had Vinicius not pulled me off her and restrained me while my sister probed her scratched and bruised flesh.

Never had I had more urge to kill someone.

XXV

THE BLADE AGAINST MY NECK

We settled into the old estate of my mother's across the river from the city. I cannot tell you how odd it was to be back in the villa where we had made such happy childhood memories before all the trouble set in. Agrippina and I – and the ever-present urn of Lepidus – were imprisoned now in the old gardener's shed, from which we could see those seats where we had sat with Nero and Drusus when they came back from the African wars. I cannot say it was a joyful homecoming. The place was full of ghosts, though the restless dead could scarce create horrors to match the ones my own head produced in the blackest nights.

Blinding, eye-searing flashes of red and white, which gradually resolve into a canopy of crimson with the brilliant sunlight of a Roman summer slashing through like a blade. The world below that shelter is a dreadful scarlet, battered and stabbed by those sharp beams of light.

The roar of a crowd is still audible as a din in the background.

I am moving, walking casually, calmly.

I am filled with a strange ennui, though that itself is just a boat of emotion bobbing upon a sea of despair that has always been there, dark and immense, threatening to engulf me. But now that is changing. The untroubled nature of my mind is cut through with new emotions . . . stark, terrifying ones.

The unexpected. A shock. Horror, even. How can this be?

My hand goes out to ward off the unseen threat. No! I am surrounded only by the trusted. This cannot happen. Such threat is the province of enemies, not friends.

Gleaming metal – blue Noric steel shining with that sickly all-pervading red glow – lances towards me. I lurch away and the blade that seeks my heart instead cuts through flesh and grinds against bone.

Agony. Flashes of agony and panic. Disbelief and terror.

There is blood. My hand comes up and is oddly black within the red of my enclosed world. So much blood. I try to react, but I am prevented. I am stopped.

We stayed there for a month – the whole court in the villa and the army encamped upon the extensive estate, as well as the Praetorian Guard. The treachery of the two legions who had made to mutiny in the north was finally forgotten. Caligula had them relieved of their burdens and reinstated their standards. I suppose it should have irked me to think of the vineyards and manicured gardens of that large estate being flattened and swept aside to become the camping ground of tired, dirty legionaries, but little affected me so directly these days. Some mornings I awoke so raw and terrified from my dreams that it took me almost an hour to gather my wits – to remember both who and where I was. Some mornings there was no need to wake at all, for I had only witnessed sleep as it came to my bed and passed me by in search of calmer climes.

As if the opening of her lips at the camp had unsealed her tongue, now Agrippina was talking again, and once more I spent every pale-skinned, watery-eyed, hateful day in that shed resisting the urge to rip out her tongue and stamp on it. She was unable to speak now without her lips dripping venom.

'He is doomed,' she would say. 'The city is closed to him and if he enters it under arms, he will become a traitor to Rome rather than a saviour.'

I grunted.

'The people are starting to hate him. I can feel it: a wave of dissent like a fog bank, rising from the streets of Rome and rolling, silent and hateful across the river to engulf him.'

Still I fought the urge to silence her for good.

'There is no way forward, Livilla,' she said in a matter-of-fact manner. 'Gaius Caligula will not see out this year. His reign is coming to an end. And he has only a girl to follow – a baby girl with a slack-witted mother.'

'Milonia Caesonia is far from slack-witted,' I snapped, rising to the bait despite my determination not to.

'An appraisal carried out by the slack-witted,' she replied nastily, and I fought once more the urge to hit her, instead sitting back and hugging my knees.

'Time to decide where your own loyalties lie, sister,' Agrippina said.

'What?'

'When our dear brother can no longer hold together his empire – when his tenuous grip on power finally fails him, Rome will be open. The empire will need a new leader. Lepidus is gone. Claudius is a stammerer and a lame creature. The senate would never serve him. I am the eldest surviving child of Germanicus and I harbour a boy. An heir who could be emperor of Rome.'

'He is little more than a baby,' I said in disbelief.

'That will change in time. I told you that this imprisonment would not be the end of me. My son will be the emperor of Rome. And every day now brings our brother's fall and my son's rise closer.'

I fell silent. So did Agrippina. But where my silence was born of nervous worry, hers was smug and self-congratulatory.

Rumour began to spread. Even in our small enclosed world, I heard what was being said in the city – lies and accusations started by the remnants of the senate and propagated among the people. That my brother had been abandoned by the gods. That even Neptune despised him enough to stop him crossing the sea. That he intended to abolish the senate and rule as an 'oriental god-king'. The longer we stayed, the worse the rumours became. My brother was starting to fret so much over it all that he was becoming quite ill, or so Vinicius claimed. Paler, drawn and more ill-tempered even than usual.

I had a momentary memory of my brother in just such a state after Drusilla's death. I could imagine how he was now feeling. The senate were goading him. And once that had started, if he crossed into the city with his army, it would be seen as war.

'Rome is lost to him, isn't it?' I'd asked Vinicius, aware that I was rather ironically echoing the words of Agrippina that had started our latest argument.

He had no answer to that. He just sat with me in the silence, his face once more disapproving of the way Caligula's rule progressed.

But my brother was no idiot. In fact, crisis always brought out the best in him, in terms of ingenuity, at least. Over that time in the villa, where people thought him sulking or hiding from the world, what he was doing was scheming. Caught between what he could not do and what Rome would not give, he sat in the villa and worked through every angle of the problem in solitude as he had so often done in the dangerous times at our grandmother's house or on Capri. And finally, one day, an answer formed itself in his mind. What Caligula planned was both grand and insane. It was audacious and magnificent and dangerous.

*

Days later we were on the move again, but there was something new, now. Where the journey from the north had been subdued and dark, negative and uncertain, now the army had an air of positivity. Shed of their burden of guilt and shame, the First and Twentieth legions had once more polished up their armour, raised their standards and marched with pride. Their rocks and shells lay gathered in the villa of my mother and now Caligula had distributed among the legions instead a donative of one hundred denarii each for their continued support. Honouring a legion can buy a man their loyalty, but it is clear to all that nothing secures fidelity like cold silver.

My brother's grand plan unfolded. We travelled south once more, bypassing Rome entirely, and moving along the coast, past the summer villas of the rich and influential. It took days to reach our destination. We could have been fast had we taken ship from Ostia, but the emperor needed his legions for this. When we arrived on the peninsula of Cape Misenum, opposite Puteoli and within sight of the towering point of Vesuvius, Agrippina and I were startled by a visit from Caligula.

He appeared on his horse alongside our rickety wagon, my husband beside him with a grim face and the German Guard all around for his protection. They watched me carefully as though I might leap from the cart and try to wring his neck. Of course, they believed me capable of just that, and I knew that Agrippina *could*.

'I have decided upon your fate,' he said in leaden tones. I felt my heart skip at the words. It had been over a year now since the failed plot had been cracked open and I had been incarcerated with my dreadful sister. While I still had awful nightmares and my life was drab and uncomfortable even compared with most plebs, I had felt oddly safe in the knowledge that I was alive and relatively healthy, and there had always been that faint hope of clemency in the future. My brother's expression tore away that last in a moment, and I knew now that whatever fate he had decreed would be unenviable, and was about to fall upon me. I held my breath. Agrippina simply sneered.

'In fact, I had decided your fate back in the villa at Rome, and could easily have enacted it there, but I am to have my triumph for Germania, and I felt it fitting that you both be here to see it, since Germania was the scene of your grand unmasking, and the plot you devised that led to the army commander there forcing my hand.'

I opened my mouth to deny my guilt, but closed it once more. There was no point. My brother would not believe me, and he had made his decision. In my imagination, I felt already the blade against my neck, waiting to cut.

'You will witness the triumph,' he said. 'The senate will not vote me one, and clearly I cannot vote one for myself, but the *army* has done so. The same army that *you* turned on me. The legions that your co-conspirator would have arrayed against me.'

Now, Agrippina did begin to argue, but my brother was in no mood to listen to her. 'Silence!' he roared, and she blanched. 'You will witness two days of glory and then you will be taken from Misenum by ship to your places of exile.'

Exile! My blood ran cold with memories of mother and of Nero, starved to death in their solitary worlds. Was this to be my fate now, too?

'Agrippina will spend the rest of her life on Pontia, in the villa where our dear beloved brother Nero was confined, and Livilla . . .'

No. Not that.

'To Pandataria, and the prison villa of our mother.'

I fell, the cold darkness of a faint claiming me.

The gulls screeched and wheeled against the featureless blue of the Campanian sky, their lofty cries melding with the sounds of an army below. The smell of men's sweat and armour oil was almost buried beneath the combined scent of salt water, olive oil and tar. But it was neither audible nor olfactory matters that truly drew the attention that day. It was sight.

And what a sight.

For the great bay of Baiae had been bridged. The three-mile expanse of water that formed the mouth of the Roman navy's greatest port, from headland to headland, had been bridged. I was sure, as my eyes strayed along that vast, seemingly endless structure, that no man or woman in the history of the world had conceived of such a thing.

Three miles. And not for the future, destined to be a reminder of my brother's glorious reign. No, this was all for one spectacular event. The greatest bridge the world had ever seen, and it would last just days.

The bridge was of boats and stretched from Baiae to Puteoli like a solid wall of jostling timber, a sight to make the gods wonder. The vessels had been freshly tarred, pulled together and filled with heavy ballast to prevent them bouncing around wildly, then tethered tight with ropes. A timber walkway had then been laid across the top, wide and straight and preserved with olive oil.

I stared in wonder. Three years earlier Caligula and I had espied this bay from our eyrie on Capri. 'They look so close,' I had said. And now they were. Had my brother been thinking of that day – thinking of me, even – when he planned this architectural marvel?

The blaring of the horns cut through the warm, salty air – the fanfare for a glorious, triumphal emperor. Half a hundred *cornu* players standing by the seashore blew their melody as the army came up from Baiae, at its head my glorious brother. He rode Incitatus, all black and shiny and proud – his favourite steed. His breastplate was burnished to a blinding sheen, bearing a gorgon's head embossed on the chest and two decorative rondels – a cuirass that was said to have belonged to the great Macedonian conqueror Alexander himself. As he reached the end of the bridge, he reined in the magnificent black beast and drew his sword, holding it aloft so that it caught the sunlight and flashed dazzlingly. The blade was a marvel of the smith's art, said to be that very one that Julius Caesar had used to conquer Gaul, that he had wielded at the Sabis and at Alesia. And atop his head was the victor's wreath.

He was on a horse for this triumph, not in a chariot as a victorious general would be in Rome. This triumph was a military one, not a civil one, and Caligula had no use for a slave in his vehicle whispering that he was no god. For he was clearly, if not a god, then a living demigod rising to rival them. He had challenged Neptune and tethered the untameable sea god.

Behind the emperor, the rest of the triumph formed up, led by his three closest companions. Vinicius, my husband, dressed as I had never seen him, like an army commander in red and gold and burnished bronze. Antiochus, the swarthy king of Commagene, in his Greek-style armour looking like a dark reflection of Alexander, with a high-crested Phrygian helmet. Julius Agrippa, his strange apparel an odd mix of Jewish tradition and Roman military. They did little to Romanise proceedings. The group looked as disparate a bunch as ever rode together – Roman and Greek and Jew, pale and swarthy, blond and brown and black of hair. If all the world had gathered together they could have not made a more fascinating group.

After them came the Praetorian Guard in their best polished dress finery, three *alae* of gleaming, white-clad cavalry and two cohorts of guardsmen on foot. Behind them, dressed in clean clothes and properly bathed and primped for the first time in a year, were Agrippina and myself. I had to be grateful that we had not been driven along in chains at the front as was the norm for captives in these processions, though this was far from a normal triumph. Agrippina had made to rest the urn on the floor of the carriage in which we rode, but the Praetorians riding alongside warned her that the emperor's words still held and she was expected to carry it until the day she delivered it to the mausoleum that would house it for eternity. She suffered dreadfully trying to maintain her hold on the heavy, cumbersome item as the carriage bounced and lurched, and all I could think of was how much I enjoyed watching her suffer.

The leading veteran cohorts of the legions brought back from the north came next, and as the emperor's sword swept down in signal, the column moved onto the bridge. More than one set of eyes in the army dropped nervously to the timbers beneath their feet, since a three-mile pontoon bridge, for all its expected integrity, had never been tested with so much weight, and the stamping feet of thousands upon thousands of boots and hooves thudding in time made the whole bridge tremble and groan. More than one man present – and notably one girl – had read Caesar's war diary and knew the tale of the collapsing bridge at Ilerda. The men and animals and carts swept away in the waters of the Sicoris, soldiers dragged to their death by their armour. And that was just a river. This was Neptune's realm – the sea itself. I shuddered.

'Domine Neptune,' I said under the lightest of breath, 'bear aloft this procession, I beseech you. Seek not the embrace of the children of Germanicus.'

Not the army. Not the Praetorians and not even our old friends. Oddly, and with a pang of guilt, I realised that I had sought Neptune's protection for the three of us and not even mentioned my husband. A foolish prayer, for certain, given that Vinicius held the cords to my heart in his hands while Agrippina could wash up grey and stinking on a foreign beach for all I cared. I needed to be more thoughtful in my prayers. Agrippina's eyebrow rose, dragging the rest of her face into one of her sneers.

'Domine Neptune,' she said in a low hiss, 'take the offering of a pointless sister and a foolish brother and bring me back to the arms of my son.'

I glared.

'He is proving them wrong. The things they said about him in Rome . . .'

I was silenced by a gesture and a hard glare from the German guardsmen who rode alongside us. I am not sure what it says about both my brother and I that even now, days from an exile that would likely mean lonely death on Caligula's order, still I defended him in the face of our twisted sibling's bile.

The people of Rome had missed out on one of the world's great spectacles, I thought as we moved. They would blame the senators, for it was because of them that the emperor bypassed Rome. But what the Roman populace lacked, the people of the Bay of Neapolis gained. Even before we left the Roman villa, while he was finalising his remarkable plans, the emperor had sent ahead a fortune to fund the inevitable celebrations. People from as far afield as Pompeii, Capua and even Formiae had come to watch, crowding into the inns and bunkhouses of the local towns and even camping on the parched grass outside the urban sprawls. The crowds were immense, hanging from every window and even sitting on the roofs to secure a good view of the spectacle. The money my brother lavished had bought enough wine to float a ship, and it was given gratis to the people who attended. Some were so drunk they fell into the sea while cheering.

Slowly, the procession moved forward, something never before seen by the people of Rome. An army on the sea. The longest bridge ever built – three miles of floating timber and, at the centre of it, the bridge rose a little where larger barges had been utilised instead of smaller hulls, creating a wide platform for uses unknown. It was incredible. It was terrifying and exhilarating all at once.

The German guards beside us were now paying little or no attention, their eyes locked on the shifting timbers beneath them, the general din of the world filling the air and assaulting the ears. I contemplated speaking to Agrippina again, though I knew whatever was said would simply make me angry, so I kept my peace and watched.

It took an hour to cross the boats. It could have been done faster, especially with the veteran soldiers present, but the whole thing was as much about appearance and spectacle as it was about achievement. As the head of the column neared Puteoli, the legions' musicians blared out the calls once more, and the army charged. As though they were racing into battle against the city itself, they charged the last quarter mile of that bridge, the legions chanting the word 'im-per-a-tor' in time with their pounding feet. They charged with weapons levelled. Panic tore through the assembled spectators, people throwing themselves into the sea in fright. And then, as the army reached the end of the bridge and passed onto the stone quayside of Puteoli, the second call went out, the charge stopped as suddenly as it started, and the emperor and his men rode and marched slowly through Puteoli to the camping grounds that had been prepared. The people did not know what to think. Rome grows and survives through its army, the greatest in the history of the world, but few of the Roman people had ever seen more than a scuffle between bandits and the urban cohorts. I doubt any present that day had even seen a legion on the march, let alone charging as though a horde of Germans stood before them. It was a spectacle for the people unlike anything they had ever seen. It was the might of Rome showed off in all its deadly and incredible glory, and at its head was my brother, like some Homeric hero of old – a warrior prince.

The panic suddenly turned to explosive laughter and applause as hearts thundered and women fainted with relief, snatching up their children from the approaching army. The emperor Gaius Caligula had conquered the sea! And that day he conquered the hearts of the people again

Word of the event reached Rome that same day, I understand, and already those same people who had called him a tyrant, abandoned by the gods, were now calling him the 'new Alexander', and saying that he was greater than the Persian king, Xerxes, who could only bridge the narrow Bosphorus.

And that was just the start. The next day was the *real* triumph. The first day had been a show of power, designed to win the hearts of the people, and it had done so in spectacular fashion. The second would be the true event that my brother had missed in Rome. We went back across the bridge, this time with Caligula in his toga on a chariot drawn by four horses, in the manner of a traditional triumph. Each of those horses was one of the prized racers of the four factions from the Circus in Rome. The chubby Vitellius had brought them south for Caligula. My brother rode like a conquering god with my husband standing behind and holding the wreath above him.

While the legions were drawn up into units along the length of the bridge, the emperor and the court gathered close to the centre where the wide platform had been built on those larger barges. The legions and the Guard were stood down and allowed to feast and drink on the bridge. The mood was good – except in the small gathering where I sat as far as possible from Agrippina and her urn, both of us hemmed in tightly by Praetorians, forced to watch the spectacle but unable to take joy in it. My brother rose then and spoke to his army. His voice, powerful though it was, would not have reached more than a few cohorts to either side along the bridge, but Caligula was no fool. At intervals along the span, slaves chosen for their voice alone echoed his every word so that no soldier that day missed his speech.

'My children,' he announced in a booming orator's voice, 'for who is more a father to the army than I . . .'

There was an appropriately loud roar of approval, and where I sat with Agrippina under guard, away from all others that mattered, I mused on the irony that *Little Boots*, the boy who had marched with his father's army, had now become their master, and they treated him just as they had the great Germanicus in his day. This speech was for the army, not the public in the cities to either end of the structure.

'I stand at the heart of a circle of the valiant and the strong,' the emperor announced. 'Beside me stands Helicon, who served the old tyrant faithfully and has never once failed in his duty to me. The German Guard, my personal force, who remain steadfast and loyal as always. The Praetorian Guard, clear now of the foul influence of those corrupt and wicked prefects, are a strong, loyal force – the best of Roman manhood. And the legions that accompany me here on this bridge have always followed their conscience, even into danger, but despite everything their corrupt masters would have had them do in Gaul, they remain loyal to their eagle, to Rome, and to their emperor.'

There was an uncertain silence. Doubtless many there wanted nothing less than to be reminded of the rebellions and plots that had almost brought them and their units dishonour. Still, they waited on Caligula's next word. I could not see him from here, or even his court, but I could imagine his face as he decided how to progress. His strange sense of humour did on occasion shoot wide of the mark and I wondered if it had done so here.

'Your loyalty has been tested, but you have not been found wanting. Not one of you.'

A general sense of relief flooded the air now.

'No emperor – not great Augustus or dark Tiberius – could claim a better, more loyal army than I. Jove, even the great Caesar himself, a soldier's soldier, had no better men than I. I salute you!'

He must have toasted the men then, for all along the bridge, even by us, men lifted a cup and drank.

'All our doubt is now in the past,' he went on once more when the cups were lowered, 'but there remain a small number of souls who were torn from their command on the coast of Gaul for their part in inciting mutiny. They have been with us throughout our long journey, a canker in the body of the army. The time has come to deal with that sickness.'

I felt a dread anticipation settle upon me, though I seemed to be alone, the mood on the bridge once more riding oddly high, given those last few ominous words.

Fires had been lit on the shore all the way around the bay and the darkness as the day faded could achieve no hold on proceedings. The assembly watched in the golden glow of a thousand beacons as a dozen ships came bobbing out of Puteoli's harbour. They were actually small rowing boats, but had been arrayed and painted to look like triremes, with Hellenic designs on small fake sails. The entire congregation wondered what was happening, for this had not been part of the planned festivities known to any observer. The dozen ships sailed towards the platform at the centre, each powered by two oarsmen with a commander standing behind. Each of them had a specially made small ramming beak on the front. They were magnificent, and the bridge roared with laughter at the sight.

'Behold, the Battle of Salamis,' Caligula announced, grinning. 'The Greeks and the Persians will fight and sink for your entertainment, all brought to you by the officers of the First and Twentieth legions.'

A dreadful end for those officers responsible for the mutiny of the legions in the north. All patricians and equestrians of Rome, they had been brought south with the army as prisoners, and that night they crewed a dozen boats in mock battle. They were to a man weighed down with heavy armour and as the battle progressed to the cheers of the crowd, those who lost, their 'ship' sinking, were pulled down to the bottom of the sea by the weight of their mail shirts. The beacon fires were so bright that for some distance all observers could see to the bottom of the clear water, and could spot the mutinous officers lying on the seabed, motionless.

I had a momentary flash of memory that dragged me from the scene. Men falling, screaming, from the balcony of Tiberius' villa on Capri, where they would slap into the water, dead before they even sank beneath the surface. I pictured that poor dismembered courier lying on the seabed below the Villa Jovis staring sightlessly up at his killer's domain.

I watched in mounting horror as men next to whom I had sat at banquets in Rome tumbled from boats that had become little more than cracking timber and plunged into the bay, screaming, their cries swallowed by the water as they thrashed all the way to the bottom, fighting to free themselves of the deadly armour. And then, moments later, they were swaying in the current at the bottom of a brightly lit sea, the sand golden around them beneath the calm surface as they expired. My fretting at the hem of my tunic became frantic. I was suddenly less appalled at the notion of a solitary island. As I watched my brother's twisted joke at the expense of his enemies steal the breath from a dozen Roman nobles, I even wished momentarily that I was on Pandataria and away from this grisly scene.

'They are *rebels*, Livilla,' said a quiet voice behind me, and I was surprised to see Julius Agrippa there. His influence was great enough that the Praetorians had not barred his way, and he had brought Agrippina and me a cup of wine each. He proffered them and I took mine gratefully, sinking the heady brew in an effort to numb my senses. Agrippina merely turned up her lip at this unexpected gesture of generosity, and so Agrippa shrugged and began to drink the wine himself.

'They should have died ignominiously in the north,' he said

quietly. 'Instead, they were given a chance. Those who are victorious tonight will be freed and their lands and honour restored. Those the gods favour less? Well, they will meet their end the way they had always been destined to.'

I was less inclined to see mercy there. Many of the vessels were already broken and most of their crew already gazing up at us, lifeless, from the seabed. There would be few men freed tonight. Some of the lucky losers clung to floating timber and were slowly making it to safety, and the emperor magnanimously forgave them as they reached the bridge or the shore, where they were collected and brought before him one by one. Across from me, one tribune who sank even managed to struggle out of his mail before he took a fatal breath. Still, there were precious few heaving sighs of relief as they enjoyed the emperor's largesse.

'It's horrible.'

'I think your husband agrees,' Agrippa said, quietly. 'I am not at all sure he is entirely at peace with your brother's sense of humour these days. He does not look amused. He and a few of his friends are even helping some of the survivors back to dry land, though the emperor decreed there was to be no help for them.'

'Will he be punished?' I asked.

Agrippa shook his head. 'Vinicius remains close to your brother and is trusted. He believes he can be Caligula's conscience. He dares not leave his side for fear that the emperor will do something dangerous. We are travelling north once more for Rome in the morning, and Vinicius will go with the emperor. He regrets that he will not see you before you leave for Pandataria – the emperor has forbidden us all from consorting with you tonight, though I felt compelled to flaunt my influence. Your husband will come soon, though. When he knows that your brother is safe in Rome and the excesses of Vespasian have been curbed. Once Rome is at peace, there will be time.

And know that both he and I continue to lobby the emperor for your freedom.'

Agrippa left when the wine was drunk and we were alone amid a sea of people once more. Once the 'entertainment' was deemed concluded, Agrippina and I were escorted to the harbour at Misenum, where we were placed on board two ships that awaited the morning tide to whisk us away to exile.

On the way, I briefly caught sight of my beloved husband helping a coughing, soaked officer along the timbers, though he did not see me. And I saw my brother, his face a theatre mask of beaming smiles that never, even for a heartbeat, reached his cold, dead eyes.

XXVI

SOLITUDE

Agrippina went north. She still bore Lepidus' urn, had done so long now that it seemed an extension of herself. She went to Rome to deliver the urn to its resting place, and then, without ceremony or pause, boarded her ship once more, prodded forward by Praetorians like recalcitrant cattle bound for market, and was taken to her place of exile.

Me? I boarded my ship with an odd mix of panic and relief. I was sore at heart that on the last night before I was taken away, Vinicius had chosen to stay and help the poor, beleaguered, drowning officers rather than come to me. That he chose curbing my brother's excess over his duty to his wife. That Agrippa chose to override my brother's orders and come and see me, but my husband didn't. I cannot complain in truth. Vinicius was being what he had always purported to be: a loyal servant of Rome, doing what he had to in order to preserve the empire we all knew.

Still it rankled.

My prison.

Pandataria is small and barely inhabited, only two miles long and eight hundred paces wide. A tiny hamlet at one end and three or four villas around the shoreline. Escape was impossible, even if I'd had anywhere to go. I was incarcerated in the same villa as my mother, which chilled me to the bone. I had last seen her as a child, walking away with her tightly pinned rippling hair and that elegant indigo palla, and now I was to be kept in the very place where she had lived out her last days alone and grieving. The knowledge was almost too much to bear.

It was a sumptuous enough place, I suppose, but a prison is a prison, no matter how gilded the bars. I explored the villa and its grounds until I was thoroughly bored with it all. I had two slaves, Horion and Annius, who cooked – almost exclusively fish caught at the shoreline by the villa – and cleaned for me, but I had no companions. A unit of mercenaries, ex-soldiers from the look of them, lived in the tiny settlement at the other end of the island, and they were paid a small stipend to check on the villa daily and make sure I was still there and still alive and – most importantly, I think – still alone.

I spent some time in those first days leaning on the sill of a window and looking out to sea, watching the birds until even their antics became tiresome. Not once did I see a boat – even that of a peasant fisherman. On the fourth day, I could see a hazy line on the horizon and realised I had spotted land. When the guard came to check on me, I asked him if that was the mainland, and he told me that no, that was Pontia, the prison of my lying sister. I closed the shutters on that window and tied them in place. I had no interest in seeing that island or thinking on its occupant.

I spent three months rattling around in that shoreside villa. In all that time I saw just eight people – two slaves and six mercenary guards. And none of them were over-friendly. After all, my exile might be paying the guards' wages, but all eight of them were stuck on Pandataria because of me, and their bitter gazes never let me forget that. The nightmares that had now become such an ever-present part of my life that I scarcely thought about them, considering them a natural part of sleep, abated briefly as I arrived on the island, making way instead for a series of odd, disjointed dreams that made little sense. But within a week the terrors were back, and I was once more spending my nights with knives and blood and screaming, my bedclothes soaked with sweat. In a way, I welcomed them back after the odd dreams. They had become strangely comforting, as though nothing that could happen in the waking world could match my imagination.

Blinding, eye-searing flashes of red and white, which gradually resolve into a canopy of crimson with the brilliant sunlight of a Roman summer slashing through like a blade. The world below that shelter is a dreadful scarlet, battered and stabbed by those sharp beams of light.

The roar of a crowd is still audible as a din in the background.

I am moving, walking casually, calmly.

I am filled with a strange ennui, though that itself is just a boat of emotion bobbing upon a sea of despair that has always been there, dark and immense, threatening to engulf me. But now that is changing. The untroubled nature of my mind is cut through with new emotions . . . stark, terrifying ones.

The unexpected. A shock. Horror, even. How can this be?

My hand goes out to ward off the unseen threat. No! I am surrounded only by the trusted. This cannot happen. Such threat is the province of enemies, not friends.

Gleaming metal – blue Noric steel shining with that sickly all-pervading red glow – lances towards me. I lurch away and the blade that seeks my heart instead cuts through flesh and grinds against bone.

Agony. Flashes of agony and panic. Disbelief and terror.

There is blood. My hand comes up and is oddly black within the red of my enclosed world. So much blood. I try to react, but I am prevented. I am stopped.

I am helpless, and it is trusted ones that seek my end. Why? What have I done to deserve this?

I shout, but that shout goes nowhere, gathered up by the limp crimson canopy and hurled back at me. The myriad voices far away cheer still, unaware that I am imperilled.

Three months passed slowly and with an almost unbelievable level of tedium. It was becoming hard to remember what day it was. Solitude does strange things to the mind, and mine had already been deteriorating since that first nightmare in Ara Ubiorum so many months ago. I spent day after day sitting or working in the front garden of my prison, waiting and watching for my husband. I threw myself into keeping the gardens tidy. I am not naturally a gardening person. They say some people have green fingers and merely have to move among the flowers to watch them flourish. I, then, have *grey* fingers. Flowers die when I water them, and plants do not thrive under my care. Of course, as a matron of Rome I have never needed horticultural knowledge beyond what looks best to decorate an atrium.

Still, I gradually learned a few things through trial and error, and I managed, with the sullen and grudging aid of Horion, to catch and tether two goats who were wandering close to my villa. I do not know to whom they belonged, but they cropped the lawns down to a pleasing level, and removing their dung and occasionally fighting them off was a small price to pay.

I weeded. I was good at that. I was to my garden what Vespasian had been to Rome, beheading proud plants and cutting down thriving weeds in swathes. I began to imagine the plants screaming with every killing blow. Solitude, again.

Slowly, over two or three weeks, the garden began to take shape. I had gathered together the various pieces of sculpture from around the villa one day when I was excruciatingly bored and painted them all in odd colours using pigments crushed and ground from whatever I could find in the villa and its gardens. They were gaudy and odd, and looked like a child had been at work. And on the end one, I had begun to experiment with sculpting, using a chisel I found in a garden shed. Some serious-faced republican statesman now had a stubby nose, one lip, one ear and a crack in his cheek. I put my marble creations proudly on display in my neat garden. Then the next day I removed them, realising how unsightly they made the place look.

I began to compose small ditties in my head as I worked. They invariably failed to rhyme, but their lyrical content was interesting, for they were born of whatever subject was on my mind at the time, which means they varied wildly from the nature of captivity to the hell of betrayal, to the loss of family, to the absence of a loved one, to why bees buzz, and so on. A quarter of a year of keeping only one's own company makes the mind stray, I can tell you.

I worked the garden as the autumn set in, and when I was tired of nursing plants, I would sit and let the late sun warm my skin to the gentle hum of bees and birds and the lapping waves. I suppose if one must have a prison, there are worse places than Pandataria. Ask any of those wretched senators who overnighted in the carcer before their head rolled down the steps into the forum.

I am to this day not entirely sure whether the villa was haunted by the *lemure* – the dark restless spirit – of my mother, or whether the pressure of solitude on my poor mind made me dream up the image, but one morning as I staggered, exhausted and grey from another sleepless night, I saw my mother, standing in the triclinium, still in that same saffron-coloured stola and indigo palla, pinned hair escaping in small wavy wisps. I'd thought I caught glimpses of her before, but this was clear as the daylight. She looked well, if sad and unearthly pale. Oddly, I felt more comforted than afraid, though a little dismayed when I spoke to her and she appeared to hear me but produced no reply. I almost reached out to touch her, but could not bear the possibility that my hand might pass through her. I left the room for a cup of water and when I returned she had gone.

That was not the last time I saw her. Indeed, she became something of an irregular, silent visitor to the villa and I became so used to seeing her, even if out of the corner of my eye, that I began to speak to her, to confide in her my feelings and ideas. She became the sounding board for my scattered, flittering thoughts.

I was on Pandataria for three months before I had any other visitor than the six surly guards who watched over the island and my ghostly mother. I became aware of the sudden activity instantly. When you have been alone for so long in a silent, solitary place, you become unusually sensitive to change. I hurried to the door to see six horsemen riding towards me. Five were soldiers in full armour . . . the other was my husband. Elation flooded through me. It was just after lunchtime when they came, and I was busy eating a plate of fruit and drinking the sour wine from the cellars while involved in a rather one-sided discourse with Mother on the nature of weeds. I had become used to the taste of the bitter wine now and barely even bothered to water it. Since that summer, I have been unable to drink good wine. The sweetness and headiness is not to my taste.

My husband dismounted, ran to the door and threw his arms around me. I had never been more grateful for an embrace. After what seemed like an eternity of joy, he stepped back and gestured to his men. The soldiers were sent into the village for the night, and we went inside.

My husband was full of news. I didn't hear it until the next day, though, of course. That evening was ours and ours alone. I had not seen Vinicius for months, and whereas I had been too busy in Rome to miss him in his other recent absences, now, in my island cell, I had no such luxury. I had missed him more than I realised I could. We shared my lonely bed as husband and wife that night, and for a few short hours the world was less horrible.

The next day, when we were secure in my triclinium, the servants absent about their surly business, we sat and talked. He took to a couch and, while I poured him a well-watered wine to disguise the sharp taste of the low-quality stock to which I was fast becoming used, Vinicius began.

'Things are turning from bad to worse in Rome.'

I frowned. Here I was exiled in solitude on a rock in the ocean. My husband had come to me for the first time in three months and he expected me to be overly concerned about Rome? You shoot wide of your target, husband. Rome could tear itself apart for all I cared. No. That wasn't quite true. Despite everything, I still cared for my brother. And he was part of Rome. He *was* Rome, to some extent.

My face must have revealed this chain of emotions and thoughts, for Vinicius frowned at me. I had spent so long with no need to hide my feelings that I could no longer really remember how to do so.

'Livilla, I am torn.'

'What is it?'

Vinicius sighed. 'I love Gaius. I always have. He has been a brother to me in more than just a familial connection. He is as close as any man in my heart, and it pains me to know that you, who I love even more, and he cannot be together, and that I cannot have both of you.'

Something about his eyes suggested that this was not the point he intended to make, so I waited silently.

'But I love Rome too, Livilla. I love your brother and I have remained loyal to him throughout everything, despite growing increasingly uncomfortable with the way he works, but I love Rome, and Rome must be preserved at all costs. And between your brother and the senate, Rome will soon perish.'

I sagged back on to a couch. 'My brother is beloved of the people. I remember how they reacted at Puteoli. They adore him, now more than ever. The senate have thrown every obstacle they could in his way and he has overcome them all. Better, he has turned them often to his advantage. And the army are behind him.' I tried not to think about that mutiny in the north, the rolling heads, the drowning tribunes . . .

'The army and the plebs are not enough, Livilla. Yes, with them Caligula is the most popular man to rule in Rome since Caesar, but the mob and the soldiers are not Rome entire. They are *part* of Rome. The senate, the consuls, the equestrians . . . these are the bones and muscle of the empire. And they are being systematically exterminated. Rome cannot exist the way your brother seems to envisage it, Livilla.'

I rubbed my cold arms and sighed. 'Agrippa told me at Baiae you were looking after him, playing the part of his conscience.'

'I *have* been, Livilla. But you have no idea what it's like. I can curb the worst, but he listens to the army and the mob and to freedmen like Callistus and Protogenes as much as to me. And Antiochus and Agrippa do not help, for their eastern monarchic ways do not meld well with ours, and in trying to help they simply make matters worse.'

He stepped towards me and grasped my hands in his.

'Livilla, the senate is down to about fifty serving men. The rift between them and your brother is irreparable. The senatorial families that have survived purge after purge have fled Rome and live in self-imposed exile as far from the capital as they can manage, hoping to maintain a future for their lines. Rome is all but run by soldiers and freedmen on behalf of your brother. I have tried to talk him around, but he is adamant that the senate ruins Rome and that it must go. He doesn't say as much in public, of course. Your brother is clever as always. He gained yet more popularity by returning to Rome and putting an end to Vespasian's bloodbath – a bloodbath for which he himself was responsible. One cannot blame the dog for killing when its master removes the leash and sets it to task, after all. But he did not *stop* the blood flowing when he tethered Vespasian. He just found new outlets for it where the people could not see. His favour is so important for survival now that the nobles of Rome are killing each other just in the hope of pleasing the emperor. The families that founded Rome and guided it through centuries of turmoil are culling themselves willingly. It is sickening to watch, Livilla.'

I was still a little uncertain how I felt about it. I loved my brother, and the noble families of Rome had given me precious little reason to prize them. They had tried time and again to destroy our family and kill my brother. I could hardly blame him for his view. But then I remembered the lifeless eyes of so many noble officers staring up at me from the waters of Baiae and it made me shudder. Was I truly willing to see the bones of Rome crumble?

'Can you not even concede the possibility, Vinicius, that those families have guided Rome to this very point. That while you blame Caligula, it is the senate that has brought this upon itself? Remember that my brother opened his reign with magnanimity. He tried to please the senate, and in return they planted a blade in his back.'

'Perhaps they saw what was coming. There have been more attempts, Livilla. The senatorial class is desperate now. Another conspiracy was unearthed last month. Five more senators died. Canus the poet died! A *poet*, by Jove! Just for a slightly mocking verse. And another smaller plot was foiled last week. Anicius Cerialis was brought low by the investigation and the Praetorians came for the suspects at his banquet in celebration of the Lupercalia. They executed three of his guests in his atrium, quite brutally. From what I understand there was so much blood you couldn't see the mosaic of the floor. Can you not see how this is destroying our world?'

'*Your* world,' I said, bitterly. '*My* world is four walls and enough sea to drown in a million times.'

'Do you remember Proculus?' he said suddenly.

Gods, some days I struggled to remember my own name. I gave him a blank look.

'Proculus,' he urged. 'He owned a house on the Esquiline that your brother forced him to sell so he could turn it into a lavish stable for that damned horse of his?'

Ah yes. Long nose, little hair, expensive clothes. The man, not the horse. Incitatus was hairier.

'Proculus bowed to your brother in the forum. Caligula merely frowned at him and asked why someone who hated him so much would bother bowing. You know what happened? The other senators there tore Proculus apart. They *killed* him in the forum, just because he hated Caligula and they hoped to curry a little favour through his death. I was there. I was behind your brother when it happened. They quite literally tore the man apart. And that is what is happening to Rome. It is being torn apart. I truly do not believe your brother will stop until the senate is a thing of the past and the entire senatorial class has been exterminated. Or rather has exterminated *itself* through fear. Because your brother doesn't do it, you know? The killing, I mean. As far as the mob can see, the upper classes are just culling themselves, and the emperor remains as popular as ever with the other people of Rome.'

'So you blame Caligula and yet you say they kill each other and that my brother is *not* the one wielding the blade. You argue with yourself, Vinicius, and I should know. I do that a lot these days.'

'He doesn't wield the blade because he doesn't *have to*, Livilla. He is more like Agrippina than he realises now – twisted and scheming. The right word slipped in at the appropriate moment and he can trigger a massacre while his own hands remain clean. And Callistus has managed to have a law passed that means even slaves can give testimony now without torture. Can you imagine what *that's* doing? Every other slave in Rome has a grievance against his master. The upper classes are going to be reaped once more, but now on the word of slaves, Livilla. *Slaves!*'

'You expect me to care deeply?' I rounded on him, irritated. 'It is not my concern. When I was sent away from Rome to live out my days on a rock, I was absolved of all social responsibility.'

'Your uncle Claudius was accused by his slaves, you know? He's a sly one, and he managed to get himself acquitted at trial, but now he mutters openly about the emperor's lack of care for his empire. Your brother's response? He had Claudius dropped to the lowest position in the senate. Of course, it's rapidly reaching the point where the lowest is also the highest, so he needn't worry too much about that. Soon he alone will *be* the senate. But now Claudius seethes and plots like a madman, and other senators are with him.'

'So another conspiracy will be uncovered, and this time perhaps our dear uncle will fall. You must know how little I care about that wicked, monstrous old snake. It is about time he went.'

Vinicius' temper flared. 'I *know* what Claudius is, Livilla. I've been with you through the whole of this. I've seen him spreading his poison through the upper classes, never with enough evidence to pin anything on him. I know him for the creature of hate that he is. But I don't have to like him to see that he's right. Your brother has to stop before he destroys the mechanisms of rule. It's him or Rome, and I have run out of ways to persuade him. Do you know he has had the more sycophantic of the remaining senatorial class and their families moved to houses on the Palatine, just outside his palace walls?'

'That has always been a sign of favour, Vinicius. Remember that he gave *us* a house close by.'

'And it means that their families are little more than hostages, and he can claim exorbitant rents for their new abodes. He seems Hades-bent on humiliating even those who still support him. When someone asked him about these houses and their rich tenants, your brother referred to the whole collection as a "brothel", for he claims they house the most degenerate and dissolute of Rome's citizens. And these are the ones nominally *on his side*, Livilla!' He sagged. 'He's removed senatorial seating privileges in the theatres and stadiums. He's banned all ancestral inheritance of honours. Livilla, unless I can find a way to change your brother's policy of extinction, by the new year there will be only one power in Rome. Either him, or the senate. Either he will finish the job and kill them all, or your uncle's cronies will find a way to get past the Praetorians and the German Guard and they will finish the task the senate started three years ago in the atrium of Minerva. Coexistence is rapidly becoming impossible.'

'Again, why should I care?'

Vinicius leaned forward. 'Because while you may not care for Rome or the senate, I know you care for me, and for your brother. I do not want to have to decide between Rome and your brother. That choice might very well kill me. But that will be the choice we're all faced with soon, unless I can find a way to bring things back from the brink. I have exhausted all possibilities. I've run out of ideas, and I've run out of people to ask. Antiochus and Agrippa cheer him on. They see the end of the senate and the consuls as a natural progression, and I think they have persuaded your brother to that view. They steer him towards turning Rome into a new Macedonia, or a new Persia, or Aegyptus, where the king is a living god and requires no ratification to carry out his every whim. Help me, Livilla. Help me find a way to stop this.'

I sat still for a while. The shade of my mother in the darkened corner went unnoticed by my husband and I conversed with her unheard, my lips moving soundlessly, for I knew that she could understand me, even if he couldn't.

How can Gaius be persuaded away from his path?

She gave me no answer. There *was* no answer.

Is there any way I can save him and Rome?

Was that a shake of her head? It was hard to tell in the gloom.

No. There was no way. I had known that, of course, but it was nice to have my conclusions borne out by my mother. Vinicius was right. A conflict was inevitable. So how did I want it to turn out? It had been a quarter of a year now since I had come to my island, and I still hadn't figured out the answer to that question. Did I want my brother to become a god-king, unopposed? At least he would be safe. I would stay on Pandataria and rot, of course, in that case. And Vinicius might well fall in the process too, given his current direction, which would be the latest in a long line of blows to my heart. But if the senate succeeded in planting a dagger in my brother's back, while I might very well be freed, it would be to a world without Caligula, and that I simply could not imagine. He was my *brother*. Ignoring Agrippina, who had betrayed my faith and turned on us all, we were the last of the siblings that came to Rome twenty-one years ago with our father's ashes. The last children of Germanicus. Either way, Rome would struggle and change, but then Rome was used to struggling and changing and it had survived the fall of the kings and the end of the Republic. I was sure it would endure, while its sons and daughters were more vulnerable.

I shrugged once more. 'There is nothing to say.'

'Then I was mistaken in coming here,' Vinicius snapped. 'I always thought you cared more than this. I thought you were a true Roman. The woman I *married* was a true Roman.'

'The woman you married was a child of Germanicus. We survived through the worst times in the history of Rome, and we did so by staying together. Fractures in that family are what brought much of this about: Agrippina's selfish attempt on him.

If she had not turned on Caligula, he would still be the man we all loved. And I would still be in Rome helping to guide things. But if you are asking for a way to *stop* my brother, then yes, you made a mistake coming to me. He may have put me here, but he is still my brother. We are children of Germanicus and I will never betray him. If the senate are waning under his rule, then perhaps it is their time. Perhaps Agrippa is right? After all, what have the senate ever done for the line of Germanicus?'

Vinicius shot to his feet with an angry glare and turned. He left my house without even a farewell.

I cried for hours, alone in that house, begging the shade of my mother to come and console me. Finally, when the sobs subsided, I was able to think once more in some semblance of coherence. I regretted that things had ended that way, but for all my tears, those years ago when we were being lined up for matrimony under the wicked eye of Tiberius, I had vowed to myself that my marriage would never stand in the way of my family. I was, first and foremost, a sister to the emperor, and while a simple ring bound Vinicius and I together, the hot blood of the Julii and two decades of surviving insurmountable adversity bound me to my brother.

I assumed that was the last I would see of Vinicius.

I was wrong.

XXVII

COLD WORDS SPOKEN QUIETLY

When my husband came again, the island was coated with a glittering crisp sheet of white frost and I was wrapped in my blankets in the bath suite of my prison. I had retreated to it as a mini-home within the extensive villa in my loneliness. The nightmares that had become my constant companions for a year and a half now had robbed me of my once healthy skin tone, left me with sunken, mad eyes and skeletal cheeks, had withered my muscle and left me looking more like a revenant than I would care to acknowledge.

I had also continued my steady mental decline since his last visit. I didn't see it at the time, of course, but I had started to eat my food in order of colour, from red to green, hot to cold. I had dug a trench around one of the gardens – I cannot for the life of me remember why. I think it might have had something to do with cavalry. I talked all the time, often to the sporadically present shade of my mother, who would nod her agreement, and sometimes just to the air to keep myself entertained. The slaves had always been monosyllabic conversationalists at best and I had early on decided that no discourse was better than that.

A physician would have labelled me mad. He would probably have been right to do so.

I had been shocked when Horion, that dour slave with the slack face who had attended me for a third of a year on

Pandataria, took his own life, no longer able to cope with the loneliness, the snide attitude of the mercenaries and my burgeoning lunacy. In fairness, my endless night-time screaming had probably been as much of a spur as anything. And *he* had a friend – another slave. I had *no one*. He simply gave up one day, threaded a rope over a beam, fashioned it into a noose and throttled the life out of himself. I suppose a slave has little to live for at the best of times, and his lot was worse than many.

A week later I found Annius – the other slave – floating in the ornamental pond with the most blissfully peaceful look on his face. If I'd imagined I was alone previously – with two slaves – I was now learning a harsh lesson about taking things for granted. Once a day I saw one of the six bitter, miserable mercenaries on the island, and they rarely deigned to exchange a single word with me. I asked them if I would get another slave. I received no reply. Somehow I doubted that word of my losses ever even reached the mainland. My only true conversationalist was either a ghost or a figment of my imagination. Thank the gods for that product of my mania, for it at least gave me a little focus.

A new servant never appeared and over the last few weeks I had had to learn new skills, not the least of which was the scavenging, preparation and cooking of foodstuffs. Through trial and error I learned to make bread. My early experiments ranged from some soft goo that set like concrete on the table and is probably still there now, to something the legions would have been happy to fire from a ballista. It was in my complete solitude that I learned to my chagrin just how pampered we of the noble classes are, and it gave me a new understanding, and perhaps even sympathy, for those who serve upon us. It also lent a little understanding as to how Mother had starved to death here. I was undernourished and painfully thin myself, and as yet I had been here only a fraction of the time she had. Had Mother had servants? Had she talked to Father's shade, painted marble faces and baked inedible bread?

I cut down my first tree that autumn. It was not a *large* tree – more of an extended shrub. But from there I moved to willowy boughs. With my wasted muscles and now-hollow frame, it was excruciating work, but if I wanted warmth in the wintery chill then I had little choice. I'd implored the guard who visited me one day to supply me with wood or charcoal, but he simply sneered, informed me that he was paid to see if I was alive and not to cut wood, and left.

So, with winter settling in, I made my home in the baths, for running the furnaces of the whole villa would have been wasteful and taken a great deal of effort. I left the bathhouse to cook, and that was about it. I made the cold bath into my bed, using all the blankets and pillows I could find, and it was as comfortable a bed as I ever slept in. I used the *apodyterium* as my main room, for eating and sitting and gently going mad.

Occasionally, Mother visited me in the baths, but she seemed to prefer the triclinium for her little appearances, and I would only brave the bitterly cold rooms outside the baths for short stints, so our discourse, such as it was, became rarer.

That December morning I was hungrily wolfing down a plate of roasted goat meat – yes, I had turned butcher as well in my self-sufficient mania, and those goats had regretted straying too close to my villa in the end. It was not well cooked, but I had managed a reasonable spiced apple sauce that helped disguise the poor quality of the meat and its unimaginative preparation.

I supped my vinegary wine with gusto. I had long since discarded the jug of water that went with it, preferring the acidic, bitter infusion neat. I no longer suffered hangovers in the morning.

I heard horses' hooves far off. I grabbed my plate of tough, apple-flavoured meat, picked up my cup, thought again, tipped it back into the jug and just took that, and scurried through the villa. I had no idea who to expect. I was certain my husband had made his last appearance. That left the unknown – probably a party of executioners, since freeing me was not high on my brother's list.

When I opened the front door and was struck by the icy blast of the sea breeze, it made me shiver. But I bore the cold with ease, my eyes locked upon the figure of Vinicius at the head of a small group of mercenary guards. I experienced one of the strangest combinations of emotion in my life. A mix of hope and dread, hate and desire, urgency and procrastination. I truly wanted to see him, hug him, love him. And I wanted to hide from him, despise him and fear him, for he was becoming my brother's opposition.

My husband dismounted in the front garden, crunched across the gravel, and stopped before me. Without addressing me, he gestured for the guards to keep themselves busy, and they led their mounts off to the servants' quarters.

Vinicius stopped by my lawn and peered past the flower bed to a small patio where there had previously been an arbour. Now there were just old scorch marks half-hidden by frost. He looked from it to me and raised an eyebrow in question.

'My slaves. One hanged, one drowned. I performed the ceremony myself, and they both occupy a small mausoleum made of scavenged stones down by the cliff, overlooking the sea. I am surprised to see you.'

Vinicius nodded oddly, then turned and crossed to me, taking me by the hand – I almost shrank away from his touch – and leading me into the villa, where he made to take off his cloak, but thought again. I took a swig directly from the wine jug and he regarded me with a little distaste.

'Why is it so cold in here?'

'I can only cut down so many trees. I just keep one furnace lit – the baths.'

'You cut your own timber?'

'It's that or freeze.'

'I will find someone in the village to come and help you. I'll pay them well.'

'I have no need of your charity, Marcus Vinicius. I am a daughter of Germanicus, not some milksop wet flannel of a girl. I am quite capable of taking care of myself.' To illustrate the point, I ripped meat from the goat bone with my teeth – with only a little difficulty.

He followed me, his expression curious, yet grave, as I led him through to the baths, where most of the good furniture now resided. I kicked off my shoes as I entered – I had long since mastered the art of keeping the floor warm rather than hot. Vinicius looked around, appreciably impressed with my survival skills. He then sank into a seat and cleared his throat.

'Things are coming to a head in Rome,' he said in a bleak matter-of-fact manner.

'And you thought you would visit me here in my seclusion to torture me with my impotence?'

Vinicius rolled his eyes. 'I did consider whether it was a good idea to come, but whatever arguments lie between us, you are my wife and I love you, as I have since that day we stood by the sea in Antium and the shout of "Feliciter" arose. The world is about to change for us one way or the other, and I could not in conscience act without either your blessing or your curse.'

A statement that boded ill in any direction.

'Do you know old Vitellius?' he asked, quietly. 'Not the chubby one with the racing obsession that used to hang around with your brother. His father, Lucius Vitellius Veteris?'

'I vaguely recall him from some occasion or other.'

'He's been governing Syria, but he's back now – recalled by the emperor. When he returned to court, he prostrated himself before your brother. I've never seen anything like it – a former consul lying in the dust at the feet of an emperor. Obviously some strange eastern custom he's brought back, thinking it would please Caligula, but it's started a whole new round of sycophancy. Now at meals, the nobles of Rome sit at your brother's feet. Like slaves, Livilla. Like *slaves*!'

'And my brother commands this?'

'Not *commands*, no. But he does nothing to stop it. It amuses him to watch the last of Rome's senators debase themselves. He holds out his hand for patricians and equestrians to kiss as he passes, and he doesn't return the gesture.'

'And why should he?' I felt odd in defending my brother when he had put me here, and in fairness, Vinicius' tidings were not wholly welcome. I could well imagine that darker, angrier, acerbically sharp-witted side of my brother becoming ascendant following the loss of everything he ever really cared about. But still, he was my brother, and I clung to the memory of the good man I had supported through all those years of difficulty. How could I not? We were the children of Germanicus, bound together by blood to the bitter end.

Vinicius' eyes flashed angrily. 'He need not kiss their hands back, I agree. But he *does* kiss the hands of the freedmen in his employ, openly placing them above the senate in his court. It is an insult bordering on the unacceptable. Yet the senate still take it and suffer, trying to regain his favour. Last month, old Vitellius put forward a motion in the senate that they confer divine honours on the emperor. While he *reigns*, Livilla, not in respect for a departed shade like his predecessors. Can you imagine that? A *god* ruling the empire, as though we were Aegyptians or Hellenes! They voted him a temple in the forum, and it's being connected to his vestibule and the palace on the hill, right through the Temple of Castor and Pollux. The senate dishonour those divine twins by turning their temple – one of the oldest in Rome – into little more than an entrance to your brother's palace.'

That *was* perhaps going too far. Had it been Caligula who

had come up with such an impious idea, or the senate? It mattered not, really. That it was done at all was what counted in the eyes of Rome.

'And your uncle?' Vinicius went on. 'Your brother treats him like a fool, dishonouring him at every turn, for he knows Claudius speaks against him and would depose him if he could, yet the man is clever and is never open to tangible accusations. I'm starting to gain a certain respect for the old goat. He's in the priesthood now, you know? He was all but pushed into the role, so that now he has to worship his own nephew as a god. He's almost bankrupting himself in doing so, too. And out east the Jews have torn down the altars to the imperial cult, but your brother commanded that a statue of himself be erected in their ancient temple at Jerusalem. Agrippa eggs him on.'

I knew the Jews would resent that. They were ever a fractious bunch, with no love of Rome and a bloody-minded unwillingness to accept the truth of the gods.

'He models himself on Alexander, Livilla. There can be no doubt now – even among the dullest plebs – that he intends to turn Rome into a monarchy once more, and this time not a noble monarchy of Etruscan foundation, but an eastern one. Worshipped as a god and with total power. Do you not see that it is like the last days of Caesar – like that towards which the dictator was working when the brave liberators stopped him?'

I did. And yet Caesar was mourned and worshipped now. And really, was my brother perhaps right to do this anyway? Certainly, the days of the honourable and noble senate seemed to have passed us by. The consuls were – what did Agrippa call them? – redundant. Yes. The consuls and the senate were all redundant. My brother was proving it by watching them destroy themselves even as they turned him into a divine king. It was enough to make me chuckle. As Vinicius had started listing these latest abhorrences, I had seen them as just that and worried that my brother had slipped from his wits. Yet a second thought suggested something else. It reminded me that my brother was clever and ingenious. He had rarely in his life – and certainly in his reign – *directly* set anything in motion, but through manipulation and suggestion he caused it to happen regardless. I could see him now, no madness afflicting him, but a simple wave of satisfaction as he watched those institutions he considered corrupt and redundant wiping themselves out and raising him among the people in the process. He was not making himself a god-king. The senate were doing it for him.

I laughed. I laughed for some time at the realisation, and I simply could not stop. Of course, I was a tiny step from madness myself in those dark days of isolation and sleepless screaming nights, and maniacal laughter was no stranger to me. When I glanced across the room at a flicker of movement and saw my mother also chuckling where she stood by the wall, I collapsed into fresh howls.

'But he is no Caesar,' Vinicius snapped, trying to cut through my laughter. 'He will not try to create that which Caesar intended or in which Augustus succeeded – a republic with a single man at the helm. No, your brother will go further. He will be a new Macedonian-style king. He will be a god with no one to check him or question him. Imagine a Rome where the emperor is untouchable. Remember Tiberius? Imagine what Rome would have been like if there had been no consuls or senators to cushion Rome or vote against the worst of his mania?'

Was Vinicius blind to what we had lived through? That *was* what Tiberius was like. No one had cushioned Rome from him or Sejanus. He had merely exiled himself.

'My brother is no Tiberius,' I said with an edge of spite to my tone. 'The people and the army love him. And he loves the people and the army. What should we care that the senatorial class are fading out? Of what use are they?'

'You sound like your brother,' my husband spat angrily.

'Of *course* I do!' I snarled back at him. 'We are our father's children. We are of the blood of Caesar. Why should we fear the end of the senate and the consuls, for they do little other than conspire against us.'

'Livilla, *I* am of senatorial rank. *I* was a consul. The people we are talking about are people like me. Can you so easily dismiss me? And your father was a consul. Your own grandfather, Drusus, yearned for the Republic restored, not a step further into despotism.'

I simply glared at him and he took a deep breath and tried again.

'Caesar, back in his day, was too confident. He went to his doom blindly. Your brother is different. He is careful and suspicious. He wears a sword at all times now. He has to die, Livilla.'

A chilling silence settled in the warm bathhouse.

Cold words spoken quietly in a cold world.

I should probably have reacted instantly. I could perhaps have stopped him. I had a heavy jug in my hand. Had I cracked him on the side of the head with it, I might have overpowered my husband and possibly even killed him. Ha, but listen to how cold I had become in my solitude, talking of killing my husband so blithely. Instead, shock had taken me, and I stared, astonished.

'He has to be stopped before he destroys Rome,' Vinicius murmured. 'I have sought all autumn and into winter to change his path, but he is decided, and I am now left with no other choice. The word among those in the know is that he plans to depart the city in late Januarius, just before the Sementivae festivals, taking ship for Aegyptus. Agrippa and Antiochus are his closest companions now and they urge him on with his monarchic vision, while the rest of the court are his freedmen who would never gainsay him. Agrippa tells me that your brother intends to stay there, in Alexandria, and found a new capital around the tomb of Alexander, leaving Rome to rot and become naught but a provincial town in his new kingdom. And the frightening thing is that the people of Rome will cheer him on, even as he strips their city of its status. He will be a pharaoh, Livilla, not an emperor. He *has* to be stopped.'

I could not speak. I simply sat agape, shivering despite the warmth of the room.

'Marcus Antonius ruled from there, you know?' he said. 'And some say Caesar had also meant to, and that only those righteous blades in the senate stopped him. And if the history of Caesar is repeating itself and your brother is walking his path, then there must be new righteous blades in the senate.'

Silence. I steeled myself.

'You cannot. He is your brother, Marcus. *My* brother.'

'He has to die, Livilla, and it has to be before he leaves for Alexandria, for then it will be too late.'

'You cannot drive a blade into him, Marcus. It would be fratricide. The gods would never forgive you. Your spirit would never rest.'

'No,' Vinicius conceded. 'I cannot wield the blade, that is true. That task will fall to Cassius Chaerea, a tribune of the Praetorian Guard who has been playing the role of executioner for your brother these past months. He is sick to the stomach of his role and will do what needs to be done. And he is a professional, a soldier who can deliver a single killing blow. I do not wish him to suffer, Livilla, even if he must be stopped. There are others, too, who are with us. I shall not wield the blade, but I *will* do my part. I shall stand by your uncle, who has brought people to my attention – people who realise the import of what we do. People who wish to see Rome go on as it always has. Preservers of Rome. Senators, Praetorians, even your brother's closest advisor, Callistus.'

I felt ice cold. Even Callistus? I had never liked the man, and it seemed that my instincts had been right.

'You cannot do it, Vinicius. You *can't!* He's my brother. Your friend. He's the emperor of Rome. So what if the senate hates him. The rot in Rome runs deep, and perhaps a king is what we *need* now? My brother could be a new Caesar. Rome will change, yes, but who says it will be for the worse? You cannot be a Cassius or a Brutus or a Casca.'

I suddenly lunged forward, dropping the wine jar and plate to the floor unheeded as I clasped my husband's hands in mine – my hands that were once manicured and courtly, and were now calloused and scarred, with nails jagged from my labours.

Vinicius recoiled as though I was something appalling, ripping his hands from mine and struggling to his feet.

'I came to try and reason with you, Livilla. I came seeking your blessing in our endeavour.'

'My *blessing*?' I shrieked in disbelief.

'You and your uncle and your sister are Caligula's last family. Claudius is with us, and Agrippina has blessed our task. I hoped you would see the necessity of what we do and join the ranks of the righteous. I could even have taken you off the island. This *will* happen, Livilla. It *has* to, for the good of Rome.'

Off the island? Really? But at the cost of blessing my brother's would-be murderers . . . could I be so bold or heartless? The temptation was strong, even as I shoved it violently away. Never. Gaius and I were the last children of Germanicus, for I could never consider Agrippina such, now.

'For the good of Rome?' I spat. 'For the good of *Claudius*, you mean. I would wager all I own – not that I own much – that my uncle already has a purple cloak and sceptre ready in his rooms, just waiting for Caligula to die so that he can neatly step into his place. Do you not see, Marcus, that this is all his doing? He is a master of manipulation just as much as my brother. He bears the same ophidian streak as my sister. He has turned you all against Caligula, so that you think you are killing a megalomaniac to preserve Rome, but in truth you are murdering a good man to put our uncle on his throne. How can you not *see* this?'

Vinicius backed away towards the door, his face dark and angry.

'Your uncle is not planning to take the throne. There are better men in line for that. Vitellius, maybe? Or even me. Or perhaps there will be a republic once more? What matters is that our ways will be preserved and a tyrant felled.'

'I wonder if Agrippina plans likewise and has a purple swaddling cloth for her *darling* boy?' I snapped. 'She is as bad as our uncle. You are not preserving the Rome you once knew, husband, you're just ripping it out of my brother's hands and passing it to the less worthy.'

Vinicius drew himself up then, strong and still the handsome man I married a lifetime ago, despite his drawn, haggard features and the pain in his eyes. 'Farewell, my wife. Despite all that stands between us, I still love you, and when your brother dies I will have you freed. The next time we meet will be the day I come to rescue you. Unless we fail . . . then I shall see you in Elysium.'

Without a further word, he turned, gathering his cloak around him, and left my house. I looked down, shaking, to see that my jug of wine had broken when it fell, and the dark liquid flowed around the floor, filling the tiny gaps between the mosaic stones. It looked so much like spilled blood that I panicked for a moment.

And then I imagined my brother lying amid it. My nightmares came flooding in even now, during the cold, wintry light of day.

Blinding, eye-searing flashes of red and white, which gradually resolve into a canopy of crimson with the brilliant sunlight of a Roman summer slashing through like a blade. The world below that shelter is a dreadful scarlet, battered and stabbed by those sharp beams of light.

The roar of a crowd is still audible as a din in the background.

I am moving, walking casually, calmly.

I am filled with a strange ennui, though that itself is just a boat of emotion bobbing upon a sea of despair that has always been there, dark and immense, threatening to engulf me. But now that is changing. The untroubled nature of my mind is cut through with new emotions… stark, terrifying ones.

The unexpected. A shock. Horror, even. How can this be?

My hand goes out to ward off the unseen threat. No! I am surrounded only by the trusted. This cannot happen. Such threat is the province of enemies, not friends.

Gleaming metal – blue Noric steel shining with that sickly all-pervading red glow – lances towards me. I lurch away and the blade that seeks my heart instead cuts through flesh and grinds against bone.

Agony. Flashes of agony and panic. Disbelief and terror.

There is blood. My hand comes up and is oddly black within the red of my enclosed world. So much blood. I try to react, but I am prevented. I am stopped.

I am helpless, and it is trusted ones that seek my end. Why? What have I done to deserve this?

I shout, but that shout goes nowhere, gathered up by the limp crimson canopy and hurled back at me. The myriad voices far away cheer still, unaware that I am imperilled.

Panic is all, now. There is nothing I can do.

That blade, given an extra scarlet tint by my life's blood, is pulling back, the face behind it feral, the teeth bared like a wolf protecting a half-eaten kill from its pack mates.

*

How could I wish for my husband to fail, since failure would mean the dreadful end of the man that I still loved despite everything he had said and done? But then I could no more wish for success, for that would mean the death of my brother.

Sometimes decisions are impossible.

In a way, I was oddly fortunate in the imprisonment that kept me from having to make this one.

XXVIII

THIRTY BLOWS

A month passed. Saturnalia came and went without my notice: the new year, when the consuls traditionally take up their posts. Winter hit its hardest on the tiny island. I barely noticed.

The nightmares took up all the hours of darkness now, the fear of their arrival keeping me wide-eyed and shaking into the night until finally Somnus enfolded my unwilling form in his arms, and then the blades and the blood would begin, wracking my precious few hours of sleep with agonies and panic and fear. I would be awake in time to hear the birds stirring in their freezing world.

Blinding, eye-searing flashes of red and white, which gradually resolve into a canopy of crimson with the brilliant sunlight of a Roman summer slashing through like a blade. The world below that shelter is a dreadful scarlet, battered and stabbed by those sharp beams of light.

The roar of a crowd is still audible as a din in the background.

I am moving, walking casually, calmly.

I am filled with a strange ennui, though that itself is just a boat of emotion bobbing upon a sea of despair that has always been there, dark and immense, threatening to engulf me. But now that is changing. The untroubled nature of my mind is cut through with new emotions . . . stark, terrifying ones.

The unexpected. A shock. Horror, even. How can this be?

My hand goes out to ward off the unseen threat. No! I am surrounded only by the trusted. This cannot happen. Such threat is the province of enemies, not friends.

Gleaming metal – blue Noric steel shining with that sickly all-pervading red glow – lances towards me. I lurch away and the blade that seeks my heart instead cuts through flesh and grinds against bone.

Agony. Flashes of agony and panic. Disbelief and terror.

There is blood. My hand comes up and is oddly black within the red of my enclosed world. So much blood. I try to react, but I am prevented. I am stopped.

I am helpless, and it is trusted ones that seek my end. Why? What have I done to deserve this?

I shout, but that shout goes nowhere, gathered up by the limp crimson canopy and hurled back at me. The myriad voices far away cheer still, unaware that I am imperilled.

Panic is all, now. There is nothing I can do.

That blade, now given an extra scarlet tint by my life's blood, is pulling back, the face behind it feral, the teeth bared like a wolf defending a half-eaten kill from its pack mates.

I am still trying to react, to fight, but I am failing, restrained. The wound that daubed the blade before me is a searing conflagration in my flesh, sending tendrils of pain throughout my body. To see my own life coating a sword . . . I catch my face briefly reflected in the oily red sheen. I do not look panicked or agonised. Just sad.

It is not that *blade I should fear.*

*

I was turning into a shadow of myself, and I had almost stopped eating entirely, unintentionally following the path of my mother. But it was neither the hunger nor the weakness, nor even the lack of sleep and the night terrors, that made that month the worst I ever endured.

It was the knowledge of what was happening in Rome. Less than a hundred miles from where I raged and wept, my husband was stalking the palaces of Rome, seeking the demise of my brother. He would not wield the knife, he had said, but he wielded the intent, which was worse in some ways, and that Praetorian tribune of whom he spoke would be with him, blade gleaming, waiting to taste the hot blood of the Julii once more.

What cared I that Caligula now sought a new way to rule Rome? Why should I show the slightest concern for the senators and the consuls who had grown fat and indolent while they plotted murder and usurpation in their opulent houses? The two men I loved most in the world were caught up in a gladiatorial bout that would only end with blood on the sand – the blood of a husband or the blood of a brother.

The agony of waiting and not knowing was too much. Some mornings, drawn and shaking, staggering from my sodden cot, I would send up prayers to every god I could name that the German Guard were as efficient and strong as my brother believed and would stop the plot, even if it meant Vinicius' head bouncing down the Gemonian Stairs – the death of a traitor. For my brother *had* to live, and that was all that occupied my thoughts as I threw down and smashed busts and defaced the paintings on the wall with violent hackings and scratchings.

Other mornings, I would hobble out into the freezing world and remember how the warmth of my husband's arms drove out all the horrors of the world. I would remember my brother's glee and the cold eyes as men drowned in armour by torchlight, and I would realise that Caligula was not the child of Germanicus I remembered now. That perhaps Vinicius was right. That whatever happened, I was so alone in the world now that I needed my husband above all things. And in my heart on those days, visible to the gods and a shame to my core, I prayed for the death of my brother so that I could be free with Vinicius.

It was vile. Every day saw new hopes and the changing of my dreams, while I continued to descend into hunger and madness, sleep coming in tiny, uncomfortable staccato bursts. I was sick often with the tension and horror – and likely with the hunger and exhaustion, too.

The boat came for me while the sea was still choppy and the island white and crusted with rime. I saw it approaching from the north and held my breath, for it had to bear dreadful news, one way or the other. Either I was to be freed and my brother was dead, or Caligula lived and I was to be informed of the execution of my husband. My heart lurched with every dip of the prow as that vessel of death ploughed towards me. Would that I could have held it back and lived another day with a brother and a husband who both drew breath. But it could not be so, and perhaps, given what that last month had done to me, it was a good thing it couldn't.

I didn't stay in the villa. I had to know as soon as possible, so I gathered up my cloak, slipped on my shoes, bade farewell to the shade of my mother, and began to hurry along the road towards the village with its dock. It was only the second time I had traversed the island, the first being when I had arrived over a year ago. There are three other villas on the island, the only one permanently occupied at the eastern end, close to the village. A few small farms lie dotted about, and cisterns are sunk into the rock all over to collect rainwater, as there are no springs on Pandataria. I noted these things in passing, my mind was naturally given to flitting hither and thither in those days.

I reached the village just as the bireme was putting into port.

I stood, my breath fast and nervous, watching the Praetorians disembark. There was no sign of Vinicius, and as the Praetorian prefect Lucius Arruntius Stella stepped down to the dock, I realised why with a heavy heart wrapped in strange strains of joy. The plot must have failed. Vinicius could not come for me, and my brother had sent his loyal Praetorian prefect to inform me. Possibly to execute me. After all, he had to at least *suspect* that I had a part in the plot.

I would die like a Roman matron, not a snivelling, cowering senator. I stood, straight-backed, and waited for Stella to approach me.

'My lady Julia Livilla, it has been a long time,' he said.

It had. I remained silent, a marble statue of a Roman matron awaiting her fate.

'Would you care to embark now, Domina, or is there anything you need from the villa?'

I almost fainted. What had happened? If my brother had died, surely Vinicius would have come for me. But I was to be freed? And yet he wasn't here?

'Tell me everything.'

'I will, Domina, but not yet. Time is apparently of the essence. I am no sailor, but the trierarch tells me that the winter currents hereabouts are treacherous, and we need to set sail for Ostia immediately if we wish to avoid any delays or dangers.'

Still shaking and confused, I descended to the dockside, waving a hand dismissively. 'I need nothing from the villa. I *have* nothing at the villa. Just take me back.'

And on the first morning of that two-day voyage to Rome, overnighting at Antium just a few hundred paces from where I had married Vinicius seven years ago, Stella told me the whole sorry tale. I played it over and over in my head that second day as we closed on Ostia and Rome and it bore more resemblance to my nightmares than I cared to think upon. Oddly, that night was the first nightmare-free sleep I had had in months. We transferred to a sleek, river-borne passenger vessel at Ostia and quickly skipped upstream to the capital. It was the kalends of Februarius when we arrived and I alighted on the dock of the water-side *emporium* with a cold knot settled in my belly that was no symptom of the weather. For half a year I had dreamed of leaving Pandataria, and now that I placed my foot once more in Rome, I found myself yearning to be back in ignorance in my island prison, or *anywhere* else, in fact, but here.

We walked. There was a litter waiting for me, but I shooed it away and walked. I was in Rome. I wanted to feel those worn, cracked cobbles beneath my aching feet. I wanted to drink in the smells and noise. I wanted . . . I wanted to leave. But I couldn't. I had to see it all. It was not enough to be told by another. I had to *see* it. Without seeing it, it would never be real. It would never have happened for me.

We crossed the Velabrum with an escort of Praetorians at my heel and made our way along the Vicus Tuscus towards the forum, the great temples of the Capitol ahead to the left and the steep slope of the Palatine to the right, the palace of my brother nestling atop that ancient mount, on the western edge. Stella had suggested the quick route up the Scalae Caci, from the flat ground to the Palatine right above the Circus, but I had declined. I needed to go the long way round, because I needed to see it. The irony that my first ever journey through Rome, as a babe-in-arms, had been along almost exactly the same route was not lost on me. I even found myself searching for a rainbow that I felt should have been there, but could not be, for the gods had torn all the colour from the world for me now. All but the red of spilled blood, anyway.

We passed the Basilica Iulia and entered the square of the forum. The new construction of my brother's was clear, rising from the frontage of the Temple of Castor and Pollux and arcing up on a sloping bridge of impressive dimensions to meet the great vestibule of the palace. Odd that this imposing edifice so dominated the forum and yet I had never before seen it. But then I had been gone a year and a half by then. Other than the new palace entrance, the forum seemed unchanged.

Except in atmosphere, though, which was dour and miserable, the populace going about their business unhappily.

We passed beneath that great stepped bridge of my brother's, through a lofty arch, and moved on to the Via Nova, where the shops pressed in on the paved road, always so full of life and gaiety when we lived here as the sisters of a glorious golden prince. Now they felt like mausolea, with dead eye-sockets for windows staring out as I passed.

I stopped, shaking suddenly.

Marcus Vinicius stood in the street, waiting, with a Praetorian at each shoulder. For a moment I felt utter confusion. Was he now protected by that elite unit too, as had been my brother, or was he under arrest? Not that there seemed to be much difference these days, since the Praetorians appeared to wield a blade against the emperor as often now as they did to defend him. My question was answered when he stepped gravely forward and the soldiers stayed respectfully in place. Vinicius was dressed well, if soberly. He wore a cloak against the winter cold, and his face was the bleakest mask of guilt. I hated him. I longed only to run forward and let him fold me in his arms, but those were the arms of a killer now, and I hated them, for all I loved the heart that drove them.

Vinicius stopped a few paces from me.

'Livilla . . .'

Unable to look at his face any longer and caught up in turmoil at the many conflicting emotions his presence drew from me, I strode past him, refusing to acknowledge his presence. Arruntius Stella followed on, his men close behind, and Vinicius spun on his heel, following me closely. I wanted to turn and tell him to leave me, and I wanted to cling to him as we moved. I wanted to cry on his shoulder and to tear out his eyes. I loved him and yet, gods, on that morning how I hated him. I know

I was shaking, and I must have looked like one of the lemure spirits that stalk the half-world of the restless dead.

'Livilla, you don't have to do this,' came Vinicius' scratchy voice.

Without turning, I replied coldly, 'Of course I do. It was *you* who didn't have to do this.'

Up we moved, onto the lower northern slope of the Palatine, skirting the imperial palace. Behind the rows of shops, the slope had been converted into a huge temporary theatre, wooden hoardings and rows of benches carefully assembled, with the rear wall and the stage at the forum end and the seats built against the slope. The rear wall had been hung with drapes of purple and white for a play that had been part of the festival of Divine Augustus.

We passed through the arched opening and into the theatre that straddled the road up to the palace. I entered the auditorium and shivered. The place was utterly deserted apart from myself and my escort. I had no idea what the play had been – it had been days now since it had ended.

Still shivering, I closed my eyes and came to a stop. Stella cleared his throat.

'Domina?'

'Wait,' I said sharply. 'And do it quietly.'

As the Praetorians came to a halt and stood silent, I let it all wash over me. I had heard the tale on the ship, and had replayed it so many times that I knew it as well as I knew my Virgil. My mind's eye was vivid with detail.

The actors on the stage are tossing back and forth inanities in theatrical tones to make the crowd either laugh or shudder. For a moment I've no idea whether it is a comedy or a tragedy. A comedy, I feel. My brother has ever loved his comedy – a symptom, probably, of such a difficult life.

The crowd boo the villain and cheer intermittently.

I can see plebs rising from their seats and making rude gestures at the actors, and the few senators in attendance, refused their privilege of specific seats, moan and grumble at the ordinary populace around them who are ruining their experience. I can see the imperial box halfway up the seating and off to the right, on the slope below my brother's palace. A passage from there up to the top is covered with crimson drapes so that the emperor can come and go from the theatre in privacy. Six seats in the box. Caligula sits in that central chair, Vinicius, Callistus, and two senators I don't know, by the names of Valerius Asiaticus and Paullus Arruntius, who have somehow inveigled their way into my brother's court. And our uncle Claudius, of course. A small party of Praetorians protect them, standing around the rear and the sides of the box, one of the tribunes among them, commanding the detail. I can see them clearly: the two senators I don't know sweating with nerves and trying to pass it off as variously the cold of the day or some minor ailment. The tribune is at the rear, just waiting for the moment, fingertips dancing on the pommel of his sword. Vinicius, Callistus and Claudius are exchanging furtive glances. Where is Helicon, I wonder. Has his oath to protect my brother been bought off by these animals, or has he been skilfully manipulated, sent away from the scene?

And there, amid the roaring crowd and the bustle and life, my brother is rising from his seat. Why? Why does he leave the theatre early? One of the actors is poor, or has got his lines wrong? Or perhaps the whole performance is off in some way, substandard, or badly produced? My brother decides it is time to retire to the baths, for that is ever his habit these days before his noon meal. Caligula rises from his seat, saying that he shall retire but return later before the performances are ended. The crowd stop cheering, but my brother, with a good-natured smile, tells them to carry on. The others in the box rise, but Caligula laughs and tells them to stay and enjoy the performance. Yet they are insistent, and my brother shrugs. Why does he not suffer even the slightest concern when Claudius, Arruntius and Asiaticus rise too? Perhaps they have an obvious reason? He certainly doesn't notice, and doesn't care. He passes from the imperial box and into that covered passageway, the pale, wintry sun held back by the red linen cover.

The covered passageway rises, I can see, to the very walls of the palace that Tiberius had built and in which my brother lives. There it turns and leaves the temporary theatre, making for the palace entrance, utilising a walkway usually left for servants and slaves.

I see it now. Vinicius fakes a stumble and, laughing with Caligula, somehow manages to slip past the emperor in the bustle and enter the corridor first. Senator Asiaticus follows his lead and manages to slip ahead too. The two are slightly ahead of my brother and to either side, talking to him constantly about inanities – probably the failings of the performance behind them. Caligula, usually so alert and careful, is distracted by this constant stream of conversation.

I want to scream a warning.

Why do they not simply attack him?

Of course, my brother has taken to wearing a sword at his side at all times. And in accordance with ancient law, none of the civilians around him are armed. Should they strike and he fight them off and draw his blade, they risk everything. So they wait, and they stick to their plan.

I see Caligula disappear into that passageway, my husband busy chattering away, the others following on behind, including the Praetorian tribune and two of his men. This tribune would be the one called Sabinus and I find it ironic that he shares a name with the man who had been responsible for my brother's break with the senate in the first place. Tribune Sabinus I can see drawing his sword just as he disappears into the passageway at the rear of the group.

I turn my head and see Vinicius watching me intently. His face is nine parts guilt and one part desperation. I realise that this is the first time he has visited the scene of the murder since it happened. Has the guilt gnawed deep into his gut? I hope so.

'I did not want it to happen as it did,' he says.

I turn, snarling, 'Then you should not have conspired and drawn blades, should you?'

'It was . . . it was worse than I could have imagined. It should have been quick. Chaerea was an expert swordsman. He should have been with the gods before he knew anything was wrong. I am so sorry.'

'Not sorry enough,' I snap. My heart feels cold and agonising, as though it is being torn apart by icy fingers, as I begin to climb the wooden steps to the imperial box. Behind me, the Praetorian prefect Stella and his men follow on respectfully. Vinicius pauses for a moment, his face a picture of misery as he weighs up whether to press me further. I wonder in passing, since Prefect Arruntius Stella and Senator Paullus Arruntius belong to the same clan of families, whether there is a connection between the two. Was Stella standing here with breath held, waiting for it to happen?

I reach the box and make my way in through a latched doorway that has been left open in the aftermath of events. The box makes me shudder. It shouldn't. There's nothing wrong with the box . . .

I move across to the exit – the corridor that leads back to the palace.

Suddenly Vinicius is close to me again and I shy away from him as though his touch would burn me. His expression is hopeless. Lost.

'You don't have to go in there,' he says.
'Yes. I do.'

I can see the imperial party up ahead, the whole scene given a ghastly red cast by the thin covering of crimson material that keeps the weather out of the passage. I cannot quite see my brother, for the rear of the group is filled with three Praetorians, their blades at the ready.

No. Suddenly the heads part and I can see it all clearly. Ahead, a figure is approaching from the direction of the palace. It is the other Praetorian tribune, Cassius Chaerea.

'Domine . . .' the tribune says urgently as he approaches, his voice loaded with warning. What is he doing? Has he changed his mind? Is he planning to put a stop to things? No, of course not. He is throwing the emperor off guard, for Chaerea has his naked blade in his hand and if he appears confident and normal, the emperor will panic and be prepared to fight. Caligula has survived so many plots by being cautious and alert. But if Chaerea appears to have discovered trouble himself and is rushing to warn the emperor, then that explains the blade. I can imagine what is going on in my brother's head. This Praetorian officer has found something . . . a plot? And he comes to warn the emperor. My brother is relieved . . . pleased, even, to see Chaerea.

His surprise is almost total as the Praetorian takes a last step towards him and raises his blade, driving it point-first at his master's chest. But my brother is still cautious and alert and, recognising something in Chaerea's eyes at the last moment, he tries to step back, his own hand going to the sword at his side. Thus the tribune's strike is not the killing blow he intended, merely wounding the emperor. There is a desperate struggle, the cries of the combatants masked to the world by the roar of the theatre crowd beyond the passage. My brother tries to draw his sword, shouting to my husband for help, but Vinicius instead clasps his hands over Caligula's, forcing the emperor's sword back into the sheath. Now, the party scatters to the sides as tribune Sabinus comes up from behind. The second blow comes in low on the right-hand side of the ribs, angled upwards, carving through intercostal muscle and into the organs beyond.

I can hear my brother gasp in horror and pain even from the far end of the passage, echoing over the days in between.

As the emperor stiffens and lurches, Chaerea pulls out his sword with some difficulty and a dreadful sucking sound, for he is panicking at his near failure and has forgotten to twist the blade, so the wound offers him resistance. As it comes free, Chaerea totters backwards and for a moment my brother is unrestrained, since Vinicius has backed away, not wishing to be party to the actual death.

Caligula lurches, staggers a step, then two. His arm reaches up to Vinicius in despair, the man to whom he has turned in his moment of crisis and the last to deliver a betrayal. The emperor tries to speak, but his voice is just a husky gurgle. I think he is trying to echo Caesar's sentiments to Brutus as his trusted friend clutches the bloody knife.

Even you, Vinicius?

For at the end, everyone has forsaken my brother. First the consuls and the Praetorian prefects, then the senate, then his own family and finally his trusted companions. He turns, sees Callistus urging the other Praetorians to join in. His eyes narrow as he sees the look on Claudius' face and knows that there is no innocence in this corridor, but then they widen again with Chaerea's second blow, which pierces the corroded and shredded remains of Caligula's heart. In some ways, for him, it is a blessing that it has stopped beating, for now he will be at peace. There is no one left to betray him.

My brother gasps again, then his legs give way and he sinks to the floor.

Vinicius is crying. His simple, swift saving of the empire is not the straightforward thing he had counted on. It is messy and bloody and agonising and takes a lifetime to unfold. For him this has been no light undertaking. For him it is the hardest thing a man can do: to betray the greatest friend for naught but cold principle.

I am aware of Vinicius and my escort breathing in the passage behind me.

I pass the spot of the murder. For this was no execution or struggle, but simply cold and calculated murder. There are stains on the ground. The colour is undetectable given the red glow that bathes the whole corridor, but they are dark, and I know what they are. They are the blood of the Julii, that which flowed out of great Caesar on the steps of the curia in Pompey's theatre, and out of Gaius Julius Caesar Caligula on the slope of the Palatine. Here my brother died, surrounded by men and yet totally alone.

'I meant it to be quick,' Vinicius says. 'It was supposed to be. One blow and it would be over. But the animals – they wouldn't stop. He dodged the first blow, so they became desperate, violent, stabbing like fury. If I had had a knife after all, perhaps I could have finished it quickly.'

'You did quite enough,' I hiss angrily.

My nightmare had come true on this spot.

The blade that robs him of his world is the unseen one. It scythes through flesh and he can feel it cutting the threads within that bind life to his earthly shell. The heart stops with a steel point transfixing it. His eyes are wide. The feral face comes closer. He is already dead, but still standing – can still feel as that animal drives in his blade once more. Another comes from behind. And another from the side. Each blow is an insult now, nothing more, for death has been dealt. Each new blow is a statement from those he loves and trusts.

Thirty blows in all. Thirty wounds that go deeper than mere flesh, carve his very soul.

He is descending now, the scarlet canopy receding, the flashes of dagger-like sunlight unable to warm him. Nothing will ever warm him again. He can see the most familiar of faces . . .

I turn my cold, bitter gaze on my husband and then tear it away again. It hurts me to look at him.

That was the worst for me . . . for my own heart, at least. It had not been the worst of the brutality visited on that day of death, though, and I had to go on. To force myself to see the full awful scale of what had unfolded because of one disgruntled Praetorian and one man who believed he was saving the world.

With the Praetorians and Vinicius still at my back, I hurried up the passage and into the palace. I knew where I would need to go, and I made for my destination immediately. Behind me, Prefect Stella coughed nervously. 'Domina, the emperor . . . ?'

'Can wait,' I snapped, and continued on my way, with the escort at my heel. Four corridors and a flight of stairs later, I found the chambers. They had been emptied, of course, and scrupulously cleaned. But again when I closed my eyes I could see it.

There, by the window on the floor, the body of the empress Milonia Caesonia, stabbed twelve times, a heap of bloodied cloth and gristle. And close by, in a tiny, decorative cot, the tattered, bloody remains of Julia Drusilla, the baby Milonia had borne for my brother during my incarceration and who he had proudly named after our poor, lost sister. I had never met the child in life.

I was glad this was my imagination, as the actual sight might have felled me. To kill an emperor is abhorrent. To kill his wife for good measure is despicable. To kill an innocent baby? Unforgiveable.

'I most certainly didn't want this, Livilla. No one did.'

I turned to Vinicius, standing in the doorway behind me. His face was pained and drawn. I shook, with rage, and grief, and terror. I still didn't know whether to run across and throw myself into his arms or to claw and scratch that troubled face until it no longer looked like my husband. For he may not have *wanted* this, but along with traitors and greedy men, he *had engineered* it.

'His family were not supposed to be killed. Chaerea didn't want to do it and it was not part of the plan. It was Claudius.'

Of course it was.

'Tell me I was misinformed and that the baby was killed cleanly, Marcus.'

He shuffled uncomfortably. 'I will not lie, Livilla. I suspect you heard correctly, especially if it was from Stella.'

Then the sickening story was true. My one-year-old niece had been dashed repeatedly against the painted plaster until her brains coated the wall. Stella had not told me *who* did it. Whoever it was would be dead now anyway. Such a man – such a witness – could hardly be left alive to tell his tale.

'I ran back to the theatre,' Vinicius said in his small, lost voice. 'There was chaos, for rumour spreads in Rome faster even than fire. Without being able to count on the Praetorians and with the German Guard having utterly failed in their role at the end,

I deployed the urban cohorts, invoking imperial authority. I tried to announce what had happened, but there was too much noise. No one was listening. No one could hear me. I was about to make a pronouncement, though I hadn't quite decided what it would be. In my desperate panic, all I knew was that you were right. In the end, Claudius had played us all in his quest for the throne. I knew he had to be stopped, so I was about to claim it myself, or possibly announce an end to the Principate and a return to the Republic. But before I could say anything, Senator Saturninus managed to call things to order.'

My husband sagged against the wall.

'Saturninus proclaimed your brother's death and denounced him as a despot, only allowed to rule by a weak, sycophantic senate. I could see how he was working up to claiming the purple for himself, so I started foolishly to argue. I told the crowd that Saturninus was one of those very sycophantic senators who had supported Caligula. I stormed across to him and we argued in public like angry schoolchildren. I saw that he wore a ring bearing your brother's image and I ripped it from his finger, displaying it to the crowd and denouncing him. Then everything went mad. Saturninus' nephew pushed me out of the way and claimed the throne for himself. Then Asiaticus, who had clearly been part of our conspiracy merely to further his own ends, claimed it for himself. Chaos reigned and I retreated to the corridor entrance and watched the crowd starting to fight among themselves as every man with a pedigree claimed the right to succeed the throne.'

I could imagine it. Vinicius clearly sought sympathy, or possibly forgiveness. He would find neither in me.

'It was awful, Livilla. I watched from the passage entrance as the Praetorians began to march into the theatre in force, pushing the crowd out of the way. They bore a litter. Your uncle Claudius was atop it wearing a purple robe and adorned with a wreath of gilded oak leaves.'

I sighed. 'I told you, Marcus, a month back on Pandataria, that Claudius would have that cloak ready. And yet you went ahead, despite my imploring you, ignoring both your wife and the plain reality of my uncle, and you tore from Rome the possibility of renewed glory under a new Alexander. And for what? To leave Rome languishing in the grip of a snarling, slavering animal like Claudius? I love you, Marcus Vinicius. I always have, but right now I cannot look at you.'

And I turned and left that palace of the damned without answering the summons of my uncle, the new emperor of Rome. Perhaps if I had, the rest of my life would have been better, but somehow I doubt it.

As I left, I could hear Vinicius rattling out justifications behind me.

'At least the senate support him, Livilla. And he respects them.'

What did I care?

'Under him, Rome will endure!'

Under an emperor, Rome should not *have* to endure. It should *thrive* . . .

The last son of Germanicus had fallen and with him, for me, Rome itself had died.

XXIX

THIS TOMB

So I was on Pandataria for half a year, banished by my brother, and I only escaped the place because Caligula was no more, murdered by those we trusted. What happened next? Why am I here again on this benighted strand with a new cellmate?

My, but aren't you full of questions, my new companion in despair.

Well, after my brother died in that passage, Agrippa and a few loyal friends managed to secure his body before anyone could ravage and dishonour it, which would clearly have been our uncle's intention. Claudius had had Agrippina and I brought back from exile, for we were both known to have been involved in plots against Caligula, and it would do his reputation good to free us. We would in some way vindicate the murder and his elevation by our mere existence. Agrippina took it better than I, of course. She was reunited with her gurgling child and immediately began planning once more, her goal to set her son on the throne of the emperors.

Agrippa took the emperor's body across the river to our mother's villa, where we had stayed that month before my brother's great stunt in the Bay of Neapolis. There he burned the body and interred the ashes with appropriate respect in the mausoleum of our family, close to his father and our glorious great-grandfather, Augustus.

It was, frankly, the only act in those months that followed which showed even a modicum of humanity. Callistus and his oily new master, Claudius, began to clear away the chaff from the new reign. The Praetorian prefects Clemens and Stella were both removed from office and sent back into obscurity where they could do no harm. There was no real suspicion that they were involved in the plot, but their men were, and so they could no longer be trusted in their role. Besides, they may well have been loyal to Caligula to the end, and if that were true then they were the last people Claudius would want protecting him. Almost everyone who had had a hand in the plot met with a grisly end. Arruntius and Asiaticus, the two tribunes who had been in the corridor, various others in the know and who had helped to engineer the day . . . all dead. All those who could have revealed Claudius' pivotal role in the death of his predecessor. With just two notable exceptions. Somehow Callistus managed to remain in the circle of power, taking much the same role for Claudius as he had for my brother. My husband, his dreams of a republican Rome – or at least of an emperor who cared for his empire – dashed, remained close to Claudius, trying to steer him the way he had previously attempted to guide Caligula. He will find he has less success there than he had with my brother, for Claudius is a hard soul. In the end, Vinicius will fall, as does anyone who comes too close to my vile uncle. Helicon, staunch bodyguard and chamberlain of both Tiberius and Caligula, who had been in the palace attending to business when his last master was murdered, disappeared in the months that followed Claudius' rise. And perhaps the only bright star in that constellation of death was the passing of my brutal brother-in-law Ahenobarbus. He died, apparently of natural causes, in one of his rural villas, though it did not escape my notice that his passing neatly coincided with Agrippina no longer needing him and his legitimacy. See how subtly she plots?

I was in Rome for perhaps half a year after Caligula's death, living in one of the family holdings, for I had no wish to cohabit with my husband. But I was not my brother, and so my fate was already sealed. In times like these, Caligula had ever managed to navigate the dangerous currents of the court. Would that he had been so adept at ruling as he'd been at surviving *other* rulers. But still, while Caligula had always found a way to survive tyrants, I am not him. I am not subtle enough, and I have no forgiveness left in me.

My uncle repeatedly brought me to court, as he did with Agrippina, parading us before the waves of newly appointed senators who had filled the ranks of the lost, displaying us as evidence of Caligula's unpopularity and the many plots against him, and by extension evidence of Claudius' righteous ascension.

But I did not play his role with aplomb as my sickening sister did. I was outspoken. When my uncle's cronies asked me why I had felt the need to make an attempt on the life of my brother, I told the truth – that I had done no such thing and had been falsely accused by my harridan of a sister. Agrippina began once more to accumulate power and influence as she played our uncle's game, and as she rose so did I fall.

I have no interest in influence or power.

I watched my uncle becoming more and more frustrated with my reticence and unwillingness to play my part, yet he dared not risk punishing me, for that would simply add a perceived veneer of truth to my story. But there were no such restrictions on his hag of a wife, Messalina. She engineered a social gathering and stuck me in a room with the playwright Seneca. There he bored me sick for an hour with tales of theatre and of provincial entertainment. The next day, at the clear instigation of Messalina, I was subjected to accusations of adultery with Seneca. As if I might have the slightest interest in that jowly, balding, boring old Spaniard.

My darling husband, of course, never opened his mouth to

defend me, and nor did my sister, who saw my fall as another stepping stone in her own return to prominence.

So there we are. By autumn I was back here, on Pandataria. My mother was not waiting for me, for it seems the island has changed. Now *you* are my only companion, and the island outside this tomb of a villa is forbidden me. No more walking under the sun and watching the waves, or tending my little garden. Did you see it when you were brought in? Is it horribly overgrown? No more goats or cooking tough stews and soggy bread. No more cutting down trees or heating the bath suite. No more *anything*, in fact. For my brother sent me to Pandataria to live out my days because he was heartbroken at my betrayal, but my uncle has sent me here to die. Simple as that.

No, they will not unlock the doors or unbar the windows. Not until I am dead, anyway. Perhaps for you they will then be more lenient?

Hades hovers over me like a shadow, and the boatman is sitting by the shore of the Styx, rapping his bony fingers impatiently.

I still wonder that I have the materials with which to soil myself, since I am in my second month of starving to death and even the water is no longer sustaining me.

I am truly sorry, but when they come and remove my body, if you ask kindly, they might clean the room. And maybe then they will unbar the doors and you will be able to eat and walk, for you are still new here and you have strength enough to survive for some time.

So you asked, if I remember rightly, before I told my tale, who I was?

I am Julia Livilla, a matron of Rome.

I am the wife of the nobleman Marcus Vinicius, the daughter of the great Germanicus and the great-granddaughter of Augustus.

I am called traitor, and yet there is no cause to call me such.

I am a child of discord and I will be the mother of Furies.

First and foremost, I am the sister of Caligula.

But I am one last thing.

I am one of the few remaining people who know the truth of Claudius' part in the death of an emperor. I am one of the very last who know how a good man was driven to ruin by betrayal and despair and fell only because of greedy, weak and misguided men. I am one of precious few bearers of the truth, and the only one willing to stand against my serpent of an uncle who occupies the throne. But now you, Locusta, are another. And while within days I will be dead, for now I sleep at night with the coin under my tongue just in case, you may live. And while you live there is always a chance you will be freed. And if you are free, then the truth is still out there to haunt Claudius.

And now, dear Locusta, I must sleep.

And if I do not make it through the night, Fortuna watch over you.

HISTORICAL NOTE

It is inevitable that history is written by the victor, and throughout the past two millennia there have been plenty of cases of good men being maligned by their successors, as well as evil men made saints by their progeny. Rome was no different, and may indeed be the very epitome of this. Being so far removed from our modern world, we have only fragmentary archaeological and epigraphic evidence to directly base our research on – that and the writings of those who lived in the era.

It is remarkably easy to find evidence of such writers tampering with the truth. In my recent research into Commodus, I have often noted that the three main sources on his reign (Cassius Dio, Herodian, and the ever-dubious *Historia Augusta*) cannot even agree with each other, let alone with visible evidence or logic. With the tiniest amount of digging it becomes possible to start exploding the myth and the hearsay and to construct a more plausible and realistic timeline of events.

Such it is with Caligula. Once the chaff is cleared away, misunderstandings and misrepresentations clarified, and the more obvious cases of character assassination discarded, we are left with a complex man who fell foul of the most influential and dangerous people in his empire. He could hardly have been the monster he is painted as, for while those powerful senators and nobles managed to remove him, the ordinary people of Rome held him up as their golden prince and the army remained his.

And while his name may have been officially struck from monuments, evidence of his popularity remains in the fact that his chariot training circuit on the other bank of the Tiber was still known as the *Gaianum* in his honour generations later.

Such a re-examination of the life of Caligula produces the story of a slightly erratic, haunted, acerbic man who suffered due to an inability to work with the senate. It also casts his predecessor and his successor automatically in a worse light. For without comparison to the 'evil' of Caligula, it is much easier to see the wickedness of the last days of Tiberius and the great likelihood of Claudius' close involvement in the young emperor's downfall.

As an example of the exploding of Caligula myth that was a large part of my process, let us look at the tale of his horse, Incitatus. The common story is that the emperor made his horse a consul, the most powerful role within the Roman political system. Yet on closer examination of the sources, their veracity is thoroughly questionable.

Suetonius notes, 'it is also said that he planned to make him consul', which very clearly shows that that author was merely relaying hearsay rather than basing this accusation on any kind of evidence. Cassius Dio claims that the emperor planned to make Incitatus a consul, and then tacks on, 'he probably would have done it'. It is worth noting that Suetonius was not even born when Caligula died, which explains something of his need to rely on tales and rumour. Moreover, Cassius Dio was writing much later still and would have been sourcing his stories from, among others, Suetonius, who, as already noted, was relaying rumour. It seems somewhat harsh that one of the most common accusations of Caligula's madness is based upon two writers who were merely spreading gossip. Such is often the case with Caligula and is the basis for my treatment of him.

In this novel I have tried to stick as close to the truth as possible, allowing for the fact that the truth is always somewhat nebulous when it is portrayed by critics after the man's death and can involve a great deal of interpretation of conflicting material and illogical explanations. I have mostly followed Aloys Winterling's reappraisal in *Caligula: A Biography* (2011), with a few tweaks of my own. Dates may not match up with other sources, because there is vagueness with the actual dates involved, and there is always going to be a little give. All the events portrayed in this work are either as they were recorded by the ancient writers or are plausible reappraisals of those events, barring one exception, noted below.

Apart from a few miscellaneous slaves, servants and citizens, all the main characters in the story are historical figures, as are most locations. I have, however, created a fictitious villa on the western end of Pandataria (now Ventotene), while the only excavated remains of such are at the eastern end near the later town. There is little record of Roman Pandataria, and so I have put together a largely fictionalised picture of the island. It was a place of exile for a number of famous Romans over the centuries (Augustus's daughter, Nero's wife and Domitian's niece for example), some living out long periods there, while others starved to death. Thus I have attempted to create a plausible site where both forms of exile are feasible. The senator's house on the Esquiline where Incitatus is stabled is fictional, though quite possible, as is the house of the auspex with his chickens. Every other location in the book is attested and real and, where there is archaeological evidence, I have tried to fit the tale within its bounds. Some sites, such as the Palatine palace and the staircase Caligula built, the Circus Maximus and the mausoleum of Augustus, are still visible today and can be visited. Others, such as the navalia docks, the suburban villa of Agrippina and the famous bridge of boats at Baiae, have left no visible evidence, though their locations are well recorded.

*

I decided from the start that this tale could not be told by Caligula himself, though I wanted it to be a first-person account, since it is much easier to portray emotion and motivation that way – and what is the tale of Caligula if not a wealth of emotion? As such, I had to find a character who was with Caligula, or at least could have been, throughout his life. They had to outlive him, so that they could finish his story, and they had to be reasonably sympathetic to the reader. The emperor's siblings Drusilla, Nero and Drusus all died early, and Agrippina is such an unsympathetic character that I know *I* would not like to read a story narrated by her, so she was clearly out. His eastern friends came in too late; Lepidus dies too early. Claudius was destined to be the villain. In the end, Livilla was my only realistic choice, and I was happy with that.

Though she is not always attested alongside her brother throughout their early life, her biographical evidence is scant, and there is absolutely no reason she couldn't have been involved, and so I chose to put her there all along. The only hiccup was that she was arrested for treason in 39AD and sent into exile on Ventotene, where she would remain throughout the last months of his reign . . .

This meant that, although she would get to witness his rise and his apex, Livilla would be absent for Caligula's fall. Initially, I had followed the generally assumed course of events and shuffled her off immediately after the plot was exposed, with the rest of the tale coming in third-party reports. Over time it became clear that the reader (and, therefore, also Livilla) needed a more direct view of later events, though I could initially see no way to do it without altering history. It was only when my editor drove me to look at the sources once again that I realised there was no specific reason to place her exile immediately after her arrest. She simply was sent to the island sometime after the events in Germany, and was there when Caligula died. Therefore she went to the island sometime between perhaps October 39AD and late 40AD. As long as I maintained those immutable facts, I was at liberty to slide events along.

I therefore reworked the tale so that Livilla would be witness to events in Gaul, Rome and Baiae, with only the last part of her brother's fall cut off from her. I simply could not bend truth enough to take Livilla from the island altogether – as historical authors, we are bound to stay within the framework of history where required and only to invent where there is no written record.

I have chosen to make Livilla innocent of the plot against her brother. This is my choice and I hope you can forgive my presumption. Her innocence lends the latter quarter of the book a sympathy that would not be there otherwise. And though I have tweaked her motivation, I have not flown in the face of the facts that surround her. She *was* arrested for treason, she *was* sent to Pandataria in exile and she only returned after her brother's death.

I have omitted certain facets of the timeline from this tale. This is not in order to change the story or motivation therein, but more an effort to keep the book concentrated on the important parts and cut out the chaff. I have not, for instance, touched on Caligula's pleasure ships on Lake Nemi – though I did have Caligula thrashing out his grief after Drusilla's death in his villa there – and I have only lightly brushed upon the dangerous business of Caligula's interference in the religious life of Jerusalem. I mention only in dispatches his campaigns in Germany which Livilla could not realistically have witnessed anyway. Sometimes a plot has to be driven forward at the expense of describing far-flung scenes that are unnecessary, no matter how exciting.

That being said, I did tweak one part of the tale. I hold up my hands in apology for playing hard and fast with the episode of Livia Orestilla and flying in the face of Cassius Dio and Suetonius, both of whom have Caligula seizing her from Piso at their wedding and then divorcing her two days later. It seems out of character in the way it is described – too impulsive and dangerous for the man who had so successfully navigated the reign of Tiberius and manoeuvred himself into power. As I noted earlier when discussing Incitatus, Suetonius was writing some eighty years after the event, and there is a hint of doubt in his account, given the fact that on this matter he tells us, 'others write that . . .'. Moreover, yet again Dio was writing two centuries after the event and had Suetonius to work from. Hearsay lent to hearsay once again. Simply, though, the strange event they describe would jar and not drive the story forward, so I combined the essence of the sequence (forced divorce, new marriage, new divorce, exile) with other accounts of Caligula's banquets in order to maintain the plot and its pace.

The possibility that Caligula was contemplating moving the centre of government to Alexandria and founding a monarchy after the eastern model may sound fantastical, but it is not quite as far-fetched as you might think. There is some suggestion of it in Suetonius, and Tacitus' writings also support the notion, to an extent. And there was a historical precedent, too. Caesar may well have been planning the same before his downfall – another set of rumours expounded by Suetonius in his biographies has Rome worrying that Caesar plans to quit the capital and move there with his armies. Marcus Antonius did oppose Augustus, using that place as his centre of power alongside his Egyptian queen. Moreover, Caligula did spend a portion of his reign in the company of Julius Agrippa (later known as Herod Agrippa) and Antiochus of Commagene, and their influence on him must have been vast, especially when added to his increasing distance from the mechanisms of Roman republicanism.

If you want to know what happens beyond the end of the novel, there is plenty of work out there to read up on. Claudius and Nero are well covered in both fiction and non-fiction, and the year of the four emperors is positively blown open, examined from every angle by a number of excellent writers. I highly recommend the novels of M.C. Scott, Douglas Jackson and Robert Fabbri in particular on the latter days of the Julio-Claudian dynasty and the rise of the Flavians.

Still, here are a few teasers of what was to come: Livilla dies on Pandataria. Her husband, Marcus Vinicius, manages another four years before Messalina (Claudius' wife) has him killed. Callistus' fate is not recorded, but he seems to have died during the later days of the reign of Claudius. Claudius himself later married Agrippina, his niece, in a traditionally Julio-Claudian mess of incest and complexity, and the baby she had borne her loutish husband Ahenobarbus became Claudius' heir, and was renamed Nero. He in his own right carried her wickedness on into history after Agrippina probably poisoned Claudius (again, just as with Caligula's life, we must be prepared to take the sources with a pinch of salt). But herein lies the subject of my last note, and a fun one to leave you with:

This tale is told as a narrative by Livilla, sitting in her prison and being executed slowly by starvation, relating her life story to a new cellmate. In it she blames Claudius for pretty much everything, and holds him up as the most wicked of all Romans. She relates the poisoning of Tiberius by her brother (one way in which it has been suggested the old man died, though the specific choice of the abrus berry – the jequirity or 'Indian licorice' – was mine as I needed a naturally occurring poison that would be unknown in the empire and yet could have made its way there). As a side note, the practice of building an immunity to poison through exposure (Mithridatism) is not always successful and depends on many factors, only working on some poisons in the best of cases, but I have not had Caligula suddenly drop dead from his experiments, for obvious reasons. Do not try this at home! And in the epilogue I have revealed Livilla's cellmate to be Locusta, who rises to infamy in 54AD when she is recorded as one of Rome's most infamous poisoners, and is said to be the woman who supplied Agrippina with the poison to kill Claudius. And so, with something of a delay, and through a twisted untold path, you might think that in the end Livilla gets her revenge.

My task is done, and now I head off to explode the myths surrounding the megalomania of Commodus. I look forward to journeying there with you next year.

Simon Turney, July 2017

ACKNOWLEDGEMENTS

A novel is not solely the work of an author. Without the aid and support of a number of people it would often remain just illegible and disorganised scribblings. I would like to thank a number of people who helped turn *Caligula* from the one to the other.

Firstly my superb agent Sallyanne Sweeney and the visionary Ivan Mulcahy at MMB Creative who took a chance on me as an author and have guided me from small places to greater heights and who first instilled in me the idea for this novel. Moreover, special thanks are due to Sallyanne for all her efforts in turning the first rough draft into a polished offering with her editorial skills.

Thanks are due also most definitely to Craig Lye at Orion, an excellent and imaginative editor who repeatedly tightened the text of this book and made it what it now is, and who never once pushed for something I did not like. Also at Orion, I am indebted to Jennifer McMenemy and Lauren Woosey for their amazing work on bringing *Caligula* to the world's notice.

My gratitude goes out also to several fellow authors and friends without whom this would not have been possible. The lovely Kate Quinn and Stephanie Dray both read the early draft of *Caligula* and offered advice and support, as did my wonderful antipodean friend Prue Batten. Some of the best authors in the genre have offered much-needed encouragement and support over the past couple of years of work, particularly Christian Cameron and Ben Kane, but also Anthony Riches, Nick Brown, Manda Scott, Ruth Downie, Paul Fraser Collard, Angus Donald, Harry Sidebottom, Rob Low, Giles Kristian and Douglas Jackson. And then there's Robin Carter of Parmenion Books, without whom I probably wouldn't have this career at all, and the talented Gordon Doherty, with whom I have shared much of the journey from wannabe to author.

Finally, there is my family, without whom not only would none of this have been possible, but none of it would be worthwhile. My wonderful wife, Tracey, who keeps me organised and alive, my children, Callie and Marcus, who supply light relief, support and love, my parents, Tony and Jenny, and my in-laws, Ken and Sheila, all of whom have offered nothing but support over the years.

Thank you all. You made this possible.

DRAMATIS PERSONAE

Agrippina the elder
Wife of Germanicus and mother of Caligula and his siblings.

Agrippina the younger
Eldest sister of Caligula and future empress of Rome. Noted for her ambition and quick wit. Mother of the emperor Nero.

Ahenobarbus, Gnaeus Domitius
Former consul, Roman nobleman and politician, distant cousin of Caligula. Husband of Agrippina the younger.

Antiochus III Epiphanes
King of Commagene, a sometime client state of Rome and buffer zone with eastern neighbours, now in southern Turkey.

Antonia Minor
Daughter of the great Marcus Antonius, mother of Claudius and Germanicus, and grandmother of Caligula. A powerful matron of Rome and opponent of Tiberius.

Caesonia, Milonia
Sister of Corbulo and wife of Caligula.

Chaerea, Cassius
Decorated former legionary centurion and now a tribune in the Praetorian Guard.

Claudilla, Junia
Daughter of the senator Silanus and wife of Caligula.

Claudius
Uncle of Caligula. An ambitious senator of imperial blood with a limp and a speech disorder.

Clemens, Marcus Arrecinus
Obscure equestrian soldier with a good military record who rose under Caligula to be one of two Praetorian prefects.

Corbulo, Gnaeus Domitius
Respected military man and popular Roman noble. Brother-in-law to Caligula via Milonia. Noted later as one of Rome's greatest generals.

Drusilla, Julia
Middle sister and closest sibling of Caligula.

Drusus Caesar
Middle son of Germanicus and brother of Caligula.

Gaetulicus, Gnaeus Cornelius Lentulus
Roman general and former consul, governor of Germania and one-time ally of Sejanus.

Gemellus, Tiberius
Grandson of the emperor Tiberius through his deceased son Drusus.

Germanicus
Father of Caligula. Respected Roman nobleman and descendent of the line of Julius Caesar. A renowned general who died in mysterious circumstances in Syria.

Lepidus, Marcus Aemilius
Son of a former consul from a very wealthy and distinguished family, friend of Caligula and young nobleman of Rome.

Livilla, Julia
Youngest daughter of Germanicus, sister of Caligula.

Longinus, Lucius Cassius
Roman patrician and politician. Brother-in-law of Caligula via Drusilla.

Macro, Naevius Sutorius
Ambitious Roman equestrian who became commander successively of the Vigiles and then the Praetorian Guard, following the removal of Sejanus.

Naeva (née Thrasylla), Ennia
Wife of the Praetorian prefect Macro, Roman noblewoman and descendent of eastern royalty. A predator.

Nero, Julius Caesar
Oldest of the children of Germanicus and Agrippina, eldest brother of Caligula.

Orestilla, Livia
Wife of the senator Piso and later of Caligula.

Paulina, Lollia
Roman plebeian and wife of a former consul and governor, who became Caligula's wife.

Sejanus, Lucius Aelius
A Roman citizen risen to be prefect of the Praetorian Guard, charged with the

personal protection of the emperor.

Silanus, Marcus Junius

Respected senator and former consul, advisor of the emperor Tiberius and later of Caligula.

Stella, Lucius Arruntius

Obscure equestrian soldier who rose under Caligula to be one of two Praetorian prefects.

Tiberius

Emperor of Rome, tyrant and recluse. Nephew of Augustus and successful former general.

Vinicius, Marcus

Former consul and respected member of the senatorial order. Husband of Livilla and brother-in-law of Caligula.

Vitellius, Lucius

Former consul and Roman politician of noted good character. Father of the future emperor Vitellius.